Praise for *The Incarnations*

New York Times Book Review Notable Book of 2015
Kirkus Reviews Best Fiction Book of 2015
Finalist for the 2015 Kirkus Prize for Fiction
Winner of a Jerwood Fiction Uncovered Prize

"A thrilling journey through a thousand years of obsession and betrayal and a vivid tapestry of the individual's struggle against the tyranny of history; this is the most extraordinary work of imagination you'll read all year."

—Adam Johnson, author of *The Orphan Master's Son*
(winner of the Pulitzer Prize for Fiction)

"Astonishing, amazing . . . It's the small sagas of Chinese history contained in the letters, together with Barker's vivid descriptions of today's China, that set this book apart as a work of considerable, if unnerving, importance. . . . Tightly wound, intensely wrought, fantastically exciting . . . Beguiling, readable, intense . . . The book's stellar narrative carries us briskly along."

—Simon Winchester, *The New York Times Book Review*

"An extraordinary novel. Erudite, intriguing and compulsively readable, *The Incarnations* takes the reader on an intimate and mesmerizing journey through Chinese history. Susan Barker, a born storyteller, has written one of the most remarkable novels of recent years."

—John Boyne, author of *The Boy in the Striped Pajamas*

"The glittering prose, dazzling details and breathtaking scope of the author's vision will reward anyone who admires superb writing. . . . A powerhouse of a novel."

—*Washington Independent Review of Books*

"A perfect conclusion brings home the writer's warning: 'History is coming for you.'"

—*New York* magazine, "7 Books You
Need to Read This August"

"Barker makes Wang and his city as vividly real—and disturbing—as any of the other versions of China. . . . One of the novel's many structural pleasures is watching Barker slowly reveal the connections between Wang's seemingly simple life and the other lives the letter writer reveals."

—*The Columbus Dispatch*

"A jackpot. This sprawling, time-bending epic somehow manages to span a thousand years while still remaining grounded and intimate. It's a monumental feat of writing; the sort of wildly engaging creativity that can never be predicted, but only embraced upon its discovery. . . . A hypnotically brilliant, emotionally powerful piece of fiction that denied classification and demanded contemplation. It is indisputably one of the best books of the year."

—*The Maine Edge*

"Highly successful as art and craft . . . *The Incarnations* uses its unique premise to combine a series of short stories based in history with a realistic account of a difficult modern life, for much more than the sum of the parts."

—*The Florida Times-Union*

"An idiosyncratic epic to savor."

—*San Francisco Chronicle*

"A hypnotic journey through 1,500 years of China's history . . . Culminates in a shocking and violent conclusion that will haunt you for weeks."

—*Paste Magazine*

"[A] stunning epic . . . Barker's historical tour de force is simultaneously sweeping and precise. . . . Effortlessly blends the past with the present, dark humor with profound sadness. A deeply human masterpiece."

—*Kirkus Reviews* (starred review)

"Barker's fluid prose makes of their tragic stories irresistible reading. . . . The stories come alive via a veritable catalog of dark and desperate details. This ambitious novel traffics in intrigue and betrayal, yet never loses its hypnotic grip."

—*Booklist* (starred review)

"A page-turning reincarnation fantasy . . . Lush historical detail . . . A very memorable read."

—*Publishers Weekly* (starred review)

"Daring . . . The novel's shifts from the distant past to the present are seamless, and the bittersweet twist at the book's finale will have readers searching back through the novel for clues to the ending. . . . Skillfully combines history, the supernatural and the everyday in a novel that suggests that the past is never really past, while providing a cracking good read."

—*BookPage*

"Reads as China's *Midnight's Children*. An utterly remarkable novel, it is certainly a very different book from Rushdie's but just as important in its historical and cultural sweep. . . . Barker's storytelling is lively and addictive. . . . She has an eye for the absurd and darkly comic."

—*The Independent* (UK)

"Suspend your disbelief, flow along with this wonderful book, like the crazy traffic flowing around Beijing's six-ring roads. . . . The book moves effortlessly from past to present and back again. . . . Masterful."

—*The Guardian* (UK)

"Barker resembles David Mitchell in the ability to weave together past and present in a convincing, and ultimately intriguing, manner."

—*The Sydney Morning Herald*

"Invigorating. To recreate convincingly a single historical period is an achievement. To recreate six is to approach virtuosity. . . . Deft, smart, various and warm: a very good book indeed."
—*The Sunday Business Post* (UK)

"Barker has that rare contortionistic imagination possessed only by the finest Chinese literary legends such as Wu Cheng'en and Yu Hua, and this book is soaked deep in the vintage mysticism of Nobel Prize–winner Mo Yan. It's a rare feat that a China-themed book could be this universally abiding. My favorite part being its setting: China is alive and deeply soulful under Barker's knowing pen, making me want to revisit this mystic land of much enchantment."
—Da Chen, author of *Colors of the Mountain* and *Brothers*

"What a ferociously talented writer Susan Barker is. *The Incarnations* is a hallucinatory ride. Highly recommended."
—Anna Hope, author of *Wake*

"Barker's remarkable new novel is ambitious in scope, scholarly in depth and absolutely riveting. *The Incarnations* works on a number of levels, pulling together so many strands of history and perspectives and drawing them into a compelling and convincing tale. Part history, part love story, with good doses of horror, comedy and philosophy, it is ultimately a thriller and a page-turner. . . . The effect is explosive."
—*South China Morning Post*

"Remarkable. . . Ambitious in scope, painstakingly researched and most importantly, a gripping read."
—*Publishing Perspectives*

Also by Susan Barker

Sayonara Bar
The Orientalist and the Ghost

The Incarnations

Susan Barker

TOUCHSTONE
New York   London   Toronto   Sydney   New Delhi

Touchstone
An Imprint of Simon & Schuster, Inc.
1230 Avenue of the Americas
New York, NY 10020

First Touchstone trade paperback edition March 2016

TOUCHSTONE and colophon are registered trademarks of Simon & Schuster, Inc.

For information about special discounts for bulk purchases, please contact Simon & Schuster Special Sales at 1-866-506-1949 or business@simonandschuster.com.

The Simon & Schuster Speakers Bureau can bring authors to your live event. For more information or to book an event, contact the Simon & Schuster Speakers Bureau at 866-248-3049 or visit our website at www.simonspeakers.com.

Manufactured in the United States of America

1   3   5   7   9   10   8   6   4   2

The Library of Congress has cataloged the hardcover edition as follows:

Barker, Susan, 1978–
The incarnations / Susan Barker.—First Touchstone hardcover edition.
pages ; cm
"A Touchstone Book"
"Originally published in Great Britain in 2014 by Doubleday."
1. Reincarnation—Fiction. 2 China—History—Fiction. I. Title.
PR6102.A7635I53 2015
823'.92—dc23
2014043145

ISBN 978-1-5011-0678-1
ISBN 978-1-5011-0679-8 (pbk)
ISBN 978-1-5011-0680-4 (ebook)

For Robbie

Contents

CONTENTS

I ask, in this boundless land,
who is the master of man's destiny?

Mao Zedong

1

The First Letter

Every night I wake from dreaming. Memory squeezing the trigger of my heart and blood surging through my veins.

The dreams go into a journal. Cold sweat on my skin, adrenaline in my blood, I illuminate my cement room with the 40-watt bulb hanging overhead and, huddled under blankets, flip open my notebook and spill ink across the feint-ruled page. Capturing the ephemera of dreams, before they fade from memory.

I dream of teenage girls, parading the Ox Demons and Snake Ghosts around the running tracks behind our school. I dream of the tall dunce hats on our former teachers' ink-smeared heads, the placards around their necks. *Down with Headteacher Yang! Down with Black Gangster Zhao!* I dream of Teacher Wu obeying our orders to slap Headteacher Yang, to the riotous cheers of the mob.

I dream that we stagger on hunger-weakened limbs through the Gobi as the Mongols drive us forth with lashing whips. I dream of razor-beaked birds swooping at our heads, and scorpions scuttling amongst scattered, sun-bleached bones on the ground. I dream of a mirage of a lake on shimmering waves of heat. I dream that, desperate to cure our raging thirst, we crawl there on our hands and knees.

I dream of the sickly Emperor Jiajing, snorting white powdery aphrodisiacs up his nostrils, and hovering over you on the four-poster bed with an erection smeared with verdigris. I dream of His Majesty urging us to "operate" on each other with surgical blades lined up in a velvet case. I dream of sixteen palace ladies gathered in the Pavilion of Melancholy Clouds, plotting the ways and means to murder one of the worst emperors ever to reign.

Newsprint blocks the windows and electricity drips through the cord into the 40-watt bulb. For days I have been at my desk, preparing your historical records, my fingers stiffened by the cold, struggling to hit the correct keys. The machine huffs and puffs and lapses out of consciousness. I reboot and wait impatiently for its resuscitation, several times a day. Between bouts of writing I pace the cement floor. The light bulb casts my silhouette on the walls. A shadow of a human form, which possesses more corporeality than I do.

The Henan migrants gamble and scrape chair legs in the room above. I curse and bang the ceiling with a broom. I don't go out. I hunch at my desk and tap at the keyboard, and the machine wheezes and gasps, as though protesting the darkness I feed into its parts. My mind expands into the room. My subconscious laps at the walls, rising like the tide. I am drowning in our past lives. But until they have been recorded, they won't recede.

I watch you most days. I go to the Maizidian housing compound where you live and watch you. Yesterday I saw you by the bins, talking to Old Pang the recycling collector, the cart attached to his Flying Pigeon loaded with plastic bottles, scavenged to exchange for a few fen at the recycling bank. Old Pang grumbled about the cold weather and the flare-up in his arthritis that prevents him from reaching the bottom of the bins. So you rolled up your coat sleeve and offered to help. Elbow-deep you groped, fearless of broken glass, soapy tangles of plughole hair and congealed leftovers scraped from plates. You dug up a wedge of Styrofoam. "Can you sell this?" you asked. Old Pang turned the Styrofoam over in his hands, then secured it to his cart with a hook-ended rope. He thanked you, climbed on his Flying Pigeon and pedalled away.

After Old Pang's departure you stood by your green and yellow Citroën, reluctant to get back to work. You stared at the grey sky and the high-rises of glass and steel surrounding your housing compound. The December wind swept your hair and rattled your skeleton through your thin coat. The wind eddied and corkscrewed and whistled through its teeth at you. You had no sense of me watching you at all.

You got back inside your cab and I rapped my knuckles on the passenger-side window. You nodded and I pulled the back door open by the latch. You turned to me, your face bearing no trace of recognition as you muttered, "Where to?"

Purple Bamboo Park. A long journey across the city from east to west. I watched you from the back as you yawned and tuned the radio dial from the monotonous speech of a politburo member to the traffic report. Beisanzhong Road. Heping South Bridge. Madian Bridge. Bumper to bumper on the Third Ring Road, thousands of vehicles consumed petrol, sputtered exhaust and flashed indicator lights. You exhaled a long sigh and unscrewed the lid of your flask of green tea. I swallowed hard.

I breathed your scent of cigarettes and sweat. I breathed you in, tugging molecules of you through my sinuses and trachea, and deep into my lungs. Your knuckles were white as bone as you gripped the steering wheel. I wanted to reach above the headrest and touch your thinning hair. I wanted to touch your neck.

Zhongguancun Road, nearly there. Thirty minutes over in a heartbeat. Your phone vibrated and you held it to your ear. Your wife. *Yes, hmmm, yes, seven o'clock.* Yida is a practical woman. A thrifty, efficient homemaker who cooks for you, nurtures you and provides warmth beside you in bed at night. I can tell that she fulfills the needs of the flesh, this pretty wife of yours. But what about the needs of the spirit? Surely you ache for what she lacks?

Purple Bamboo Park, east gate. On the meter, 30 RMB. I handed you some tattered 10-RMB notes; the chubby face of Chairman

Mao grubby from the fingers of ten thousand laobaixing. A perfunctory thank-you and I slammed out. There was a construction site nearby, and the thoughts in my head jarred and jangled as the pneumatic drills smashed the concrete up. I stood on the kerb and watched you drive away. Taxi-driver Wang Jun. Driver ID number 394493. Thirty-one, careworn, a smoker of Red Pagoda Mountain cigarettes. The latest in your chain of incarnations, like the others, selected by the accident of rebirth, the lottery of fate.

Who are you? you must be wondering. I am your soulmate, your old friend, and I have come back to this city of sixteen million in search of you. I pity your poor wife, Driver Wang. What's the bond of matrimony compared to the bond we have shared for over a thousand years? What will happen to her when I reappear in your life?

What will become of her then?

2

Wang Jun

Through the windscreen of his taxi, Wang has seen the city change. He has seen the wrecking balls swing, bulldozers levelling streets to rubble and dust, and skyscrapers rising like bamboo after the rain. Land and planning permission is bought and sold. Property developers draw circles on maps and, in weeks, all that is circled disappears, the residents exiled to the far-flung suburbs and demolition crews moving in to clear out the rest. In the decade Wang has been a taxi driver, the city has changed radically. And as the dust of construction gusts across the city, sheet after sheet, he often wonders when it will end.

Pedestrians wave him down and Wang drives them all over Beijing. He is mostly silent throughout his twelve-hour shift, and most passengers behave as though he's not there, or as if he's a mechanical part of the car, like the gear stick or steering wheel. They don't censor what they say in the back seat, and some of the conversations lure Wang's attention in. Investment bankers bragging of profits of millions of yuan. A middle-school student with metal braces on her teeth, describing to a saucer-eyed friend how she lost her virginity ("I bled, but not that much . . ."). Scientists from the Institute of Meteorological Sciences debating the ethics of cloud-seeding—the Weather Modification Office's strategy of firing silver iodide up into the clouds to wring out some rain. ("Man must defeat the Heavens," the woman scientist insisted, quoting Mao.) Money is what his passengers talk of most. "How much per square metre?" "How much for the upgrade?" "How much do you earn?" "How much?" "How much?" Beijingers are richer now than when Wang first started out as a driver, and his fares click compulsively at shiny metallic laptops and fidget with the latest gadgets in the back. They are shallow, materialistic and vain. But Wang would like to be wealthy too. To own a modern high-rise two-bedroom apartment. To send his daughter, Echo, to private school and have braces put on her teeth.

Confident that Wang is no one of importance, passengers rarely exercise caution in his cab. Wang has been privy to the offering of bribes to men in suits. To the haggling down of the price of women, bought and sold in bulk. To the trading of forged passports and negotiation of human-smuggling fees. Once a guy in his twenties hired Wang out for an afternoon. When it became apparent, as they drove from address to address, that he was dealing drugs, Wang asked what he was selling. "Cocaine," the dealer had said. "How does it get to Beijing?" Wang had asked. "Flown to Kazakhstan in drug mules," he was told. "Stuffed in condoms in stomachs. In the soles of shoes." "Aren't you afraid of the death penalty?" Wang asked, and the dealer had laughed: "When it comes to the police, there are ways of getting off the hook."

Lovers quarrel in his taxi. They fight about sex and abortion and extramarital affairs. Sometimes they remember he is there: "Shush . . . *the driver* . . ." "Fuck the driver! What does what he thinks matter?" And they go on with their row. Wang knows how manipulative the lovesick can be. The recklessness of those afflicted with the mental illness of romantic love. Wang's back seat has known more melodrama than any far-fetched TV soap.

Sometimes, late at night, when passengers are drunk and lonely and heading home to an empty bed, they unburden themselves to Wang, pouring out their unhappy personal lives to this safe, anonymous taxi driver. They ask his advice. Sometimes they ask for more than his advice. One woman in her thirties, whose boss had recently ended their affair, had said casually to Wang, "Can you take me somewhere and fuck me? I need cheering up." When Wang had protested that he had a wife and child, she had laughed and said, "That's never stopped any man I've ever known." The woman was plain-looking, but fiery and bold, and Wang could see what had attracted her boss. He imagined driving her to an empty car park, and shifting back the driver's seat so she could hitch up her skirt and straddle him, and he was tempted. But he couldn't do it. The woman stared out at the drizzly night streets of Beijing as he drove her the rest of the way home, not saying a word. Wang offered to waive her fare, but she made a point of paying him in full.

They are careless, his passengers. Not only do they spill intimate secrets in his taxi, they leave possessions behind too. Umbrellas, gloves, scarves, tubes of lipstick, cigarettes, cough drops and keys. Vials of Viagra and strips of birth-control pills. Tickets to the Beijing opera. Maps and guidebooks in Arabic, Hebrew and Japanese. Minutes from the annual meeting of the Optometrists' Society of Tianjin. More than once Wang has leapt out of his bones at a shrill ringing in the empty back seat.

The ID on the fare receipts means any theft would be traced back to him, so Wang turns everything in to the taxi company's lost-property depot. In nearly a decade he has stolen only one thing: a self-assembly kite in a box, the frame slotting together to make a magnificent dragon with a one-metre wingspan. Wang saw the forgotten kite in the back seat. Then he saw the receipt of the old man who owned it, poking like a tongue from the meter at the journey's end. A stroke of luck. That weekend Wang and Echo flew the kite together in Chaoyang Park, the crimson dragon fluttering its tail as it darted over the lakes and trees. As he watched Echo that day, smiling and gazing up to the kite in the sky, Wang thought of the old man and tried not to feel bad. What's the good of one person clinging to his morals when everyone else is so corrupt? What's the good of that?

* * *

Wang is driving east down Workers Stadium Road when, squinting in the sun, he flips down the visor above the driver's seat and an envelope falls onto his lap. Must be Baldy Zhang's, he thinks. Then he sees his name. Wang pulls over into the bicycle lane and slides his thumb under the adhesive seal. The letter is printed on four sheets of A4. As he reads, a woman dragging a suitcase on wheels taps on the window. Wang switches off the for-hire sign and waves her away. After reading the letter he refolds it and stuffs it back in the envelope. Workers Stadium Road reverberates with engines as cars flow to the east and to the west. Ignitions growl, rickshaw bells *brrring* and horns beep. Migrant workers with greasy hair and padding spilling out of ripped jackets trudge up the pedestrian overpass, shouldering heavy bags. The street seems changed somehow. As though everything is a façade for something hiding beneath. He wants to call Baldy Zhang but knows that he sleeps until dusk. Wang smokes a cigarette, then calls his wife instead.

Yida is at work and the phone rings and rings. Wang sees her in one of the private rooms at Dragonfly Massage, under the sensual, dimmer-switch-on-low lighting, standing over a customer on the massage table in her clinical white uniform. Wang sees her as a customer sees her. A pretty twenty-nine-year-old masseuse with bronzed skin and a wilderness of curls that tumble and fall from any barrette or butterfly clip she uses to hold them back. Firm calves. Lips that don't need lipstick. Hazel eyes flecked with gold. "Where are you from?" customers ask when they hear her accent. And as she tells them, they nod and recoil slightly, as though the soil and toil of peasant life still clings to her skin. There are facts about his wife's occupation Wang can't stomach. The fact that her male clients strip to their underwear. The fact that with her bare hands (moisturized, the nails clipped) she kneads and caresses every part of the male flesh. Shoulders, lower back, buttocks, inner thighs. Her upper-arm muscles rippling with strength as she attends to her bare-chested customers in the aromatherapy-oil-scented room. Wang knows what's on a man's mind when he is massaged by a pretty girl. And so does Yida. When she was a teenager, new to Beijing and ripe for exploitation, she worked in a parlour where bringing a client to a climax with her hand was an ordinary part of the massage routine. She'd wiped up the semen afterwards, she confessed, as casually as a waitress mopping up a spilt drink in a café.

She answers on the seventeenth ring.

"How come it took you so long to answer?" asks Wang.

"The phone was in my locker . . ."

"Were you with a customer?"

"No. I've had no customers yet . . ."

She sighs, weary of her husband's jealousy. "What is it, Wang? Is something wrong?"

"No. Nothing's wrong . . ."

And Wang changes his mind about telling her. He says, "I was thinking of you. That's all."

Yida softens. "Are you sure that there's nothing wrong?"

"Yes. I'm sure."

In the Public Security Bureau in Tuan Jie Hu, there are three policemen behind the enquiries desk. Two of them are Wang's age. Thugs with crew cuts, fogging the police station with wreaths of cigarette smoke. The third policeman is sixtyish with kind-looking eyes. Wang takes the letter to him. He tells him where he found it and describes the contents. The policeman reads the first page: "I don't understand." Wang shows him the part where the writer confesses to stalking him.

"Do you remember driving a fare to Purple Bamboo Park? After talking to the recycling collector?" the policeman asks.

"No. I don't remember."

The letter is put under the photocopier lid and reproduced for police records with mechanical whirrings and flashes of light. The policeman then asks for Wang's ID card. He taps his ID number into the computer and Wang's personal file comes up on the screen. When the policeman looks at Wang again, the kindness has gone from his eyes.

"Mr. Wang," he says, "why don't I take a look at your car?"

The policeman checks the door handles and windows for signs of forced entry. He opens the glove compartment and, rummaging about, finds Baldy Zhang's baijiu. He opens the brand-new bottle and sniffs, then pockets it without a word. He looks at Wang as though he is wasting his time.

"Well," he says, "someone is having a joke with you."

"Whoever it is has been following me. They know where I live. They've been watching my wife and child."

"Unless a law has been broken, there's nothing we can do."

Passengers slide in, front seat or back, sighing with relief to be in the stuffy car-heater warmth. As Wang navigates the streets of Beijing, steering through the arrhythmic stop-start of traffic, they *tap tap tap*, messaging on phones. They crack knuckles, popping sockets of bone. They yawn and yawn again. They struggle in with backpacks, unfolding German maps, naming a street in strange Teutonic tones. They scowl at Wang, blaming him for slow traffic. A teenage girl points to a plastic bag cartwheeling in the wind and remarks dryly, "That bag will get there before us." The radio says, "There are 66,000 taxi drivers in Beijing. A figure the government intends to reduce by a third by 2010."

The sky is stark and white as though bled dry. A woozy woman, her head swathed in bandages, staggers in from outside a plastic-surgery clinic. Mute, she hands Wang her address on paper. Throughout the journey Wang senses her watching him through the eyeholes in her gauze mask. He imagines the reconstructed face beneath. The surgeon's stitches and the sag of age drawn taut. He longs to call it a day and go home.

The canteen is east of the Third Ring Road, between a carwash and a garage. Crowded around Formica tables, cabbies hunch over bowls, chopsticks tugging noodles to mouths. Smoke from the poorly ventilated kitchen and crimson-glowing cigarettes swirls above them in a stratum of clouds. Hacking coughs cut through the dinnertime clatter, and lighters spark and flare as though pyromania, not nicotine, is the addiction here. Wang stands in the doorway, his pupils dilating in the dimness. Cabbies are not a healthy breed, slouching and overweight and in the high-risk category for coronary thrombosis. Irritable from hours of grinding traffic and liable to fly off the handle at the slightest thing. Wang hopes he doesn't look too much like these bad-tempered, whey-faced men in the canteen. "It's freezing! Shut the fucking door!" shouts Driver Liang. Wang steps inside.

Baldy Zhang grunts at Wang, frowning beneath his bald, ridged cranium as he peels a clove of garlic and grinds it between his molars. Baldy Zhang can get through a bulb of garlic a night and leaves the taxi so pungent Wang has to wind the windows down before his shift to air it out. ("Germ-ridden, passengers are," Baldy Zhang once explained. "Garlic protects me from the germs.") Baldy Zhang has been a cabbie since the eighties, back when Beijing was a city of bicycles and driving a taxi a prestigious job, and though he is arrogant and rude, Wang likes co-renting with him. Baldy Zhang never works during the day, for one, which means Wang hasn't worked a night in three years. Though fares are fewer, Baldy Zhang prefers the nighttime, when there are less of the things that he loathes: traffic, policemen and people. ("There's too many people in China," he says. "The one-child policy isn't enough. They should ban childbirth for a few years.") Baldy Zhang usually works from dusk until dawn, parks the Citroën outside Wang's building, then goes home to down a few beers and sleep. Baldy Zhang isn't married. ("Women aren't worth the hassle. Not even prostitutes. This right hand is all I trust," he says, waggling his fingers at Wang.)

They each own a set of keys, and Wang avoids him most days. But today he texted, asking to meet.

"Know anything about this? I found it in the sun visor."

Wang tosses Baldy Zhang the letter, watching for a spark of recognition in his eyes.

"What is it?" Baldy Zhang asks.

"Read it."

Baldy Zhang skims a page, then tosses the letter back, lacking the patience to read on. "What is it?"

As Wang tells him, Baldy Zhang reaches for Wang's pack of Red Pagoda Mountain, sticks a filter between his lips and sparks the lighter. "Mutton noodles!" calls one of the Sichuan girls who works in the kitchen. "Who ordered mutton noodles with chillies?"

"I once knew a driver who got a letter like this," Baldy Zhang says. "Driver Fan was his name. Few days after he got the letter he was found dead in his taxi. Murdered."

"Murdered?"

Baldy Zhang slits his eyes as he inhales, tobacco and cigarette paper crackling.

"Stabbed fourteen times in the chest. The inside of his taxi was like an abattoir. Everything sprayed with blood. It was on the news. Never caught who did it . . ."

Wang falls for it. Only for a second, but that's long enough for Baldy Zhang. He wallops the table and guffaws. Other cabbies look over.

"Very funny," says Wang.

He waits for the cackling to die down. He has a headache from the stale, recycled air and can't wait to get out of the canteen and breathe in the cold winter sky.

"Tell me the truth. Is this letter anything to do with you?"

"'Course not. Do I look mad?"

"How did it get there then?"

"A piece of wire's all it takes to pick the lock. Done it myself when I've locked in the keys."

Tilting his chin, Baldy Zhang blows a plume of smoke to the ceiling, then smiles.

Yida is in the kitchen. Rice-cooker steam fogs the window and the radio talks of Beijing's preparations for the Olympic Games. A cotton rag pulls back Yida's tumbleweed curls, and one of Wang's old T-shirts hangs loosely from her slender frame as she slices a green pepper on the chopping board. Standing in the doorway, Wang watches her move between the kitchen counter and stove, adding the peppers to the onions sizzling in the wok, as rings of flame blaze beneath. Wok handle in one hand, spatula in the other, Yida looks over her shoulder. "That you, Wang?" Wang says that it is.

The TV is madcap with cartoons. A hyperactive playmate that Echo ignores as she sits in her Zaoying Elementary tracksuit, copying illustrations from an anime comic into her spiral-bound pad. She is pretty like her mother, but her eye-teeth have come through crooked. Little Rabbit, they call her at school, and Wang winces at the orthodontist's bills yet to come.

"Ba, you're back," she says, not looking up from the spiral-bound pad.

Echo wants to be a comic-book illustrator when she grows up, an ambition of which Yida disapproves. "Stop praising her. Don't encourage her to waste time on art," she tells Wang. "Not when her grades in every other subject are so poor." Yida is harsh on Echo. Back when she was pregnant, she had bribed a doctor to give her an ultrasound. When she was told the foetus didn't have a penis, Yida had debated having an abortion. "But what if the ultrasound was wrong?" she fretted. "What if I abort a boy?" "Carry the baby to term then," Wang suggested, "and if you give birth to a girl, drown her in a bucket." Wang had shamed her into keeping the baby, and he suspects Yida is strict with Echo because she regrets not having a son. But Wang has no regrets at all. He couldn't be prouder of Echo. He pats her messy hair, thinking he couldn't have been blessed with a better child.

"Not so close. You'll ruin your eyes and need glasses. Then you'll never get a husband," he says.

"Good," says Echo. "I don't want a husband."

"You will," Wang says. "Finished your homework?"

"Yes," she fibs, knowing he is too lazy to check.

After dinner, Wang opens his laptop and scrolls through blogs online, mentally fidgeting, his attention span narrowing with every click. Yida curls up on a cushioned chair, her baggy, holey jumper tugged down over her knees, her wire-rimmed reading glasses perched on her nose and a best-selling paperback on Confucianism on her lap. Yida has started misquoting *The Analects*, and Wang can't wait for her to move on to something else.

On the living-room wall is a framed photograph of Wang and Yida, nine years younger, posing in the marble foyer of a five-star hotel. Yida is in an ivory wedding dress and Wang in suit and tie selected randomly from the photography studio's clothing rails. They don't look like themselves in the photo. Their smiles are forced and unnatural and may as well have been pulled off the rack with their clothes.

The actual marriage had been months earlier. Wang was twenty-two and Yida twenty, and they had been together for six weeks. Wang remembers how young Yida looked that day at the registry office, her hair scraped up in a ponytail, not a scrap of make-up on her joyful face. Afterwards they had ordered steaming-hot bowls of Lanzhou noodles at a nearby stall. "This is our wedding banquet," Wang had told the noodle maker, and he had poured out shots of baijiu and they'd all drunk a toast. Wang and Yida had drunkenly kissed, and an old woman had scolded them. Yida beamed and waved the marriage certificate at her: "We got married today. Here's the evidence. I'm allowed to kiss my own husband, aren't I?"

They were proud of their wedding day. It was proof they were far more in love than the couples with dowries and guest lists and parental approval. Which was why, when Yida later confessed her regret that they'd not had a traditional ceremony, Wang was disappointed. They went to a photography studio for some professional wedding portraits, to make their marriage seem more conventional. They were nowhere near as ecstatic on the day of the photo shoot as the day they were married. A miscarriage and many late-night fights had brought about a loss of innocence, the sadness of romantic expectations fallen short. Yida is pregnant with Echo in the photo. Queasy with morning sickness and holding a bouquet to hide her bump. The fact that she is also in the photo, as a foetus in the womb, fascinates and delights Echo. Every so often she points at the slight bump visible under the bouquet and cries, "There I am. Tucked away in Ma's belly! Guest of honour on your wedding day!"

Echo is sleeping when they go into the bedroom at ten, in her narrow bed against the wall. Her cheeks are flushed as though she is overheated, and Wang tugs down her heavy duvet and strokes her brow, thinking how lovely she looks when she sleeps.

Wang and Yida go to the larger bed they share by the window. Yida pulls her baggy, holey jumper over her head and, standing in her thermal underwear, massages almond lotion into her arms, calves and thighs. Once moisturized, Yida bends at the waist so her hair sways upside-down and drags a wide-toothed comb through curls so abundant you could lose a hand in them. Sometimes Wang hears the comb teeth ping as they break.

Wang reaches for her as she slides between the covers beside him. He pins her down beneath him and reacquaints himself with the parts of her body that he loves: the hollow at the base of her throat, the curve of her hips and her breasts that he cups and squeezes in his hands. He kisses her in that generous, wet and open-mouthed way they kiss now only when in darkness and in bed. "Shuuush," she whispers in his ear, though he hasn't yet made a sound. Wang longs for the abandon she used to have, back when they were newly-weds. Back before Echo was born. Now she is rigid and tense beneath him. But when he parts her thighs, his fingers slide inside her with ease, and he knows she is ready. "Shuuush," she says again as he thrusts up inside her. And Wang moves as silently as he can, stifling his moans in her hair.

Wang forgets time and place, until Yida digs her fingers in his shoulders. "*Echo*," she whispers. He pauses, hears a mattress creak and a child's hollow cough from the other bed. "That's enough, Wang Jun," Yida whispers. "She's awake." Wang pretends not to hear. He waits for a few moments, then starts up again. Silently. Stealthily. He does not last for much longer and as he comes feels Yida's eyes spitting at him in the dark. He sheepishly kisses her damp forehead, then peels himself away.

Wang remembers a line from the letter. Something about Yida satisfying *the needs of the flesh* and little else. Whoever wrote that knows nothing about his love for his wife, he thinks. He reaches out and sets the alarm for six o'clock. He falls asleep pretty much straight away.

3

The Second Letter

As biographer of our past lives, I recount the ways we have known each other. The times we were friends and the times we were enemies. The times lust reared its head, and we licked and grazed on each other's flesh. Once you were a eunuch. Your mother bound your wrists behind your back, laid your pubescent organs out on a chopping block, and severed you from the ranks of men. Once you were a Jurchen. The Mongols invaded our city, charging in on horseback, raping, beheading and capturing slaves. They reduced Zhongdu to ruins and cluttered our gutters with cadavers and severed limbs. They drove us forth across the Gobi Desert, and we fled during a sandstorm and sheltered behind rocks smooth as prehistoric eggs, jutting up to the sky.

Once you were a Red Guard, rampaging through Beijing, intent on destroying the Old Culture, Old Society, Old Education and Old Ways of Thinking. You raided the homes of class enemies, carting the "Ill-Gotten Gains of the Exploiting Classes" off in wheelbarrows, after beating the rightists in a gang of teenage girls.

Months later, I aided and abetted your suicide. You bared your thin, blue-veined wrists to me in the school toilets, and shouted, "Long live Chairman Mao!" as I slashed each one with the blade.

Then you plunged your wrists into the mop bucket, and your pa-triotic blood turned the water red as our national flag. I wanted to rip tourniquets out of my shirt and staunch the flow. But a promise is a promise, and I severed my own wrists with the sting-ing blade. Once. Twice. And the darkness roared, like the Great Helmsman's fury, that I had taken my fate into my own hands.

Can you guess where I am as I write this, Driver Wang? Hint: Baldy Zhang's Mao Zedong pendant hangs from the rearview and in the map-holding compartment of the door is a wallet of family snapshots. Echo aged three in Mickey Mouse ears. Yida on your lap as you smile together in a photo booth. That's right. I am in your taxi, outside Building 16.

A security guard patrols your housing compound. Three times he has passed your cab, shining his flashlight into the bushes and startling the stray cats. Three times he has failed to see me in the driver's seat, straining my eyes under the dim overhead light. There are a thousand fading scents here: cheap perfume, nylon tights, cigarettes, the man-made fibres of winter coats and, be-neath all this, your distinctive odour of hormones and sweat. Other remnants of you remain here too. Follicles, and scales of dead skin on the headrest. Molecules of breath.

Building 16 is in darkness. There is no one at your window now, but I have seen your wife and daughter there during the day. Yida hanging machine-damp laundry on the balcony rail. Echo fogging the glass with her breath, then dragging her finger through the condensed steam. Last week I saw you washing the windows. Sleeves rolled up to the elbows, splashing soapy water on the pollution-smeared panes, squeezing out the excess from the sponge. Ephemeral rainbows glistened in the soap bubbles, spec-trums of colour that imploded against the glass. Your cigarette smoke billowed in your eyes as you worked. Washing windows you have washed a hundred times before and will wash a hundred times again.

There is no one at your bedroom window now, because the three of you are sleeping. Echo in her bed in the corner. You and your wife in the larger bed. Cages of ribs rising and falling, as lungs inflate and deflate. Eyelids palpitating with the stimuli of dreams. Three separate minds processing the day's events. Three warm-blooded mammalian bodies at rest, regenerating cell by cell. Snoring as you breathe into the dark.

I understand your need to be with your wife. Yida is a woman who stirs up in men the animal instinct to fuck and procreate. Tempting men as spoiled fruit tempts flies. But sleeping with Yida must be a sad and lonely experience, for the pleasure and the rhythm of coitus do not amount to intimacy. Your soul detaches when you conjoin with her and looks away. And I don't blame your soul for averting its gaze. The thought of you with your wife repulses me too.

Please do not misunderstand me. You aren't the one I am disgusted by. In other incarnations I have explored every inch of you, with tongue and fingers and eyes. No matter how dilapidated, scarred and mutilated your body, I have always found you beautiful, for it is the soul beneath I seek.

The sky is lightening now. In twenty minutes your alarm clock will ring. At quarter past seven you and Echo will leave the building together, bundled in your winter coats, fogging the air with your breath. You will climb into the driver's seat. You will see this letter. You will wait until Echo is in school before tearing open the seal and reading it. Certain emotions will possess you. Anger. Scepticism. Fear. But these sentiments are transitory. Once reacquainted with your past, you will be grateful for my hard work.

To scatter beams of light on the darkness of your unknown past is my duty. For to have lived six times, but to know only your latest incarnation, is to know only one-sixth of who you are. To be only one-sixth alive.

4

Estrangements

Yida wakes on Sunday morning, shivering and burning up with a temperature so high she half expects the duvet to burst into flames. The fever is incandescent on her skin, and when Wang lays his hand on her brow, she is scalding to the touch. He slips a thermometer under her tongue and mercury expands in the calibrated glass tube. "You're a furnace in there," he says, reading the scale. He makes her a cup of lemon and ginger tea and holds it to her lips. Yida's throat, sore and inflamed, undulates as she drinks it down. Echo peers through the shadows at her mother, then bounds over in her pyjamas and bounces on the bed. She peels a satsuma and feeds the segments to Yida, one by one. "There there, the vitamin C in this orange will make you better," she sings. "Go away, Echo," Yida croaks, "or you'll catch my bug."

Mid-morning Wang hacks up a medium-sized chicken with the cleaver and simmers the carcass with herbs to make a soup. As the pot bubbles on the stove, Echo sits at the table in dungarees, her rabbit's teeth sticking out as she sketches a machinegun-toting vixen with a sexy hourglass figure in her spiral-bound pad. This doesn't strike Wang as the right sort of thing for a child to be drawing but, unsure of how to broach this, he says nothing. He stirs the pot and his thoughts drift to the letter. At the police station they had asked him for a list of people who might play a practical joke on him. Wang's mind had gone blank. Who does he know who is capable of writing such strange letters? Such sinister stuff about reincarnation? The letter makes Wang feel as though his privacy has been violated—as though the writer has keys to Apartment 404, and enters in the night to watch his family as they sleep. "Someone is stalking us," he told the police. "What can you do?" They had suggested that he get a car alarm fitted. They told him to warn his family to be vigilant, but Wang hasn't yet. Something holds him back.

At noon Wang wakes Yida, props her up with pillows and places a bowl of chicken broth on a magazine on her duvet-covered lap. He and Echo have lunch at the table, slurping out of the bowls and stripping the carcass of meat. On TV, camouflage-smeared Communists run through a twig-snapping forest, pursued by Japanese soldiers. "The TV is a time-machine," Wang says. "Every day you can travel back to the War of Resistance against the Japanese on one channel or another." Echo nods and picks at a chicken bone. Then she asks, unexpectedly, if he will take her to the park. Unexpected, because Echo is not a child who likes to play outdoors. Wang prepares his excuses. Beijing is submerged in a heavy fog and a temperature five below zero. He wants to potter about the centrally heated apartment and click about online. But Yida has overheard and calls out weakly from the bedroom, "Take her, Wang. She's been cooped up indoors all morning." So Wang and Echo pile on jumpers, button up coats and wrap on scarves, and Echo pulls on a bobble hat with flaps that hang over her ears. They call goodbye to Yida, but she has lapsed back into fevered sleep, and doesn't reply.

They walk to the park through fog as dense as descended clouds. They walk past skeletal cranes jutting into the sky, and tall ply-wood walls surrounding a construction site, a photoshopped utopia of villas and trees hiding the pit of mechanical diggers within. "How's school?" Wang asks. Echo tells him about the Hygiene, Homework and Politeness Monitors, eight-year-old bureaucratsin-training, who deducted points from her Young Pioneers pass-book this week because she forgot to wash her hands and has been "separating from the community" during break. Echo is one of the few students not yet invited to join the Young Pioneers, and Wang, suspecting that he has passed his inability to fit in down to his daughter, feels responsible for this. "How are your friends?" Wang asks, knowing full well Echo has only one friend, a chubby and awkward boy called Xiu Xing. Echo tells him the girls in her class won't sit near her because she is "ugly and has rabbit's teeth." "I hate my teeth," Echo confides to her father, and her small voice pierces his heart. "Don't listen to those girls. You aren't ugly!" he says. "When your teeth are fixed you'll be very pretty!" It pains him that Echo has to go to school and suffer the bullies, and the teachers, drilling her into becoming a loyal, obedient citizen of the PRC. But Echo needs an education. He has no choice.

They reach the south end of Chaoyang Park Road and Wang tells Echo that they have to call on her grandfather and Lin Hong and invite them to the park too.

"Do we have to?" Echo asks.

"Yes, we do."

Wang is firm and resolute, though he feels exactly the same way.

Before motor aphasia slurred Wang's father's speech, making him sound permanently, paralytically drunk, he liked to remind his son of the money he'd wasted on him over the years. Hundreds of thousands of yuan in boarding-school fees, and then tuition for the university Wang never graduated from.

"Such a privileged education," he laughed, "and what do you end up as? A taxi driver!"

Wang Hu's government official's perks meant he could more than afford the expense, but he liked to remind his son of what a failure he was. So when he married Yida and started a new life, Wang resolved not to see his father again. They had barely been on speaking terms since his mother had died anyway, and had already had a long period of estrangement, stretching five years.

The second time around, Wang had expected the rift to last for good.

Then one day in 2004, when Wang was twenty-eight and hadn't seen his father in four years, his stepmother Lin Hong called to tell him Wang Hu had had a stroke. He was now paralysed on his left side and had reduced motor function on the right. The doctors said the damage was irreversible. "Your father wants to see you," Wang's stepmother had said, and Wang went to their apartment the next day. His father was crippled now, slumped in a wheelchair, with a bib to catch dribble tucked into his collar and an incontinence pad bulging under his pyjamas. His once-commanding speech had deteriorated to a garble only his wife could understand. Wang had looked at his father, struck down at the age of fifty-eight, and felt conflicting emotions. He had expected to feel vindication—that his father had suffered the fate he deserved. He hadn't expected to feel so sad.

Wang would never love his father, nor even like him much, but his stroke stirred his sense of filial duty, and he began to visit him again. He brought Echo, then aged four, to meet her grandfather for the first time, and Echo had cowered behind Wang's legs. "Say hello to your grandfather," Wang had urged. "Go on, say hello." Upon hearing this, Wang Hu, with evident physical strain, opened his fist to reveal some glitteringly wrapped sweets. Echo shrank further back. "Don't want to," she whispered. "He smells funny." The old man looked so hurt by this that Wang understood the stroke had changed him. That his once-domineering mind, moulded by quotations from Sun Tzu's *The Art of War*, had become mushy as the mashed-up peas and carrots Lin Hong spoon-fed to him. That Wang Hu was harmless now.

The stroke transformed Wang Hu's relationship with his second wife too. They had been married for nineteen years, and for the first fifteen Lin Hong had had no say over how her husband lived his life. She had no say over how much he smoked and drank, or how many whores he fucked and mistresses he financially supported. "I'll have my lawyer prepare the divorce papers" was Wang Hu's response to her complaints of marital neglect. He'd made her sign a prenuptial agreement and, should they split, Lin Hong would be left without a fen.

But now that her husband can barely wipe his own backside, Lin Hong has the final say over everything. She is his primary carer, and "for his own good" exacts her revenge for fifteen years of misery. She scolds her husband for soiling his incontinence pad, for drooling and other mishaps he can't control. Cigarettes, alcohol and coffee are banned. She forbids his favourite Sichuan cuisine and feeds him over-boiled vegetables. She turns off the TV at the first hint of any gunfire or sex or anything that could raise a man's heart rate (claiming the overstimulation would trigger another stroke). She "puts him down" for his nap at two o'clock every afternoon.

When Wang and Echo call on them to invite them to the park, Wang sees a new framed photograph on the sideboard. "We had it taken at a studio," Lin Hong tells her stepson when he asks, "to celebrate our wedding anniversary." In the photo Lin Hong grips the handles of her husband's wheelchair as he slumps beneath her. Incarcerated in his semi-functioning body, Wang Hu looks downright suicidal. But Lin Hong, in contrast, is smiling and radiant. At forty-one she has outlived Wang Hu's first wife by three years. Tough as nails and in her prime, Lin Hong beams at the camera, confident she won't suffer the same tragic fate.

As they enter the east gate of Tuan Jie Hu Park, the fog hangs over the lake and bridges and paths and breathes sparkling drops on their coats and scarves. The fog is breathed in by them and resides for a few moments in the warm dark living cavities of their lungs. They have not brought Wang Hu in his wheelchair. Though Wang's father had been shut in all week and wanted to come on the outing, Lin Hong insisted he was overtired and "put him down" for his nap. She regards the park and the fog critically. She tugs her fur stole closer around her and stamps her spike-heeled boots.

"Why do you want to go to the park on a day like this?"

Why do *you* want to go to the park? Wang is tempted to remark.

But he knows why. Though Lin Hong is not a blood relation, she regards Echo as her granddaughter, showering her with affection, gifts and inappropriate "how to be a woman" advice.

Though the weather is freezing, there are other park-goers strolling around. Only children, bundled up like little Eskimos, wander around the park's fairground—the roller-skating rink, trampoline and merry-go-round—with an entourage of parents and grandparents following close behind. Most of the rides are nearly empty. A solitary boy steers about the dodgems as his father documents his progress with a clicking digital camera. A girl straddles a horse, holding a candy-striped pole as it goes round, a lone rider on the carousel of empty-saddled horses. The boating lake is translucent with ice.

"Echo, why don't you go on a ride?" suggests Lin Hong.

Echo stares up at the Ferris wheel, the top carriages lost in the mist. She shakes her head, but Lin Hong eventually persuades her to go on the trampoline. Wang and Lin Hong stand shivering as Echo jumps up and down with a wobbly smile, her pigtails bouncing under her bobble hat and her woolly socked feet barely straying from the cross marking the centre of the canvas sheet. Though she wears a duffel coat over her sweater and dungarees, Wang thinks his daughter looks cold, and he regrets not having made her put on another layer before leaving home.

When the allotted time is over, Echo stumbles dizzily down and pulls her fleece-lined boots back on.

"Wasn't that fun! Another ride?" asks Lin Hong.

Echo says no and wanders ahead down the foggy path. The amusement-park rides don't interest her. Instead she gathers frost-veined leaves and blades of grass, razor-edged with ice, and inspects them in her palm. At the lakeside she taps at the ice floes with her boots so they fissure and crack. She kneels and lifts a thin sheet of ice out of the water, holding it up, staring at the bubbles trapped in the translucent white. "Careful!" cautions Lin Hong. "That's dirty!" Echo slides the ice back in the lake, floating it on the surface like a raft.

A boy appears out of nowhere, underdressed for the cold in

tennis shoes and a zipped-up tracksuit. No coat or hat or gloves or scarf. "Little Rabbit!" he calls to Echo. "Little Rabbit!"

"He goes to my school," Echo says, waving at him.

"Where are your parents?" Wang asks the boy.

"At home," the boy answers.

"And they let you come to the park on your own?" Wang asks. The boy nods. Wang and Lin Hong sit on a park bench as Echo and her friend chase each other about. The boy lifts an ice sheet from a puddle, shatters it with a headbutt, and Echo covers her mouth and giggles.

"Feral child," remarks Lin Hong. She asks Wang where Yida is. Wang tells her she has the flu.

Wang's teeth are chattering, his toes numb. Conversing with Lin Hong on the park bench is not so much an exchange of words but of icy gusts of air. She has a personality like fingernails on a chalkboard, setting his nerves on edge. Wang watches his daughter and the boy poking about in the shrubbery with twigs, gathering frost-baubled spider's webs. He thrusts his hands deeper in his coat pockets as Lin Hong continues with her scathing remarks. He hopes Echo will soon want to go home.

Wang was fourteen when he first got to know Lin Hong. He had been at boarding school since his mother's death and hadn't seen his father in over a year. Wang Hu hadn't bothered to let his son know he'd remarried, so when a beautiful young woman came to his all-boys boarding school one Sunday and announced she was his stepmother, Wang was very surprised. Lin Hong was twenty-three and desperate for Wang to like her. A botched abortion had left her infertile and, devastated to learn that she would be childless, she sought out her stepson as the next best thing to a son of her own. The first time they met, Wang was wary of Lin Hong and her low-cut blouse, gold-hoop earrings and flirtatious ex-hostess manners. Out of loyalty to his mother, Wang was sullen and mute. So Lin Hong laughed and tossed her auburn-highlighted bob about, compensating for Wang's hostility with chatty exuberance until visiting hours were up.

Determined to make friends, Lin Hong visited again and again, presenting her new stepson with a Nintendo Game Boy, Nike Air Max, imported junk food and other trophies coveted by China's richest children. Lin Hong enhanced Wang's status in other ways too, as boys crowded around him after visiting hours with smutty questions about his striking, provocatively dressed stepmother. Year after year, Lin Hong visited his boarding school at weekends and public holidays. And gradually, Wang Jun came to trust and like her, and stepmother and stepson forged a friendship of sorts.

When Wang Jun was eighteen he was offered a place to study history at Beijing University. His father, who had barely finished middle school, was proud of his son's achievement and invited Wang to spend the summer holidays in the guest room of his brand-new apartment. Wang had spent every summer since he was thirteen in the boarding-school dormitory but was no longer allowed to stay there after graduation. He thought about his father's offer and decided he didn't care about the years of paternal rejection. He needed a place to stay. So after a five-year absence, Wang went back to his father's home.

At high school Wang had studied punishingly hard, depriving himself of sleep and friends in his single-minded preparation for the gaokao. To recover from this, he spent most of the long hot summer of '94 lazing about, reading paperbacks and playing video games. Wang's father was never home. Weekdays he worked until late and slept elsewhere, and weekends he was away at the beach resort of Beidaihe. Wang's stepmother, however, who had no job or social life, was in the apartment day and night. Whenever Wang slipped out of the guest room for a glass of orange juice, or to grab some food from the kitchen, Lin Hong would be there, flipping through a fashion magazine in one of her floaty summer dresses, strands falling loose from her piled-up hair. Or lounging on the balcony overlooking Chaoyang Park, her long slim legs stretched out in her denim cut-offs, her crimson-painted toes wiggling in the shade as she nibbled slices of watermelon and spat the pips over the rail. Though the east wall of the living room was entirely glass and the apartment heated up like a greenhouse, Lin Hong never turned on the air conditioning. The soles of her bare feet kissed the marble flooring as she wandered aimlessly from room to room. "I like to sweat," she told Wang, pulling her hair up from her perspiration-damp collar bone.

In the evenings Lin Hong mixed pitchers of cocktails, and she and Wang stayed up drinking until late on the balcony, gazing out at the tenth-floor view of thousands of lights twinkling in the city, as burning coils of mosquito repellent scented the air. Though the vodka and gin went some way to lessening Wang's awkwardness, he was still very shy, and Lin Hong dominated the conversation most nights. Lin Hong liked to talk. About her lonely sham of a marriage. About how her romantic life was over at the age of twenty-seven. About how worthless she was. Wang nearly fell out of his chair reassuring Lin Hong she was beautiful and clever. All she needed, he assured her, was the courage to live her life. Every night he listened sympathetically to her monologue of sorrows. Every night he was aroused and confused by her flirty little games.

"Why don't you have a girlfriend, Wang Jun?" she asked. "You're a handsome, eligible bachelor, right? I bet you could screw any girl you wanted."

Wang said nothing and blushed.

"You must da feiji all the time," she added with a knowing smile.

Da feiji. Beat the aeroplane. Wang wanted to spontaneously combust with shame. Did Lin Hong know it had become his habit to do this, twice a day, while stripping her of her sundress and cotton bikini briefs in his mind? His stepmother smiled.

"One day you'll do it for real. Why don't we wait and see . . ."

One evening in August Wang's father showed up at the apartment. He called his son out of the darkened lair of the guest room.

"Shower! Shave! Put on a clean shirt. And you can borrow a pair of my shoes. I'm taking you for a night out on the town. You can't spend the whole summer holed up playing computer games."

As Wang went to take a shower he saw, out of the corner of his eye, Lin Hong flounce into her bedroom and slam the door. But he put it out of his mind. His father was a stranger to him, and the opportunity to visit his shady nocturnal world was too interesting to pass up.

The nightclub, the first one Wang had been to, had a dance floor of pulsing neon and a lounge of faux-brocade-upholstered chairs and velvet curtains. Father and son sat at a table and a waiter immediately brought over a bottle of whisky and a tray of sashimi, sliced Kobe beef and other gourmet snacks. Wang's father stuffed a Vietnamese spring roll in his mouth and nodded approvingly at the hostesses in spangly dresses on the dance floor. The teenage girls had white gardenias tucked behind their ears, and the way they wobbled in their stilettos reminded Wang of little girls dressed up in their mothers' shoes.

When his colleagues arrived, Wang Hu introduced his son with pride. "He's going to Beijing University this year. Graduated first in his class at high school. Inherited his old man's intellect, eh?" Other work associates joined them. Some CEOs of agribusinesses, one of whom Wang Hu jokingly introduced as a Dirt Emperor, a billionaire of peasant origins who'd made his fortune manufacturing fertilizer. The Dirt Emperor wore a brick of gold on his finger and when he congratulated Wang in his thick Shanxi accent, nuggets of gold winked in his teeth.

After the introductions, Wang sank back with a beer and watched his father. Now forty-eight, Wang Hu had aged remarkably well. His hair, dyed politburo black, was thick as ever, and the lines on his face, instead of diminishing his handsome looks, lent them a distinguished air. Wang Hu was in his element in the company of other powerful men. He was outgoing and charismatic, with a deep and easy laugh that rumbled up from his belly, and a natural ability to strike up a wise-cracking, back-slapping camaraderie with just about anyone. Wang was bewildered by how different he was from the cold and distant stranger he had known as a child. Noticing his son watching him, Wang Hu leant over and grinned. "Do you like those girls dancing? Pick one. I'll invite her over to talk with you."

Wang shook his head. "No thanks." His father beckoned over three of the hostesses with a wave of the hand.

As his father was preoccupied with whisky and profiteering, Wang sat with the coquettishly giggling girls. They were Wang's age and younger, and up close he could see the smoke and mirrors used to create an illusion of sophistication and sex appeal: the pancake make-up covering teenage acne, the push-up bras and the crookedly glued-on fake lashes. The girls were well trained, smiling and full of questions, and oohing and ahhing at everything Wang said, but he could not relax in their company. He looked about at the other men basking in the attention of hostesses, inhaling flattery as naturally as they breathed air. "Drink more!" the hostesses cajoled, but Wang refused. The last thing he wanted was to become intoxicated. The last thing he wanted was to be seduced by this pretend world.

After midnight his father's mistress turned up, a willowy Russian with long blonde hair and curves spilling out of her dress. The girl smoked cigarettes and sipped a glass of cognac, sitting beside Wang Hu as though her sole purpose was to offer her thigh as a resting place for his hand, while he and the Dirt Emperor negotiated contracts. Wang kept glancing at the Russian. Why was she so mute? Couldn't she speak Chinese? Was she bored acting out the part of the Russian doll? Wang Hu caught his son staring at his mistress and, mistaking his gaze for desire, winked at him. Wang was suddenly exhausted. He rose to his feet and told his father he was going home. Wang Hu's silver-threaded eyebrows shot up.

"Go home? It's still early!"

Wang said he was tired. His father handed him a key with a room number on the key-ring tab.

"Go and rest then. I reserved you a suite in the hotel next door." Wang Hu's gaze slid to the hostesses, and he added in a low voice, "Which one do you want to take with you?"

"I don't want to stay in a hotel. I want to go home."

"What's wrong with you? You're a man, aren't you?"

For the first time that evening, cracks appeared in his father's joie de vivre. He looked frustratedly at his son. The Dirt Emperor chuck-led at the father and son dispute, his gold-plated molars glinting.

"There's nothing wrong with me. I want to go home—that's all."

"Don't be so ridiculous," his father reproached. "The room's all paid for. All you have to do is walk a few steps next door."

"No, I am going home," Wang said.

Wang Hu laughed indulgently. "Go then! All the men you see here, we all work hard. We deserve our fun. We don't want some puritanical virgin looking down his nose at us."

As Wang walked away he heard his father joking to the Dirt Emperor, "Kids, eh? Where'd he get that prudish attitude from? Not from me!"

His father was angry of course. But he hid that well.

The light was on in the kitchen when Wang got back. Lin Hong was on a stool by the counter, her blue silk robe gaping over her lacy negligee and alcohol-flushed chest. On the counter was an empty jug and a cocktail glass with a flamingo-pink paper um-brella leaning on the rim. As he entered the kitchen, Lin Hong ignored him and stared at the humming fridge with a tragic look in her eyes. Straight away Wang was guilty and concerned.

"Have you been crying?" he asked his stepmother.

Lin Hong sniffed and refused to meet his eyes. She slurred, "What do you care?"

"C'mon, Lin Hong. What's the matter?"

She looked at him in disapproval, as though he was the one who was drunk.

"Have fun tonight? Drinking whisky with your father's cronies and sixteen-year-old whores?"

"No," he said. "I didn't."

He stood in front of her stool, his hand resting on the coun-ter. He could smell white rum and pineapple juice on her breath. Sugar and alcohol rushed through Lin Hong's bloodstream, flush-ing her pretty, angry face.

"You're a lousy liar, Wang Jun. Of course you had fun. Like father, like son. You are just like him. I see that now."

The accusation was too far from the truth to offend Wang. He sighed at his stepmother, lashing out in her lonely rage.

"C'mon, Lin Hong. You know that's not true . . . If I had known how upset you'd be, I wouldn't have gone."

But her stepson's kindness only encouraged Lin Hong.

"Just so you know, Wang Jun, your father was using you tonight to get at me," she said. "He wants you on his side. He knows how important you are to me, and he wants to destroy what we have . . ."

What we have. Wang's heart quickened at the notion they *had* something.

"Lin Hong, I don't think my father thinks that way . . ."

Wang censored the rest—that his father probably never thinks of her at all. Lin Hong's paranoid imaginings that her husband was out to destroy their relationship were far more palatable to her than the truth, which was his indifference. Lin Hong scowled.

"You don't know your father," she spat. "He's an awful man. He deserves to go to jail!"

The shimmering blue silk of her robe slipped off her shoulders as she pulled forcefully at the counter drawer, and Wang looked away from the swell of her breasts beneath her black lacy negligee. Lin Hong removed an envelope from the drawer and handed it to him. The letter was addressed to the Central Discipline Inspection Committee. Wang quickly read the contents.

"I'll post it tomorrow," Lin Hong said. "Anonymously, of course, with a copy of our bank statement showing deposits from various businesses. I have sent other letters before, but they ignore them. They never discipline him. I keep writing to them, though, because maybe one day someone with morals will read one of my letters and investigate him."

Wang returned the letter to his stepmother, thinking it a waste of time. The odds of a government official being punished for corruption are the same as the odds of their being struck by lightning.

"Be careful," he warned. "He'll kill you if he finds out."

Lin Hong smiled. "If he ends up in prison for my murder, then it would have been worthwhile."

Wang laughed, but Lin Hong did not laugh with him. She hadn't forgotten where he had spent the evening.

"Which girl was he with tonight?" she demanded, shattering the confiding mood. "The Russian? The girl from Shanghai?"

Wang's instinct was to protect her feelings and deny there had been a girl. But he was loyal to her now, over and above his father.

"She was Russian."

Lin Hong looked sickened.

"Was she pretty? Blonde?"

"Why do this to yourself?"

"I bet she had big breasts. He likes women with curves."

"She was nothing special," Wang said, "and she didn't say a word. He may as well have hired out a blow-up doll."

"But she was young, though, right? Eighteen or so? Younger?"

Tears welled in Lin Hong's eyes, spilling over and sliding down her cheeks.

"Don't cry," Wang groaned. "Not over him."

"Do you know your father hasn't kissed me in two years?" More tears chased their predecessors down her cheeks. "What's wrong with me?" she asked. "What's wrong with these lips? Are they as disgusting as he thinks they are? Are they?"

On her stool, Lin Hong looked at him expectantly. Under her lacy negligee her perspiration-damp chest was rising and falling, as though in anticipation. Her brown eyes seemed to be challenging him, demanding something of him. Heart hammering in his chest, Wang gazed at her, and for one agonizing moment thought he hadn't the guts to act. Then, in a surge of courage, he lunged and clumsily banged his mouth against hers. The kiss had been inevitable—she'd been baiting him for weeks and, inexperienced as her stepson was, he was still red-blooded and male. But Lin Hong reacted as though shocked. She gasped, pulled away and slapped him across the cheek. The message was loud and clear: she was not the instigator of the kiss. Blushing, Wang stuttered apologies then shuffled away to the guest room. He didn't even feel the sting of her slap he was so consumed by disgrace.

* * *

A quarter of an hour later, Lin Hong entered the darkness of the guest room without knocking. She slipped under the bedsheets beside her speechless stepson and kissed him full on the mouth with her sweet, rum-scented lips. Her loose hair tickled his collar bone as she moved her head down, licking his chest, her tongue circling a nipple, her hand sliding under the waistband of his shorts. Wang had fantasized about her for weeks, but now that she was kissing him and writhing on top of him, he froze. The memory, long repressed, of the last time he had shared a bed with a woman, resurfaced, inhibiting lust or any emotions other than panic and fear.

"What's wrong?" Lin Hong asked, groping at his lack of arousal. "You can touch me if you like."

Wang couldn't speak. She took his hand and pressed his fingers to the moist folds of flesh between her legs, and he felt as though she was forcing him to finger a festering open wound. But he couldn't protest. His heart was beating out of control and his lungs couldn't take down any air. Struggling to breathe, he shoved her off the bed and she thudded to the floor. Then, his head spinning, he staggered out of the bedroom, through the living room to the balcony, where he leant over the railing and gasped at the night air like a man surfaced from drowning. Only then did his heart slow down and the panic subside.

The furious slam of the bedroom door shuddered through the apartment. Wang knew Lin Hong well. He knew she was shaking with anger, shame, indignation and disappointment. Rejected by father, now rejected by son. She would never forgive him for this.

Wang couldn't go on living there. He went back to the guest room, packed two suitcases, wrote Lin Hong a note and was out of his father's apartment at dawn. He stayed at a friend's place until late August, when he moved into his new dormitory room at Beijing University. Then the first semester started and Wang threw himself into lectures, hanging out with new friends and dating girls his own age. The incident with Lin Hong became a distant, embarrassing memory. And, like his father, he seldom thought of her at all.

*　*　*

Thirteen and a half years later, they sit on a bench in Tuan Jie Hu Park, watching his daughter play. In the years that have passed, what happened that summer night has not once been mentioned or alluded to. Wang suspects that if he brought it up, Lin Hong would deny it and laugh in his face. But he knows it's there, like an acrid odour in the air between them. Wang has forgotten what it was like ever to be attracted to his stepmother, whose chemically pale skin and surgically tightened forehead have given her a permanently startled look. Bitterness has ruined her looks too. Her dissatisfaction with the days of caring for her invalid husband, and the nights of alcohol and sleeping pills.

"Echo needs a proper winter coat," Lin Hong is now saying. "That cheap jacket your wife bought won't keep her warm . . . I can take her shopping to buy a new coat next weekend, and replace the one your wife picked out . . ."

"The coat Yida bought her is fine."

Wang has had enough of Lin Hong and the freezing park and is ready to go home. He stands up to call Echo, but before he can shout for his daughter, she rushes over. She is bawling like she hasn't done in years, her screwed-up face a tight ball of angst. Wang strides over to her and holds her shoulders firmly with his gloved hands.

"What's the matter, Echo? What's wrong?"

He looks her over. She seems unscathed, though the fleece-lined boot is missing from her left foot. The boy from Echo's elementary school stands behind her and looks sheepishly at Wang.

"What's going on?" Wang says sternly to the boy. "Why is she crying? Where's her boot?"

Lin Hong stands up in her spike-heeled boots and looms over the boy.

"You son of a turtle!" she shouts. "What have you done to make her cry?"

The boy backs away. "Nothing," he says defensively. "Bye, Rabbit," he calls to Echo. "See you in school." And he turns and runs off.

Leaving Lin Hong to comfort Echo, Wang rummages about in

the shrubs where the children had been playing. He pokes about for several minutes, but there's no sign of the missing boot. He sighs. The boots had cost 50 RMB and were meant to last another couple of winters. Yida had bought them a size too large and stuffed cotton wool in the toes.

Wang goes back to the bench and interrogates Echo: "What did that boy do to your boot? Did he throw it somewhere?"

But Echo shakes her head tearfully and won't say what happened. She can't walk home with only one boot, so Wang lifts her up, troubled to see his daughter in such a state. She wraps her arms around his neck and hides her face in his coat.

Quarter past seven, Monday morning. Beneath one of the taxi's windscreen wipers is a brown package. Wang lifts the parcel out from under the wiper and rips the adhesive flap to see what is inside.

"My boot," Echo says.

She stands behind her father and does not sound pleased to see her boot again. There is a letter in the parcel too, folded up. Wang knows he should rip the letter up and throw it away. But he doesn't. "C'mon," he says to Echo, holding open the passenger-side door. He slides the letter in his pocket, knowing he'll be reading it the minute she is in school.

5

The Third Letter

History is coming for you. Do you hear it, coming up behind you in the dark? Dragging its iron chains and shackles, up the concrete stairs of Building 16? History taps you on the shoulder, breathes its foggy thousand-year-old breath down your neck. "Here I am, Driver Wang. Why don't you turn around? Look me in the eyes?" But you pretend not to hear. You whistle. You fumble the key in the keyhole. You slam the door of 404, turn the lock and hook on the security chain. There was nothing in the stairwell. Nothing but the dark.

There are others like us in Beijing. Once I bought a ticket from an attendant in Wangjing Station, who was formerly a servant to the Empress Dowager Cixi (blinded in one eye when the Empress lashed out with her long nails in a fit of pique). Once at the National Library, the due date was stamped in my book by a librarian who was a graverobber during the late Ming (a depraved man who had carnal relations with the cadavers he dug up).

Some of the past incarnations rise up from the depths. They crawl up the throat of the host and peer beguilingly out from behind the eyes. They manoeuvre the host's mouth, taking over the vocal chords and tongue.

"I was a Peking Opera singer, who had his feet bound at the age of six to play female roles. I became addicted to the opium I smoked to ease the pain."

"I was an eighteenth-century Urumqi camel herder, with a goitre and three wives."

Then, having made themselves known, they sink back down, leaving behind the host stunned by the temporary possession by the other selves within.

When I encounter one of our kind, I tally the former incarnations as a woodcutter counts rings within a tree. I date the soul as a Geiger counter dates carbon. Last week I met a shoe-shine boy in Wangfujing, who was first made flesh during the Neolithic era, when men were cave-dwellers and dragged their knuckles on the ground. When men danced around fires and had no language other than violence and grunts. The higher reincarnates, who have lived hundreds of times, tend to live as hermits far from the human fray. To meet one in the hustle and bustle of Wangfujing was rare. But there he was, beckoning me over to the wooden box where he crouched, a rag in his polish-blackened fingers. As he buffed my boots, I told him who I was and of my hopes of reunion with you.

"Patience is a tree with bitter roots that bears sweet fruit," he opined.

He shone my boots to perfection and charged me five kuai.

Many of our kind go from cradle to grave ignorant of who they are. Some are now confined to asylums and subject to medication, electroconvulsive therapy and round-the-clock supervision by white-coated medical professionals. Those who have known fame and notoriety in their former lives often struggle with anonymity. They roam the streets, bragging of the feats they accomplished back when they were Mencius or Li Bai or Sun Yat-Sen, until they are arrested and locked up, or heckled and beaten by drunks.

Fantasist. Mythomaniac. Liar. What names do you call me in your mind? No matter how scathing, I am not offended or deterred. My undertaking, as biographer of your past, is not one I take lightly. I work hard for your enlightenment. I am patient, diligent and devoted to the role.

I came back to Beijing to find you, Driver Wang, gusting back to the city with the Gobi sands. Once I knew your whereabouts, I rented a room nearby, on the eleventh floor of a run-down tower block. The room is a tomb of cement, with a mattress, a table and chair. The windowpanes are myopic, grimy with the polluted breath of Beijing. The melancholy glass weeps in heavy rain, and stagnant pools of tears leak onto the inner sills. The central heating is broken, so though I come from a region of China thirty degrees colder than the capital, I suffer the cold more here. Migrant workers from Henan Province live above. They gamble and chatter and scrape chair legs over the ceiling throughout the night. Living here is often unbearable. But I remember my higher purpose and I endure.

Once I had found a room, I bought a secondhand computer, as dusty and old as an archaeological find. For days on end I shiver in a shroud of blankets, hunched at the screen. Every so often I pause my typing to briskly rub my hands and breathe warmth onto my icy fingers. I don't know a soul in Beijing. The computer is my only companion, the overheating machinery spinning its internal fan. Sometimes the machine breaks down, goes silent and black. I reboot and pace nervously back and forth, waiting for the resuscitation of my only friend. The machine comes back to life and my heart leaps with relief. I resume my work and, as your biography takes shape on the flickering monitor, I am full of hope.

I watched you today, wandering with your daughter through the frozen wastes of Tuan Jie Hu Park, wrapped up against the January cold and blowing cigarette smoke into the fog. I saw your fatherly pride as she explored the paths and lake and bounced on the trampoline. I saw your concern as she wept over her lost boot. I saw how important Echo is to you. How you love her most.

But here's the truth, Driver Wang. Blood, though thicker than water, never lasts beyond the span of one life. When the heart ceases to beat, blood oxidizes to rust and flakes away. And the other things that bind you to wife and child—the marriage and birth certificates, and legal documentation of family life—will be dust in a hundred years.

Our bond, however, transcends the death of the body, though we are hosted by flesh and blood, viscera and bone. Though we eat and sleep, laugh and weep, sneeze and catch colds, we differ from those condemned to live only once. When they die they are dead. After we die we live on.

Listen. Do you hear that? Outside the door? Strain your ears above the TV and the washing machine's spinning drum. The chained beast of history is breaking loose. Do you hear his deep and ragged breathing in the dark?

History is knocking for you, his knuckles striking the door. Don't pretend not to hear. Don't pretend he's not there.

Open the door, Driver Wang. Let him in.

6

Night Coming
Tang Dynasty, AD 632

I

Strangers knock in the night. The common folk of Kill the Barbarians Village, seeking out your mother to confess the torments of the soul. You, a boy named Bitter Root, huddle with the Runts in the corner, and peer through the darkness at the Sorceress Wu as she lowers her hawkish nose, shuts her piercing eyes and listens to the tales of woe. Envy and lust. Wrath and revenge. Flames leap in the hearth, and the sorceress chants in an ancient tongue and tosses into the fire a mysterious dust that flashes sulphurous and bright. She decants into vials potions to cure heart-sickness, abort a foetus or punish a husband who rapes the twelve-year-old servant girl. She sells bottles of deadly nightshade, and hallucinogenic venom extracted from the heavy-lidded toad she keeps in a bamboo cage. She sells amulets and anti-lust charms. She sells a poultice to the cabbage-seller to grow back his amputated foot.

A husband killed by bandits. Too many mouths to feed and nothing but steamed grasshoppers to feed them. These are the misfortunes that forced your mother to turn to the dark arts.

And what she lacks in supernatural ability, she makes up for with nerves of steel. For sometimes the strangers come back, accusing her sorcery of being a sham and demanding refunds. The sorceress blames the meddling of evils spirits and offers to sell them anti-demon charms. She curses them and slams the door. The sorceress never backs down.

You are Bitter Root, named thus to trick the demons into thinking you are vile-tasting and bad to eat. You are thirteen years old and wild, with never-healing scabs on your knees and your eye-teeth knocked out from falling out of trees. Your hair is filthy and gnarled as roots, and your sun-darkened face grubby and snarling. You are a solitary child. You scorn your pot-bellied little brothers and sisters, whom you call "the Runts," who splash about in the river Mudwash and dare each other to gobble spiders up. You spend your days roaming the Neverdie Forest, toughening to leather the soles of your bare feet. A hunter-gatherer, you steal eggs from nests and trap birds and animals for the stew pot. Stealthy and brave, you part the bamboo saplings and swoop your snake-catching net down on serpents coiled bellydown in the grass. You carry the captured snakes, in a fury of thrashing in your net, to your mother. The sorceress kills them and slits their bellies, slicing from fanged head to tail, and extracts the gall bladder and poison sacs for medicinal use.

You are not Sorceress Wu's firstborn. You have an elder sister, whom the sorceress named Brother Coming, to encourage fate to bring her a son. One year older than you, Brother Coming is a mute and too dim-witted to do even simple chores, such as raking ashes in the hearth or fetching water from the well. Solitary like you, Brother Coming spends her days in the forest, wandering through the maze of trees and whistling with a blade of grass in mimicry of birdcall. But Brother Coming is not predatory. She is a scavenger, not a hunter. She gathers bird skulls and scapulae, dark feathers and jagged stones, and stows her treasures in tree-hollow hiding places. Toads *ribbit* in her tunic pockets and beetles scuttle in her knotty hair. The Neverdie Forest embraces Brother Coming. When she curls up to sleep on a bed of moss, the trees above her shed a blanket of leaves should the air turn chill. The canopy shifts to shelter Brother Coming should some rain begin to fall.

When you encounter Brother Coming in the Neverdie Forest, you ignore her. Your idiot sibling is of no interest to you and you pass her without a nod. Then one day in your thirteenth year you catch Brother Coming stalking you through the trees. Whereas you are forest-coloured, streaked with greens and browns, Brother Coming is pale and conspicuous. Twigs snap and leaves rustle under her feet, frightening the snakes away. "*Go away!*" you hiss. You hurl clods of mud, which splatter her because she is too feeble-minded to dodge them. You run over and clobber her until she hobbles away.

But an hour later she is back. Stalking you through the trees. You charge at her and knock her down, and as you roll over with her on the leaf- and twig-strewn ground, you notice the swellings on your fourteen-year-old sister's chest. Curious, you pull up her tunic. You tweak and peek. You poke and pry and probe her with your tongue. As you grope her, Brother Coming lays beneath you, quiet and unprotesting. As you have your way with her, her eyes register neither pleasure nor pain.

Many cycles of the moon go by. Starry constellations come and go in the night sky. Skinny Brother Coming is fattening up. As you lie together in the forest, you sink your hands into the ever-swelling bump to push it flat. But the mound of belly grows fatter by the day, warning you things have gone awry. The Runts notice the change in your sister too. "Fatty Coming! Fatty Coming! Waddling like a duck!" they tease. At supper the Sorceress Wu serves Brother Coming an extra ladle of rice gruel. She prepares nourishing herbal soups for her. The Sorceress Wu narrows her eyes at you, her hook-ended nose flaring in suspicion when you are near.

"Bitter Root! Bitter Root!"

The sorceress is calling, so you fling your fishing pole down by the edge of the river Mudwash and hurry past the Runts (who are squealing, "Worms! Worms! Worms!" and chasing each other with dangling earthworms). You run up the hill to the mud-walled dwelling, eager to please the sorceress, who lately snarls at the mere sight of you.

"Here I am," you announce.

The sorceress is pacing the trampled-earth floor. She looks up and trepidation flashes in her eyes before the return of her habitual cast-iron will.

"Ma?" you ask. "What do you want?"

"Take off your clothes," the sorceress commands.

You obey. You stand there naked. A fire blazes in the hearth and the brass pot bubbles and boils. She tells you to kneel. She binds your wrists and ankles with rope. She plunges the blade of the snake-eviscerating knife into the boiling pot. Suddenly, you understand what she intends to do. Weeping, you beg for mercy.

"I'll never touch Brother Coming again! I swear on the graves of our ancestors!"

Tied up like a pig for a spit-roast, you wriggle to the door. The sorceress grabs your hair and presses the knife-edge to your throat. "Don't you dare! Or I'll slit you from ear to ear."

You kneel by a chopping board. She grabs your penis and testicles and roughly pulls, threatening to kill you if you don't hold still. Her other hand holds the knife, raising it high. She is shaking with nerves, but her teeth are gritted with intent as the blade swoops down. You see the blood splatter her pale cheeks before you feel the pain. When the pain comes, you scream. You scream with such violence it curdles the air. The sorceress is trembling and bathed in perspiration. The castration is harder than expected. Like beheading a chicken whose stubborn head won't detach. She hacks and hacks, and at last she pulls her hand away in exultation and relief. The knife clatters to the floor and she opens her blood-soaked fist. And what you glimpse before you lose consciousness will haunt you until the day you die. Your blood-glistening organs in the palm of your mother's hand. Her smile of triumph at having severed you, at the age of thirteen, from the ranks of men.

Months later a man with a donkey comes from the Kill the Barbarians Village to collect you. You are wearing a hemp tunic and carrying a bundle of clothes. Hanging from the belt of your tunic, in a leather pouch, is a silver trinket box with your embalmed genitals inside. The sorceress hands the donkey man a string of copper cash and issues her instructions.

"All the way to the city of Chang'an?" asks the donkey man.

"All the way to the gates of the Imperial Palace," says the Sorceress Wu.

"And then what?"

"And then you say, 'This is Eunuch Wu. A gift to the Emperor.'"

Foot in stirrup, you clamber up on the donkey, grimacing as you straddle the saddle (though the stump has healed, when pressured it hurts). The sorceress turns her back on you and returns to the mud-walled dwelling. The donkey man grasps the reins of the donkey bridle and leads you away.

II

The very day you leave for Chang'an, water gushes out from between Brother Coming's legs. Her mouth rounds into a cavern of pain as she keels over, wracked by the spasms within. "It's time," observes the sorceress, and sends the Runts to fetch pails of water from the Kill the Barbarians Village well. A short while later, I am born. A baby girl with a vigorous cry in her lungs and no deformities visible to the eye.

As a child, I have no name. The sorceress calls me "Girl" or "She-Brat." And later, when I am of crawling age, the Runts call me "Doggy." They pat my head and throw sticks for me to fetch and carry back to them in my mouth. When I am of walking and talking age, the Runts have grown up and gone away to labour on pig farms or be the wives of pig farmers in the other villages of Blacktooth County. Leaving me behind with Brother Coming and the Sorceress Wu.

My childhood is much the same as yours. Strangers knocking in the night. The chanting of spells and magnesium flares in the fireplace. For much of my childhood I am under the impression that Sorceress Wu is my mother and Brother Coming my mute idiot sister. The peasants of Kill the Barbarians Village call me the Wu Child and, owing to the sorceress's reputation for evil-doing, forbid their children from going near me. I am very lonely. Brother Coming won't play with me and when she goes into the Neverdie Forest, won't let me tag along. Rejected and hurt, I bully Brother Coming on our bamboo-mat bedding at night. I slap her, and pinch her black and blue, and get away with it, for she never makes a squeak of protest. I abuse Brother Coming for years, until the evening the sorceress looks over as I am twisting her ear and says slyly, "That's no way to treat your mother, She-Brat."

Shocked, I let go of Brother Coming's ear. The sorceress laughs. "Yes, that's right. You weren't squeezed out of *my* loins, Girl. You are the progeny of incest and rape. Your father was the good-for-nothing rapist and your mother the imbecile next to you. No wonder they spawned a she-brat such as you."

My grandmother makes no secret of her wish to be rid of me and, afraid of being sold into slavery or married off to a pig farmer, I toil for the sorceress. I cook and clean for her, sweeping the floor and scrubbing the pots and pans, keeping our rammed-earth dwelling spick and span. I am filial and obedient and never answer back. But it's no good. The year I am thirteen, Sorceress Wu tells me of the arrangements she has made.

"Girl. You are now betrothed to the Young Master Huang of the Huang family of Goatherd Valley. You are to be wedded next week."

"But I don't *want* to be married," I complain in a small voice.

The sorceress scoffs, "Want? Want? Want is neither here nor there! The Huangs are the most prosperous family in Goatherd Valley. A she-brat such as you ought to be on her knees with grati-tude!"

The next day the man with the donkey comes from Kill the Bar-barians Village. He hoists me up on the saddle, and we clip-clop away from Blacktooth County. No one, not the Sorceress Wu, Brother Coming, nor the Runts, comes to bid me farewell. I never see any of the Wu clan again.

III

The grandeur of the Huang family mansion is such that I cling to the donkey reins, too intimidated to dismount. The manor has a glazed-tile roof and the walls are lacquered wood (unlike the sorceress's mud-walled dwelling, which a thief needs only a pail of water to break into). A servant boy leads me through parlours and halls to a shady courtyard of cypresses and a shimmering pond of carp. I am exhausted from riding on donkeyback for three days, plodding along the river Sveltedeer to the foothills of Mount Weep. I am barefoot, in a tattered robe stitched from a discarded rice sack. A girl with no name. Having inherited the sorceress's humpbacked nose, I lack even prettiness as a saving grace. What if the Huang family are disappointed and send me back? What bloodcurdling punishment would the sorceress mete out should that happen?

"She's here! She's here!" a woman chimes.

Master Huang and his wife enter the courtyard, a handsome couple in black damask robes of mourning, both tall and stately, with unpocked skin and fine sets of ivory teeth undamaged by rot. Wife Huang claps her hands in delight. She sweeps towards me and gathers me into her sweet, fragranced embrace. "Welcome to the Huang family, beloved Daughter-in-Law!"

Wife Huang then releases me and gazes upon me at arm's length. "Oh you are lovely!" she beams. "How lovely you are!"

Master Huang is more muted in his reception. Sotto voce, he says to his wife, "The girl is ugly. Horrendously hooked of nose."

"Oh shuush!" scolds Wife Huang. "Can't you see we are blessed? Once the dirt is scrubbed off she will be a passable bride!"

As Wife Huang fusses over me and Master Huang frowns, I am too timid to utter a word. Young Master Huang, to whom I am betrothed, is nowhere in sight. Shyness prohibits me from asking where he might be.

A pretty maidservant named Duckweed conducts me to a bed-chamber with rosewood furniture and a four-poster bed with a canopy of chiffon, where I am to rest before the wedding the following day. Incense braziers burn patchouli and myrrh, and goldfish swim in a flower-and-bird-painted porcelain bowl. I daren't touch anything, lest I grubby it with my hands.

As Duckweed bathes me in a brass claw-footed tub of water sprinkled with rose petals, she smirks and wrinkles her nose. Granted, I am skinny and flea-bitten and turn the water black, but her rudeness offends me. I am about to marry into the most prosperous family in Goatherd Valley. Who is this servant girl to act so haughty and superior? After my bath, I change into a clean linen robe, and Duckweed brings me a tray with bowls of steaming rice, stewed meat and pickled vegetables. Famished, I bolt everything down, pretending not to care as Duckweed titters behind her dainty hand.

Later, as I lie in bed, Wife Huang enters the bedchamber like a visitation from the Goddess of Mercy. She kneels at my bedside and strokes my temples with a gentle smile. Not once in my thirteen years of girlhood has anyone touched me with such tenderness. A lump forms in my throat.

"Sleep, beloved Daughter-in-Law," she whispers. "Tomorrow is the wedding. A day of joyous festivity. You need your rest."

Daybreak. A sunny morning of birdsong, fragrant breezes and cloudless sky. In my wedding robe of embroidered red silk, my hair elaborately braided into the Anticipating Immortals style, I am radiant. In fact, I will shun modesty and own that I am beautiful for the first time in my life. Looking over the guests in the courtyard, I understand the wedding ceremony is to be an intimate affair, with only Master Huang, Wife Huang and an uncle and aunt in attendance. Evidently there has been a recent death in the family, for they are wearing mourning robes of black and are very solemn indeed. The Buddhist monk arrives and speaks in hushed tones with the Huangs. A cockerel is strutting around, cawing and pecking at the ground. Odd, I think. Why is it on the loose? Young Master Huang has not yet come, and I am jittery and dying to know what my husband will be like.

"May the ceremony begin," intones the Buddhist monk. A stable boy comes forth and catches the cockerel, which squawks and flaps. The boy squats beside me, pinning the cockerel's wings down and holding it steady. Where is Young Master Huang? The monk holds up a copper censer by a chain and sways it over the squawking bird and me. Strange blue smoke pours out of the censer, chokingly pungent and stinging my eyes. The monk begins to chant and, with an ear attuned to sorcerers' dialects, I hear he is chanting not Buddhist sutras but ancient dark magic. He is not a monk, but a shaman. A necromancer, conjuring spirits, summoning the dead. The black-robed wedding guests are silent, except for Wife Huang, who sinks to her knees, sobbing and beating her chest. Where is Young Master Huang? The shaman's eyes roll backwards in their sockets and, as he ululates, I hear the ancient Chinese for "marry" and understand I am being joined in holy matrimony with the bird.

The wedding banquet is a sumptuous feast served with silver ewers of wine. Not a morsel passes my lips and I don't speak a word. The bridegroom, however, is in high spirits, throwing his wattle-and-combed head back and crowing vociferously, scampering about on clawed feet and pecking up the grain Master Huang scatters for him. Wife Huang has recovered from her sobbing. Whenever our eyes meet across the banquet table she beams and raises her goblet of plum wine: "To our son's new bride!"

After the banquet, Duckweed the maidservant leads the cockerel and me to the bridal chamber. She bolts the latticed door when she leaves, locking the newly-weds in. Unperturbed, the cockerel hops and squawks and flaps up on the conjugal bed. He struts in a half-circle then defecates on the bedspread. Has the son of the Huangs died and been reincarnated into this bird? Is that what the ceremony was about?

"Young Master Huang?" I call experimentally.

The bird claps its beak and blinks its beady eyes. I shake my head at my foolishness then decide to call the cockerel Young Master Huang anyway, as he responds to it.

As the cockerel puffs up his feathers and swaggers about, I sit on the edge of the four-poster bed in my red silk wedding gown, wringing my hands on my lap as I ponder the fate that awaits me. Am I really to spend the rest of my days wedded to a bird? What a preposterous destiny! Then, out of nowhere, I hear the low cackle of the Sorceress Wu: "Wretched she-brat! Character determines destiny. Fate is the excuse of the spineless and weak!" And though it was my evil grandmother who sold me into this strange predicament, her words lend me strength.

Dusk creeps into the bridal chamber, and I plot and wait as the shadows thicken. My spouse is quieter now, grooming his plumage, plucking out the odd feather not to his liking with his beak. When at last the bolt slides back and the door creaks open, the bridal chamber is completely dark. It is Duckweed, bringing the supper tray. I needn't see her face to know she is smirking. Duckweed lowers the tray on a rosewood table then turns to the dresser to light the oil lamp. I waste no time. I leap up, grab the water carafe from the tray and smash its neck against the bedpost. At the shattering of glass, Duckweed gasps and spins round. I knock her head with my knuckles and drag her to me by her hair. I touch the jagged edge of the carafe to her throat.

"Don't scream," I warn her, "or I'll stab out your eyes!"

Duckweed whimpers. In the flickering oil-lamp light her eyes are frantic. Not so high and mighty anymore.

"Tell me what is going on. Speak!"

Duckweed speaks. A breathless rush of words. Young Master Huang died in a tragic hunting accident the year before. He'd passed on before marrying, so his parents wanted to find him a bride, a companion for the afterlife. I was the Spirit Bride in a Spirit Wedding and the cockerel the stand-in for the Spirit Groom. Then, with some satisfaction, Duckweed adds that the eminent Huang family would never have wed me to their handsome son were he alive.

"Now let me go!" Duckweed weeps. "I have told you everything."

"Liar!" I spit. "What happens next?"

Duckweed won't say. I scratch the broken glass of the carafe against her cheek, drawing blood. "Oh no! Not my pretty face!" she wails. The maidservant then reveals the final stage of the Spirit Wedding: the Sacrificial Ceremony. The following morning I am to be ritually slaughtered then laid to rest beside the corpse of Young Master Huang in the Huang family mausoleum, joining him in eternal sleep. I thank Duckweed, then I beat her with my fists until she is limp and barely conscious. I rip off my accursed silk wedding gown and change into Duckweed's servant robes and woven reed sandals. Out of spite I snatch up the Spirit Bridegroom, tucking him under my arm. I slip out of the unbolted door and make my getaway.

IV

I flee through the night. The runaway Spirit Bride, dashing pell-mell through paddy fields of croaking frogs, leaping over ditches and streams. "Run! Run! Run!" squawks Young Master Huang under my arm. And I obey, hurtling through the darkness without pause for breath or to ease the stitch in my side. The Huang family owns a stable of horses and will come galloping for me at dawn.

Where in the Middle Kingdom am I fleeing to? As far away from Goatherd Valley as possible. And then, who knows? As I tear through the night, I think of you, the father I have never met. Eunuch Wu of the Imperial Palace in Chang'an, loyal servant to the Emperor Taizong. I decide to go to Chang'an and find you. I am your daughter, and perhaps our blood bond will oblige you to find me lodgings and work. Perhaps you will find me a position as a chambermaid in the Imperial Palace. Perhaps the Emperor Taizong will fall in love with me, and I will ascend from servant girl to empress. And with these fatuous thoughts of fame and fortune in my head, I run and run, wishing I could grow wings and fly to Chang'an.

By sunrise I am staggering beneath the strange turquoise peaks of the Tiltingsky mountain range, following the Turnabout River to its end. Under my arm Young Master Huang stabs at me with his beak, wriggling to be set free. Fed up with his squirming, I wring his neck. Widowed at the age of thirteen, I tuck my spouse's feathered corpse back under my arm and stagger onwards, not daring to stop. At sundown I build a fire, pluck Young Master Huang, then roast and eat him. He is delicious. As I suck the marrow from his bones and lick bird fat from my fingers, I contemplate the journey ahead. The city of Chang'an is three years away by foot, and one year by horse and cart. A thousand-league journey I must rise at the crack of dawn to begin. Sated with bird, I fall asleep, full of uncertainty but grateful not to be in the Huang family mausoleum, dead.

The next day, by a stroke of good luck, I meet an expedition of merchants travelling northwards to Chang'an. There are eighty merchants in the caravan, riding in eighty horse-drawn wagons carrying exotic spices and fabrics, frankincense, silver ewers, sky-blue Syrian glass, delicate ostrich-egg cups and countless other frivolous trinkets for the capital's rich. As well as these exquisite trifles, the merchants have collected many marvels of the plant and animal kingdom to sell to the nobility of Chang'an. Curiosities such as albino frogs and a wise and ancient monkey who can do sums with an abacus. Russian conjoined twins fused at the head (like one man resting his temple against a mirror) and a bare-breasted Japanese mermaid, her tail curled up in a barrel of salty water, weeping bitterly to be so far from the sea. In the very last wagon, a cyclops and a wolfman, both shackled at the ankles, play a never-ending game of chess. The wolfman furrows his furry brow and deliberates for hours on end before moving a chess piece with his shaggy paw.

The journey to Chang'an lasts three hundred days and the caravan passes through every landscape of the Middle Kingdom. Terraced hillsides where water buffalo pull ploughs. Holy mountains with peaks so high they penetrate the cloudy realm of the gods. Vast stretches of barren nothingness where not even the wild grasses grow. As the scenery changes by the day, the heavens above us change by the hour. The Gods of Thunder brew up dark lagoons of cloud that the Gods of Rain turn into heavy deluges and floods. The Gods of Wind bluster and chase flocks of clouds across the sky, until the Gods of Bright Skies clear the firmament for the sun.

During my time in the merchant expedition I am wretchedly miserable, as for three hundred days I ride in the wagon of the Merchant Fang, who'd taken a fancy to me and rescued me from the roadside when every other wagon had rolled on by. The old merchant is blotchy with gout and has many yellow rolls of fat under his robes cut from fine expensive cloth. The merchant calls me "wench" and likes to fondle me on his lap and tickle me with his beard. Needless to say, my passage to Chang'an is not free of charge, and within months I have a bulging belly. By the time the caravan enters the gates of Chang'an and proceeds up the Vermilion Bird Avenue with much trumpeting of horns, clashing of cymbals and weeping of merchants affected by the homecoming, I add to the cacophony a cry of pain as the Merchant Fang's baby prepares to come out. As the merchant already has a wife and a brood of eleven children, to him the progeny in my womb is a bothersome thing. So when the baby is born lifeless in a boarding house on Drum Tower Lane, the Merchant Fang sighs with relief. "Well, that's that then," he says, pulling a blanket over his stillborn son. He tosses the midwife a string of coppers, bids me farewell and is on his way.

V

Springtime in Chang'an, the tree peonies in blossom. Bleeding, weeping and limping, I stagger about the streets of the twelve-gated city to the Imperial Palace in the north. In a daze, I roam in and out of the city wards, gazing in wonderment at the sights. Row upon row of wooden houses, vertiginously soaring up to three storeys in height. Avenues of horse-drawn carts, clattering at breakneck speeds, and magnificent palanquins borne aloft on the shoulders of manservants, velvet curtains hiding the distinguished noblemen inside.

The Eastern Market teems with common folk and Uighurs and

Persians and Europeans trading their wares. I wander by stalls of millet, bamboo shoots, pigs and Tibetan slaves in pens. Arabian stalls of alfalfa, pomegranate, spices and wool. I wander into the market square, where magicians in dark booths sell python's bile for melancholia and dragon's bones for fatigue. Troupes of buskers strum zithers and pipas, and a dancing bear shambles on his hind legs as his master waves a birch wand. A storyteller has attracted a crowd with his tale of the Sea-Dragon King who lives in a palace under the ocean and feasts on opals and pearls.

I ask passerby after passerby, "Excuse me, which way to the Imperial Palace?"

And in this manner, I gradually find my way there.

I arrive at the gates of the Imperial City at sunset. Though I am tired and aching to the marrow of my bones, the magnificence of the palace rejuvenates me. Stone lions roar at the Vermilion Gates and the palace rooftops, curved elegantly from ridge to eaves, shining gold in the setting sun.

I accost an armoured guard at the gate.

"Excuse me. Could you pass on a message to Eunuch Wu? Could you tell him his long-lost daughter has come to Chang'an to see him? I don't mind waiting here while you fetch him."

The guard beats me so hard with his spear he knocks out a tooth, and this is how I learn that commoners are not meant to approach the gates of the Imperial City without an invitation bearing the imperial seal. I would have to contact you through other means.

VI

I spend a night shivering in a ditch, then in the morning return to the Eastern Market to look for work. I go to Butchers Lane, Ironmongers Lane, Axe-Makers Alley and Cloth-Weavers Lane, in and out of every shop. "I am hungry and strong," I say. "I am willing to work for a crust of bread." But no one wants me. Not even the human-waste collectors who trundle wheelbarrows from privy to privy. I am starving. I go over to the gangs of beggars rattling begging bowls in the market square. The first gang of beggars tells me to go away. "Only those with missing limbs can beg here," they say, waving me away with stump-ended arms. The second gang tells me to get lost too: "Only the blind or one-eyed allowed here." I glance over at the third gang, swatting at the flies buzzing over their pustule-weeping skin, and realize I lack the requisite skin disease.

I am at my wits' end. How will I survive in this black-hearted city? I may as well crawl back into the ditch and wait to die, as the Heavens must have decreed. Then, out of nowhere, I hear the cackling of the Sorceress Wu—borne by the Daemons of Wind from that mud-walled dwelling over a thousand leagues away. "Wretched she-brat," she cackles. "Character determines destiny. Courage and boldness. Not fate." And goaded thus, I holler at the top of my lungs, "Has anyone any work for me? I am hungry and strong! I can work as hard as any man. I will toil like a dog! I will toil until I sweat out my blood! I am willing to do anything!"

"Anything?"

A pedlar of candy apples with scheming eyes and hog bristles spouting out of his chin stalls his pushcart nearby. The pedlar holds out a sugar-coated apple on a stick, and my stomach growls.

"Anything," I repeat.

I stumble to him. I snatch the sugar-coated apple and, light-headed with hunger, I take a bite. The pedlar shows his stumpy brown teeth in a sly grin.

"Then come with me."

VII

"I see you've lost your virtue then," says Madam Plum Blossom as she peers between my legs. "Pity. Customers pay a fortune to defile a girl with her purity intact."

She orders me to strip for inspection. She prods and pokes. Tweaks and peeks. She squeezes my breasts and tuts.

"Sallow complexion . . . Humpbacked nose . . . Sour, down-turned mouth . . . Knocked-out tooth . . . Chest like a boy . . ."

But in spite of her harsh and negative appraisal, Madam Plum Blossom likes me.

"There's some fighting spirit in you," she says. "The gentlemen callers like a girl with fire in her belly. *Night Coming*. That will be your name. Night Coming. Yes. Can't think of a better sobriquet than that!"

When the pedlar said he would take me to a brothel in the Gay Quarters of Chang'an, hopes of fame and fortune rang out in my head. On the long journey to Chang'an the Merchant Fang had waxed lyrical about the Gay Quarters and their legendary brothels, such as the House of Willowy Enchantresses and the Parlour of the Golden Peaches, frequented by aristocracy, imperial scholars and literati.

According to the Merchant Fang, the courtesans of the Gay Quarters are classical beauties with lunar skin, scallion fingers and tresses dark as ravens' plumage. They flutter about like exotic birds in an aviary, in the finest, most intricately embroidered robes. Such is their beauty, boasted Merchant Fang, that should they happen by your hometown, the common folk of Kill the Barbarians Village would mistake them for immortal goddesses and lay sacrificial offerings of slaughtered pigs at their feet.

Not content with mere pulchritude, the courtesans of the Gay Quarters have many talents and accomplishments. They are gregarious hostesses and poetesses, enlivening banquets with witty repartee and verses composed on the spot. They sing like songbirds and are skilled musicians, strumming the zither and playing the lute and flute. They are intellects educated in the Five Classics and Daoist and Confucian philosophy, and keen to engage in verbal jousting and philosophical debate. The life of a celebrated courtesan, whose patrons and admirers are the most powerful men in Chang'an, was very appealing to me. So my hopes were dashed when the pedlar brought me to the Hummingbird Inn in Old Temple Lane, which makes no pretence of being a high-class establishment.

"We don't put on any airs and graces here!" laughs Madam Plum Blossom. "We're a lowly brothel, for commoners! For scoundrels, rascals and ne'er-do-wells. Hiring our cunts out. That's our job. We make no pretences to the contrary. We can't sing or dance and the only verse we compose is doggerel and bawdy rhymes. But our customers come to our parlour and have themselves a rollicking good time! I'll teach you all the tricks of the trade, Night Coming. I was an excellent whore in my day. A veritable snake-charmer . . ."

Proprietress of the Hummingbird Inn for twenty years, Madam Plum Blossom is a cheerful woman with a loud and raucous laugh. The pastimes she is most fond of include ale drinking, gorging herself with cakes and tutoring Master Xing, her Burmese parrot, to curse and sing vulgar little ditties for the gentlemen callers. Proud of her voluptuous figure, Madam Plum Blossom is often tethered to a brass mirror, admiring her wide hips and the ample cleavage she flaunts with a low-cut décolletage. Though most madams of the Gay Quarters have a reputation for being mean-spirited and quick-tempered, quoting Confucius as they beat their girls for alleged wrongs ("Those!" *whack* "who err!" *whack* "on the side of strictness!" *whack* "are few indeed!" *whack*), Madam Plum Blossom spares us the rod, being too jolly of temperament for such corporal spite. Though most madams keep their daughters imprisoned under lock and key, Madam Plum Blossom encourages us to venture out into the hustle and bustle of Chang'an on daily constitutionals. The warm-hearted proprietress quickly becomes like a mother to me.

The other two prostitutes at the Hummingbird Inn, Moonglow and Heavenly Lotus Flower, are nowhere near as kind. "Stinking southerner," they mutter, pinching their noses when I am near. But Madam Plum Blossom tells me to pay them no heed.

"Don't mind them, Night Coming. They've no right to put on airs. Heavenly Lotus Flower used to be a scullery maid called Appleseed, and Moonglow's husband is a dissolute wastrel who sold her to pay off his gambling debts."

As I am a fledgling in the bedchamber, Madam Plum Blossom prepares me for brothel life by having me tryst with the young stablehand from down the lane. She stands at the bedside as the boy and I fumble together, clumsy and maladroit, haplessly muddling through the conjoining of our yin and yang parts. Though we go at it until I am quite saddle-sore, Madam Plum Blossom casts a critical eye over the proceedings. Her arms crossed, her lips a thin line of disapproval, she scolds, "Don't be so coy, Night Coming! There are more ways to make Clouds and Rain than by lying on your back, y'know. And why are you flinching? That's his Jade Stalk he's stabbing you with, not a dagger!"

Exasperated, she teaches me how to straddle the stablehand and rise up and down in a style known as Riding the Unicorn Horn. "This position is very good for the elderly and infirm," she advises. "As well as veterans who have fought in many battles and are missing their limbs."

The tutorial underway, Madam Plum Blossom drills the stable boy and me with step-by-step instructions, through the Raising the Yin to Meet the Yang position, the Two Dragons Who Fight until They Drop, and the Silkworm Spinning a Cocoon. The stable boy and I are soon quite knackered, pink in the cheeks and out of breath from flailing and contorting our limbs. The first tutorial reaches its climax when Madam Plum Blossom is teaching me the best technique for Playing the Jade Flute, and the stable boy, no longer able to contain his excitement, spurts the Jade Liquor into my mouth. Madam is very cross when I gag and grimace and spit.

"Impoliteness!" she scolds. "One mustn't spit the Jade Liquor as though it scalds the tongue. One must swallow and smile." After twenty years of whoredom, Madam Plum Blossom's knowledge is as boundless as the sea. "Men have all sorts of peccadilloes," she tells me. "Some men like to Penetrate the Red during a woman's moon cycle, or piddle on a woman out of the Jade Watering Spout. Some men like to poke a woman in the back passage, which is called Pushing the Boat Upstream."

When she suggests I attempt to Push the Boat Upstream with the stable boy, I protest I cannot imagine a more agonizing suffering. But I then try it, and it's not so bad once I am used to the clogged-up sensation in my rear end.

"They come here to do the things their wives won't do, you

see," Madam Plum Blossom says, "unless they have a delightfully wicked and depraved wife, who may come to watch her husband go at you, and then Mirror Dance with you, which is how two women enact the Clouds and Rain."

The stable boy is fifteen and his family name is Hogspit. Though he takes pains to wash and comb his hair before coming to the Hummingbird Inn, he is still a mucky boy who stinks of horse sweat and manure, and in spite of his passion in the bedchamber, my Peony Pavilion never moistens with dew. Madam Plum Blossom likes the stable boy, however, as he has stamina and obeys her command not to spill his yang essence until the lesson's end. Only once does he get swept away in the act of Clouds and Rain and deviate from the tutorial. A rapturous look in his eyes, Hogspit the stable boy hoists my legs over his shoulders in the Starving Horse Rushes to the Trough position and thrusts his slobbery tongue in my mouth. Madam Plum Blossom calls him to heel, smacking his buttocks with a birch wand and warning him to make Clouds and Rain only in the manner that *she* dictates *or else*.

After the third lesson of the bedchamber the stable boy confesses that he has fallen in love with me. This is very bothersome. Especially when he starts bringing me small tokens of his affection, such as the skull of a rat he found in the stable and a pig's trotter pickled in brine. One night I am woken by a hail of stones on my window. The stable boy is outside in the cobbled lane.

"Elope with me, Night Coming!" he calls. "Run away with me and leave your life as a common strumpet behind!"

Disgruntled to be woken, however, I shout down that a life of harlotry is far preferable to the family name of Hogspit and go back to bed.

Meticulous and thorough in my education, Madam Plum Blossom supplements the practical tutorials with theoretical lessons. During the day we peruse the Manual of the Bedchamber, the leather binding creaking as we flip through hundreds of illustrations of the two-headed, eight-limbed beast.

"Endowments come in all shapes and sizes," Madam Plum Blossom says, "and some are very curious indeed. Endurance also differs from man to man. Some men spend their yang essence in very few strokes, like our customer Ten-Strokes Li. And an unfortunate few, such as Hopeless Chen, spill their yang before even penetrating the Vermilion Gates. And then there are men who need tens of thousands of strokes to spend. Men such as these are *nuisances*, and you'll be at it until cockcrow unless you clench the lotus shaft and use some tricks to hurry them up!"

While gleeful on the subject of Clouds and Rain, on the subject of love Madam Plum Blossom gets a cold and steely look in her eye.

"Beware men who swear eternal oaths of love, Night Coming! Men speak all kinds of devilry in the throes of lust. They'll promise to marry you, or take you as a concubine. But at the end of the day they want a wife from a respectable home, with her Vermilion Gates *intact*. Two of my girls have fallen ill from lovesickness. Heavenly Snapdragon shaved her head and went to live in a nunnery, and Celestial Moonbeam suicided by swallowing needles. Armour yourself, Night Coming, against men who'll try to swindle you with blandishments and declarations of undying love. Or else the dalliance won't end in a wedding song . . . but a funeral dirge."

The tutorials end one evening as I am Riding the Unicorn Horn with the stable boy, whose eyes are rolling around in ecstatic bliss. Madam Plum Blossom, standing in her usual spot at the bedside, for the first time has no critique or suggestions to make. She nods swiftly with approval.

"Very good, Night Coming. You are dexterous and skilled. Agile, nimble and spry. This session will conclude your lessons of the bedchamber. You are now ready to begin your life as a whore."

VIII

Afternoons at the Hummingbird Inn are spent in the courtyard, drinking jasmine tea in the shade of the cherry tree. Moonglow and Heavenly Lotus Flower prattle to each other as they pose at easels, daubing brushes over mediocre paintings of butterflies alighting on azaleas, or peacocks with fanned-out tails. Madam Plum Blossom reads erotic poetry and nibbles cakes, and Master Xing the Burmese parrot scuttles to and fro on his perch, until the door knocker sounds, and he squawks, "Here are the guests! Pour the ale! Light the candles!" and our working day begins.

A jovial and convivial hostess, Madam Plum Blossom makes no distinction between rich and poor as she serves plum wine, thrusts her bosom about and holds forth with charming small talk. All men (except known bandits and vagabonds) are welcome in her parlour, and her lack of pretension warms the hearts of many. Moonglow and Heavenly Lotus Flower are delightful too, with a knack for being silly and fatuous and making the guests roar with laughter. During my debutante nights at the Hummingbird Inn, I am timorous and shy, and some of the gentlemen callers ask Madam Plum Blossom if she has cut out my tongue. Madam hoots with laughter and playfully slaps her accuser.

"Oh, you wicked scoundrel! I've done no such thing! Night Coming's a mere apprentice. But soon she'll be the most popular courtesan in the Gay Quarters. Just you wait!"

Before long I have contorted my limbs into every position in the Manual of the Bedchamber, played over a hundred Jade Flutes and had the Jade Liquor spurted into every orifice (and splattered on other parts, such as my bellybutton or hair). Some men are handsome devils, for whom my Peony Pavilion becomes drenched with dew. Others look and smell as though they haven't bathed in a year, and Raising the Yin to Meet the Yang with them is an odious chore. Out of professionalism, though, I serve every customer alike, and most with no particular sentiment at all.

During the day I wander around Chang'an, frittering my earnings on frivolities such as puppet theatres, sugar-spun birds on sticks and fortune-tellers ("This won't be your only life," predicts one physiognomist, stroking the hump of my nose. "You will be reincarnated many more times yet.") Though my new life as Night Coming has begun, I am still determined to find you. Once a week

I go to the calligraphy shop on Old Temple Lane and dictate to the old bearded sage there (the one literate person I know) a letter to you.

"To the Honourable Eunuch Wu," the letter usually begins. "This is your long-lost illegitimate daughter, Night Coming . . ."

The letter ends with my whereabouts and a request that you come and visit. Then I seal the letter and hire a messenger boy to deliver it to the gates of the Imperial Palace. Week after week, the old bearded sage writes my letters in his best ink-brush calligraphy. And week after week, I dispatch them to you, though you never reply.

As the nights of carousing and merry making accrue, I come into my own as a hostess. I at last find my voice, which rings out in the parlour like a tinkling bell, mellifluous and gay.

"What a charming young wench you are!" the patrons say. "Where in the Celestial Kingdom do you hail from?"

I regale them with tales of Kill the Barbarians Village and the wicked Sorceress Wu. I tell them of the sorceress grinding up concoctions of bat's gonads, centipedes and menstrual blood with pestle and mortar. I tell them of Turnip-Seller Chen who came cradling the turnip he thought was his wife, begging the sorceress to reverse the "fox fairy curse" (in truth, his missus had eloped with a goat herder from Magpie County). I tell them of Pigbreeder Liu, who begged the sorceress for an anti-lust charm to cure his habit of engaging his sows in the act of Clouds and Rain. The guests laugh uproariously and thump the wooden table with their fists.

"Bravo! What funny little tales, Night Coming! How ignorant these silly, superstitious country folk can be!"

I abhor false modesty, so I shall speak plainly: I am a masterful storyteller. A first-rate raconteur. Kingfisher feathers in my chignon, in flowing satin robes, I stand at the head of the candlelit table of guests, open my mouth and the extraordinary tales of the common folk of Blacktooth County flow forth. Macabre tales of sorcery and blood-spattered revenge. Romantic tales of tragic star-crossed lovers. Erotic tales of lusty bed-hopping and adultery. I do not exaggerate or embellish. The truth, as witnessed by the grand-daughter of the Sorceress Wu, is far stranger than any far-fetched imaginings. I have been privy to thousands of people begging for magical intervention in their darkest hour. I have witnessed the sorceress's cruel and pitiless exploitation of their need.

As I gain in confidence my tales become theatrical performances. I create an atmosphere of suspense, like a striptease artiste, building up to the finale, the climactic scene. I imitate the Sorceress Wu's shaman act with a sacrilegious thrill, ululating in tongues, eyes rolled back in sockets. I impersonate the country bumpkin accent of Cabbage-Seller Qin, buying a poultice to grow back his amputated foot. I am a wit, a comedienne, my humour slapstick or refined. My performances soon last throughout the evening, until the candles have sputtered down to pools of wax.

The legend of Night Coming the Tale-Spinning Courtesan spreads throughout the Gay Quarters and every night the Hummingbird Inn is packed. The guests crowd in and drink jugfuls of wine, perhaps fondling Heavenly Lotus Flower or Moonglow on their laps as they listen spellbound to my spine-tingling tales. Silver piles up in our coffers and Madam Plum Blossom is well pleased.

As my star ascends, shining high above Old Temple Lane, I add to my repertoire the Tale of Bitter Root and Brother Coming. I tell of the Neverdie Forest and my conception by sibling incest sixteen years ago. I tell of the Sorceress Wu's barbaric punishment for your sins against Brother Coming. I tell of how I fled to Chang'an.

"Gentlemen, my quest here in the city of Chang'an is to be reunited with my father, the Eunuch Wu. I beg of any gentlemen here with imperial connections to let it be known that Night Coming of the Hummingbird Inn wishes with all her heart to meet her father. Pass on this message for me, kind sirs, and I'll be forever in your debt!"

Patience is a tree with bitter roots that bears sweet fruit. This is the motto I live by. Patiently I wait for my message to spread from the Gay Quarters to the imperial household, and to the ears of my father. I come to be known as the Eunuch's Daughter, much to my delight.

IX

"Night Coming!" trills Madam Plum Blossom. "A gentleman caller is here for you." Her voice drops to a whisper. "*A eunuch from the Imperial Palace.*"

A year has gone by since I came to Chang'an. A year of life at the Hummingbird Inn. A year of changing seasons, and now spring is here again. How remarkably apt! My heart leaps and rejoices at the granting of its deepest wish. My father has come!

"One moment, Madam Plum Blossom!" I call back. "Do serve our guest some tea."

I am in my bedchamber, having risen after a night of spinning fables and Playing the Jade Flute of a gold merchant from Samarkand. Madam had interrupted me as I stood at the mirror, idly attending to my coiffure and toilette. I stare into the polished oval of brass. Am I a long-lost daughter to make a father proud? I am no longer the starving waif who arrived in Chang'an a year ago. My cheeks are rosy and plump (thanks to Madam's epicurean tastes and fondness for plying others with cakes), but many late nights of ale-drinking and sinning have tarnished the bloom of my youth. The purity and innocence I once had has vanished, and a knowing, wise-beyond-her-years look haunts my eyes.

I change my scarlet gown with plunging décolletage for a peony-embroidered robe, modest and high in the neck, as becoming a young girl. My lofty chignon cascades down as I pull out the combs of rhinoceros horn. I arrange my loose hair into two chaste plaits and rub the rouge paint off my lips, smearing a white linen hanky as red as a menstrual rag. Shaking, I take a deep breath. "Father, here I come . . ." Down the creaking wooden stairs I go.

The eunuch peering into the deep stone well is not you. Call it intuition of the blood, but I know this at once. He nods his turbaned head and strides towards me in a swish of fine robes cut from imperial cloth, and I hide my disappointment behind a warm and welcoming smile. The eunuch has a blue-tinctured pallor and looks ethereal as a fox fairy or spirit, and out of place in our sunny, cherry-blossom-fragranced courtyard. On his perch Master Xing ruffles his feathers and puffs out his chest: "A guest is here! A stinking castrato!" The eunuch's face wrinkles as he smiles, showing neat rows of little teeth. Under his turban, his eyebrows are feathery and light.

"Eunuch Talent," he says. "An honour to meet you, Night Coming, the Tale-Spinning Courtesan. I have heard of your magnificent storytelling. You are fast acquiring a mythical status in the Gay Quarters."

Eunuch Talent is slight as a boy child of about twelve, and his lack of masculine traits suggests he was neutered before puberty. His high and fluting voice is an octave below falsetto, and in it one can detect years of training to restrain its crow's screech.

"A pleasure to meet you, Eunuch Talent," I say. "As you can see, I am but a poor and ignorant country girl. The reputation that you hear of is not one I deserve."

Madam Plum Blossom bustles into the courtyard with a tray of jasmine tea and cakes of sticky rice and sweet dates. She narrows her eyes at Eunuch Talent, as she has a low opinion of the castrati ("Never met a neuter who weren't a malevolent fiend!") and won't waste her charms on him. She sets down the tray and goes away.

Beneath the pink blossoms of the cherry tree, Eunuch Talent and I sip at tea and nibble little cakes. Isn't the spring weather fine? Aren't the cherry blossoms exquisite? Isn't the brevity of their flowering expressive of the transience of life? What splendid cakes these are! Etiquette demands the point of his visit be delayed with trivial and meaningless chatter. But impatience wears my politeness thin.

"Why have you come to see me, Eunuch Talent?" I ask. "Are you acquainted with my father, Eunuch Wu?"

"*Yesssss*," he hisses, and I half expect to see the flicker of a forked tongue. He gives a smile, thin and calculating.

"He no longer goes by the name of Eunuch Wu, but Eunuch Loyal One. He is the head of the Department of Housekeeping in the Imperial Palace, and a trusted servant and confidant of the Emperor Taizong. A very powerful castrato indeed."

"Does he know of me, his daughter, Night Coming?" I ask anxiously.

"Not yet. But I shall tell him. Tomorrow."

"A thousand blessings to you, Eunuch Talent!" I gush. "Oh what a kind-hearted soul you are!"

I am not so naïve of course. There is something he wants in exchange. The eunuch smiles, basking in my praise. Then he sighs wistfully and gazes upon me with affected romantic longing.

"How lovely you are, Night Coming," he says. "It's obvious how an enchantress such as you has every man in the Gay Quarters under her spell. One night with Night Coming the Tale-Spinning Courtesan would be an honour I would cherish for the rest of my life."

He strokes his beardless chin and waits for my response. Cast in a role that would challenge even the most skilled of actresses, I smile. "Eunuch Talent, the pleasure will be all mine."

May you sleep with a eunuch! is a curse spat by courtesans who wish evil upon each other, but what "to sleep with a eunuch" means, and why it is a curse, is a mystery to me. How does a eunuch perform the Clouds and Rain? How does a eunuch compensate for his lack of manhood? What does the courtesan do with the mutilated stump? Eunuch Talent ends my ignorance.

To sleep with a eunuch is to be stripped and leered at as the eunuch keeps on his robes. To sleep with a eunuch is to become a scratching post for a neutered cat, to be stabbed with your own rhinestone-studded hairpins and strangled with your own beads. To sleep with a eunuch is to be bitten and grinned at with blood-stained teeth. To see the eunuch's pale whey face light up as he penetrates you with a balled-up fist, punching its way inside. I clamp down hard on my tongue. My shadow writhes on the wall of the bedchamber, but I won't give him the satisfaction of tears or a cry of pain.

Eunuch Talent sneers, "I saw how you smirked when I asked to spend the night with you. 'How can this emasculated fool make love to a woman?' you scoffed. Well, is this not making love? Don't I penetrate you far deeper than your average man?"

When Eunuch Talent's vandalism is over, purplish marks of strangulation circle my neck and bite marks throb on my breasts and buttocks; crescents of teeth, upper and lower sets, are embedded in my flesh. On his way out, Eunuch Talent glances back at the blood-spattered bed where I am protectively hugging my limbs. He smiles, proud of the damage he has done. He will request an appointment to see Eunuch Loyal One, head of the Department of Housekeeping, the next day.

"However," he adds, "I can't guarantee he will acknowledge paternity of a low-breed slut like you."

Then, in a swish of imperial robes, Eunuch Talent is gone.

"Night Coming! Damn you, child, for not calling me! How could you let that horrid teapot without a spout torture you so? How?"

Sighing and cursing under her breath, Madam Plum Blossom swabs and dabs ointment on my wounds and orders a few days of bed rest. But I won't hide in my room as though I am ashamed. I surrendered my body to Eunuch Talent in exchange for his services as a messenger. I am not a victim here.

I stand before the polished oval of brass, open a jar of dove's droppings and rub the snowy-white powder on my cuts and bruises. I change into a sapphire gown and arrange silk scarves over the purple throttle marks on my neck. I colour my blood-drained cheeks and lips with rouge paint, bind my chignon with bright ribbons and go down to the parlour that very evening. I am a whirl of merrymaking, witty banter and joie de vivre. The gentlemen callers, in high spirits, raise their goblets of ale: "To Night Coming," they say, clinking in toast. "Gay as a canary, she tickles the very soul!"

I stand at the head of the table and, eloquent and silver-tongued, compliment every gentleman in turn. I am aching, my body hot and shivery as though infected by the Eunuch Talent's bites. But my joy and jubilation are genuine. My father is coming to see me. You are on your way.

X

Three quarters of a year go by and you do not come. Many moons wax and wane in the night sky over Chang'an and, convinced you have rejected me, I sink into hopelessness and despair. In the evenings in the parlour of the Hummingbird Inn, I drown my sorrows in plum wine and drunkenly slur morality tales of fathers abandoning daughters and meeting ruinous ends.

"Is that a jug of vinegar she is drinking instead of ale?" the gentlemen callers ask Madam Plum Blossom. "Have you been feeding her nettles and wasps? What happened to the charming and clever Night Coming we used to know?"

In the morning, when I am moaning and groaning and cradling my throbbing head, Madam Plum Blossom scolds me. Hand on hip, standing in my doorway, she says, "What has become of you, Night Coming? Why do you insult the gentlemen callers and drink till you can't stand? Soon you will be unfit to work in even a notoriously lowly brothel such as ours!"

My head hurts so much I can't look up at her. Go away, I think. Then, in a gentler tone, Madam Plum Blossom says, "Didn't I warn you never to trust a man, Night Coming? Not even those teapots without a spout. Forget that Eunuch Whatsisname from the palace. You have no need of him. We here at the Hummingbird Inn are all the family you need . . ."

Wincing at the stabbing pain behind my eyes, I glare up at her. "You common whores aren't my blood kin! I have imperial connections. I am but one degree of separation from the Emperor Taizong!"

"Well!" Madam Plum Blossom sniffs. "Who's been shooting vinegar up your Peony Pavilion? Ain't no shame in being a whore. We here at the Hummingbird Inn are proud of what we are! And we may not be your blood kin, Night Coming, but we love you far better than him . . ." Madam Plum Blossom turns and leaves, and I hear the wooden stairs creaking as she goes down. Meddling old hag, I think.

And I bury my head in my hands and cry.

* * *

Then, one midwinter day, hope returns. I am gazing out of my window at the mesmerizing swirl of snowflakes in the sky when a magnificent palanquin appears in Old Temple Lane. The palanquin is borne on the shoulders of eight men, proceeding slowly over the cobbles, and a scaly dragon, sinuous and fierce, roars on the side. The insignia of imperial affairs. The bearers lower the carriage at the gates of the Hummingbird Inn. A pale hand from within parts the velvet curtains, and my heart misses a beat as I intuit that my fate is about to emerge.

The winter garden is chilly. Snow flutters to the ground. You stand by the stone circular well in robes of deepest purple, the wide-cuffed sleeves hanging to your knees, and the sight of you stalls my breath. Majestic and imposing, you have come a long way since the days of Bitter Root. Beneath the low black turban wound around your head, you are handsome, your eyes darting and quick. Your skin begs comparison to porcelain or milk, but you are nothing like the Eunuch Talent, who was effeminate and slight. You are manly enough to make the palace ladies whisper and regret Eunuch Loyal One can't be seduced. You are your mother's son. You have the Sorceress Wu's humpbacked nose and, beneath your composure, I sense the fighting spirit of the Wu clan, strong and indomitable within.

Fearing you would grow impatient with waiting and leave, I rush down to meet you without changing my cicada-wing lace nightgown or combing my messy hair. I look as though called away from a gentleman caller, and I blush with shame.

"Night Coming," you say, "at long last we meet."

Your speech is as commanding as your presence. How can you be so steady on your feet? How can your heart not be vaulting up in the air? I bow to you, long and deep with respect.

"Eunuch Loyal One," I say, "I am honoured that you have come to meet me."

You smile and wrinkles spread out from the edges of your eyes. You are not yet thirty but, like most neuters who lack the yang essence, are beset by premature ageing. "How are the Sorceress Wu and Brother Coming? How do the Runts fare these days?"

"They fare well, Eunuch Loyal One."

Then I tell you how the sorceress sold me to the Huangs of Goatherd Valley to be slaughtered as a Spirit Bride. You shake your head with a weary sigh. "The wickedness of the Sorceress Wu never ceases to appal."

I nod and, loath to waste more time on the atrocious Wu clan, say, "Eunuch Loyal One, did you read the letters I sent?"

Snow whirls into the courtyard, settling on the bare branches of the cherry tree. You blink as a snowflake catches in your eyelashes. "Forgive me, Night Coming," you say. "As head of the Department of Housekeeping, I have many duties and responsibilities. I have not had time to read your letters."

I recall the hours spent composing the letters with the old sage in the calligraphy shop, and I lower my eyes, bewildered and hurt. You clear your throat. "Allow me to speak frankly, Night Coming," you say. "I won't insult your intelligence with less than the truth. I have no paternal feelings for you. Fatherhood is the fate of other men. To be a eunuch and serve the Emperor is mine."

You speak as though there is truth and integrity in what you say. But you are denying paternity of me. Where's the truth in that?

"Fatherhood *is* your fate!" I protest. "You are my father. I am your daughter. How can you deny the fact of me?"

Disagreement shows in your eyes, but you are calm. "You misunderstand me, Night Coming. Of course I accept that we are related. But I can't be your father. I will never love you as a father loves a daughter. I have neither the time nor inclination. My life is devoted to serving our Son of Heaven, the Emperor Taizong."

Your dark eyes shining with emperor-worship, you tell me how honoured you are to serve His Majesty. You tell me how His wisdom and judiciousness make Him the greatest emperor the Celestial Kingdom has ever known. You tell me how proud you are that He who loathes sycophants and flatterers has chosen you as His confidant. Your love of the Emperor crowds your heart. Crowding out your only child.

"I admire you, Night Coming," you say, "for coming to Chang'an with nothing more than your quick wits and tale-spinning skills and becoming a renowned courtesan. But the Imperial Palace and the Gay Quarters are two worlds that ought not to collide . . ."

You summon forth a manservant, lurking in the gateway, carrying a wooden chest. The chest is lowered on the stone table and the lid unlocked with a key. Under the lid are rows of silver coins. A fortune. Enough to feed, clothe and shelter me for the rest of my life.

"One thousand tael," you say. "My gift to you."

I am speechless. You misinterpret my shock for joy and are pleased. "And from you, Night Coming, I beg a small favour in return. I beg of you to be silent about the fact that you are my daughter."

You are disowning me. I reel as though slapped. "You are ashamed that a prostitute of the Gay Quarters is your daughter?" I ask.

You clear your throat again, the wide cuff of your sleeve hanging down as you cough into your fist. "I am head of the Department of Housekeeping in the Imperial Palace. The tale of Bitter Root and Brother Coming is injurious to my reputation. Bitter Root was a feral beast, and I am grateful to the Sorceress Wu for . . . severing me from him. She freed me from the libidinous throbs and urges of men and purified me for the higher purpose of serving the Emperor."

Your calm and reasonable manner is infuriating. I would prefer your honesty. A sneer. A nose wrinkling of disgust as you sling me out, like night soil from a chamber pot.

"Tell me," I say bitterly. "Does the Emperor repay your sycophantic and fawning love of him with love in kind?"

Annoyance flashes in your eyes. Then you regain composure with a condescending smile. "My love for Emperor Taizong is not a possessive love that demands love in return. My love of the Son of Heaven transcends this ordinary, selfish love. But this is more than I can expect a simple girl from Blacktooth County to understand . . ."

Snow is tumbling out of the sky. The crystals of ice melt against my cicada-wing lace gown and my skin, heated by the tempest in my heart. I am trembling, but not with cold. "Very well, Eunuch Loyal One," I say. "I will never speak of Bitter Root again. You have my word. But I don't want your money. Please take the silver when you leave."

You are relieved. Now the embarrassing chore of severing ties with your illegitimate child has been taken care of. You are eager to return to the imperial household.

"Farewell, Night Coming," you say.

You nod at the manservant and you both proceed to the gate, leaving the chest of silver behind. Insulted, I am about to shout after you, when a fierce and sudden wind gusts the snow sideways. A cackle of laughter, borne by the Daemons of Wind from over a thousand leagues away, startles both of us. You stiffen and pall. A primal fear creeps into your eyes.

"Wretched she-brat," the sorceress laughs. "Are you going to let him get away with treating you like dirt?"

A gust of wind directs my gaze to the leather pouch on the belt of your robe, containing the silver trinket box of your embalmed genitals. I run over and snatch the pouch, and to my delight it comes away in my hand. Aghast, you lunge to grab it back, but I skip away, giggling. I swing the leather pouch by the drawstring in front of you, as though tormenting a starving cat with a dead mouse dangled by its tail.

"You'll rot in Hell without these," I laugh. "The Gatekeepers of the Otherworld will turn you away if you don't have your precious jewels!"

You turn pale with superstitious fear. I giggle again, giddy to have the upper hand.

"Brother Coming," you shout, "return those to me at once!"

"I am *not* Brother Coming!"

Offended to be confused with the imbecile Brother Coming, I dash over to the stone well and swing the leather pouch over the dark hole. My fingers are numb and stiffened with cold, and though I do not intend it, the drawstring slips out of their grasp.

There's a moment of silent descent. Then, *splash*. I throw my hands over my shocked mouth. Snowflakes eddy and spin into the dark hole. You are horror-stricken. You run and leap up onto the circular stone ledge. You perch there like a bird in purple robes, peering into the depths.

"Master!" shrieks your manservant. "Master, wait! Let me fetch a slave to go down for you."

You ignore him. Your manservant dashes into Old Temple Lane, calling for the palanquin bearers. There are hand- and footholds on the inner wall that Well-Dredger Wang uses to climb down, to scoop out branches and drowned birds with his net. But in midwinter the inner walls are slippery with ice, and to go down is to risk life and limb. Determined to recover your precious jewels, however, you position your foot into a foothold and begin to descend. I say nothing. I gloat at the sight of you demeaning yourself.

A count of three is all it takes before you lose your footing. A scream. A swish of robes cut from imperial cloth. *Splash*. I lean over the well's stone wall and peer into the dark abyss.

"Eunuch Loyal One?" I call. "Bitter Root?"

I stare into the silence and fathomless dark. The Daemons of Wind moan, and once again I hear a loud and malicious cackling, borne across the Middle Kingdom from a mud-walled dwelling a thousand leagues away.

XI

I was charged with manslaughter and sentenced to a life of exile in a Daoist nunnery on the Flowery Mountain, where I lived for another twenty-nine years, to the ripe old age of forty-five.

Twenty-nine years of celibacy, prayer and silent meditation. Twenty-nine years of singing scriptures and shaving my head. The older nuns taught me to read and write, and I worked in the nunnery's silk farm, where I acquired some skills other than performing the act of Cloud and Rain. Every day I fed the silkworms leaves plucked from the mulberry bushes. Every day I watched them grow fat and spin silken thread for me to harvest and sell in Chang'an.

For the rest of my life I was wracked with guilt over your death. During the first eighteen years in the nunnery I was completely silent in repentance. Then I grew old, lost some teeth and warts and hairs bristled on my chin. I became a wrinkled old crone. When my fingers became too arthritic for spinning silk, I sat on a tree stump near the nunnery, on a path up to the holy mountain peak. I started to speak again and tell of my past. I accosted travellers and pilgrims, inviting them to come and rest a while and listen to my stories. The Tale-Spinning Nun, I came to be known as. A legend of the Flowery Mountain. There is reference to the Tale-Spinning Nun in the Tang Dynasty records in the national archives. Go and look me up.

I died while pruning the mulberry bushes on a rainy afternoon in the twenty-eighth year of the Gaozong reign. Many wept. But, to be honest, I was rather relieved.

7

Year of the Rat

"What are you reading, Driver Wang?"

Wang blinks up at her. Rain—her name is Rain. Seventeen years old. "Hip-hop baby" T-shirt and acid-washed, hip-hugging jeans. One of the not-so-pretty ones, but not from lack of lip gloss and efforts with the curling tongs. Rain taps her foot. Her eyes are so bored and vacant they verge on hostility. The transition from past to present disorientates Wang. Reading? He looks down at the pages he has spent the last two hours shuffling in his hands.

"A story," he says.

"What kind of story?"

"A Tang Dynasty folktale."

"Oh."

"Not interested in history?" he asks.

Silver earrings jingle as she shakes her head. She has a dishcloth in her hand. "I need to wipe the table."

Rain is from the same Sichuan village as all the kitchen girls and came to Beijing to take over from her pregnant cousin, knocked up by Driver Li. Recently graduated from junior high, Rain's cheeks had dimpled on her first working day as she smiled at the drivers, full of good cheer. But four months in Beijing have changed her. Now during the lunch rush Rain has the same attitude of the other sourpusses. Humourless and efficient. Sullenly dragging her heels against the fate of marrying a driver.

"You're here late, Driver Wang," Rain says. "It's three o'clock. Don't you have a job to do?"

Wang curses. Three o'clock. Scraping back his chair, he stands to leave.

"Happy New Year," says Rain.

"Happy New Year," he says.

The other girls are chattering in Chongqing dialect, humming Taiwanese pop songs and dreaming of brighter futures than being stuck in the kitchen of a taxi-driver canteen. They see Driver Wang is leaving but don't wave goodbye.

The story is a work of plagiarism—Wang is certain of it. Stolen from a book or printed off the Internet. But by who? Someone from boarding school? University? Wang has lost touch with everyone he knew back then—mostly out of pride, because he knows they will pity what he has become. But he ought to track a few people down anyway and find out if the hoax has been perpetuated amongst others too. Wang swigs bitter tea from the flask, planning this in a hazy way, doubting he will follow through.

Through the taxi windscreen he watches scavengers picking over the rubble of a demolished building, looking for bricks, wiring and pipes to sell. A recycling collector pedals by, wobbling beneath a two-metre-high stack of polystyrene, like an ant carrying a huge leaf. Skyscrapers loom in the distance, casting no shadow under the smoggy sky. Wang stares at the corporate monoliths of glass and steel, the multimillion-RMB deals taking place within them a mystery to him. The Beijing of street level is what he knows best. The Beijing of hawkers and hustlers, where the have-nots scrabble over the scraps of the haves.

Fireworks. The explosions began around noon. Bright flashes showering golden sparks. Through the window recently cleaned by her father, Echo watches the day fireworks, her fingers pressed against the pane. Lightning in reverse, shooting from earth to sky. The fuses ignited by Beijingers too impatient to wait for darkness to detonate their gunpowder hoard. Echo awaits the booms and bangs with suspended breath. Evil spirits, she thinks—the fireworks are scaring the evil spirits away. She breathes on the glass and watches the flashes of creation through the steam.

Yida is cleaning. Every lunar New Year's Eve she capitulates to superstition and sweeps and dusts the previous year's bad luck out of Apartment 404. She borrows one of Wang's ragged old shirts, bundles her curls into a red bandana and gathers cleaning sprays and dusters, like weapons for a battle to be fought. Rubber-gloved, she scours the kitchen, clattering pots and pans as she purges the cupboards of past-the-sell-by-date tins. She scrubs the counter as if it is a guilty conscience she is determined to purge with scalding water and bleach.

When she has finished, she strips and stands under the shower, the hot spray needling her scalp. The last of the purification rituals, the soaping of dirt from every pore.

In the evening Wang prepares drunken empress chicken, steamed sea bass with ginger and spring onions and stewed pork belly with aubergine. Fireworks blast like heavy artillery as they eat. Car alarms wail like the sirens of war. The TV is dominated by the snowstorms in central and southern China. Millions of migrant workers travelling back home for the Spring Festival, to see family not seen all year, are stranded in crowds of tens of thousands outside railway stations. Wang flips between TV channels. Wen Jiabao making a patriotic speech outside a train station in Changsha. A montage of scenes of People's Liberation Army troops bounding heroically through the snow. A stranded migrant worker unable to return to Hunan to see his wife and child, who says, "This is a natural disaster. We Chinese have more than our fair share of natural disasters, but we always rise up and overcome."

"One hundred million stranded," Yida murmurs. "Or was it two hundred million?"

A newscaster says the death toll so far is one hundred.

"Not so many. . ." Yida says. "*Echo*, eat your fish!"

At ten to midnight the Wangs go out into the freezing cold to detonate their 200 RMB of fireworks. The night blazes with light, as though all of Beijing has banded together to fight an enemy in the sky. Sneezing at the gunpowder smoke and watching in excitement as the rockets whiz-bang up to the sky. Wang is in charge of lighting the fuses. Amid the carnage of exploded fireworks, charred red paper tubes, trampled and flattened underfoot, he crouches, sparks a lighter, steps back. Yida stands behind Echo, her arms protectively around her, her hands covering Echo's small ears as she screams in delight.

The pandemonium of midnight comes and goes. Kneeling to light another fuse, Wang realizes that he is completely and utterly numb. That the empty and mechanical state of mind he lapses into behind the wheel has stayed with him hours after leaving the taxi and spending time at home with Echo and Yida.

New Year's Day will be the same as last year. Firecrackers at dawn as the neighbours' kids rush out to celebrate the first day of Spring Festival. The lion dance at the Dongyue Temple Fair, candyfloss and games. Then a visit to his father, punctually at four o'clock, the time they agreed. Wang Hu dribbling in his wheelchair, and Lin Hong wrinkling her powdered nose as she hands them hongbao and expensive gifts in department-store bags. Chocolates from a Belgian chocolatier. A red-and-gold stuffed toy rat for Echo. They will stay and make polite small talk for twenty minutes, then leave. Back home they will fill dumpling dough with minced pork for New Year's jiaozi. They will watch more song-and-dance extravaganzas on TV.

When they go to bed, Wang's ears are ringing hard, the inside of his eyelids incandescent with eruptions of light. He can feel it dragging him down again. The lethargy and apathy and ebbing of desire to be in the world that broke him down years ago.

"Yida?" he whispers.

Beside him, Yida mumbles but does not wake.

Sleep won't come, so he stares into the darkness as the city explodes.

8

The Wedding Photo

W hat was your mother like?" Yida asked, back when they were newly-weds and her desire to know him kept her awake throughout the night. Wang pulled a photograph of his parents' wedding day from a bundle of documents bound with an elastic band. Bride and groom and Ministry of Agriculture work-unit colleagues, sternly attired in Mao suits of utilitarian grey. A solemn gathering, as though not celebrating a marriage but mourning a death. On the wall above them is a portrait of the Great Helmsman, omnipresent throughout China back then. The Chairman overseeing the proceedings, ensuring that no one so much as smile.

The date on the photograph's reverse is 3 May 1975. An anniversary, Wang told Yida, not once acknowledged in the thirteen years of marriage to come. On the wedding day the bride was not in love with the groom. Love, she told her son years later, was not such a priority back then. In the photo they look an ill-matched couple, the bride, to put it bluntly, not pretty enough for the tall and handsome groom. Straining her eyes at Wang's twenty-five-year-old mother, Yida remarked, "She's so innocent and wide-eyed." But Wang knew better than that. The bride was not as submissive as she appeared. Studying the photo two decades later, Wang could detect the shadow of a smile on her lips.

"What was she like?" asked Yida, elbow on pillow, tousled head propped in hand, lovely and naked under the sheets. Possessiveness over his past, as well as curiosity, glinted in her eyes. Rivalry of her predecessors in her voice. "Tell me about her . . . Go on . . ."

Childhood. First come the images, like the weave of smoke from one of Shuxiang's menthol cigarettes, spiralling, amassing into the shape of the past. Apartment 404. Dishes in the sink. Curtains pulled over the rails. A message to the day: *Keep Out*. Shuxiang's round, childish face, and her narrow range of sloe-eyed expressions. Deceptively ingénue, for an innocent his mother was not. She knew the truth about what people are like. A truth from which she did not protect her son. Kneeling by him, pouring cups of water from the basin over his head, rinsing away the suds of shampoo, she said, "Don't be fooled, Little Bear, by the so-called civility out there. All our morality could blow away tomorrow like a fart in the wind. I saw it happen before."

The boy blinked, the shampoo stinging his eyes. He believed everything his mother said when he was only a single digit in age.

The days of Wang's early childhood were as unstructured as a dream. Days of waking at any hour. Days of pyjamas, Shuxiang's pale agoraphobic complexion and sweet, musky scent. Not ruled by the tyranny of clocks, they ate when hungry and slept when sleepy (her metabolism slow, Shuxiang was often sleepy). Absent-minded in her child-rearing, for her the boy was often a dazed afterthought. "Are you hungry?" she asked. "When were you last fed?" She sniffed at him when a rankness stirred her nose. "Are you dirty?" she asked. "Do you need a bath?"

She called him Little Bear and said this was because Wang was born as a bear cub and later shed his fur. Shuxiang had a wicked sense of humour. Sometimes when he tapped her shoulder to wake her from a nap, she stilled her breath, pretending to be dead beneath her shroud of hair. He shook her and wailed "*Mama!*" on the brink of tears, until she smiled, her sentience betrayed by the curve of her lips. Cruel jokes are the funniest jokes, she once told him—the jokes that, before the punchline, stop the heart. She creaked her eyelid open a crack: "Leave me alone. I want to sleep."

"Mama, I'm bored . . ."

"So?"

When Shuxiang cradled her son in her arms, he could smell the cigarettes and baijiu on her breath. Tobacco and cheap liquor were habits she'd acquired as a Sent-Down Youth, seeking comfort during the frozen winters in the Great Northern Waste. Habits she hid from her husband, who, though a drinker and smoker himself, considered the vices deplorable in women ("Only prostitutes smoke," Wang Hu said—and he should know). Shuxiang hid her illicit substances under the mattress of Little Bear's cot. When he asked to smoke one of her cigarettes, Shuxiang lit one for him, creasing up with laughter as her five-year-old spluttered and choked. "Practice," she said. "That will go away with practice, Little Bear."

Shuxiang often disappeared into the books stacked around her bed. "Read to me," Little Jun begged. But reading was a solitary pleasure for Shuxiang. "These are grown-up books, not for bear cubs," she told him. But sometimes Shuxiang narrated her own invented tales, in which her son was the hero. A warrior during the Warring States era, or a labourer building the Great Wall. Sometimes, when she was in the mood, they played together, knotting bedsheets to climb the Tibetan Plateau, or cantering on horseback in an army of two. He adored his mother during these games. Shuxiang did not play like a bored adult indulging a small child, but acted out every role with gusto. Throughout these adventures her son was her sidekick, following the twists and turns of her imagination. They were co-conspirators. A gang of two against the world.

Shuxiang didn't like to go outdoors, which often led to encounters with other people and the narrowness of their minds. But they had to go out sometimes, to shop for weekly rations of vegetables, meat and cigarettes. Passersby greeted her. They commented on the paleness of her little boy. "He is white as a glass of cow's milk," they'd say, mentally tutting and thinking, He needs more sun. Shuxiang was not deaf to the mental cluck of tongues. "Cow's milk?" she said to Little Bear. "Well, who'd know better than one of the lowing herd?" They lived in a housing compound where all employees of the Ministry of Agriculture were housed. The wives of her husband's co-workers did not like Li Shuxiang. They did not invite her to be part of their gossipy clique, with a hierarchy based upon their husbands' positions and salaries. They shunned her and, offended by her indifference, condemned her as mentally deficient and strange.

Yida's eyes widened in fascination, pupils swallowing the dark. "What about your father? Tell me about him."

She shifted slightly on her side. He stroked a hand along the curved length of her body, from shoulder to hip, under the sheets.

"What do you want to know?"

"Anything. Go on."

Throughout Wang's childhood, his father was promoted through the ranks of the Ministry of Agriculture, his status rising annually. Socializing was part of his job. Banquets, baijiu and beer. He was home in the evenings only once or twice a week. Bleary-eyed from overwork, alcohol and forty cigarettes a day, rubbing broodingly at the stubble the razor never completely banished from his jaw. His wife and son were not used to him. Both preferred it when he was not there. Wang Hu was critical of them, his lip curling at his wife as he chastened her, "You are lazy as a goat, Shuxiang. Look at this fucking mess. What do you *do* all day?"

Little Jun was nervous of him. Though his father hung up his suit jacket and loosened his tie, he never stopped being a stranger. Sometimes he rumpled his son's head and smiled with tobacco-tawny teeth. But mostly he was polite and distant, as though the boy was someone else's child. He scowled at Shuxiang's meals. Accustomed to banquets hosted by contract-seeking agribusinesses, he grumbled about Shuxiang's cooking. "This is prison slop," he told her. "Worse than what they serve in Labour Reform camps."

"Don't eat here then," she replied.

Wang Hu complained that his son was not like other boys his age. Not boisterous and rowdy enough. Not enough rough and tumble in him. *A Mama's boy.* "Send him to play outdoors more," he ordered Shuxiang. "The kid needs to get into some scrapes." The closeness of mother and son bothered him. "You spoil the boy," he said. "Eight years old and his breath still smells of mother's milk."

Little Jun's bed was in the corner of his parents' bedroom. Mama went to bed the same time as him, but Baba came home much later. Sometimes he slipped in quietly. Sometimes he slammed doors, cursed and spat. Unzipped his fly and pissed around the rim of the squat toilet. He broke things accidentally. He broke things on purpose. He knocked an ashtray onto the floor. Shattered the teapot in the sink. Mama and Little Jun did not investigate these destructive fits of rage. They stayed in bed, wakeful and tense, until Baba staggered in and was snoring drunkenly. Some nights when Baba came to bed, he turned into a beast that devoured Shuxiang. Wide-eyed in the dark, Little Jun watched from the other side of the bedroom as the humpbacked ogre reared up. Panting, out of breath and shuddering the bed frame, until he grunted and collapsed. ("A bad dream," Mama said when Little Jun asked about Baba the morning after. "You were having a bad dream.") Little Jun sometimes woke from nightmares. Mama stroked his brow, brought him to her bed and cuddled him back to sleep. One night she dozed off before carrying him back, and Baba pulled back the bedcovers to find mother and child in a sleeping embrace. He dragged his son out of bed, nearly pulling his shoulder out of its socket as he threw him across the room. "It's time he crawled out of your womb," he shouted at his wife. "Or he'll be stuck up there for the rest of his life."

Wang Hu was gone when they woke in the morning. Washed, shaved and out the door. His career was founded upon his ability to be drunken and sociable at night, then resurrect himself from the ruins of a hangover and be first in the office the next day. Once he was gone, mother and son trod carefully about the apartment. They cleaned up. Soaked up the puddles of urine with old newspapers. Swept up the shards of glass. "Love for a man must extend to the crows on his roof," Shuxiang intoned flatly. But neither of them loved him to start with, thought her son. Never mind with crows.

"I am Lin Hong."

The girl blocked their path in the street. Mean-looking in stilettos and a little black dress. Rouged lips. Fight-picking eyes rimmed in electric blue. Mother and son were walking home from the supermarket. They stared at the girl, standing with a hand on her hip, proud of her beauty and height. She smiled at Shuxiang.

"On the nights your husband doesn't go home to you," she said, "he is with me. In the apartment he rents for us both. I thought you ought to know."

Wang Hu's mistress paused to measure the effect of her words. Shuxiang blinked as though a gust of wind had blown up in her face, but was otherwise impassive. The young boy at least had the sense to look intimidated. Lin Hong patted her brand-new corkscrew perm (she had gone to the beauty parlour that morning, with a photo of her favourite Cantopop star clipped from a magazine). She smiled again. She then announced to Shuxiang that not only was her husband cheating on her, but she (the mistress) was now pregnant with his child. Wang Hu had a new family now, and Shuxiang should expect her husband to leave her any day soon. The girl waited, expecting tears and devastation. Denial and rage. But there was none of that. Calm, and not flustered in the least, Shuxiang said, "Congratulations. I wish you the best of luck."

The malicious look faded from Lin Hong's eyes. Thrown, she had wobbled away on her high heels, looking very silly and young. Wang looked at his mother after the girl was gone. He could tell Shuxiang's mind was now turning away from the confrontation, to other things.

"Is Ba going to leave us?" he asked.

"No. He will force that girl to have an abortion."

They had continued walking home.

*   *   *

85

August 1988. Twelve-year-old Wang cycled home from his middle school in Dongcheng every afternoon, the wheels of his Flying Pigeon spinning, his satchel thumping his side. He locked his bike up in the shed, rushed into Building 16 and up four flights of stairs, blinking as he entered the smoky apartment. Shuxiang had been on her own all day. Sitting at the table, littering her ashtray with filters. Wang pulled the curtains wide and Shuxiang flinched in the daylight. He opened the windows to let the smoke escape. Though Shuxiang was thirty-eight now, her face was obstinately childish and round.

"What did you do today, Ma?" Wang asked.

"Nothing," she said.

Wang resented her. He resented her for sooting up her throat and the recesses of her lungs with cigarettes. He resented her when she murmured, "What they teach you at school is a pack of lies, Little Bear. Every lesson is to brainwash you." Wang resented her for the fact he did not fit in, which he knew to be the fault of his isolated childhood. He rolled up his sleeves and washed the dirty crockery in the sink. He bought meat and vegetables from the stall, and cooked them shredded cabbage in sesame oil and pork dumplings. Shuxiang rarely had an appetite. She prodded at the pork dumplings with her chopsticks.

"What are you thinking, Ma?"

"Nothing," she said.

For years, Shuxiang had been a recluse, her one companion her young son. But as the heat of the summer faded away, she changed her agoraphobic ways and roamed the communal yard. Everyone was surprised to see her out and about, with her cardigan buttoned up wrongly over her frock and her hair in need of combing. Her hectic eyes and purposeful stride prompted people to ask, "Where are you going in such a hurry, Li Shuxiang?" But she behaved as though she had neither seen nor heard them. She charged out of the housing-compound gates with a sink plunger in her hand, deaf to the laughter in her wake. ("A plumber now, is she? Whose toilet is she going to unblock?")

One afternoon Wang returned to an empty apartment, then rushed back out to look for her. She was in none of her usual haunts, so Wang returned home to wait for her, scared that something bad had happened. Half an hour later there was a knock at the door. It was Shuxiang and two men from the Residents' Committee. Grey-headed, retired factory workers now volunteering to protect the harmony of the community. Shuxiang was drenched, the hem of her coat dripping puddles about her bare feet.

"Your mother was wading in the Liangma River," one man said. "Up to her waist."

"The river is dirty and polluted," said the other. "Not for swimming."

"My shoes are missing!" Shuxiang blurted. "I put them on the riverbank and a thief stole them."

She was outraged, as though the theft of her shoes was the scandal here. "Your mother is not well and needs to see a doctor," the grey-headed men told Wang. "She needs supervision during the day." Did Wang's father know about her eccentric behaviour? Wang lied that he did. Shuxiang nodded, and they continued to discuss her as though she was not there, which was partly true.

They travelled backwards in time, mother and son, back to the days before Wang was of school age, though now the roles were reversed. Wang stayed home from school to care for her, his world shrinking to the shadowy, curtained rooms of Apartment 404. He cooked her rice porridge for breakfast, then rubbed a damp flannel over her face and brushed her teeth over the sink. Though she was a distracted listener, he read passages out of her old classic novels to her, wanting to occupy time in a meaningful way.

Wang came to understand the tedium of caring for a small child. How thankless children are. How slow the passage of time when punctuated only by repetitive tasks. He resented Shuxiang for what she had become, but caring for her exaggerated his love for her too into a fierce, protective breed. He brushed her hair before bed every night. He covered her with blankets when it was cold. His mother was his burden and sorrow now.

* * *

When Wang had to go to the market, he locked her in so she couldn't escape. But one day in December he returned to the compound and discovered that this was not precaution enough.

"There he is. That's her son."

Entering the gate with a bag of shopping, Wang saw the crowd by Building 16 and, sensing the atmospheric disturbance, the thrum of something out of the ordinary in the air, hastened over. Heads turned towards him. Security guards, the man from the vegetable stall, old women with dogs on leashes and mothers jiggling babies on hips. "She needs to see a doctor," he heard. "Wrong in the head." The crowd parted for Wang, and he looked up at the object of the communal gaze. Shuxiang was standing naked in the window of the fourth-floor balcony. The pale winter sunlight fell through the glass, illuminating the thickness of her hips, her dangling breasts and the dark pubis that reminded him of documentaries about primitive tribes. But Wang knew the most obscene thing about Shuxiang was her smile. She smiled as though her indecent exposure was for exhibitionist kicks, but Wang knew this was not the case. There was no provocation or perversion in her stance. Lost in her own world, Shuxiang had no idea of her effect on the crowd gathered four storeys below. But the crowd did not know this. They flattered themselves that her nakedness was for them. Wang muttered an apology and rushed into the building. After he was gone, the crowd neither dispersed nor stopped gawking up at the nude woman behind the glass. "Outrageous," they whispered. "Ought to be locked up." They stared on and on. They could not drag their eyes away.

Wang ran into the bedroom and threw a bedsheet over her shoulders, as though putting out a fire that threatened to burn the apartment down. He pulled her back from the window, out of public view, not caring when she lost her footing and stumbled. He was angry enough to slap her.

"Everyone saw you! Everyone was looking at you and your disgusting body!"

She glanced at him, as unabashed by her nakedness as a cat or a dog, the burden of shame her son's alone. Taller than his mother now, Wang lowered his face to hers. "*Why can't you be normal?*" he shouted. She said nothing, didn't even flinch. The bedsheet slid from her shoulders. Her skin was goosepimpled, her nipples erect in the chilly air.

"You shouldn't be a mother," Wang said. "I should never have been born."

This remark had some effect on Shuxiang, and she looked at her son.

"Yes, it would be better if you had never been born," she agreed. "Being born into this world is hell. You will be crushed with countless millions all your life long."

Shuxiang went to the bed, pulled back the covers and got in. Then she held up the bedspread with her arm, making enough room for her son to crawl in beside her. "Come to bed," she said. Wang stared at her body in the shadows. No way, he thought. But they had shared a bed when he was a child. Back when Shuxiang used to look after him, and not the other way around. And Wang was tired. He was tired of worrying. Tired of the anxiety of what she might do next. So he went to the bed, slipped under the bedcovers and rested his head on the pillow beside hers. He had on a jumper and old school trousers. The fact he had clothes on, he decided, compensated for the fact that she did not. At first he was tense with the strangeness of it. But Shuxiang was not tense. Shuxiang was sleeping. The rhythm of her breath lapped at him like waves against a shore. Lulling him to calmness, lulling him to sleep.

Wang lapsed in and out of consciousness, waking to the darkening sky and lengthening shadows as the earth spun away from the sun. Waking to the nearness of Shuxiang and her mouth slackened by gravity. Waking to sulphurous breath, rising from her stomach's gastric pit. Shuxiang's hands were in prayer, her body in a loose foetal curl. They were not touching at first, but her body moved to his, seeking him out. She gathered him in her arms with a protectiveness she lacked in waking life and slept on. Wang drowsed, the sounds of children playing in the yard drifting in and out of his hearing. But he did not hear the key in the lock. He did not hear the front door clicking open.

They were not woken when the quilt was tugged off them. They were not woken by the bloodshot, caffeine-sharpened eyes staring down at them. They were cleaved to each other, mother clasping son in a tight embrace. On the pillow their parted mouths nearly touched. The blood-capillaried eyes bore into them, until Wang's father could not stand what he saw a moment longer. His thick knuckled hand reached down and dragged his twelve-year-old son up by a fistful of hair. Wang screamed as his scalp lifted and short dark hair ripped out from the roots. Shuxiang leapt up, her bare chest heaving as she slapped at her husband, shrieking at him to stop. Wang Hu hurled the boy from bed to floor, then fell on him. Blow upon blow upon blow. When he was done, and the boy near unconscious, he turned on Shuxiang, who had been hitting him throughout. "Shut up," he said and hit her so hard her screaming stopped. Then he threw her on the bed and unbuckled his belt.

Wang was sent to a boarding school, north of Beijing. After eight weeks at the school his father came to visit and told him his mother had died from the pneumonia she caught after swimming in the Liangma River on a freezing January night. Father and son were in an empty classroom, loaned to them by the headteacher, to allow Wang Hu some privacy to break the tragic news.

"The funeral was three days ago," Wang's father said. "We didn't want to interrupt your schooling. It was very depressing. Your mother wouldn't have wanted you there anyway."

It irritated Wang Hu to see that his son's dislocated shoulder still hadn't healed and remained in a sling. He should have recovered weeks ago, he thought. The boy's stubborn as a crooked nail that won't hammer flat. For appearances' sake, Wang Hu sat with his son for another twenty minutes before getting back in his BMW and heading back to Beijing. It was the last time Wang would see his father for several years.

9

The Alley

Springtime. The city is thawing. Beijingers shedding coats and scarves and other woollen armour in the battle against the cold. The scenery of winter, the roadside oil drums of foil-wrapped baked potatoes and the heavy quilts over supermarket doors retiring from view.

Gobi dust billows in the sky. The city suffocates under the haze of pollutants, the smog burning the back of Wang's throat. He streaks the tissue he blows his nose with into black, but with a mental shrug lights another Zhongnanhai from a pack left by a fare. The shadow in his lungs will worsen anyway. What difference will one more cigarette make?

East Third Ring Road, the digital Olympic clock counts down the seconds until the Games. Billboards of athletes leap over hurdles and somersault through the air, China's national heroes, muscles rippling and taut, holding up cans of Coca-Cola mid-jump. Throughout Beijing renovations are underway. The polluted façades of buildings are being repainted. Millions of empty flowerpots line the streets, waiting to be filled. *One World, One Dream. Remaking the Environment Benefits the People. The Olympics Unites You, Me and Him.* The slogans are everywhere.

Passengers come and go. The destinations are far and wide.

Nanluoguxiang, the courtyards renovated into overpriced boutiques and tourist shops. Babaoshan cemetery. The Chairman Mao Memorial Hall, and the undercover-police-surveillanced expanse of Tiananmen Square. The affluent gated residences of Shunyi. Desolate regions of the Great Wall. The vast sundial of the Millennium Monument, casting no shadow under the sun-bereaved sky.

A westerner slides into the back seat with a beautiful girl. Wang watches the couple in the rearview. The man is fortyish, with toady eyes and the broken thread veins of alcoholism in his large meandering nose. The girl is in her twenties, with a sugar-frosting of make-up on her pretty face. How can she let him put his hands on her? wonders Wang. For what? Money? Status? A US fiancée visa? The man has a proprietorial hand on her knee and the smirk of one who thinks his own charisma has won him his trophy, and not the charisma of the West.

An official in an expensive tailored suit, his hair dyed an inauthentic black, flags down Wang's cab outside a government building in Jianguomen. As Wang drives him, the radio news talks of the Toxic Dumpling Incident. Fourteen people in Japan are sick in the hospital after eating dumplings imported from China that were contaminated with pesticides.

"Sabotage!" says the official. "They are poisoning our dumplings to make China look bad."

"Really?" Wang says. "You think the Japanese would poison their own citizens?"

"They are an evil race."

"I've met some Japanese," Wang says. "They don't seem so bad."

"Driver!" snaps the official. "Didn't you study the War of Resistance against the Japanese at school?"

"Of course I did."

"Well, go back to school and study it again! You obviously know nothing about our *history*. You wouldn't know our history if it slapped you in the face!"

At the forceful spit of the word "history," Wang stiffens, hands tightening around the steering wheel. Then he looks in the rear-view at the indignant official, and the suspicion passes. He has to get a grip. He has to keep his paranoia in check.

The market. Vegetable stalls of pesticide-sprayed spinach and earth-clodden turnips. Racks of carcasses hanging from hooks, ribs and spinal cords exposed. A butcher in a bloodstained apron slams his cleaver, seasoning a joint of pork with ash spilling from his cigarette. Wang roams from stall to stall, gradually filling his bag with items on Yida's list. Bean curd. Spring onions. Vinegar. The ground is slippery with plums fallen from a fruit stall and trampled to pulp. The children of the migrant vendors chase about, skidding through the mess as they play tag. Wang buys two jin of rice. The rice seller hands Wang his change without looking away from the old Bruce Lee movie on his laptop, perched above the till.

The dusk is balmy and suffused with spring. Wang detours down an alley behind the Golden Elephant pharmacy, passing a Uighur selling fake Rolexes and a shifty-looking man lurking by the tobacco and liquor store, on the lookout for police. Wang has seen him before and knows he is a seller of identities: student IDs, graduate diplomas and other papers. Documents, both stolen and forged, used by migrants to gain employment in the capital. Another man nearby is peddling blank receipt booklets from hotels and restaurants for officials to claim fraudulent expenses. He rustles a wad of banknotes, hinting at a profitable day's trade.

Farther down the alley, neon-lit shops cater for the darker pleasures of the flesh. An "Adult Health Store" has shelves of rubber and latex sex toys and powdered "male power enhancers." In a glass-fronted massage parlour, girls perch on stools, skirts ridden up to the shadowy meeting place of their thighs. The whores are heavy-lidded with boredom as they wait behind the glass. A teenager in leopard-print catches Wang's eye with a gap-toothed smile, and he reddens and looks away.

A pole of red, white and blue stripes spins by a barber's doorway. Inside, a man in his thirties and a teenager on a laptop slouch on leatherette chairs. The thirtyish man has his boots up on the ledge under the mirrors, stretching out his long, denim legs. He reminds Wang of someone he once knew. But older. And with shorter hair and smoker's wrinkles around his eyes. Out in the alley Wang stares through the glass. No, he thinks. Can't be. But on the man's bicep is an emerald dragon. On his forearm is a knotty gnarl of scar tissue. Who else has that tattoo? Those scars?

Wang's heart is beating hard. The wisest thing to do would be to walk on by. But he does not do the wisest thing. He opens the door and enters the barber's.

Leaning back in his chair, Zeng Yan looks over, weary at the arrival of another customer. Then recognition widens his eyes and he swings his heels down from the ledge and stands. He is taller than Wang remembers, and thinner, his jeans sliding off his narrow hips.

"Wang Jun!" he laughs. "Is that really you?"

Wang nods and sways slightly. He feels as though reality is disjointed, as though he's knocked back several glasses of baijiu in a row.

"Long time no see," he says.

"How long has it been?" Zeng smiles. He pauses to cough. "Nine years? Ten?"

"Ten," Wang says.

They look each other up and down, taking in a decade of change. Wang has become softer and rounder, the hair sparser on his head and the stubble coarser on his jaw. Zeng is gaunter, more angular, but his hair wavy and thick. Zeng Yan has lost the handsome looks he was so proud of at twenty—a loss Wang knows must have been painful for him.

"You look well, Wang Jun."

"Liar," Wang laughs. "I'm balding. I've gained weight."

"Bullshit! You're handsome as ever."

"You look much better than I do."

Zeng coughs at this, his congested lungs protesting Wang's lie. Looking at how haggard Zeng has become, Wang suspects something worse than heavy smoking and late nights. Some chronic illness lurking within.

The teenager on the laptop has stopped chatting on QQ and

stares at Wang with a hostility that makes him shift awkwardly. He looks around the run-down barber's. The linoleum floor is peeling at the edges, scattered with tufts of hair. Duct tape mends the rips in the fake leather chairs. The cords of the hairdryers are frayed electrocutions waiting to happen.

"How long have you been working here?" he asks Zeng.

"Two years."

"I live in Maizidian. Just round the corner. How come we haven't seen each other in the street?"

"I've seen you," Zeng says, "with your little girl."

"And you didn't say hello?"

"You're a family man now. I thought it better to leave you be."

Zeng lowers his eyes in shame. Still in the same line of work he was in as a teenager, but now on the lowest rung. Wang can tell he doesn't have wealthy men throwing money at him anymore. Now Zeng has to haggle over his fee with working-class men or migrants from outside Beijing.

"Would you like a haircut?" Zeng asks.

Wang went to the barber's three weeks ago, but he nods. "Sure."

"Go clean up the back room, Wu Fei," Zeng orders the teenager.

The boy shunts his chair back and exits through the beaded curtain, the strands swinging aggressively in his wake. Zeng shakes out a hairdressing cape and holds it up so Wang can thread his arms through. Wang then sits in one of the ripped leatherette chairs, and Zeng squirts shampoo and water from a plastic bottle on to his scalp and lathers it up.

"How long you been married?"

"Nine years."

"Long time," says Zeng. "What's your wife's name? What does she do?"

"Ma Yida. She's a masseuse at Dragonfly Massage." Wang then asks, "How about you? Married?"

Zeng's laughter lapses into a coughing fit. His chest revs like a car that won't start.

"I'm still a bachelor," he laughs, thumping his sternum. "I'm not the marrying kind."

Wang leans back into the washbasin, and Zeng cradles his head, kneading his temples and digging his thumbs behind his ears. Wang shuts his eyes as Zeng's strong fingers go to work on his scalp. The massage is part of the seduction routine. Many men wander into the barber's on a whim. *Only a haircut*, they tell themselves. But Zeng's fingers persuade them to stay for more. "Look what we do to your scalp," they say. "Think of what else we can do."

"How long have you been driving a taxi?" Zeng asks.

Wang opens his eyes. He stares at Zeng's upside-down face. "How do you know I'm a taxi driver?"

"I've seen you in your cab."

"Really? When?"

"Sometime last year, near Liangmaqiao."

Water sprays from the nozzle, rinsing the lather out.

"How many times have you seen me?" Wang asks, his heart quickening. "Do you know where I live?"

Zeng starts at Wang's tone. "No," he says. "I only saw you twice." He continues rinsing in silence, and Wang's suspicion recedes.

Zeng rubs Wang's head dry with a towel, then combs his sparse, damp hair. Wang watches, reversed in the mirror, as Zeng starts to cut. He stares at the deep scar, from elbow to wrist, on the inside of Zeng's forearm. They'd been rallying a Ping-Pong ball in the hospital yard when Zeng had told him how he punched out a window when his boyfriend, Dragon, dumped him. Some nerve endings were severed, and Zeng couldn't make a proper fist. He had put down the Ping-Pong paddle to show Wang the looseness of his grip.

"Should have punched with my left hand. Certain things I could take care of on my own I can't anymore."

Zeng had grinned, then admitted, "Some people are as good for you as a bullet in the head, but you want them anyway. Know what I mean?"

And Wang had nodded. He was beginning to understand.

* * *

Zeng Yan is blasting the blow-dryer when Wang's phone buzzes with a message. Yida, waiting at home. Wang signals for Zeng to turn off the dryer.

"I have to go," he says. "How much do I owe you?"

"Nothing."

Zeng removes the cape and brushes off the collar of Wang's polo shirt. "Come back whenever you like. I will always cut your hair for free."

"Thanks," Wang says. Though he doesn't feel gratitude. Only an addict's fear of relapse.

"Well," says Zeng. "See you around."

But Wang isn't fooled by his casual, offhand tone. Zeng looks as though he can't bear to see him leave.

"Sure," he says.

Wang picks up his shopping and walks out of the barber's and into the alley. He doesn't say when he will be back, but they both know that he will.

10

Mindsickness

Nothing seemed seriously wrong at first. A few days of struggling through lectures and campus life. A seasonal depression as the earth moved farther from the sun and the hours of darkness lengthened. Then one morning Wang couldn't get out of bed. Under the blankets, he lacked the strength to move. He shut his eyes but could not sleep, because his thoughts wouldn't grant him a moment's rest. They mocked his defects and weaknesses. They scorned his punctual and eager attendance at lectures, pen grasped in hand to note down everything the lecturer said. They ridiculed Wang's ambition to be a history professor—he who was so pathetic he couldn't even get out of bed.

Under the blankets Wang stagnated. His physiology slowed down to the point of stasis. Waste filtered through his kidneys, seeping from bladder to sheets. His heart pumped so weakly, blood silted up his veins.

Vanishing under the duvet to recover from a hangover, a cold or a broken heart was a norm of dormitory life. Three days went by before Wang's roommates recognized something was wrong. They crowded around Wang's bottom bunk, shivering as the windows were flung wide to clear the air. Wang could hear them debating what to do, their voices filtering down to his new subterranean level of reality, where the meaninglessness of everything was bleakly exposed. They shook Wang's shoulder, then withdrew from his limp unresponsiveness. There was laughter as they threw a glass of water over him. Then confusion as Wang did not so much as flinch or blink.

"What's wrong with him? It's like he's *died*."

Wang's father came to collect him the following day. A commanding figure in his expensive suit, Wang Hu went to the student accommodation office first and handed over an envelope stuffed with cash for the "inconvenience" caused. He was charming and apologetic, slick and experienced at bringing disagreeable situations under his control. Wang Hu then went to his son's dormitory with two security guards from the Ministry of Agriculture, who heaved Wang out of bed. The guards stripped Wang under his father's watchful eye and dumped the soiled clothes and bedsheets into a bin bag. Then Wang Hu told them to stand him under a shower.

"Be as rough as you need to be. Make sure the water is *cold*."

The shower got Wang functioning again, putting one foot in front of the other and moving in the direction that he was told.

During the medical checkup Wang did not answer a single question. Clinical depression, diagnosed the doctor. A high suicide risk. Owing to his deteriorated mental state, twenty-one-year-old Wang sat out in the waiting room as, in hushed conspiratorial tones, his father and doctor determined his fate.

"What's your madness?" The elderly man peered at Wang through the opalescence of his eyes.

"Don't know," Wang said. "Dr. Fu has it in his notes."

A frozen wind gusted through the wrought-iron bars of the window, and Wang smelt the sourness of the old man's estrangement from water and soap. The old man squinted his cataract-clouded eyes at Wang. "Neurasthenia," he decided. Then he shuffled away, remarking loudly to the empty hall, "His mother was here once. She pretended to be a cat and peed on the floor. What a hiding the nurses gave her."

Wang was leaving his room for the first time that day, holding his breath as he passed the urinals on the way to the common room. He stared through the doorways into the other dorms. Six iron bedsteads and one wardrobe per room. The walls empty, no photographs or calendars to count the days. Not even a potted plant on the sills. The patients huddled under blankets or stared about with the idleness of nothing to do.

The illness of some of the men in the common room was evident in their smiles. Others were deceptively sane-looking as they watched the TV news bulletin, wearing long johns and mildewy jumpers coming apart at the seams. It was 1997. The year Deng Xiaoping died and Hong Kong returned to the motherland. Wang was certain that neither historical event had even for a moment shaken the patients out of their lassitude.

Eleven o'clock was personal-grooming hour. A nurse clipped an old man's nails, nagging him to keep his splayed and liver-spotted fingers still. Another nurse was cutting a patient's hair over sheets of the *People's Daily* spread under his chair. Wang saw some electric clippers on the table and asked her to shave his head. The nurse refused. Skinheads were against regulations. Why not go for a short back and sides? Wang scratched his head.

"My scalp is itchy. I've got lice."

He sat before the nurse and bowed his head. The buzzing clippers vibrated against his skull, tremors descending vertebra by vertebra down his spine. Wang felt like a sheep being shorn. Fleeced. Afterwards he rubbed his hand over the stubble, waving away the nurse's offer of a mirror. The palm of his hand had told him all he needed to know.

The clinic was a low building with wrought-iron bars over the windows. *Kindness, Friendship, Tolerance*, said the breeze-fluttered banner stretching across the entrance. Sometimes Wang stared out from between the bars at the suburbs of Beijing. Fields of poorly irrigated crops, fertilized by sewage. The dust-blown sign of the near-empty-shelved corner shop creaking in the wind. A bus stop where a bus from the city stopped twice a day. "A temporary stay," Wang was told. "A month or two at the most."

The world shrank to the hospital grounds. Restricted, regimented, confined. Bells rang at six. Yawning, the patients trudged to the canteen at quarter past. Breakfast was rice porridge. Tea. On Sundays a hard-boiled egg. The day nurses yet to arrive, the Level One patients struggled to put spoons in their mouths, dribbling the porridge back out. At seven they washed and brushed their teeth in the bathroom of Ward B, spitting in the scum-filthy sinks. There were no mirrors, and as he dragged the toothbrush about Wang stared at the cracks in the wall.

Eight o'clock, outdoor exercises in the yard. Thirty patients in padded winter jackets followed the tracksuited Dr. Fu as music played on a cassette player. Hands to toes. Hands on head. Jumping jacks. They queued for medication at eight thirty. Otherwise speech-stunted patients were fluent in the language of pharmaceuticals, the polysyllabic names of psychotropic drugs—chlorpromazine, perphenazine, trifluoperazine, clozapine and diazepam—rolling with ease from tongues. Eight fifty-five, Wang swallowed his anti-depressants. Nine o'clock was cleaning time. Wang swept and mopped on automaton, changed the bedsheets soiled by incontinents in the night. Ten o'clock, a mid-morning nap until lunch. After lunch, a nap until dinner. Another dose of medication. Television. A cigarette smoked in the yard. Bells ringing at eight thirty. Lights out. Bed.

Within weeks Wang felt as though he had been a patient for years. There was no rehabilitation or occupational therapy, but the lack of meaningful activity did not bother him. All he wanted was to sleep around the clock. And at the clinic, he got away with this, almost.

Bells rang at eight thirty. Lights out. Sleep quotas met during the day, the patients were untired at the scheduled hour for sleep. Each night Wang lay awake in his cot, his blanket pulled over him, listening to the voices of his roommates in the dark.

"Look closely at the pills they give you," whispered Gao Ling in bed two. "Are they different in size, colour or shape? Spit them out if they are. The doctors are testing out new drugs for pharmaceutical companies. They are experimenting to find out which ones make our brains haemorrhage. Don't be a lab rat. Spit them out."

"Down with Gao Ling!" chanted Wei Hong in bed four, "running dog of the Guomindang!"

Wei "Serve the Red" Hong had been sacked from his job as an elementary-school teacher after making his class of seven-year-olds write "Thought Reports" to expose their anti-Maoist thoughts then leading a struggle rally against a little girl, encouraging the rest of the class to slap her and smear her with black ink.

"You know the Cultural Revolution ended twenty years ago, right?" called Gao Ling. "You know Mao Zedong is dead?"

"Stinking capitalist!" Wei Hong shouted. "Chairman Mao will live for ten thousand years!"

"Quiet now," scolded Old Chen. "People need to sleep."

Old Chen in bed three was not mentally ill but a homeless vagrant swept up by the police in a street-cleaning campaign before the National Day parade of 1989. Institutionalized for eight years, Old Chen was glad of the shelter, regular meals and medication for his Parkinson's and, not in any hurry to return to the streets, he faked an episode of dementia at every threat of discharge. "After eight years of living with the insane," he confided to Wang, "I impersonate them well."

In the spring Wang came out of hibernation and went out in the yard, where the patients gathered and spoke of their pasts. They spoke of husbands and wives, sons and daughters. They spoke of careers as schoolteachers, bus drivers, post office clerks and engineers.

"I was somebody once," they insisted, "before they put me in here."

Wang came to know of many kinds of madness. The madness of those who thought they had magic powers and could levitate. The madness of disciples of religious cults who communed with their leaders through emissions of alpha waves. There was the madness of those arrested for running naked through the streets.

The madness of the woman who chased the head of her Neighbourhood Committee with a frying pan. There was the madness of those who opposed the government. The madness of petitioners who had come to Beijing from other provinces and queued at the Bureau of Petitions to lodge complaints about the seizure of land by local officials or a husband beaten to death by hired thugs. Some of the petitioners lived in a shantytown near Beijing South Railway Station and, clearly suffering from psychosis, went to the Bureau of Petitions every day. They were a threat to public security. The police rounded the worst of the psychotics up for the mental home.

There was the madness of those who had lost the ones they loved (the wife who left for another man, the child killed in a hit and run), and there was the madness that had caused the loss of the ones they loved. Qi Rong, a schizophrenic with razor-scarred wrists, showed Wang a photo album of her twenty-seven-year-old son. Photos of her son as a baby. Photos of his graduation in mortar cap and gown. Photos of her son and his pregnant wife.

"He's now a chemical engineer for Sinopec," Qi Rong boasted of the man who three years ago dumped her in the home of demented, broken souls and has never visited—not even to introduce her to her grandson. "I'm so proud of my boy. He was always the cleverest in his class. Not like his crazy old ma!"

There was the madness of the president's mistress, who danced about the hospital yard, spinning round and round in the arms of an invisible partner, her skirt flaring up and showing her pale, varicose-veined legs. As she danced she recounted a life of banquets and private jets, giddy as a sixteen-year-old girl.

"Jiang Zemin and I waltzed together in a Russian ballroom," she called out to Wang, "when he took me to meet President Yeltsin in Moscow. We drank champagne, and oysters slipped down our throats." The president's mistress then grinned, showing the black holes where her teeth used to be. "He's coming for me," she whispered to Wang. "Any day now he will come and whisk me away."

Later that day she saw her lover on TV, touring a factory in Shandong Province. She walked up and touched him tenderly on the screen, deaf to the other patients shouting at her to get out of the way.

Aware of Wang's privileged background and prestigious education, white-coated Dr. Fu was more deferential to him than to other patients. He smiled warmly at Wang from across his desk, considering him one of the few patients to be treated with respect. Potted plants trailed vines from the window ledge and on his desk was a thousand-page edition of the *Chinese Classification of Mental Disorders*, scuffed with the overlapping ring marks from hundreds of cups of tea. *Serve the Patients*, instructed the needlepoint hanging on the office wall.

"How have you been feeling lately, Wang Jun?" Dr. Fu asked.

"Tired," said Wang. "Low."

The doctor nodded sympathetically.

"But you have improved. When you came here in November you barely ate or spoke and spent most of your time in bed. You are much more sociable now. I see you out in the yard every day, chatting with the other patients."

Wang shrugged.

"There's not much in the way of intellectual stimulation here, is there?" continued Dr. Fu. "Don't you want to return to the university and finish your education? You have been here for four months. Wouldn't you like to try, Wang Jun?"

Wang's gaze hardened. "I am not ready to be discharged," he said. Then, after a pause, "Can I go?"

Before Dr. Fu could nod his consent, Wang had scraped back his chair and stood up. Though the doctor was offended, he did not insist Wang stay and discuss the matter further. As well as paying the monthly fee, Wang's father was making generous donations to the hospital and would continue to do so as long as his son was resident there. Progress meeting adjourned.

"Toothpaste?"

Wang looked at Zeng Yan in his vest, silver dog tags and faded jeans, holding his forefinger out. He grudgingly squeezed some toothpaste out of the tube onto Zeng's finger and Zeng grinned and rubbed the toothpaste on his teeth. Wang ignored him. He leant over the sink and washed his face.

Wang hadn't spoken much to Zeng but knew of him. The boy from the south who had chased his dreams of pop stardom to Beijing, only to end up selling his body in karaoke bars. Zeng was handsome enough to be on magazine covers and TV, but Wang had heard him singing Faye Wong ballads and knew his ambitions of becoming a professional singer wouldn't amount to much. "Stop torturing us! You can't sing!" some of the patients yelled.

"What do you madmen know about singing?" Zeng yelled back. Though they were the same age, Wang hadn't gone out of his way to make friends with Zeng. Wang didn't know much about homosexuals but had heard they had AIDS and other diseases and thought it safest to avoid him entirely.

Zeng gargled and spat in the sink. He wiped his mouth with the back of his arm and said, "I heard you're a rich kid. That your father is a Communist official."

Wang shrugged.

"Why didn't your father send you to a proper clinic then?" asked Zeng. "Somewhere they actually treat patients so they get better, instead of drugging them and locking them up?"

"He is punishing me," Wang said.

"For what? He must really *hate* you," said Zeng. "If I were you I'd get the hell out of here. Run away."

Wang countered, "Why don't *you* run away?"

Zeng laughed. "After they arrested me, I was *lucky* to be sent here and not to Re-education Through Labour. Run away and I'll end up in prison. But you should get out, Wang Jun. The police won't go looking for you."

Wang rubbed his face with the towel. Arrested for what? he wondered. Sodomy? Singing in public? Zeng leant his hip against the sink, tilted his peroxide-dyed head to one side and watched Wang with interest.

"Why are you here anyway?" asked Zeng. "You don't seem ill to me."

"I had a breakdown at my university."

"Didn't you go to Beida? You must be a genius. I heard the cleverest people in China go there."

Wang thought of his classmates and laughed. "The richest," he corrected. "The ones with the best guanxi. The ones who are good at passing exams. Students at Beida spend a lot of time in the library."

"Yeah? How much time did you spend in the library?"

"Seven hours a day," said Wang, "more during exams."

Zeng hooted. "No wonder you went fucking crazy!"

The bell rang for lights out, and Zeng sauntered out of the bathroom, shaking his head and laughing: "Seven hours a day!" And Wang had to admit he had a point.

Wang had never had a friend like Zeng before. At university Wang's friends were similar to him, studious and hardworking, the passing of exams the focal point of their lives. They lost control sometimes—spraining an ankle during a drunken fall or getting in trouble for sneaking a girl into the dorms. But never to the extent that it wrecked their lives, or even got in the way of their handing an essay in on time.

Zeng, in contrast, was as out of control as a car skidding on ice. He had dropped out of school at fifteen when a sleazy older boyfriend convinced him he didn't need a high school diploma to succeed. The boyfriend then pimped Zeng out, exploiting him for over a year. When they split up, Zeng went to work as a host in a Guangzhou nightclub. He bragged to Wang of how desired and sought after he was there, and of the money and extravagant gifts his patrons had showered him with: leather jackets and stereos, gold chains and rings. A millionaire from Hong Kong had even rented a luxury apartment for Zeng to live in as his "second wife" (an arrangement that ended after six weeks, when the Hong Kong millionaire came home unexpectedly to catch Zeng and his boyfriend in the Jacuzzi together). Zeng boasted of his rich and powerful clientele, hoping to impress Wang. But Wang saw nothing to envy in the career of a prostitute.

Zeng told Wang he was six when he knew he was gay. "I was in the acupuncturist's waiting room with my father, and there was a diagram of a man on the wall. The male body. Full-frontal, back and sides. I stared and stared at that diagram, and I have always known, since that day . . ."

When he was a teenager, Zeng's mother had attempted to cure him of his effeminacy. She had crushed up herbal pills and sprinkled them into his meals behind his back. "I had an upset stomach and diarrhea for months. I didn't know what was wrong, until I caught her one day, stirring the pills into my soup. She wasn't sorry. She said I was abnormal. She said I had too much yin and not enough yang, and the medicine would even me out. She said I had to stop being such a girly boy, or I'd never find a wife. I told her straight. 'Ma,' I said, 'I will never marry.' She lost her temper and screamed that I was an unfilial son. That I would dishonour our ancestors by not continuing our family line." Zeng rolled his eyes. "I said, '*Fuck* our ancestors, Ma. They are dead in their graves. What do they care if I walk like a girl?'"

Before Zeng, Wang had never spoken of his past. "Boring," he said, when friends asked what his childhood was like. "Just a housewife," he said, when they asked about his mother. The past had a power over Wang, silencing him and crippling him with shame. But there was no need for censorship with Zeng. He was the first person Wang confided in about his mother's breakdown. The first person he told about his father wrenching his shoulder out of joint. As he recounted his father's abuse, Wang became panicky and short of breath. But then he looked up and saw Zeng, listening on the end of his bed, and the power of the past was somehow lessened. Zeng had been through this stuff too. Zeng's mother had drunk a bottle of weed killer when he was twelve. His father had beaten him and thrown him out on the streets when he found out he was gay. Zeng spoke of these incidents dismissively, laughing at his parents and the damage they'd done and encouraging Wang to do the same.

"What were you arrested for?" Wang asked.

They were sweeping the yard on a breezy morning in March.

The Secretary-General of the United Nations was on the bench in his pyjamas, waving his hands about as he chaired a summit on Third World hunger. Two young women had abandoned cleaning duty for Ping-Pong, giggling as they missed the ball, over and over again. Zeng leant on the handle of his broom.

"I burnt down a shed in an alley in Dongcheng."

"Why?" Wang asked.

"I saw my ex, Dragon, moving about behind the windows. So I poured lighter fluid on the door and struck a match. By the time the firemen got there the shed had burnt to the ground."

Wang was shaken by this. "Was Dragon in the shed?"

"No. He was in Shenzhen. I just imagined it."

"But you started the fire because you *thought* Dragon was there? You wanted to burn him to *death*?"

Zeng's brow knotted. "I knew Dragon was in Shenzhen," he decided, "but he was on my mind when I started the fire . . . I was mad at him, and setting fire to the shed was something to do . . . like a release . . . I regret it now."

Wang was disturbed. People didn't go about starting fires for "a release." Zeng looked down at his mutilated forearm. The scars were deep and destructive, as though repeatedly slashed with a knife, and he stroked them with a masochistic pride. Though they had broken up years ago, Zeng still wrote letters to Dragon, which he bribed a dishwasher in the kitchen to smuggle out and post to the Shenzhen nightclub where he was a bartender. Two weeks ago, when they were queuing for medication, Zeng had shown one of the letters to Wang. The letter listed his ex-boyfriend's crimes: the times he'd cheated on Zeng, the money he'd "borrowed" and the lies he'd told. Then, near the letter's end, Zeng swung from hate to love. Dragon was his soulmate. His love for Dragon, like the tattoo on his arm, would never fade.

"Do you think he reads your letters?" Wang had asked.

"No," said Zeng. "He throws them away."

"Then why bother?" Wang asked, baffled. "Why waste your time?"

And Zeng, with a pitying look in his eyes, had said, "The problem with you, Wang Jun, is that you've never been in love."

In the yard, Zeng bent over his broom, the stiff bristles scratching concrete as he swept cigarette ends and burnt matches into a pile. Were all gay men like this when they were "in love"? Wang wondered. Irrational? Obsessive? Deranged? Wang knew no other homosexual men to compare Zeng to but decided this was probably the case. As though reading Wang's mind, Zeng said, "Don't think badly of me. I've changed. I don't care about Dragon anymore. I'm over him now."

Zeng didn't look up, and his head was a tangle of dark roots and peroxide as he swept.

"Yeah?" said Wang. "How come?"

"I only think of you these days."

Bent over his broom Zeng's gaze was indecipherable. The women from Ward C giggled as they swung their paddles wide of the Ping-Pong ball. The Secretary-General of the United Nations struck the bench as he argued with the President of France and the Prime Minister of Japan. And at a loss for what to say, or even what to think, Wang Jun went back to sweeping up the cigarette butts scattered in the yard, putting what Zeng had said out of his mind.

11

The Watcher

Yida is working nights at Dragonfly Massage. She leaves home at 4 p.m. in her clinical white uniform and flat-soled shoes and works through the hours of darkness until dawn. Her shadow moves across the walls of private rooms with the lights dimmed low as she massages body after body. Due to shyness, lack of curiosity and fatigue, Yida does not talk much with her customers. She knows the bodies of her regulars, the skin-braille of moles, the birthmarks, stretch marks and post-operative scars, but not the jobs they do or the lives they lead. She knows the flaws and frailties of the flesh, hidden under her customers' clothes, but she doesn't know their names.

Wang dislikes Yida working nights, as he knows the sort of men who go to Dragonfly Massage after dark. Men who drunkenly swagger through the heavy glass doors, eager to strip off the noose of work ties and tobacco- and-sweat-stale shirts and be serviced by a woman's sensual touch. Men with lewd, alcohol-loosened tongues and wayward, groping hands that Yida has to remove from her hips and thighs again and again. Even at the "proper" massage establishments, the masseuses offer extras. Stuff goes on. The late-night drunks would not go there otherwise.

By the end of her shift Yida is exhausted, her lower back aching from bending over the white-sheeted massage tables and her arm muscles cramped. She leaves work as the sun rises and is back at Apartment 404 by quarter past six, to get her husband and daughter ready for work and school. Before changing out of her uniform, she goes to the kitchen, puts saucepans of eggs and rice porridge on the gas burner and washes the dishes from the night before. She makes Wang's coffee and puts his hard-boiled eggs in a bowl. As she puts his breakfast on the table, she sees the tightening of her husband's jaw.

"What?" she says.

"Nothing."

Yida is so exhausted she wants to lay her head down and weep. She can feel the rings darkening around her sunken eyes, and her youth draining out of her, onto the tiled floor. He behaves as though she has wronged him, through her physical proximity to other men. But she has done nothing wrong. Only the job they pay her to do.

"The men who want that sort of thing don't come to Dragonfly Massage," she says. "They go to the teenage whores at the place down the road." Then, too tired to fight, she backs down and placates: "I know you don't like it. But you can't deny we need the money."

Wang knocks a boiled egg against the bowl so the eggshell cracks. He can't deny that they need the money, but he'll never get used to how it is earned.

As Yida is working, Wang and Echo have takeout noodles from a nearby Lanzhou place for dinner, eating out of the plastic containers. Wang has bought Echo a can of lychee juice but, when he catches her stealing sips from his bottle of Yanjing, pours her a third of a glass. After dinner Echo goes to the bedroom to do her homework, and Wang goes to the kitchen. Cold yellow light spills out of the fridge as he takes out another beer. He levers the cap with a bottle opener and gazes out the window at the buildings of Maizidian as he swigs. The mid-nineties high-rise office and apartment complexes are nowhere near as tall as the skyscrapers in Guomao, but the effect of them at night, with the dozens of floors randomly lit, is striking. Wang cracks the window open to air the stuffy kitchen but smells the greasy cooking odours from the ventilation fan below and slams the window shut again.

Heavy footsteps thud across the ceiling, and the gunfire of Call of Duty, the shoot 'em up played by the teenage boy next door, rumbles through the walls. Wang drinks half the beer in one long swallow. He is restless. His heart, lungs and legs are bursting with longing to be striding through neon-lit streets, amongst revellers, music and noise. To drink whisky in the side-alley bars and shoot the breeze with strangers. But it would be irresponsible to leave Echo. He'd never forgive himself if something happened to her.

Wang sparks a lighter and inhales the flame into a cigarette. Ten days have gone by since the barber's and, though he hasn't been back in person, he casts his mind back there a hundred times a day. He wants to talk to Zeng. Nothing more than that. He is not one of those men who likes other men. He is attracted to women. Zeng has never cared for women. "What are they for?" he once joked.

Back when Wang drove his taxi at night, he sometimes picked up gay men from nightclubs near the Workers Stadium. Men in Day-Glo T-shirts sweaty from the dance floor. Men with abnormally dilated pupils and loopy grins, sucking on lollipops and squealing, high-pitched, in the back seat. Once, two men got in his taxi and were all over each other. Mouths slurping and hands groping at the crotch bulges in each other's jeans, as though Wang wasn't there. Wang had nearly pulled over and ordered them out. Why behave like animals? Why can't they control themselves for ten minutes?

The high-rises of Maizidian sway like bamboo in the breeze and Wang realizes he is slightly drunk. He can't call his mind to heel. Can't stop his thoughts from returning, again and again, to Zeng. Ten years ago, in the hospital. Ten days ago, in the barber's. To his wry smile and the dark blades of hair scything his brow. To the emerald of his dragon tattoo and the grotesque, self-inflicted scar on his forearm, as good as a warning to stay away.

112

* * *

When Wang looks in on Echo around nine, she is in bed in her pyjamas and reading a comic book. He leans on the door frame, his perspective of the room tilting slightly from the beer. Alcohol has turned up the thermostat of his body, flushing him red.

"Done your homework?" he asks.

"Yeah."

"Are you sure? Remember you told your mother you'd study harder and improve your grades . . ."

Echo has been in Yida's bad books since the parent–teacher meeting at Zaoying Elementary last week, where they found out that Echo ranked thirty-second in her class of thirty-five. "A day-dreamer," Teacher Ling had said. "Echo has poor concentration and consistently low grades. She has no community spirit and does not mix well with other children. She won't get into a good junior school at this rate."

When they got home, Yida shouted at Echo that she was lazy and spoilt. She smacked Echo and threatened to throw her artist's sketch pads and colouring pencils in the bin. "I got poor marks at school," she shouted. "I didn't work hard enough. And look at how *I* ended up! You'd better study harder, Echo, or you'll end up with a life like *mine*!"

Remembering the scene that Yida had made, Echo looks at her father from the bed and says quietly, "I finished my homework an hour ago."

"Okay. Good. You brushed your teeth? Washed your face?"

"Yes."

Wang asks Echo what comic she is reading, and she holds up the cover. The myth of the Goddess Chang-e and her palace on the moon. Wang approves, but it's a school night, so he says, "Put that away now. Time for bed."

"One more page . . ."

"No. I'm putting the light out. No more reading." Wang reaches for the light switch, and Echo calls out, "Ba, can you leave the light on? Just for tonight?"

"Why?" Wang asks. "I'll only be next door . . ."

"Please, Ba . . ."

"What are you scared of?"

Echo won't say, but looks at her father with panicking eyes.

"What is it, Echo? Tell me. What are you frightened of?"

And Echo whispers, as though fearful of being overheard, "The Watcher."

"The Watcher? What's the Watcher?"

"The person who is watching me."

Wang steps nearer to the bed. "What person?" he asks carefully. "Where does he watch you?"

"Everywhere. In the street, and the park, and school . . ."

Wang goes over and grabs Echo's arm. "Why didn't you say anything?" he cries. "What does he look like?"

Echo stares back, trembling at her father's bloodshot, intense eyes.

Wang squeezes her arm and shakes. "What does he look like? Is he skinny? Does he have strange hair? Tell me, Echo!"

"Ba . . . You are hurting me . . ."

Wang loosens his grip, but his voice remains insistent, demanding. "Look, Echo, it's important that you tell me right now. This man could be dangerous. You have to tell me what he looks like so we can report him to the police."

"You . . . you can't tell the police . . ." Echo stammers. "The Watcher is a ghost."

"A ghost?"

"Yes."

"The Watcher isn't real?"

She shakes her head and whispers, "*No.*"

Wang is relieved. He feels terrible for shaking her so hard, and he says he is sorry, but she gave him a scare. She shouldn't make up things like that. She shouldn't let her imagination run wild. She shouldn't read horror comics anymore, because they are a bad influence. Now if she ever *does* see anyone watching her— an actual man—she must tell Baba at once. Understood? Because Baba wants to keep her safe. Wang strokes her hair and promises to leave the light on until he comes to bed. But just for tonight.

Because sleeping with the light on is a bad habit, and she is not a little girl anymore.

"Ba?" Echo whispers. "Is it true that you used to be mad?"

Wang starts and hesitates. Echo is too young to know about the time he was in the hospital. He and Yida had agreed. "Who said that to you?" he asks. "Lin Hong? One of the neighbours?"

"The Watcher."

He is angry enough to shake her again. "Echo, stop making up silly stories! Who said that to you? Tell me now!"

Echo sniffs, and Wang's heart tightens to see more tears trickling down her cheeks. He knows he won't get a word out of her when she is upset like this. Lin Hong, he thinks. Who else?

"Well, it's a lie," he says. "I was never mad. Next time anyone says so, tell them they don't know what they are talking about and walk away. Understand?"

Echo nods. Wang had meant to speak calmly, but his words had seethed out, drunken and ranting. He steps back from the bed. "'Night, Echo," he says.

Echo lies down and pulls the duvet up to her chin, staring up at him. Wang sees the fear and mistrust of him in her eyes and knows tomorrow he will be remorseful for losing his temper. But tonight, alcohol and righteousness course through his veins. "'Night," he repeats.

Then he turns and walks out, flipping the light switch before shutting the door and leaving his daughter in the dark.

12

The Fourth Letter

Today is my tenth day of exile. Newsprint blocks the windows and electricity drips through the cord into the 40-watt bulb. The machine wheezes and gasps, as though protesting the darkness I feed into its parts.

For ten days, I have abstained from you, Driver Wang. No letters. No visits to Apartment 404. No riding in your taxi or watching you in the street. For ten days, I have been chained to my desk, preparing your historical records, my fingers stiffened by the cold, struggling to hit the correct keys. The machine huffs and puffs and loses consciousness. I reboot and wait impatiently for its revival, several times a day.

The Henan migrants gamble and scrape chair legs in the room above. I curse and bang the ceiling with a broom. I don't go out. I hunch at my desk and *tap tap tap* at the keyboard, as single-minded as a prisoner tunnelling out of solitary confinement with a spoon. Though I have kept away from you, Driver Wang, you are my every waking thought.

Do you remember what it was like to die? Though your death count is higher than average, your departure from the host body is harrowing every time. Your soul, overcome by grief, floats above the rigor mortis–stiffened corpse. You mingle with the gases of decomposition rising from the rotting flesh. You leap back into the stopped heart with such force the cadaver jerks (to the fright of workers in the morgue). However, to stay in the host body past the expiration date is a serious offence. Latecomers to the Otherworld are disciplined, and so you leave.

Our souls have never met in the Otherworld. We suffer for our prolific sins against each other separately, and our paths never cross. After incarnation is when we meet. After the hand of fate has snatched up our souls and placed them in the womb to be born again, kicking and screaming into the human world. Fate throws us in the same family, the same harem, the same herd of slaves. But fate sets us against each other. Fate has us brawling, red in tooth and claw. Fate condemns us to bring about the other's downfall. To blaze like fiery meteors as we crash into each other's stratosphere, then incinerate to heat and dust.

Now the time has come for my exile to end. For me to go out into the city, to the housing compound where you live. Past the junk mail–stuffed letterboxes, electricity meters and Internet cables, and up the concrete flights of stairs to Apartment 404. I will stand with palms and ear against your door, my eardrum straining at the sounds within: the TV selling cars and fast food; the water heater banging; the clatter of Yida washing dishes in the sink. My eardrums will strain to pick up the sounds. You and your wife and child a mere heartbeat away.

The time has come to deliver this letter. For in your sixth and current incarnation, Driver Wang, we must rebel against fate. So read on. Fate must be outwitted. It must no longer stand in our way.

13

Arise, Slaves, Arise!
Jin Dynasty, 1213

A turnip in the gutter. Purplish white and wrinkled, with dirt clinging to the furrows and roots. A miracle in our famine-stricken city, that a vegetable could survive this long, even interred in the ground. I think I am hallucinating. But you have seen the turnip too and stare at me rivalrously. Hunger gnawing in our guts, we size each other up. Two Jurchen boys with starved-mutt rib cages and eyes bulging in our gaunt skulls. Your face has been mutilated by a branding iron, with three wide scars burnt on each cheek. The brandings are tribal and deliberate and a warning that you are much tougher than I am.

You stiffen and clench your fists. If we fight I will lose, so I pretend that I am deranged. I growl and gnash my teeth (wobbly teeth in bleeding gums, too loose to break your skin). I claw the air, as though ready to rip your throat into geysers of blood. I toss my head this way and that and howl, shuffling wolfishly towards the turnip. Are you afraid? Or could that be a smile on your lips? A smile in this city of hunger-deadened wretches; that would be the second miracle of the day. Now or never, I think, and pounce

118

at the turnip. And there is no mistaking that you are smiling now. You swing your fist, and the battle over the turnip has ended before it has begun.

I come round on a hard wooden floor. You are standing over me, gnawing the turnip raw. "Here," you say, and toss what remains to where I lie. I devour the vegetable, dirty tangled roots and all. Maggots have burrowed inside. Wriggling maggots. I devour those too.

We are in a glassblower's workshop, with a workbench of crucibles, scales and long glassblowing horns. Vases, elliptical bottles and paperweights glint on the shelves. A wind chime of glass pendants tinkles above. The beauty of the glassware does not move me, however. Glass cannot feed a man, after all. Breathing ragged and shallow, you collapse beside me like a sack of bones. The branded scars on your cheeks are like barren riverbeds. How sickening it must have been to smell your own flesh sizzling under the metal of a branding iron.

"Who are you?" I ask.

"Tiger."

Your brandings are like tiger stripes. Your name is apt.

"I was Glassblower Hua's apprentice," you lie, "but he's dead now. We were fishing in the river when he fell in and drowned."

You stare at me, challenging me to challenge you. You were never apprentice to Glassblower Hua. Those hands of yours have never painstakingly crafted glass. You are savage as a stray cat. Clever in the way of rogues and thieves and those who live by their wits.

"Who are you?" you ask me.

When I was a child, they called me Boy. After my mother died, and I came to live in the Craftsmen's District with Uncle Lu, they called me Carpenter Lu's Boy. "Turnip," I decide. "I worked for Carpenter Lu. Though he is dead now too."

In his sixth decade, Uncle Lu suffered greatly when the famine began. A filial child would have sliced off and cooked a piece of his own flesh for his starving master, but I was too cowardly. I went out scavenging for Uncle Lu instead, and last week I came back to find him glassy-eyed on the workshop floor. I lay beside him until nightfall. Then I took him by wheelbarrow to a nearby field, dug a hole as deep as I stood and buried him there. Afterwards I lay on the mound, protecting the unmarked grave for a night and a day. Over my dead body would cannibals dig him up. Uncle Lu had been like a father to me.

"Why have you brought me here?" I ask you.

"Better here than the gutter, Turnip," you say. "Better here than where the corpse-snatchers can get you."

My head throbs from where your knuckles flew at me. My buttocks and back are grazed from where you dragged me through the streets. I murmur, "Do you mind if I sleep now, Tiger?"

But your eyes are shut. You are already sleeping.

For many moons the city of Zhongdu has been under siege. The Mongol hordes came from the north, and our city walls are now surrounded by ox-skin yurts and cattle-dung fires, and tens of thousands of Mongol warriors, patrolling on horseback so no one can flee. They watch politely as famished Jurchens abseil down the city walls on ropes, before impaling the escapees with a cloud of arrows. They are breaking down our defences, starving the million citizens of Zhongdu to death. Beyond the city walls, camel-mounted kettledrums beat day and night as within the city hunger-weakened Jurchens keel over. Every beat, another dead, another dead.

Before the Mongols came, the markets of Zhongdu were thriving and bustling, selling every beast and fowl and grain. But now our stores of millet, barley and rice are gone. Every animal was eaten long ago and not one remains. Not a cat or a dog, nor a sparrow or a rat. Not even a pet cricket chirruping in a cage.

The famine-stricken citizens of Zhongdu think only of food. Staggering about the streets, their hollow stomachs rattle with stones, twigs and bark. Mouths chew at nothing, masticating empty air, or chew grass to an indigestible cud. The famine has made insectivores of us, gobblers of grasshoppers and ants. And now a moral quandary has descended like a dark cloud upon the citizens of Zhongdu.

Do we eat or bury our dead?

We spend two days and nights on the workshop floor. We are delirious. We drift in and out of consciousness. We don't talk. We barely move. The glass beads of the wind chime tinkle as they sway gently above. Sometimes I creak my eyelids apart. Through the light and dark coming through the window I track the passage of time. I shiver with cold. I swallow the air, hoping there is sustenance in the emptiness. My stomach gurgles with it. The air burbles through my intestines and splutters back out as flatulence. I swear to take revenge on the Mongols as a ghost after I am dead. But, to be honest, my heart's not in it. Apathy's all I feel as my life slips away.

On the third day you speak: "Turnip, I am going out to find some food."

I hear footsteps. I hear the door slam. I try to lift my head. Or perhaps I dream I do. I can't find my head anyway.

Night. The smell of cooking meat summons me back from the brink of death. I open my eyes. You are squatting by the fireplace, holding two metal skewers of meat over the flames. A groan escapes my lips. My saliva glands are a bursting dam. Hearing I am awake, you hand me a skewer by the wooden handle.

"Tiger . . . what meat is this?" I ask.

"Cat."

"Cat? But there are no cats left in the city."

"I know where they live. I know where to hunt for them."

I stare at the skewered pieces of semi-raw meat. The edges are charred. The meat trickles blood onto my wrist and hand.

"If you don't eat it," you say, "I will."

For twenty minutes there is no sound but our chewing and swallowing. You sink your teeth into your cat kebab, your eyes slitted, your tiger scars smeared with grease. After the meat is eaten we pick at the fibres caught between our teeth. We lick the juices from our palms. My stomach is convulsing with joy.

*   *   *

Thereafter our days are like this. During daylight we rest. We watch the sunbeams drifting through the window and shifting in golden bars across the workshop floor. We watch the rise and fall of our chests and swat at the flies buzzing around our ulcerated legs. We listen to the Mongol drums beating beyond the fortress of city walls. We think our thoughts, hunger-weak thoughts that crawl feebly through our minds. Then, after dusk, you vanish into the night to go cat hunting. Tiger by name, tiger by nature. Hunter-gatherer, you stalk one down and return with a skinned flank of meat.

"Where is the cat's head, Tiger?" I ask. "Where's the fur and limbs? The tail and paws?"

"I tossed them to some starving orphans," you reply.

Petals of blood spill from the meat as you carry it to the workbench. On hands and knees I lick them up with my thirsty tongue. You slam a cleaver into the cat, portioning it up. Then we each hold a skewer over the fire, salivating as the flames lick the rawness away. I can hardly wait for the meat to be cooked before gobbling it down.

Before grilling the meat we lock the door and windows, for the smell of roasting flesh brings interlopers. They knock politely, begging to be let in. They scrabble like rats and whine, "Let us have some meat. We are starving out here. We have children to feed. Out of the goodness of your hearts . . ."

You snatch up the cleaver and go to the door. How terrifying you are, with your scarred cheeks and wild, lice-ridden mane. The blade of the cleaver and your eyes glint as one.

"Come on in," you smile, opening the door wider. "Here I am, waiting with my cleaver to chop your children up. I will scoop out their livers and kidneys and boil them for soup."

And the starving beggars slither back into the shadows. Though your threats are horrifying, I admire your bravery. Man eat man—this is what our city has become. And you are brutal in our defence.

*   *   *

122

When I regain strength, I wander around our city and see how Zhongdu has descended into depravity. The good people have starved to death and the moral conscience of the city has died with them. Cannibalism is now the norm, the wicked feeding on the corpses of the good. They don't even wait for cover of darkness before shamelessly dragging the dead away. The kitchens of the body snatchers are fragrant with roasting meat. The maddening aroma wafts about the streets, diminishing willpower in the few places where willpower remains.

At night we are woken by shrieking in the Craftsmen's District: "Fiend! You ate our boy. You ought to rot in Hell."

"Who had a bite when they thought I wasn't looking? Who deserves to rot in Hell as much as I do?"

"Liar! Liar!"

I recognize their voices.

"That's Swordmaker Fu and his wife," I whisper. "They had a young son, but from the sounds of it he is now dead."

You sneer in the dark, "Cannibals. Too lazy to go out and hunt a cat."

I shut my eyes, but I am too haunted by Swordmaker Fu's macabre words to sleep. I lie awake instead and count my blessings that I am with a fellow believer in the sanctity of human flesh.

Every day the Mongol battering rams strike the city gates and the citizens of Zhongdu hold their breath as the beast pounds. Ah, this time we are done for, we Jurchens think. This time they will break our defences. But the Jurchen army, armed with arrows and bows, somehow keeps the wolves at bay for one more day.

One afternoon, as the battering rams pound, you ask, "Turnip, have you seen a devil's horseman before?"

I confess I haven't.

"You've never climbed the city wall?"

"Not since the Mongols came. It's too dangerous."

"Come with me, Turnip," you say. "I know a place we can watch them."

We stagger through the empty streets, two young men with gargantuan heads on spindle limbs. The few Jurchens we encounter scurry by with a hunted look in their eyes. We go to the east of the city, to a crumbling stone stairwell in the rear of a weed-choked temple garden. We go up to the stone battlements of the city wall and peer out. I am stunned when I see the enemy camp. Thousands of ox-skin yurts and cattle-dung fires and helmeted Mongol warriors on armoured horses, as far as the eye can see. The Mongols have devoted a city to their siegecraft. You are enraged. Your eyes narrow to vengeful slits beneath your gnarled and tangled hair.

"*Barbarians!*" you spit. "One day I'll rip off their heads and piss down their throats. I'll fuck their mothers and daughters to a bloody squealing pulp . . ."

Way down below, a devil's horseman trots towards us on his mare. His skin looks as though it has been flayed off, lime-cured in a tannery then sewn back on as human leather. His nose is flattened between his cheekbones and his yellow eyes glare up from beneath his helmet. Hearts hammering and legs shaking, we crouch down. "Has he seen us?" I whisper.

An arrow soars whistling over our heads in answer to my question. We flee down the stone stairs back into the accursed city of Zhongdu.

That night you go out cat hunting. When you get back we cook and feast on your kill. After supper we laze on the floor and I watch you in the flickering firelight. I watch you pick fibrous strands of cat meat out of your teeth. Sprawled by the fire, your eyes are lazy and slitted as a tiger basking in the sun. I reach and stroke the iron-scorched markings on your cheeks. The scar tissue is hard and shiny under my touch. "Who branded you?" I ask. You do not open your eyes. "Where do you come from?" I ask. "Who are your people?" Your robe is open and I move my hand over your famished chest. Your rib bones and tautening nipples. The jut of shadows in your skeletal frame. My stomach tightens. Now or never, I think, and move my mouth to yours. A jerk of your chin warns me this is not what you want. Your hand pushes on the back of my head, pushing down. Down past your sternum, down past your sunken stomach, to the rags about your groin. I loosen the rags and bury my face in the thatch of hair and what lies beneath. I take you in my mouth and feel you come to life. Swelling, growing engorged inside me, against my tongue. The smell of you, unwashed for months, is musty and intoxicating. I glance up. Your eyes are still closed. I move over you, my rhythm quickening until you spurt your bitter seed. Swallowing, I pull my wet and glistening mouth away. Sprawled on your back, your eyes are shut, and you look peaceful, as though having a pleasant dream. As much of a stranger as you were before.

The Fall

The hooves wake me at dawn. The stampeding hooves of tens of thousands of Mongols galloping into Zhongdu on horseback. I shake you awake: "Tiger! Tiger! Listen!" You sit up and listen to the kettledrums out in the streets. The yodellings of war cries and the bloodcurdling screams of Jurchens dragged from their homes. "Hide, we must hide!"

Shaking, we hurry up onto the roof. I am shuddering hard, pale with fright. "O Lord Buddha, have mercy on our souls," I plead, over and over, though the mantra brings no peace of mind. You are silent, keeping your wits about you as you watch the Mongols rampaging through Zhongdu. Narrowing your eyes and thinking of how to save our skins.

The Mongols are orderly and systematic. They plunder our city, ward by ward, street by street, house by house. From the roof, we watch them haul a wealthy merchant's family out of hiding in the next alley, thrusting spears to their throats and commanding them to bring out their valuables. The family obey. They scurry back and forth, fetching porcelain vases, wooden puppets, silk gowns, paintings, ostrich-feather fans and other family heirlooms. They plead for mercy as they lay the offerings at the Mongols' feet. But our conquerors have no mercy. They rape the screaming wife and daughters, penetrating and ejaculating in a few thrusts. Then they execute. For many moons the Jurchens have been wasting away slowly from starvation. But now death strikes the city like lightning as throats are slashed and hearts impaled by arrows at close range. The Mongols then set the houses of the slaughtered Jurchens ablaze, smoke darkening the sky as Zhongdu goes up in flames.

The devil's horsemen gallop into our alley and we flatten ourselves against the roof as screams rise up from below. You curse as an axe smashes through the bolted door of Glassblower Hua's workshop, and I shake and beg the Lord Buddha for mercy. I shut my eyes, awaiting death by suffocating smoke (should fate be lenient), or by burning (should fate be cruel). You shake my shoulder.

"Look, Turnip, look. They are letting the craftsmen live!"

In the alley the Mongols are rounding up the craftsmen of Zhongdu: stonemasons and carpenters and glassblowers and metalworkers, a group of miserable old men with black and swollen eyes being trussed up with ropes.

"We must surrender," you say. "Stay up here and we will burn."

"Tiger, no! They will kill us!"

"Stay then. Burn in the flames."

Though I am terrified, I go where you go. So, on shaking legs, I follow you down. In the alley you crash to your knees before a Mongol with flaring nostrils and yellow skin.

"I am Glassblower Hua and this is Carpenter Lu! We offer our skills as craftsmen to our conquerors and rulers, the Mongols!"

A traitorous Jurchen in Mongol robes translates our surrender into Mongolian, as you kowtow, knocking your forehead to the ground. The Mongols seize us. They smite us with their fists, but they do not kill us. They bind our wrists with rope and march us and the other craftsmen down the central avenue of Zhongdu. Massacred victims of the fall are everywhere. Corpses young and old, flung in the dust. And stunned and bereaved and frightened as we are, we know that we are better off than them.

The Mongol Juggernaut

The wagers of war ride on horseback and the slave-drivers lash their whips, driving us Jurchens forth like herds of cattle, away from Zhongdu. Oxen drag the yurts where the high-ranking Mongols reside on wheeled platforms. Sixteen warhorses pull Genghis Khan in his magnificent palace yurt, surrounded by a battalion of ten thousand warriors, defending the "Lord of Mankind."

The Mongols want to civilize their barbarous lands and have herded up Jurchens with knowledge and skills: bonesetters and physicians; artisans and engineers. They have gathered labourers too: young boys to tend to the animals and put up the Mongols' yurts; young girls to milk the cows, gather dung for fires, cook meals and serve the Mongols' voracious physical needs. After months of starvation, many Jurchens fall in the dust, too weak to march. The Mongols whip them and, when they don't stand and walk, slash their throats. Throughout the day we stagger on and the Mongol juggernaut sheds corpses like a balding man sheds hairs.

At night we slaves sleep on the bare earth under the sky. When light rains fall we shiver and curve our spines against the drizzle, hugging ourselves in the cold. When there are thunderstorms and heavy rain beats the earth beneath us to mud, we abandon hope of sleep. Lightning illuminates our writhing sea of slaves, mud-drenched and with chattering teeth.

At daybreak the Mongols lash their whips and we drag our weary bones from the earth. Slave girls ladle rice gruel into our bare hands, and a leather flask of water is passed amongst the herd. The Mongols lash their whips once more and our dark swarm of humanity moves on, the sun beating down and dragging our shadows out from under our feet.

The Mongol caravan journeys north by hoof and wheel and blistered foot, kicking up a storm of dust. I walk by your side, stride for limping stride. The nearness of you, the rhythm of your breath and your stoic, determined face is a comfort to me.

"I can't go on, Tiger . . ." I say, as my skull throbs and the weals from Ogre's thrashing whip ache on my back. "I am at the end of my strength . . ."

"No," you say, "there's strength in you yet. Keep going and there will come a time when we are free. Surrender now and you will die a slave."

I would have fallen down long ago and let the ground drink the blood of my slit throat, were it not for you. So long as you are by my side, I can endure. You ease the stoned-to-death feeling in my soul.

Though the Jin Dynasty has fallen and they stagger in rags, the craftsmen of Zhongdu brag of their former renown.

"My swords were so sharp they sliced human bone as though it were tofu," boasts Swordmaker Fu. "Warlords came from thousands of li away for my weapons."

"My Lady Mu dolls fetched a hundred silvers each," says Doll-Maker Wan, whose dolls once lived in the bedchambers of the princesses. "Lady Mu Flies a Kite. Lady Mu Plays with a Little Dog. I have crafted thousands over the years . . ."

The craftsmen are distinguished indeed. Gem-Cutter Hu's necklaces were worn on the lily-white necks of the Emperor's concubines. Stone-Carver Peng's fearsome tomb gargoyles protect the dead in the imperial mausoleums. There is a saying, "He who stands upright does not fear a crooked shadow." Well, Tiger and Turnip have much to fear. For we are not who we say we are and our shadows are crooked as bent nails. But the craftsmen of Zhongdu don't tell on us. The Mongols don't know our language, and to speak to them is to risk aggravating their tempers and fists. So long as we don't antagonize them, the craftsmen leave us be.

The Mongol in charge of our herd has a name that's some guttural sound in the throat. We do not call our slave-driver by his name, though. Ogre is what we call him. Ogre rides with his leather boots in stirrups and a coat of dog skins over his shoulders, and his mare is equipped with a hook-ended lance and a horsehair lasso. Your iron-branded scars are nothing compared to Ogre's battle scars. One fault line cleaves Ogre's face in two, from forehead to chin, as though someone once pickaxed his head. His nose has been fractured so many times it's hardly worth calling a nose. The only word he knows in our Jurchen dialect is "Go!" which he shouts often, as he is impatient with stragglers. When the elderly

Fan-Maker Zu fainted in the heat, Ogre reached down from his mare and stuck Fan-Maker Zu's chest with the hook-ended lance. Ogre gurgled with laughter and dragged him through the dirt until he was quite dead. He has a gallows sense of humour, it can be said.

At dusk the Mongols stop and rest. They drink fermented yak's milk by firelight as captured Jurchen jugglers and acrobats perform for them. The Mongols laugh and jeer but never applaud.

"I can't walk another step. My knees are aching. My heels are weeping blisters. I am dying of thirst. I've not had a sip of water all day . . ."

Gem-Cutter Hu is at the age when humans start to shrink, when the spine buckles and the skin wrinkles and grows slack. He bends over his staff as he grumbles, his hair white and his eyes near-sighted from a lifetime of squinting at precious gems through a magnifying lens. Someone tells the gem-cutter that water-drinking time is near. Master Hu scoffs, "Ha! There's just spittle in that flask by the time it gets to me. I'll drop dead of thirst in no time, just you wait and see . . ."

It's drizzling and the thousands of hooves and wheels ahead of us have trampled the grasslands to mud that squelches through our shoes and splatters our legs. Staggering by my side, you look daggers at Master Hu. The old man brays on: "The Mongols ought not to treat us this way. Don't these ignorant barbarians know who we are? They are marching us to our deaths. Won't be long until I fall down and they cut my throat . . ."

"Good," you mutter. "Fall down dead and spare our ears your whining."

Master Hu spins round, squinting accusingly. "Who said that? The Tiger Boy? The boy with the branded face? You donkey's afterbirth! How dare you speak to me like that! You are not one of us. You should have been killed in Zhongdu."

Shut up now, Tiger, I think. But you laugh in Master Hu's face.

"I heard you kept slaves in Zhongdu," you say. "I heard you beat them, and when they ran away, you caught them and cut off their ears. I heard you imprisoned your slaves in your cellar during the famine. Then you cooked and ate them, one by one."

Master Hu wheezes as though his heart has seized up.

"If the Mongols slash your throat, Master Hu," you say calmly, "then that will be less than what you deserve."

Gem-Cutter Hu shakes his crooked staff at you. "You are a liar and imposter! You are not Glassblower Hua! I knew Master Hua, and you are not him. I will tell the Mongols about you!"

"Tell, and I'll wring your neck."

"Not if I beat you to death with a rock first!" hisses Sword-Maker Fu.

You laugh at the swordmaker. "And then will you eat me? Like you ate your own son?"

The herd of old men turns on you. "Shut that evil Tiger mouth!" they curse. "Imposter!" "Lowbreed mongrel!"

You open your mouth to lash your tongue once more, but I grab you and say, "Tiger. *Shut up.*"

You shut your mouth, but your eyes are amused. You won't be civil to men for whom you have nothing but contempt. You let that be known.

Every slave dreams of escape. Some daring souls flee into the northern wilderness, only to be shot down by Mongol arrows. Two Jurchen princes gallop away one night on stolen mares, only to be recaptured, rolled up in blankets and kicked to death (for the Mongols are superstitious about spilling the blood of royalty on the ground). Suicide is the means of escape for some. They weigh their tunic pockets down with stones and hurl themselves into fast-flowing rivers. Or they goad the Mongols into losing their tempers and beating them to death, and die smiling and satisfied.

Puppetmaker Xia, whose beloved Concubine Sparrow is now a girl slave, is the most suicidal of our herd: "After the famine stole my wife and sons away, I prayed to the Lord Buddha to spare Concubine Sparrow. But now I regret that Concubine Sparrow did not die in the famine too, for death would have spared her the yoke of the Mongols."

The puppetmaker calls for Concubine Sparrow in his sleep, ordering her to bring his slippers and draw his bath, then wakes distraught because she isn't there. One evening, when the Mongols are setting up camp, he sees Concubine Sparrow crouched behind the hindquarters of a cow, shovelling dung into a bucket. He stumbles over to her.

"Sparrow," he calls. "Come here, my love . . ."

But before the concubine hears Master Xia, a Mongol warrior strolls up behind her and drags her up by the hair. The bucket rolls sideways and the look on Concubine Sparrow's face is one of weary resignation as the Mongol throws her over his shoulder like a rolled-up Persian rug and saunters into a yurt. Puppetmaker Xia turns pale as his own ghost.

"How can she betray me like this?" he cries. "I should've carved up her pretty face whilst I had the chance . . ."

The puppetmaker reaches for the nearest rock and dashes the sharp, jagged edge across his wrist, over and over, drawing blood. Other slaves rush over to restrain him, grappling the wrist-cutting stone from his suicidal grip. It is a pitiful and tragic sight, but when I look at you, you are shaking with laughter, your eyes creased up.

It's just like you, Tiger, to find the humour in the bleakest of scenes.

When the night is clear and starry constellations are scattered across the sky, the slaves sleep deeply as a battlefield of slain men. I lay behind you in the dark and breathe in your rankness, my heart thudding against your spine. My fingers count your ribs. They explore your bones, protruding under your stretched-taut skin. Your hip bones, your sacrum, your shoulder blades like wings. I reach down to your groin and stroke you to life. Slowly. Cautiously. One ear listening out. I clench my fist around your stiffness, and your breathing quickens as I draw it back and forth. After your warm, sticky release, I lick my hand clean. Then I bury my face in your wild, stinking hair and hold you. To hold you is to be at one with you. To be at one with the starry cosmos of ancient gods above.

As I hold you I will the night never to end. For our oneness fades with the disappearing stars. And by daylight you are other again.

As the Mongol juggernaut moves north the grasslands become sparse and wither away. The earth becomes bone dry and rocks burn under our bare feet. The Mongols raid and lay waste to nearby villages. They steal two hundred head of camel and thousands of leak-proof barrels and leather casks. At the lake at Dolon Nor every barrel and cask is filled to the brim. The Mongol juggernaut splits up. Most of the caravan, Genghis Khan and the seventy thousand horseback warriors, journey to the west, to battle and conquer other lands. One hundred slave-drivers and a thousand Jurchen slaves trudge with the camels up to the north. You and I are amongst those bound for Karakorum.

"Are we in Mongolia yet?" I ask you.

"After we cross the desert we will be in Mongolia," you say.

"What desert?"

"The Gobi, you fool."

The Wilderness of Stone

The Gobi is a furnace of burning rocks, dry and monotonous and flat. We journey for a day without seeing a plant or a tree. We journey for a day and encounter nothing more than the scattered, sun-bleached bones of perished animals. The sun above the Gobi is swollen, brighter and fiercer than the ordinary sun. The Gobi sun blazes as though it wants to incinerate every living creature from the earth.

The scorching winds are strong enough to knock you from your feet and make walking near impossible. But walk is all we do. We shroud our faces against the sand gusting from the western dunes with strips torn from our robes, and our eyes are gritty and red. The horseback Mongols are as stupefied by the heat as those on foot. The creaking of axles and wheels, snorting camels and our dragging feet are the only sounds. At dawn and noon and dusk we are allowed a few swallows of water from a leather flask. Ossified inside and out, we dream of water. We dream of an overcast sky. We dream of the shade of a single tree.

At night in the Gobi the temperature plummets and we shudder with cold. We Jurchens don't have slave girls and coats of animal skins to keep us warm like the Mongols do, so we huddle together on the scorpion-scuttling earth, skin against parchment-dry skin. Our tusk-like collar bones and hips knock together as we sleep, and we wake in the morning aching and bruised.

The Puppetmaker

On the second day of staggering through the Gobi, many slaves keel over and, even after Mongol whips have crisscrossed their backs with deep, bleeding welts, don't stand up. They are left for the razor-sharp beaks and claws of the carrion-eating birds.

Our herd limps on, our robes the colour of dust, our bloodshot eyes dull and wretched with suffering. The one exception is Puppetmaker Xia, who has turned strange in the heat. As we drag our feet as though in heavy iron shackles, Master Xia swings his limbs like one of his own puppets, jerked by strings. His eyes are shining, aberrant and rapt. His rag has slipped loose from a wide grin that looks carved upon his face. The puppetmaker laughs, then says in a spirited voice, "My friends, I have an announcement to make!"

We ignore him. Our shadows stretch out behind us, as though longing to break free of us and go back the way we came.

"Concubine Sparrow is with child!" Master Xia cries. "I saw her this morning. Her belly was swollen and she waddled as expectant women do. I am going to be a father!"

The puppetmaker and bleak reality have parted company, and no one squanders breath on speaking to him. Most of the herd stopped speaking days ago anyway.

"My sons died in the famine," Master Xia continues, "and I feared that there would be no heir to continue the Xia family line. But now another Xia is on the way . . ."

Puppetmaker Xia witters on and on about his "son and heir"

and the herd ignore him. But you grind your teeth in irritation. You can't suffer fools. You can't stand delusions and lies. You tug the shroud from your mouth and iron-branded scars, and spit, "If you had even half your wits about you, Master Xia, you'd stab Concubine Sparrow's belly with a knife. For that's a bastard Mongol child she's carrying. Not yours."

The puppetmaker laughs. "The child is mine! I know it in my bones. The child's a Jurchen and mine!"

"Tiger, shut up . . ." I warn.

But you won't shut up until you have cured Master Xia of his delusions.

"Whose seed do you think is planted in her belly?" you continue. "Your impotent old man's seed? Or the seed of one of the hundreds of Mongols who raped her? Open your eyes, Master Xia!"

The puppetmaker shakes his head. "No," he moans. "*No no no no . . .*"

The herd turns on you. They curse you with their elderly, creaking turtle-mouths. "Donkey's afterbirth!" "Evil mongrel!" "Should have died in Zhongdu!" You laugh at them. You laugh as though their hatred invigorates you. You spit defiantly, "Master Xia must accept the child isn't his. The child's a bastard Mongol's and—"

Puppetmaker Xia leaps at you and his knuckles thud against your skull. You stumble from the blow, and I rush to Master Xia, holding him back as he flails his old man's arms to attack you again.

"The child is yours, Master Xia," I say anxiously. "We believe you! The child is yours! Tiger here was just making trouble. Ignore him."

Blasting sour breath in my face, the puppetmaker shouts, "I'll kill you, Tiger Boy! I swear to God, I'll kill you dead!"

His words strike fear into my heart. But you laugh and say, "Go on then, Master Xia. Kill me. It won't make that child yours."

Puppetmaker Xia roars and lunges for you again, and Ogre, who had been dozing in the saddle, snoring out of his axe-battered nose as his mare plods at the herd's rear, wakes up. He lashes his whip and we all move apart. Not even the puppetmaker is mad enough to defy Ogre and his hook-ended lance.

Our herd staggers on through the furnace of burning rocks. You shroud your face again, your remorseless eyes staring out over the rags. You don't care about making enemies. You care only about dragging out the truth, consequences be damned.

Night. Descent of darkness and bitter cold. Slaves huddle against the winds howling across the Gobi's barrenness. Outcasts from the herd, you and I sleep apart from them. And as weak and thirsty as I am, I lie in your arms and go to sleep a contented man.

Daybreak, and you are gone. Disappeared into thin air. I look around and see you a few paces away, rubbing at some overnight bruises from the hard, stony ground. Hungry, we go to a slave girl ladling gruel out of a pot, holding out our cupped hands. Soon every slave is up and slurping gruel. Except for one. A lazybones who won't rise and shine. The slave shudders as Stone-Carver Peng kicks his backside. "C'mon, wake up, or Ogre will whip you." But the man does not stir. Stone-Carver Peng bends over for a closer look.

"Oh, the Lord Buddha have mercy on his soul!" he cries.

Stone-Carver Peng has some tragic news. The slave is Puppet-maker Xia, and he is not sleeping. He has been strangled and he is dead.

The Singing Dunes

Around noon we enter an ocean of sand, the waves not lapping at a distant shore but frozen into luminous peaks and shadowy troughs. No scorpions scuttle in the dunes, and the carrion-eating birds that stalked us all the way from Zhongdu are no longer circling and swooping overhead. Here and there rocks jut out of the sand, like the tombstones of mass graves.

The dunes slow the Mongol caravan down. The wheels of the oxcarts get trapped in the sand and the Mongols put us slaves to work pushing the carts from the rear, as the oxen, hooves slipping, pull with ropes in front. We slaves are not very strong. Wasted by starvation and charred by the sun, we are hardly worth calling men. We are gristle and bone. We are the parts the Mongol juggernaut has spat out, the parts not good to eat.

Onwards the Mongols and Jurchen slaves creep. The sand dunes are long and narrow, stretching for a journey of many days to the west and one day to the north. But as we toil, knee-deep in the ever-shifting sands, I fear that there's no end in sight.

The landscape fades in the gathering dusk, and our weary bones creak and sigh as we sink down upon the supple bed of sand. We keep apart from the herd, who glare at you, their breath fouling the air as they mutter, "Murderer!" "Strangled the puppet-maker!" "Better watch no one throttles him in the night!" The threats make me nervous, but you aren't scared. You turn your back on them and drift off to sleep.

The stars are brighter in the Singing Dunes. The silvery glow of the moon is iridescent upon the waves of sand. As you sleep you become a young boy again, and your iron-branded scars no longer seem menacing, but the marks of brutality and suffering. As you sleep, I vow to protect you, and I watch the craftsmen until every last one of them is out cold. During the famine of Zhongdu they slaughtered and ate their servants. They are cannibals. They are evil through and through.

I am drifting off to sleep when the spectral lullaby begins, nudging me back to consciousness. I sit up in the moonlight and stare about me. The singing is eerie and ethereal, and not in any language of humans but that of some other species of being. Where is the singing coming from? I listen and listen until it becomes apparent. The singing is coming from within the sand. I shake you awake.

"What is it, Turnip?" you say groggily.

"Listen, Tiger! The sand is singing!"

You listen.

"I don't hear a thing," you say, and go back to sleep.

I look around the dunes. The herds of Jurchen slaves are dead to the world, starved limbs as white as bones under the pale moonlight. The Mongols watching over the herds, huddled under the skins of wolves and swigging koumiss from leather flasks, show no sign of hearing the strange, otherworldly song.

I shiver in the cold night. I lie down and shut my eyes to sleep. But sleep is impossible. I can no more sleep on the dunes than on a bed of knives. I lie awake and listen to the spectral singing. I watch the sand.

On the second day in the dunes our progress is once more sabotaged by sand, as the wheels of the oxcarts and wagons are brought to a staggering halt and the Mongols force us to toil under the broiling sun, pushing the carts up slopes and lowering them with ropes down the other side. Around noon we pass some tall and craggy rocks called the Three Wise Men. A landmark we passed the day before. Orienteers consult maps and compass needles in dismay. We are straggling in circles. Lost in the foreverness of sand.

Tempers are frayed in the blistering heat. At water-drinking time Stone-Carver Peng drops the flask as he passes it to you, spilling precious water. You curse him for dropping it. He curses you for murdering Puppetmaker Xia. He shoves you, and you shove him back. Master Peng glares at you, his nostrils spurting rage.

Master Peng is old and wizened and would lose if he fought you on his own. But Master Peng is not on his own. The herd of shuffling, elderly slaves surrounds you. "Shame on you!" they cry. "Shame on you for murdering Puppetmaker Xia!" Ogre is standing with his brethren by a snorting camel, swigging water from a leather flask. *Whip them, Ogre!* I think. But Ogre watches with a lazy smirk as his herd turns on one of their own. Though the craftsmen are weak from marching to the brink of death, mob outrage lends them strength. They close in on you, stabbing you with their gnarled old men's fingers. "Shame on you!" "Brute!" "We'll beat you till there's nothing left to bury!" You laugh at first, at the stabbing fingers and threats of the white-haired old men. Then your face darkens as they begin to strike you. *Thud. Thud. Thud.* You struggle to fend off their blows

My heart beating wildly, I run into the fray. "Leave him be!" I shout as I am beaten by their fists. "Leave him be!" I drag you out of the scrum of old men. I drag you away with all my strength, and we tumble onto the sand. Your teeth are clenched and bared, and you are glaring, keen to go back and fight. I heave myself on top of you, holding you down.

"Sixteen against one," I say. "You will lose. They will beat you to death, and the Mongols won't stop them."

The will to fight drains out of you, but you glower at the old men.

"I'd rather die fighting," you hiss, "than let those fiends push me around."

Sunset. The sky is blood-coloured, as though bleeding from the Death by a Thousand Cuts. We stare at the massacre in the sky and you say, "The sun needs a tourniquet."

The Mongols are spooked. The haemorrhaging of the sky is a portent of something bad. At dusk, they gather around fires of camel dung, praying to their animistic gods for protection and tossing in handfuls of sacred dust. When the shamanistic rituals are over and the fires die out, they go into their yurts.

The moon hangs low in the sky, casting its phosphorescence upon the dunes. I lie down, but I can't sleep. When the spectral song of the sand begins, I am desolate. Though surrounded by a thousand men, loneliness wells up in me and spills out as tears. A sob, primal and deep, shudders in my chest as I suddenly understand why the souls under the sand are singing, and what they want me to do. Sobbing, I dig at the dunes with my hands. I dig and dig, like a dog burrowing for a bone, until you are shaking my shoulders and saying, "Turnip. Stop. This is madness."

You pull me down. You hold me tight, binding my arms against my sides.

"Shut your eyes," you command. "Go to sleep."

But how can I sleep? I listen to the spectral melody. I watch the sand.

In the morning Stone-Carver Peng is dead. Strangled. A choking gasp is his death mask, and his tongue is thrust out from the root.

Ogre wrinkles his axe-battered nose at the corpse, as though it's a dead cockroach or rat. He kicks sand into Master Peng's staring eyes before the Mongol caravan moves on, through the Singing Dunes.

Around midday the camels start behaving strangely. They gaze to the sky and moan. They bellow and snarl their lips back over their teeth. They sink to their knees and refuse to walk another step. One camel, possessed by terror, overturns a cart as he breaks out of his leather harness and gallops wildly across the dunes.

At first we are mystified. Then we see it, the dark and ominous cloud on the horizon, like a plague of insects swarming towards us. There is a roaring in our ears, growing louder and louder, as though the dark cloud is wrenching the heavens apart as it approaches. The Mongols have no time to put up yurts. They shelter behind the kneeling camels or under rugs of animal skins. The slaves huddle in groups. Outcasts from the herd, you and I crouch together, staring with foreboding as the turbulence draws near.

Everything turns dark when the storm is upon us. Tempests of sand, swept up by cyclonic forces, howl and shriek about us. The wind is deafening and the sand is everywhere, choking us and grazing our skin and robbing us of sight. I can no longer see the Mongols and oxcarts and slaves. All I see is you, who I cling to for my life. The Singing Dunes are attacking the Mongol caravan for trespassing. They are throwing a tantrum and hurling rocks to punish us, of this I am convinced. As the wind spins around us and a rock smashes against my temple, I shout in your ear, "We are done for. This storm will kill us!"

"No!" you yell back. "The storm is on our side. Now is our chance to escape." Though the choking dust has blinded us, and the howling wind blown all sense of direction away, you drag me to my feet. "Run!" you shout. "Run!"

We run into the storm, and the sand and rocks, the teeth of the vengeful wind, rip our robes and lacerate our skin. I don't know where we are going. I don't know if we will survive. All I know is wherever you go, I go. Even if you are leading us to a certain death.

* * *

We run and run until the howling wind dies down, the thickness of sand thins out and the sun reappears through the yellow haze. Storm-bludgeoned and concussed, we gaze at the empty dunes stretching around us, smooth and unmarred by a single hoof or footprint. The caravan is nowhere in sight. The thousand Jurchen slaves and hundred Mongol slave-drivers are gone.

"At last," you say, "we are no longer slaves. We are free."

But there's no joy in your eyes, for we are still lost in the Singing Dunes, under the man-slaying sun. Your head is bleeding and gashed, as though you fought the storm and lost. I touch the soreness of my cheeks and my fingers come away bloody, and I know I look as battered as you.

We stagger on. We don't speak, because there is nothing to say. There is not a bird in the sky, nor any other sign of life. Only the sun, blasting like a furnace in a crematorium, determined to reduce us to ash and bone. The sun knocks the breath out of us, our strength and will to go on, and my heart is breaking with the presentiment that we will perish here in this silent, godless place. In my grief my only consolation is that at least I will die by your side.

When the lake appears in the distance, shimmering in the dunes, I think I am hallucinating. But you are staring at the apparition too. My throat a cracked, aching pipe, I croak, "Let's go there, Tiger."

You look at me with deadened eyes, which life is slowly departing from. Your voice husky and low, you say, "The lake does not exist. Why waste our time chasing a mirage?"

"But the lake is due north," I say, "on the way to the end of the dunes. So why not head there? What do we lose?"

As we stagger nearer and nearer, the lake of shimmering blue does not evaporate into the sky as expected. The illusion gains in substance and reality, separating into objects of the natural world. Trees. Plants. Rocks. Grasses. A lake in the shape of a crescent moon. We can't believe our eyes. The miracle restores our strength and we start to run. We run and trip over, sprawling onto the sand. We laugh and stagger to our feet, and run again.

The Lake of the Crescent Moon

We drink the cool, clear water and our bodies rejoice. We drink and drink as though the lake could at any moment disappear. We drink until we can drink no more, then fall on our backs and laugh at the vast blue sky. The sun is no longer our mortal enemy now that we have water and shade.

The lake is curved as a sickle and surrounded by trees. We strip out of our ragged robes and round our shoulders over our pitiful nakedness. We have been starved to mere shadows of our former selves—our skin so taut over starkly jutting bones we are painful to look at. But as we slide into the lake, the water laps forgivingly at our wasted bodies. The water caresses our sores and ulcers and festering wounds, and tears of gratitude well in my eyes. Though our limbs are weak we thrash them about in joy. The filth of slavedom dissolves, and we reclaim our bodies from Mongol chattels. We swim for a while, then emerge from the waters, purified and reborn, and go to sleep naked under a tree.

We wake up hungry at dusk and rummage through the vegetation around the lake. After the monotony of the yellow and rust-coloured Gobi sand, our eyes feast on the leafy greens of the foliage. We pick and eat the bitter-tasting leaves from a low plant, and though our empty stomachs can't digest them, they cry out for more.

"Look!" you cry, pointing up at a tree.

Small brown birds are hopping about in the branches. The tree is not very tall, and you reach for a low bough and climb up, your legs dangling from the crotch of the tree as your head disappears into the leaves. You come down again with a bird's nest of speckled eggs, and one newly hatched pink and featherless baby bird. The eggshells crunch between our teeth as we chew the slimy bird foetuses and swallow them down. The baby bird opens its tiny beak, chirping with fright as you lift him from the nest. You tear into the bird's naked, defenceless body with your teeth, detaching the head and handing the half with the feet to me. I chew up the raw and tender meat and newly formed bones, and swallow them down. I wish there was more.

"The other trees will have nests too," you say, spitting out the bird's tiny beak. "And tomorrow we can trap the bigger birds."

The onset of darkness chases us back to the shore of the lake. The moon is silver and bright above, and its paler, terrestrial imitation sways upon the waters. You are half in shadow, half in moonlight as you lean back against a tree. Your handsome eyes drift over the rocks, plants and trees as you think your thoughts. Who are you, Tiger? I wonder. Where do you come from? Who mutilated your cheeks? Though we have survived so much together, you are still a mystery to me. I reach and stroke the iron-branded scars. I stroke the wildness of your hair, snagging my fingers in knots only a knife could get rid of.

"Stop it, Turnip," you growl.

But I don't, and you lunge for me. You knock me over and we wrestle each other on the ground. As we play-fight, exchanging cuffs and blows, I feel your stiffening against my thigh and my heart swells in anticipation of what is to come.

Beyond the Lake of the Crescent Moon and our fortress of trees, the sorrowful dirge of the sands has started up again. But it is not so loud and is easy to ignore.

At daybreak we go to the lake and drink and bathe. You are quiet and subdued, but your mood improves as we plot to capture the brown birds.

"Right now we are too weak for the journey ahead," you say. "We need the meat to regain our strength."

I nod, though I am dubious of this "journey ahead." Here by our lake we have everything we need. Food, water, each other. Returning to the Singing Dunes is suicidal folly. But you will come round.

We gather reeds and weave them into bird-trapping cages. Then we lie on our stomachs under some bushes and wait for the birds to wander into the rigged, grub-baited traps. Though the birds are not used to predators, they are deft and quick. But we are patient and, after some hours, trap and kill six.

We return to the water's edge and I pluck the feathered corpses as you make a fire out of wood. We skewer the birds by thrusting sticks down their throats, and roast them slowly over the flames. The meat is tender and satisfying. We strip the carcasses then lick the bones clean. You are silent as you eat. Moody and withdrawn. When you finally speak, you say, "I don't like it here. The sooner we leave, the better. Something's not right."

I laugh at this. What a joker you are.

"Yesterday we were dying in the dunes. Today we have water and shade and food. What's not right, Tiger? This is paradise."

You shake your head but are unable to express your misgivings in words.

"Think of all we have suffered," I continue. "First the famine and fall of Zhongdu. Then the Mongols lashing us with whips and forcing us to march. Then the mob of old men, baying for your blood . . ."

You nod, turning your skewer of charred, sizzling bird over the flames.

"Those old bastards would've murdered you," I say, "had I not stopped them. You should be happy, Tiger. You have much to be thankful for . . ."

You stiffen and look up from your skewer. A strange look comes into your eyes as you say, "It was you, wasn't it, Turnip? It was you who strangled Puppetmaker Xia and Stone-Carver Peng."

Did you know that our senses have a memory, separate from the memory of the mind? My hands twitch with the memory of squeezing their necks. My nose wrinkles at the spoiled meat of their breath and the whiff of elderly incontinent bowels. I shudder all over with the memory of their flailing, death-resisting limbs.

"I did it to protect you," I say.

They were evil men through and through, and deserved to die. So why are your eyes so harsh and unforgiving, as though strangling them was somehow wrong? You drop the skewered bird in the fire and the greedy flames gobble it up. You stand up and back away from me.

"Tiger, where are you going?"

"Stay away from me," you warn.

You disappear into the trees.

You go up into the branches. The soles of your feet, dirty and pale, dangle from a bough as the rest of you is obscured by leaves. You are in a filthy temper, so I stay out of your way. I hunt for birds' nests in the trees farthest from you. I go and swim on my own in the lake but, lonely without you, thrash my limbs with none of the joyousness of the day before. I am worried about you. Should I take you some water? You must be very hot and thirsty up in that tree.

The sunset is a lake of fire in the sky when you at last climb down. I leap up in relief as you come over to the water's edge.

"Tiger," I say, "come and eat. I fetched you supper."

You ignore the bird's nest of speckled eggs and pink baby-bird corpses I am holding out to you. You go to the lake and drink long and deep from its waters. Then you gather up the ragged robes you shed the day before, pulling them over your nakedness as though they are the last shreds of your dignity.

"I am leaving," you say.

"Leaving?"

You nod and I take a deep breath. I must dissuade you from this foolishness.

"We can't leave now. We are not strong enough yet. Why don't we stay here longer? Rest more, eat more . . . We will die out there in the Singing Dunes . . ."

"*I* am leaving," you say. "Without you. The time has come for us to part."

I shake my head. Every part of me feels as though it is sinking in dismay.

"Why don't you want to stay with me?" I ask.

"You are a murderer."

"But aren't you a murderer too? You fed us dead men in Zhongdu."

"Taking flesh from the dead is not the same as taking life from the living."

The descending sun is an inferno in the sky. You stare out at the dunes, casting your mind to the journey ahead, and I am in agony, because I can no more make you to stay than spear your shadow to the ground.

"Don't go," I beg. "You can't go. You will die out there."

You gaze back to me and say, "Do you want to know how I got these scars, Turnip?"

I nod. Since the day we met, I have wanted to know.

"When I was a child," you say, "I was sold into slavery. I ran away when I was twelve, but had only a few days of freedom before my master caught me and brought me back. He branded my face as punishment. He warned me the second time I ran away he would slit my throat. But the threat of death didn't stop me from escaping again . . ."

You stare at me, your eyes blazing. "Because I would rather *die* than be a slave. I am a slave to no one. Not to the Mongols. Not to the Lake of the Crescent Moon. And not to you."

"You are not my slave!" I protest. "I am *your* slave and you are my master. There is nothing I wouldn't do for you!"

You shake your head, as though I have failed to understand. Then, without even a farewell, you stroll out to the dunes. Sand gusts to the sky in the blustery winds, and you walk into the distance. You can't go. We are brothers. I will die without you.

"You are not leaving!" I shout after you. "Over my dead body are you leaving!"

The sand is singing now, histrionic and shrill. My heart is thudding, valves slamming as blood surges within, and my chest heaves with the fight yet to come. For I won't let you go without a fight.

"*Wait!*"

You don't wait. So I run and leap on your back, and we crash to the sand. Over and over we roll, and you fight me off with your fists. Your skull butts my skull. Your knee thuds my groin. And though I am in pain, I cling to you. I won't let you go.

Other than our grunts and the dull thud of knuckles, we fight in silence. Over and over we roll, until I am straddling your chest as you are bucking beneath me, panic in your eyes as my hands close around your throat with a strength that is not my own but lent to me by the Singing Dunes. *Kill him! Kill him!* shrills the sand. Blood vessels bulge in your temples, and you flush with blood as I throttle you. Tears shine in your eyes, and I am stricken, for it's the first time I have ever seen you cry. But they won't let me stop. I wring and wring your neck, until there is nothing left to wring out.

The sun descends beneath the Singing Dunes. The flaming sky above fades to darkness and stars. The moon rises and scatters its lunar beams upon the sand. I cradle your limp body in my arms. I speak to you gently and reproachfully. What madness possessed you to make you want to leave, Tiger? We had everything we needed here at the Lake of the Crescent Moon. Why did you have to spoil everything? I admonish you, weeping tears on your branded cheeks. Then I dig a shallow grave in the sand and bury you there.

Away from the Lake of the Crescent Moon I go. I stagger through the night, the stars pulsing brightly overhead and the demons that possess the sand serenading me with their song. I walk until daybreak and I have reached the end of my strength. Then I collapse upon the Singing Dunes and spread my arms wide to embrace the sand.

"Very well," I say. "Take me away."

14

The Birthday Gift

Thirty-one days is the length of time Wang's willpower holds out. Thirty-one days of driving in frustrated circles around Beijing as passengers slam in and out of his cab. Thirty-one days of being excessively irritated by roadwork, drilling and engine-thrumming traffic jams. The worst days were when the polluted sky threw a cloak of invisibility over the city, obscuring buildings a hundred metres away and darkening Wang's mood. The pollution seems like a curse to him, the curse of the million-year-old fossils, excavated out of seams deep in the ground and burnt as fuel. The spirits of the ancient trees and animals, protesting at being dug out of their resting places with lung-blackening particulates that poison the air.

On the thirty-first day of driving around Beijing, Wang caves in. He parks the taxi and walks down the side-alley, neon lit at dusk, past the baijiu and tobacco sellers and the prostitutes behind glass. Alone in the barber's, Zeng beams as Wang pushes through the door. Zeng, with the fading handsome looks. Zeng, with the sinewy, wiry body of a contortionist, making Wang self-conscious of his middle-aged sag and spread.

"Driver Wang. What can I do for you?" he asks and, before Wang can even respond, shakes out the hairdressing cape.

Wang hands himself over to Zeng. Allows Zeng to cape him, swivel him in a chair, lather him up with shampoo, rinse him in the sink, trim and blow-dry. And then finally, wordlessly, lead him to a back room, a room of shadows and secret extramarital goings-on, messy with tissues, foil strips of condoms and pump-action dispensers of lubricant. Wang sits on the clean-sheeted, firm-mattressed bed, and Zeng sits beside him and strokes his cheek. He leans to Wang and kisses him, chastely, on the lips. "I have been waiting for you," he says. "I have been waiting for the past ten years." And Wang rests his confused and weary head on Zeng's shoulder and closes his eyes. He does not know how long Zeng holds him for. He does not know how he ends up lying back on the bed with Zeng moving over him, his lips grazing his neck, his tongue blazing a trail of goosebumps as it roams, his hands sliding under his shirt and the waistband of his jeans. It's as though it's predestined and out of his control. Later, they lie side by side, staring up at the ceiling and the halo of light cast by the lamp's round shade as they speak in murmurs. Wang speaks of the emptiness of driving around Beijing. He speaks of feeling only half alive. "Except for now," Zeng says. He shapes cigarette smoke in his mouth and blows it out in concentric rings. Then he leans on his arm, propping his head up and gazing at Wang as though his eyes are made of electricity. Wang has to break from Zeng's gaze. Shifting his eyes back to the ceiling, he says, "I liked your letter."

"What letter?"

"The one with the story," Wang says. "I know you didn't write it yourself. Where did you steal it from?"

"Story?"

"The one about the slaves."

"I don't know what you're talking about, Driver Wang."

"Why are you lying?"

"No. Honestly. I don't."

Wang's phone beeps in his jacket, on the coat hook on the door.

"What time is it?" Wang asks.

"Eight o'clock," says Zeng.

"Shit. I have to go," Wang says.

But he lacks the strength to get up from the bed. The mattress, though deceptively firm, has the undertow of quicksand.

"Happy birthday, by the way," says Zeng.

"You remembered my birthday?"

"April fourth, isn't it? Your thirty-second."

"I'm an old-timer now," says Wang. "Not long for the crematorium . . ."

Zeng, who turned thirty-two a month earlier, laughs.

"Thirty-two is the best age there is," he says. "Wait and see, Driver Wang. Your life has only just begun . . ."

The wave of remorse hits Wang as he walks through the door. Half past eight and the apartment is full of the aromas of his thirty-second-birthday banquet, simmering under various pot lids on the stove. On TV an auditorium of dark-suited Communist Party officials are gathered for some event. As the camera pans out for a wide-angled shot, the officials look as identical as laboratory-made genetic clones.

"Ba! We've been waiting two hours!" shouts Echo. "We're starving to death!"

Yida stands at the gas stove, yet to acknowledge her husband's late homecoming. In the kitchen doorway, Wang pleads his case. He had to drive a fare twenty kilometres to the Fragrant Hills. Got caught in a traffic jam on the way back, then the credit ran out on his phone. Yida is dishing up in an efficient manner, with none of her characteristic domestic languor. A warning to Wang that she is unconvinced. She pours a boiling saucepan of longevity noodles—handmade that afternoon from her mother's Anhui recipe—into a colander. Geysers of steam rush up from the cold aluminium kitchen sink, pinkening her skin. Tendrils of damp curls fall across her eyes and she pushes them back with her forearm. At last, she looks at her husband and remarks, "Another haircut, Wang? Getting vain in your old age."

"I'm starved!" yells Echo. "Can we eat now? Before I die?"

The dishes are arranged on the table: phoenix-tailed prawns, spicy chicken wings and Tianjin cabbage with chilli peppers. A bottle of lime-coloured fizzy drink which Yida pours out into paper party cups (to be rinsed after dinner and stacked in the cupboard for reuse). Later there will be pink-iced sponge cake, chosen by Echo from the Good Fortune Bakery. There will be candles and a round of "Happy Birthday to You."

Hungry, they commence eating without fanfare. Yida watches Wang as he attempts to slurp up each noodle in its entirety (a superstition from childhood, to ensure a catastrophe-free year ahead), and noticing her contempt, Wang bites. He is nostalgic for his twenty-second birthday, when his young wife's only gift to him was her teasing laughter and her lovely slender body, which he had dragged by the ankles across their bed. He thinks of the way he rested his weary head on Zeng's shoulder. The way he felt when Zeng had held him, as though it was the only place that he truly belonged.

After dinner Wang unwraps his presents. An air-freshener for his taxi. A bootleg DVD of a Hollywood action movie. A comic book that Echo has made for him, called "The Beijing Taxi Driver." The comic is eight pages long, each page divided into four strips. The main character is a cartoon version of Wang: a superhero taxi driver who fights racoon-masked criminals. ("I'll rid this city of corruption if it's the last thing I do!" his alter ego shouts.) Echo is anxious and expectant as he turns the stapled pages, and Wang smiles to reassure her.

"Very impressive, Echo! When you are a world-famous artist, this comic will become a collector's item, worth millions of yuan!"

Each panel is painstakingly illustrated, and Wang is proud and touched by the effort she has made. He reads aloud from "The Beijing Taxi Driver," and Echo interrupts to expand on plot lines and the good or evil nature of the characters. But as Wang listens to her chattering and praises her hard work, Zeng and the narcotic undertow of the back room seeps into his mind. And he smiles and nods, struggling not to seem too distracted as the simple, uncomplicated joy he derives from Echo's company begins to fade.

* * *

At ten o'clock that evening the phone rings. The landline rings infrequently, and Yida answers in a surprised tone of voice. She passes the receiver to Wang. "Lin Hong," she mouths.

Wasting no time with greetings, Lin Hong tells Wang that his father wishes to see him. That he would like to wish him happy birthday.

"Now? Isn't it past his bedtime?"

"I am just the messenger. Whether you come or not is your own concern."

Lin Hong does not wish Wang happy birthday herself or even enquire how he is.

Wang puts on his coat and walks to his father's apartment. He walks at a brisk pace down Nongzhanguan North Road and Chaoyang Park Road. When he arrives at his father's his heart is pumping and his cheeks bright. Lin Hong opens the door, unsmiling in an herb-infused muslin facial mask, showing a glimpse of lacy negligee beneath her cherry-blossom kimono robe. She juts her chin in the direction of the living room, billowing Japanese silk as she turns on her heel back to her Mandarin-dubbed Korean soap opera and pillow-arrayed queen-sized bed.

The east wall of the living room is made entirely of glass. The view of Beijing from the tenth floor is of thousands of lights in many wattages of brightness and car headlights gliding up and down the Fourth Ring Road, shining through the dark. Looking out at the cityscape, Wang senses the electricity surging through the grid and being consumed by the district of Chaoyang. The living-room lights are out, and the nighttime view is so mesmerizing that Wang does not immediately see his father, the dark hump of him parked in the shadows. When he does, he starts and turns on a lamp. His father blinks, and Wang wonders if this once-intimidating man, who once commanded the attention of a room, is sad to have gone unseen.

"Ba," says Wang, "you wanted to see me?"

His father smiles at him, slumped in his blue-striped pyjamas,

151

his chin resting on his collar bone. A fleecy blanket is tucked over his lap and his hair is neatly combed and parted on the left. Wang knows that if he were to lean down and hug his wheelchair-bound father (though they are not and were never on hugging terms), he would smell toothpaste and soap. He'd smell aftershave and the talcum powder sprinkled on him when his incontinence pad is changed. Lin Hong is irreproachable in matters of grooming, and Wang's father would pass the most rigorous of hygiene inspections, at any time of night or day. But Wang isn't fooled. Her attention to cleanliness is just an excuse for the many petty indignities she visits upon him in his debilitated state.

Wang stands there expectantly. "Ba? Is everything okay?"

Across the night sky aeroplane taillights blink in arcs of descent. Wang's father's mouth comes ajar and a strand of saliva threads his lips. He has a book on his lap. He holds it out and Wang takes it. It is a hardback edition of *The Book of Odes*, red and pocket-sized. The spine creaks as Wang opens it and turns the brittle yellow pages of traditional script in faded ink. Second edition, 1908. The book is a century old. Why has his father, who is not a reader, given him a gift of poetry? Wang thanks his father uncertainly.

"Your mother," says his father. "It was hers."

In the nineteen years since her death, he has only ever mentioned Li Shuxiang in passing, to make sneering comparisons: *Like mother, like son.* Wang stares at his father, sees the shimmer of regret in his eyes and is disgusted. What a cliché, Wang thinks, that the crippled old man is getting sentimental in his old age. Why didn't he feel the sting of conscience back when it mattered, when she was alive? Wang is not convinced. Restore the strength to his legs, and the motor function to his left side, and he'll be back to his ways of cruelty, philandering and excess at once. Wang puts the book in his jacket pocket. He thinks back to when he was a child, to the stacks of books around his mother's bed. He can't remember ever seeing *The Book of Odes*.

He thanks his father. Out of politeness, he stays for another ten minutes, before apologizing for keeping him up past his bedtime and seeing himself out the front door.

* * *

After midnight Wang arrives home for the second time that day. Echo and Yida are asleep in their beds. Slouched in the bedroom doorway, fists rammed in his jacket pockets, he watches over them like an intruder in his own home. His father's mawkishness has left him with a bitter aftertaste. But who is he to cast moral judgements? *Like father, like son.* There and then, in the bedroom doorway, he resolves to be a loyal husband and father, no matter what. But, for all his good intentions, he can't get Zeng's voice out of his head.

"Thirty-two is the best age there is. Wait and see, Driver Wang. Your life has only just begun . . ."

15

Sleeping Pills

Six o'clock, bells ring. Time for breakfast at quarter past. Bowls of rice porridge, cups of tea. On Sundays, an egg. Eight o'clock, exercises in the yard. Cassette tape in the battery-operated stereo, they jogged on the spot. Eight thirty, they queued for medication. Tongues poked out for inspection by the nurses, supervising the swallowing of pills. Eight thirty-five, a woman from Ward C dived to the floor, dodging bullets. *"They are cracking down again! They are shooting at us! Get down or be killed!"* she yelled, grabbing at the legs of other patients until the doctors rushed over with a hypodermic syringe.

Summer in the hospital, and there was no escape from the heat. Most of the patients became lethargic, as though tranquillized. They stripped to damp vests and sagging underpants and lay on the cement floor, limbs stretched out in a plea for mercy. The heat was an amphetamine to others, who paced the ward, hyperactive and loud, and it was mescaline to those who shrieked of scorpions, shaking out bedclothes and banging shoe heels on the walls. The heat intensified paranoia in the minds of some, who accused the doctors and nurses of poisoning the drinking water and the other patients of stealing their clothes.

Caged fans whirred but barely moved the suffocating air, and the breeze wasn't tempted through the open windows into the wards. Wang couldn't escape his own sweat and was slippery night and day. Showers brought relief, but as soon as he turned off the spray, dampness seeped up again through his pores. The whorls of his fingers marked everything he touched. When he ran his tongue over his upper lip he tasted brine.

Reality slowed in the heat, but Zeng Yan was perpetually on the move, shuffling cards, rattling mahjong tiles, chasing Ping-Pong balls in the yard and never breaking into a sweat. "I'm a southerner," he said, explaining why the heat didn't knock him out. "This is winter in Guangzhou." Every day, Zeng looked for Wang, and they talked for hours. Wang watched Zeng's sharp cheekbones and sensual mouth as he talked, and saw how he could oscillate between genders, how a few strokes of make-up would transform him into an exquisite drag queen. Zeng was blasé about what he did for a living. When talking about his profession to Wang, he was matter of fact.

"Get in, make money, get out," he said. "Better than working in a factory. Better than doing the job of a machine. Everyone sells something about themselves, and I sell my body. But only while I am young and good-looking. Those older men in their thirties are pathetic. They make a pittance! Who wants to fuck those ageing losers? I'll quit long before then. By the time I'm thirty I'll be the boss of my own company."

When Zeng spoke of his experiences, Wang listened, rapt. Zeng the hustler, in parks and bars. Zeng the houseboy, a domesticated pet for wealthy men. Zeng on his knees for a policeman in the public toilets near Tiananmen Square. Zeng in a steamy sauna with a group of Hong Kong CEOs. He had been raped and beaten, but he spoke of this with detachment.

"One bastard made me take pills, to get me high. Then back at his place a gang of his friends were waiting . . . Bastards. They threw me out onto the street afterwards. Crippled and bleeding . . ." Zeng shook his head, wincing at the memory. "Some won't pay afterwards. Complain the service was poor after shooting a wad in your mouth. That's why I have this story about my mother having breast cancer and needing money for hospital fees. Cheat or be cheated. That's how it goes."

Zeng wanted to know about Wang too. He asked about his past lovers, and Wang reeled them out. There was the girl he dated in his first year, who wrote bad poetry and had long centre-parted hair. A sly exhibitionist, the girl had liked to serenade the drunken dregs of parties with folk songs strummed on her guitar. She liked to gush about her emotional depth, and Wang's reticence frustrated her. "The more time I spend with you, the less I know you," she complained, then dumped him for a bassist in a rock band. The girlfriend in Wang's second year had wanted Communist Party membership and a stable "iron rice bowl" job. She had said so on their first date. She had pressured Wang into arranging work experience for her in his father's department and he had broken up with her in disgust. Wang rarely thought of these girls anymore, or the awkward dorm-room fumblings with bra clasps and condoms, the rushed and unsatisfactory sex. Shuxiang is the woman who dominates his past.

"What was she like?" Zeng asked.

"Strange. One in a billion."

"Tell me about her," Zeng said. "Go on."

Wang remembers how her eyes shone black and how cigarette smoke seeped from her mouth. Shuxiang had a round and motherly face, but she was not like other mothers.

"Ignore what the teachers say," she said, when she picked her son up from school. "Forget what they teach you in those lessons. They teach nothing but nationalist lies. They are training you to be sheep." Looking around the playground at the other children, she said under her breath, "Little emperors, constantly demanding sweets and toys. As bad as babies, screaming at you to wipe their faeces and feed them milk, night and day." Then she glanced at her solemn young son, and had to concede, "But you are better than most, Little Jun. You are one of the very best six-year-olds there are . . ."

Sometimes they went to the market, riding there on the bus.

Little Jun would run amongst the stalls, sniffing at the fish guts and spilt chicken's blood and dough sticks frying in oil. "Don't touch," Shuxiang warned. But he touched everything. At the rice seller's he slipped his six-year-old hands into the barrels, sifting the grains through his fingers. At the stall where spices were weighed out on old-fashioned scales, he dipped a finger in the chilli powder and licked, tearing up as his sinuses burned.

"Like fire ants, eh?" laughed the spice seller. "Fire ants up your nose."

One day at the market he decided to run away and become one of the street kids who begged for a living. He wouldn't have to go back to school and not fit in. He wouldn't have to go back to the shadowy apartment and the strange, bitter things his mother said. They had been about to leave the market, and Shuxiang was paying for a jin of tofu when Little Jun crawled under the noodle stall. The noodle maker was kneading and slamming dough and the table wobbled. He did not have to wait long before he heard his mother say, "You seen my son?"

Under the table, Wang saw her feet, strapped in her sandals. His heart skipped with the thrill of concealment.

"No, not today," the noodle maker said.

His mother walked her feet away. Wang peeped out. She was asking the butcher, his cleaver suspended over bloody cuts of meat, if he had seen her boy. The butcher said no. Shuxiang turned away and Little Jun saw the furrow of worry on her brow. In his hiding place, Wang was pleased by her pain. Proof she must love him as much as he loves her.

Round and round the market she went, calling for him and accidentally bumping into other market-goers. "Seen my son?" she asked the shoe mender. "Seen my son?" A lump grew and stopped up Little Jun's throat. The filth under the stall, the vegetable rot and flies, was nauseating. The time to come out had long passed, but now he was too scared.

Then she saw him, under the table. They locked eyes, mother and son, the boy's eyes trembling, the mother's turning to stone.

"Still looking for your little boy?" the tofu seller asked.

"No," said Shuxiang.

Then she turned and walked out of the market.

It was dark when a neighbour brought him back to Maizidian. She was a Ministry of Agriculture wife, and out of loyalty to his mother, Wang had refused to take her hand. The neighbour was Shuxiang's age and had recognized Little Jun because she was the kind of woman who took notice of small children. She had fumed out loud, "Fate is unkind to give a child to a woman like Li Shuxiang, and to me none."

She knocked three times, loud and angry, at the door of Apartment 404. Shuxiang opened it, and the boy darted in like a cat streaking out of the rain. The woman opened her mouth to tell Shuxiang off, but Shuxiang, without thanking her, let the door slam shut.

"Don't look so scared," she said, turning to her son. "I won't smack you."

A bowl of soup and a steamed bun were put on the table in front of him. She told him to eat, and she sat at the table too. Hungry, he chewed mouthfuls of bread and slurped out of the bowl. Mentholated smoke leaked from the edges of Shuxiang's mouth and the cigarette in her hand.

"Have you learnt your lesson?" she asked.

Wang Jun nodded.

"I was rude to that woman, wasn't I?" she said. "Her name is Rongrong, and during the Cultural Revolution, I saw her stab a girl in the head with scissors. That woman has blood on her hands. That's why I was rude."

Little Jun shuddered. The woman had offered him one of her bloodstained hands, and he was glad he'd refused it.

"She has no right to look down on me," Shuxiang said, "but she probably doesn't see it that way. Everyone has amnesia about that time. But not me."

Wang nodded solemnly at his mother. He was on her side against that woman. He sided with her against every one of her enemies. Shuxiang exhaled through her nostrils, bluish snakes of smoke winding into her eyes, which softened as she looked at her son and said, "Leaving you there was as hard for me as it was for you. But I have to prepare you for the world out there. You have to be ready for what it'll be like after I am gone."

Bells were ringing. Time to go to the canteen and queue for dinner. Across the hospital patients rose up from napping, staring at the TV and other forms of inactivity. Except for Wang and Zeng. They lay on the shower-room floor. Neither of them was hungry. Neither of them stirred a limb.

"How old were you when she died?"

"Twelve."

"You must have missed her."

"She was all I had."

"But things are different now," said Zeng. "Now you have me."

Wang said nothing to this, and the words hung in the dusk, waiting for his response. When none came, Zeng reached for Wang's wrist and cuffed it with his hand. It felt strange to have his wrist seized in this way. But the strength of Zeng's grip, and the heat and pulse of his blood, was comforting too.

"Do you think we'd be friends if we hadn't met in hospital?" Zeng asked. "Would someone like you, who goes to Beijing University, be friends with someone like me?"

"What does it matter?" Wang said. "I met you here."

"After the hospital, do you think we'll stay friends?"

"Sure."

But he wasn't sure. For the first time, it occurred to him that staying friends with unstable Zeng, who sold his body in karaoke bars and burnt down a shed to kill an ex-boyfriend, was a bad idea. Zeng smiled.

"Then I have a business proposition for you, for after we get out of here. Why don't we open a bar together?"

"A bar?"

"We could rent a place in Sanlitun. A place with a dance floor. We'll have a DJ booth and a cocktail menu. Lots of cool people will come. Artists and musicians and foreigners . . ."

He could imagine the nightclub Zeng had in mind, with a flashing strobe-lit dance floor heaving with sweaty dancers. Wang's head ached just to think of it.

"Where would we get the money from?" he asked.

"Isn't your father stinking rich?"

Wang laughed. "He won't lend us a fen."

"I'll find an investor then," Zeng decided. "I'm well connected. I know the richest men in Beijing."

Zeng shone with enthusiasm, and knowing there was no steering him back to reality, Wang said nothing. Zeng's attention would soon flit to something else.

"We could move in together too," Zeng went on. "It'll be fun. We could cook meals together, and watch TV and play mahjong. We could be together every day . . ."

Wang's heart beat strangely at this. The thought of being "together every day" with Zeng both excited and disquieted him. Zeng's hand now felt like a handcuff around his wrist, shackling him to a future he wasn't sure about. He tore his wrist from Zeng's grasp and sat up.

"We can't live together."

"Why not?"

"Because two men can't live together. It's not normal."

Zeng sat up and stared at Wang in confusion. "You shouldn't care what people think," he said. "Being happy should be the most important thing . . ."

"What makes you think living with you will make me happy?" Wang said. "I'm not like you. I don't want to live with a man."

But Zeng was not deterred. He leant in closer and stroked the line of Wang's jaw. He gazed into his eyes as though reaching into their depths, and said, "Why aren't you honest with yourself?"

Wang glared at him. "*Don't!*" he warned.

But Zeng grabbed the back of Wang's head and banged his mouth against Wang's with such force his lip split against his teeth. Then his tongue was inside, probing about, and Wang was paralysed for a moment, before he shoved him back roughly. He was breathing hard, and his heart was beating against his sternum. His mouth tasted of Zeng's saliva and blood.

"What are you doing!"

Zeng said nothing, but stared back at Wang with a certainty that scythed through him. Then, with the same quiet confidence, he got up and walked into one of the toilet stalls. Wang sat and stared at the stall's open door for a while, with Zeng waiting inside. Then, awkward, messed up and sick with desire, he followed him in.

Three times they were nearly caught. Twice by other patients, stumbling in on night visits to the toilets. They froze in the stall, breathing suspended for as long as it took for the intruder to empty his bladder and leave. Once Nightwarden Guo came in and knocked on the door. "Who's in there?" Wang's mind had gone blank with fear, but Zeng, no stranger to these predicaments, flattened himself against the back wall and gestured that Wang go out alone. Wang squeaked open the door, slipped out. "What were you doing?" the nightwarden asked. "Using the toilet," said Wang. His heart was beating so wildly he thought he would throw it up. "Liar," said Nightwarden Guo. "You were beating the aeroplane. I heard you." A headshake of disgust. "Go back to bed, pervert. They should lock you in your room."

"This can't go on much longer. When I leave here, I want to be normal. I don't want this."

He swept out his hand, to stand in for what he could not say.

"I understand," said Zeng. "Tell me when you want to stop, and we'll stop."

"I'm not like you."

"I know."

"This hospital has messed me up. When I get out of here I want to get better."

"I understand."

But Wang looked at Zeng and saw he didn't understand. That he thought it was only a matter of time.

*   *   *

"Pass the remote, *faggot*."

Wang was slouched in a chair in the common room, watching the news. Heat flushed his cheeks, and his ears and scalp tingled. "What did you call me?"

"You heard," said Liu Xiaoliang. "Everyone knows what you are up to with Zeng Yan."

The other TV watchers smirked and looked at Wang. Zeng Yan, who was playing poker with Old Chen, said nothing. Wang snapped, "What are you talking about?"

"Everyone's seen you both sneaking about in the night," said Liu Xiaoliang. "It's no secret."

"What do you know about anything?" said Wang. "You think you fought the Japanese."

Liu Xiaoliang, who suffered recurring flashbacks of the Japanese occupation (though he was born in 1970, and his traumatic "memories" came from dramas on TV), took offence.

"*Faggot*," he said.

Wei Hong pointed at Wang and said, "Homosexuality is a crime against the people and homosexual diseases are highly contagious. I want him out of our room. I don't want to catch anything."

Old Chen looked up from his playing cards, and said, "You can't catch AIDS from sharing a room, Wei Hong. You only get it from blood transfusions and sex."

"I'm with Wei Hong," said Gao Ling, perched on his chair on his toes. "Wang Jun can't sleep in our room. We've got to ask the doctors to remove him."

No one was watching TV anymore. They were staring at Wang and Zeng, who was studying his fanned-out playing cards.

"Go fuck yourselves. I'll sleep where I like."

Wang glowered at them. What did it matter what these mental patients, cast out from society, thought of him? They hadn't half a functioning brain between them. Wang got up and walked out of the common room. When he heard footsteps chasing him down the hall, he knew they were Zeng's but didn't stop.

"Wait!" called Zeng. "Why are you letting them get to you?"

"Leave me alone," Wang said, without looking over his shoulder. Zeng didn't catch up.

It had to stop. So Wang cut Zeng dead, shunning him with his eyes when they passed in the hall, swept the yard or queued for medication. In the canteen, when Zeng sat near him, Wang moved with his rice bowl and chopsticks to another table. The message was clear.

Evading Zeng in the hospital could be done with coldness and determination, but Wang couldn't evade Zeng in his dreams, where he reappeared night after night. Wang woke in arousal and tenderness from dreams of Zeng in the darkness of the stall, the smoothness of his skin and scent of hormones and sweat. He woke from dreams of the time Zeng clasped his wrist as they lay together on the floor, the heat and pulse of his grip reminding him of the muscle of Zeng's heart, banging away in his chest. Wang woke from these dreams aching with a loss he hadn't known since Shuxiang died and he'd lain grieving every night on cold, damp dormitory sheets.

The hospital was lonely without Zeng. But this could be endured. He had lived with loneliness for twenty-two years before he met Zeng, and he could go back to it. What he couldn't live with was the shame. What he couldn't live with was the guilt and disgust.

A shadow descended on the copy of Tang Dynasty poems Wang was reading on the bed. He didn't look up.

"You think you can just ignore me?"

Wang ignored him and turned a page. He read the first verse of a poem over and over, not comprehending a word. Zeng broke the silence again.

"Say something. I won't go away until you do."

And, knowing that Zeng would stand over him until he spoke, Wang responded without lifting his eyes, "You're blocking the light."

"What happened, Wang Jun? Why have you changed?"

"You promised me that when I wanted to stop, we would stop."

"But why stop being friends? Why stop speaking to me?"

"I just can't anymore."

Wang turned another page. He could sense Zeng searching for the words and reasoning to show him the error of his ways.

"You know what I think, Wang Jun?" he said. "I think you are lying to yourself. You are scared of who you really are."

Wang's head snapped up in agitation and he started to see how pale and enervated Zeng had become. But his suffering wasn't enough to shift the anger in Wang. Zeng's suffering was his own fault.

"What you think is wrong," Wang said. "I know who I am, and I'm not like you. When I get out of here I want a normal life. I told you before."

"In my work I meet lots of *normal* men like you," said Zeng. "They come to me because they are miserable with their normal lives. They come to me to feel alive." He paused to let this sink in. Then he continued in a gentler tone, "Stick with me when we get out of here, and that won't happen to you."

Wang slammed his book shut and stood up. It had been a mistake to talk to Zeng. It had been a mistake to think anything but silence would work.

"When I get out of here," Wang said, "I want to forget I ever knew you. And while I am still here, I want nothing to do with you. Don't speak to me. Don't come near me. Don't even look at me. Got that?"

Wang watched Zeng's face slacken in dismay then tighten with rage.

"You know what you are?" spat Zeng. "You are a eunuch. A eunuch who has castrated himself. You are so frightened of what other people will think you cut off your own genitals."

Laughter and the sounds of Ping-Pong in the yard drifted through the window. Nervous of Zeng making a hysterical scene and attracting a crowd, Wang took his book of poetry and went out the door.

"Go then, Wang Jun," Zeng called after him. "Go and live like a eunuch then. You'll regret it."

"I don't think so," muttered Wang.

"You will," said Zeng. "You will."

Old Chen shook him awake the next morning. "He's overdosed," he said.

"What?" Wang yawned as he sat up, rubbing his bleary eyes.

He could hear the shriek of trolley wheels out in the hall and the nurses shouting at patients, "Go back into your rooms! Go back into your rooms!"

"Your friend, Zeng Yan," said Old Chen. "They found him on the shower-room floor."

Wang got out of bed and reached the corridor in time to see Dr. Ling rushing by, white coat flapping over his pyjamas, a mechanical stomach pump in his hands. A bilious taste seeped into Wang's mouth and his stomach spasmed, as though in anticipation of the pump being used on him. He stumbled after Dr. Ling, until a nurse shouted through the early-morning gloom, "Go back inside your room, Wang Jun!" She dashed into the shower room, slamming the door.

When they emerged with Zeng on the trolley, he was unconscious, and his skin was pale and shiny with the pharmaceutical toxins his body was sweating out. He looked pathetic as a drowned child. The trolley was pushed out of sight and the patients woken by the commotion had lots of questions. How had he broken into the medical supplies? How many pills had he swallowed? What was his motive? Would he live, or would he die? Everyone looked at Wang, searching his face for guilt or complicity, grief or remorse. But Wang betrayed nothing. He went back to bed, pulling the bedsheet over him and facing the wall.

The night before, Zeng had slipped a note into his collection of poems, a scrap from an envelope on which he had scrawled in his disturbed hand, "You will see me again. We are destined to be together. I will come back to you in dreams, or another life."

Wang had torn the note up in irritation and thrown it away.

* * *

Wang was on his best behaviour when Dr. Fu called him into his office. In the role of polite, well-educated young man, he answered the doctor's questions, denying knowledge of how Zeng got the sleeping pills or what he had planned.

"He is under surveillance, for he is a high suicide risk," Dr. Fu said gravely. "But, fortunately, the psychiatric ward of the hospital he has been transferred to has a doctor who specializes in his disorder. They say he is responding well to treatment. The liver damage should be reversed in time."

"I hope he recovers soon," said Wang.

"You must be upset," said the doctor. "I understand you were close."

Wang made a neutral sound in his throat.

"Well, no doubt you will choose your friends more carefully in the future. Zeng Yan's disorder is very severe. He was corrupted in his teens, and his life has since been a downward spiral, with mental illness and a high incidence of criminal behaviour. Zeng Yan has to undergo extensive treatment to cure his deviancy."

Dr. Fu hesitated, then said carefully, "There was discussion about whether you needed treatment too."

"I am not like Zeng!"

"Yes, I advised against it," Dr. Fu said briskly. "You came under Zeng Yan's bad influence at a vulnerable period in your life, and picked up his bad habits. But once you are discharged, you will avoid men like Zeng Yan and drop these bad habits? Am I correct?"

Wang nodded.

"You are a bright young man with a promising future ahead of you," said the doctor. "You have had a minor setback, but are bound to make your mark one day . . . just like your father."

Dr. Fu smiled, lines crowding his face, and Wang nodded, as though becoming his father was his greatest ambition.

"Your father called this morning to discuss your discharge. He has arranged for you to re-enroll at Beijing University. How do you feel? Ready to move on with your life . . . ?"

* * *

Wang walked out of the hospital one morning in July with a rucksack of clothes on his back. None of the patients or doctors had come to say goodbye, but Wang didn't mind. He went to the Ministry of Agriculture sedan waiting in the road and, before he got in, he looked back at the low building where he had lived for the last seven months. He looked at the weeds straggling up through the cracks in the yard and the wrought-iron bars over the windows, detaining the wards of patients cast out of the world and unlikely to find their way back.

He got into the car and, as the driver pulled away, Wang hoped he would have forgotten Zeng in a year or two. That he would have forgotten what Zeng looked like, and the things they had said and done. He was looking forward to the day when sad and destructive Zeng wasn't constantly on his mind. It couldn't come soon enough.

16

The Torch

In the darkness of the living room, the screen of the muted TV casts a spectral glow on Wang as his eyes dart over the pages in his hands. Furtive as an alcoholic with a secret bottle of baijiu, he rereads the letter about the Jurchen slaves staggering through northern China and the Gobi dunes. Though it's after two, the Jin Dynasty story quickens Wang's heart, jarring him into wakefulness. He is confounded by Zeng's strangeness. What does he want?

Wang reads and reads, then tenses at a creak in the other room. He looks up nervously. Yida rolling over, or Yida getting out of bed? Yida does not appear, but his palms are sweating and his conscience uneasy, so he refolds the letter and stuffs it back in his jacket pocket. He lights a Red Pagoda Mountain and thinks of how exhausted he will be behind the wheel the next day. He castigates himself as he smokes for not going to bed with Yida at eleven. But he is not willing to bet tomorrow night won't be the same.

Wang is stubbing out the cigarette when he hears the cough out in the stairway—loud and clear as knuckles rapped on the door. He stands up in an adrenalized surge and thinks, *Zeng*. Quietly, he goes to the door. Eye to the peephole, he sees nothing but magnified dark, but he senses the living, breathing presence on the other side. He slides out the security chain, pulls the latch and wrenches open the door. For a moment he is convinced that Zeng is standing there. But the shadowy figure recedes into nothingness, and Wang understands he has ambushed empty air.

There is a thud of footsteps one or two flights below and, without thinking, Wang is bounding down the steps, three or four at a time, in pursuit. Each flight of stairs bursts into brightness as he activates the motion-triggered lights, the impact of his bare feet on concrete jolting his knees. When he reaches the bottom, he rushes out through the exit into the yard. But Zeng is nowhere to be seen.

Wang catches his breath outside Building 16, his gaze sweeping over parked cars, the rows of bicycles in the shed and the outdoor exercise machinery, the pedals, levers and wheels utterly still. The compound is silent under the low security lights, but Wang knows he is there somewhere, hiding and watching. "*Zeng?*" he calls, and stares into the shadows as though he can summon Zeng out by sheer force of will. Shivering, Wang looks over the yard one last time, then goes back inside.

The ceiling lights spring on as he climbs the stairs, back to 404. As Wang locks the front door behind him and slides the security chain into the slot, something strange occurs to him. There had been darkness ahead of him when he chased Zeng down. The lights' motion sensors are sensitive even to the wind blowing through the windows, and not to have triggered them in his descent, Zeng must be substanceless as a ghost.

The next morning he wakes to sulphurous light and goes blinking to the window. The sky over Beijing is yellow with a haze of sand, and the sun is so pallid he can stare directly at it. The sand is falling imperceptibly, in near-transparent layers, on rooftops and cars, and the heads and shoulders of dog walkers, and old men jogging in a clockwise shuffle in the compound below. Somewhere in Gansu or Inner Mongolia, a landscape of sand has been dragged up and herded by the winds over northeastern China, to hang suspended over Beijing, gilding the sky.

Yida and Echo are eating breakfast and watching something on the laptop in the living room. When mother and daughter are side by side, Wang is often struck by the similarity of their heart-shaped faces and cascading curls. Mother and daughter both reside on the same timeline of beauty, Wang thinks, with Echo looking as Yida once did, twenty years in the past, and Yida looking as Echo will, twenty years in the future.

"I overslept," Wang says. "Why didn't you wake me?"

"I shook you," says Yida, looking up from the laptop. "You were sleeping like the dead."

Wang's coffee and boiled eggs are on the table, but he's not hungry. He sits and taps a cigarette from his pack.

"Ba, you should quit," says Echo. "The pollution is bad enough for you already."

"At least the chemicals in tobacco are listed on the packet," Wang says, lighting up. "Only the government knows what chemicals are up there in the sky."

"What kind of excuse is that?" Yida says. Then she turns to Echo. "Don't ever expect him to quit. *Crooked branches can't be straightened*, after all."

Wang leans towards the laptop. They are watching grey, drizzly skies and angry Caucasian faces, people waving banners and shouting abuse. A scene of the Olympic torch relay in London. White-skinned protestors break through the security barriers, chanting "Free Tibet! Free Tibet!" as they attempt to wrestle the torch away from the torchbearers.

"Hypocrites," says Yida. "Look at how they invaded and bombed Iraq and Afghanistan, and they think they can shout at us about Tibet. They know nothing about Tibet. Tibetans were illiterate, dirty and backward before China developed the region. But they don't care about the facts. They just want an excuse to attack us."

Echo sips her soybean milk, then licks her white moustache. "Why do the laowai want to attack us?" she asks.

"China will be number one in a few years," says Yida, her eyes flashing darkly. "Why do you think?"

Wang taps his cigarette in the ashtray. When they were newly-weds he had liked this fierce, patriotic side of Yida. He had liked to see his young wife's pretty face become fiery and passionate with her beliefs. But now her righteousness wears him out. What does Yida know about Tibet? She's only seen the propaganda about it on TV. She's as bad as a blind man groping at an elephant's trunk and screaming that the elephant is a snake.

"They think they are so civilized with their democracy, but look at them, rioting in the streets!" she continues. "What good's democracy if the government can't keep the people under control?"

Echo frowns at one of the protestors, who is waving a placard. Echo, who has been studying English that year with Teacher Chen, translates it for her mother: "'Free . . . China . . .'"

"What?" Yida says. "The people of China *are* free! Do they think we are prisoners here? That we are in chains? They're so ignorant in the West."

Throughout the day sand falls out of the sky and the windscreen-wiper blades sweep the layers into thin yellow arcs. Wang blinks and the grit under his eyelids scratches his corneas. The sand is like dandruff in his thinning hair, and he knows that that evening he will stand under the shower and watch swirls of yellow disappearing down the drain. The passenger in the back seat of Wang's cab, a short man with a barcode of thin hair combed over his head, checks the Rolex on his wrist and sighs. The taxi has been stuck in a sea of Hyundais, Volkswagens and black government official Audis for twenty minutes now.

"I'm half an hour late," he snaps at Wang. "You should have gone the way I told you to!"

Wang ignores him. In front of his cab is an exhaust-spluttering bus overcrowded with bodies. An old man stares out of the back window at Wang with a look of crushed suffering. A news bulletin on the radio speaks of a public ban on spitting, swearing, smoking and queue-jumping during the Olympics. The Four Pests, the campaign has been called, after the Mao-era policy to eradicate sparrows, mosquitoes, flies and rats. Wang remembers Shuxiang telling him how, during her childhood, gangs of children chased sparrows from tree to tree, banging tin trays until the birds fell out of the sky, too exhausted to beat their wings and fly. The man with the barcode head shouts into his phone, "Look, I am *really late*. The taxi driver didn't listen to me and now we are stuck in traffic . . . *Stupid cunt*."

Wang waits until they have crawled up to Beixinqiao Station before pulling over. He takes 3 RMB, enough for a single subway journey, out of his wallet, and leans around his headrest. He thrusts the money at the man in the back.

"Take Line 5 three stops north, then change to Line 2," Wang instructs. "One stop west and you are at your destination. Now get the fuck out of my cab."

The man hesitates, then accepts the 3 RMB. There is 20 RMB on the meter and, interpreting Wang's waiving of the fare as an admission of wrong, he says, "You really need to do something about the stink of garlic in here!"

Then he takes his briefcase and slams the door. Wang is 23 RMB out of pocket but, as he watches the man's barcode head disappearing into the subway entrance, he doesn't consider it a loss.

The alley is different in the light of day, when the dirt and dilapidation are no longer veiled by dusk. Rotten cabbage leaves, wooden skewers from yang rou chuar and polystyrene takeout containers are strewn about, and the liquor store front is smeared, as though destitute alcoholics have been rubbing their noses up against the glass. The folding tables outside the Xinjiang restaurant are covered in last night's beer bottles, and the hole-in-the-wall grill is black with soot. Behind the glass of the Heavenly Massage a teenage girl in a Supergirl T-shirt sits on a pink polyester sofa, her knee bent to her chest as she paints her toenails. In the evening's red-bulb glow, the girl would seem temptingly exotic and other. But in the stark light of day she looks very plain, and much too young. She's someone's daughter, Wang thinks, probably hiding from her mother and father how she earns her living in Beijing. And one day, she'll be someone's wife, hiding from her husband her sexual past. A bronze statue of the Goddess of Mercy stands on a shelf above the sofa. Wang can't remember what the goddess's powers are but knows they aren't enough to protect the girls.

Wang sees Zeng's co-worker through the barber's door, leaning into his laptop and weaving from side to side as he pilots a virtual jet through a craggy mountain range. He opens the door, and the boy looks over, narrowing his eyes in recognition. How ugly he is, Wang thinks, looking at his round, belligerent face and spiky hair. The fighter jet crashes and explodes into a ball of flames, and the boy scowls harder.

"Zeng Yan's not here."

"Where is he?" Wang asks.

"Out."

"When will he be back?"

"Don't know."

"Can I wait here?"

The boy wants to say no, but can't. So he abandons his fighter jet, grabs a broom and sets about sweeping up cuttings from the linoleum. Wang stands out of his way by the wall, under two laminated, fake-looking diplomas from the "Beijing No. 1 Hairdressing Academy," and watches him sweep. The boy has studs in his ears, too much gel in his spiky hair and fiery eruptions of acne on his neck. Though young, he has none of the manipulative beauty that Zeng had in his youth, and Wang doubts he commands much money from his customers.

Some rain splatters against the window, and Wang looks out at the stormy sky and wills the rain to come down harder and rinse the sand into the sewers of Beijing. His attention then snaps back to the barber's as one of the wheeled chairs crashes into the wall beside him. Zeng's co-worker has shoved the chair aggressively with his broom, which he is banging about, taking his frustration out on the linoleum. Wang wonders if he considers him a rival for Zeng. He can't remember the last time anyone considered him a rival. Not in love, or anything.

"You're not from Beijing, are you?" Wang says, hoping to strike up a conversation. "Where's your hometown?"

173

"I know who you are," mutters the boy, not looking up from his sweeping. "I know what you did to Zeng Yan in the hospital."

Wang lurches inside at the mention of the hospital.

"Whatever happened to him in the hospital was his own doing."

The boy slams the broom upright, leans towards Wang and says, "You must have a hole where your conscience should be! He went through hell because of you. Why have you come back into his life, harassing him again? What do you want?"

Outside, sheets of rain are crashing down, dissolving the city in polluted waters. Wang shakes his head at him. No, he thinks, you have it wrong. Zeng is harassing me, not the other way round. But Wang won't argue with the boy. He knows how love blinds people to the truth about the one they are in love with.

"Look," Wang says. "All I want is to talk to Zeng Yan. I am not here to harass him. I want to speak to him, then I'll go, and I won't come back. You have my word . . ."

"Come back," the boy says, "and I'll tell your *wife*."

Wang is angry enough to hit him. He opens his mouth to tell him how sorry he'll be if he goes anywhere near Yida, when the door swings wide. Zeng is out of breath and soaked by the downpour. Beads of water drip from his wet hair and glide down his cheeks.

"Wang." Zeng smiles. "Good to see you."

Wang can't smile back. Though Zeng is casual, the longing that drove him to Apartment 404 last night shows through his eyes. Zeng looks between Wang and the boy and sees at once what's been going on.

"Wu Fei, we need shampoo," he says. "Go to Jingkelong and buy three bottles of the stuff we bought last week. And gel spray too."

Zeng peels a 100-RMB note from his wallet and hands it to Wu Fei. The boy throws down the broom and storms out into the rain without a jacket or umbrella. He is drenched in seconds.

"Please understand," says Zeng, "he has no family in Beijing. No friends. I'm all he has. He's protective of me."

Out in the alley, Wu Fei turns his head and shoots one last

hostile look at Wang through the rain. Wang shakes his head. I am not your enemy, he thinks. You are your own worst enemy, boy.

The back room is dark and stuffy, and the bedsheets, though pulled straight, bear the residual stains and odours of men who have come and gone. In the low-wattage light Zeng reaches for Wang's cheek and leans in. Wang pushes him back, his fingers in Zeng's dripping-wet hair. "That's not what I am here for," he says, though part of him, the weak, libidinous part, wants to give in, the way he had before.

Zeng doesn't pressure him. He nods in acknowledgement of the changing rules and steps back. He pulls out his cigarettes and offers one to Wang, who refuses, wanting to make a habit of saying no. All day Wang has been unnerved by Zeng and his stalking. But now that Zeng is in front of him he sees there's nothing ominous or menacing about this slight and angular man offering him a cigarette.

Mattress springs creak as Zeng sits down. He pats the bed beside him, but Wang shakes his head and remains standing. Zeng shivers in his soaking T-shirt and flicks the cog of his faulty lighter over and over, trying to spark a flame.

"Why did you come to my home last night?" Wang asks.

"Huh?"

Zeng's cigarette remains unlit in his fingers as he looks up.

"Last night, why did you come to my home?"

"I was nowhere near your home last night. I don't even know where you live."

"Bullshit. I saw you with my own eyes."

Not exactly true. But Wang wants him to know there is nowhere to hide.

"Then you were mistaken. I was here last night, Wang Jun. Sleeping in this bed. Ask Wu Fei . . ."

"I've come to warn you not to come near my home again," Wang says, "because next time I will go to the police. I will show them the letters too."

"Letters? What letters?"

"The letters you have been leaving in my taxi."

"I don't know about any letters . . ."

Wang clenches his jaw. "Where do you steal the stories from?" he asks.

"What stories?"

"The past-life stories. Where do they come from? Books? The Internet? I know you don't write them yourself."

"Past-life stories?" Zeng widens his eyes. "You're scaring me, Wang Jun."

Zeng does look shaken, but Wang warns himself not to be taken in.

"You forget how well I know you, Zeng Yan," Wang says. "The letters, the stalking—this is your way of getting me back for the stuff that happened in the hospital, isn't it? I know you well, Zeng. I know how your mind works. You need help."

Zeng flicks the cog of his lighter again, and it finally shoots out a flame. The cigarette shakes in his hand as he lights up.

"I don't need help," he says. "I'm not the same person you knew back in the hospital. That was ten years ago. I've changed." He takes another drag. Smoke drifts out of his nostrils and his eyebrows hunch over dark, troubled eyes. "I haven't been stalking you. And I never wrote you any letters, because I can't write. Not with a pen and paper. Not on a computer. I can't even fill out a form. Wu Fei has to do it for me. What they did to me in that other hospital, the one I went to after the overdose, messed up my brain for good."

Zeng expels smoke from his lungs. "They never cured my 'abnormality,' but they left me illiterate, and with killer migraines and blackouts too . . ."

For a moment Wang aches with pity for Zeng. Then doubt kicks in. When he was younger, working in Guangzhou, Zeng used to pretend that his mother had cancer to trick men into donating money for "hospital fees." "Cheat or be cheated"—that was once his motto in life.

"You are lying," Wang says. "You are making this up."

"I'm not lying," Zeng says. "I don't know where you live. I

have never written you any letters. And I would never harass you or your family. I care for you too much, Wang Jun. I care for you now as much as I did back in the hospital . . ."

And Wang knows the last part of what Zeng says is true. That Zeng is just as obsessed with him as when they were twenty-two.

"You know what I want you to do?" Wang says.

Zeng looks at him miserably.

"I want you to leave me alone. No more letters. No more stalking. Come near my family again and I will go to the police, and they will arrest you and put you back in the mental hospital where you belong."

Zeng slumps on the bed, looking too dejected to speak. But he nods at Wang and says, "Okay."

17

The Fifth Letter

Did you know Yida is a reincarnate too? In her first life she was a flea who lived in the fur of a stray dog. She guzzled the dog's blood and used her hind legs to leap out of harm's way when the mongrel's claws scratched at the itch of her. In Yida's second life she was a tapeworm, hooked onto the intestinal wall of a cow. She grew to two metres in length on the cow's ingested grass and caused a gut ache so severe the beast lowed in constant pain.

Though human in her third life, Yida is still a parasite. She saps your energy as you sleep, Driver Wang, so you wake exhausted, feeling as though another decade has been dumped on you in the night. She weakens your immune system, which is why your lungs are losing the battle against the carcinogenic air. Yida has a degenerative effect on her customers at Dragonfly Massage too. They lie on the massage table and she kneads her hatred and malcontent into their backs. She pummels their muscles and they become knotted, misshapen and wrought. Under her fingers, cells fissure and split. Benign lumps of tissue turn malignant. Blood pressure rises and the blood thickens with thrombosis clots. Yida's customers hobble out of Dragonfly Massage bent out of shape, but they think that the stiffness and aching is part of the healing process.

Unaware of the damage Yida is doing, they return to her week after week, caught in a deteriorating cycle of pain.

We are all dying, Driver Wang, degenerating cell by cell. But living with Yida is hastening your demise. Only when you leave her will your life expectancy recover. Only by leaving her will you survive.

As your biographer, I resurrect our past incarnations. I summon our scattered ashes with my beckoning hand and they gather on the creases and fate furrows of my palm. I breathe life into our remnants, bringing about a slow reversal of death. Our dust turns into bones. Our skeletons calcify and grow plump with meat and blood circulates in capillaries and veins. Our muscle fibres strengthen and reattach to ligaments and bones. Our skin, teeth and hair grow back, lustrous and strong. Our hearts resume beating, and we rise up once more as living, breathing vessels of soul. Writing your third biography has been more punishing than the others. Deep, scalpel-carved wounds, stitched up hundreds of years ago, have been reopened with much darkness and agonizing pain. But I am willing to endure. For this torturous journey through the suffocating dark is the only way to get to the light.

18

Sixteen Concubines
Ming Dynasty, 1542

I

A fledgling, not yet fifteen years old, borne in a palanquin through the Forbidden City's west gate. Chair bearers lower poles, the curtains divide and you emerge. Girl in a silk robe, plaits coiled into spirals, three-inch lotus feet bound tight as buds. The harem keepers greet you, usher you into the Inner Palace. Through peepholes poked in the wax-paper windows of the Palace of Earthly Tranquillity, we peer out. We see through your eyes the magnificence anew. The acres of grand halls, deepest red with thrones and ceremony within. The endless armada of yellow-tiled roofs.

Whispers Imperial Consort Luminous Moon, "She has an inauspicious face. A widow's peak. The harem physiognomist must be sleeping on the job."

Elsewhere in the chamber, tea is sipped, ivory mahjong pieces shuffled about. A eunuch messenger appears at the door. The Emperor requests three bedmates for tonight. Names are named in a falsetto, and blood drains from faces, fingernails digging crescent moons in palms. The tea soothes me with breath of steam, the coal-fired kang warms my backside. I have not been summoned to the Leopard Room in years. I am one of the fortunate few.

II

The Imperial Gardens on a midwinter day. Frozen silver-baubled spider-threads dangle from the gnarled branches of the juniper trees. The winding pebble-mosaic path is slippery with frost. I sit on a chair of deer antlers in the Belvedere of Crimson Snow, the seat polished wood, the chairback entangled horns curved to embrace the sitter, threatening to stab the sitter in retaliation for any false move. My fingers fiddle with embroidery, fumble with needle and thread. I abhor needlework and would like to read stories instead, but they keep us harem slaves as illiterate as she-goats.

The tapping of wooden-heeled slippers on the stone path disturbs my thoughts. Every so often the wooden heels cease tapping as one of the twenty pavilions is peered into. The Pavilion of Melancholy Clouds. The Pavilion of the Immortal Birds. The Pavilion of a Thousand Autumns. I scowl as you enter the Belvedere of Crimson Snow. Why have you come to disrupt my peace? I risk influenza for these solitary hours. To flee the idle gossip and stifling unhappiness of concubines.

Your pretty face is pink with cold, and a shawl of winter mink is thrown over your robe. You bow deep and low. "Boundless happiness to my Elder Sister Concubine Swallow."

I murmur, "Boundless happiness to you, Concubine Bamboo."

Needle and thread jerk up. You peer curiously at my embroidery: tufty feathered mandarin ducks on little slippers for maimed feet. You stand respectfully but within pace restlessly to and fro.

"Concubine Swallow, I saw a girl dash out her own brains last week."

Your voice is tight and high. Thread slips from the eye of the needle. Saliva glistens on the tongue-dampened thread as I poke it through again. "Ah yes, Imperial Consort Virtuous Purity."

"Yes. Her. Aged only twenty she charged into a lacquered pillar of the Gate of Divine Prowess. Staved in her own skull. I saw her brains splashed scarlet in the snow."

I tut. "I know. I saw. A dreadful mess."

"Ethereal Dawn scraped the gold paint from her jewellery box. Swallowed it and died from poisoning."

"So I hear."

"Pale Sapphire slit her wrists with a jade-handled letter opener. She survives nursed by eunuchs in the palace infirmary. But when she recovers she will be executed for betraying Emperor Jiajing. Two deaths, back to back . . ."

You tremble with fear and say, "Beloved Elder Sister, why do so many girls in the harem want to kill themselves?"

Needle tugs thread taut. The second web-footed duck is nearly complete. Yellow-beaked bird with feathery tufts of green and blue.

"Brain fever," I say.

A glare. Another tug of cotton thread.

You whisper, "I hear things about His Majesty. That he tortures concubines in the Leopard Room. That he 'operates' on them with scalpels. That he has dispatched two hundred palace ladies early to the grave . . ."

Chin quivers and tears fall. O why did you come here, foolish child? Spoiling my solitude with your woes. One of the eunuch servants, Hunchback Guo, creeps near, cowering beneath his craggy hump of spine, sweeping the already swept pebble-mosaic path.

"What do you want from me?"

Silence. More tears. Sprinkling tear ducts that rouse disgust.

"Listen to me, Concubine Bamboo. To be born a woman is to be born into suffering. Our feet are mutilated claws. Our cunts bleed. Wombs suffer cramps, childbirth. Sex too brings pain, but a night with the Son of Heaven is an honour worthy of the Death by a Thousand Cuts. Pray to the Goddess of Mercy if you must. Grow a spine. Endure."

Gathering up embroidery, I leave the deer-antler embrace of the chair. Out of the Belvedere of Crimson Snow, I spit at the feet of smirking Hunchback Guo. I hiss, "You crooked teapot with a broken spout. Repeat a word of what you just heard and I'll cut out your tongue and boil it for soup!"

Without a backward glance, I go to the Pavilion of a Thousand Autumns. Sit on a stone bench by a statue of the Lord Buddha. Embroidery hoop on lap, glaring at the arched doorway. Pull the thread so hard it snaps.

III

Drumbeat in Drum Tower signals the fall of night. The beginning of First Watch.

"Draw the bolts! Mind the lanterns!" cry the eunuch guards as the Forbidden City seals its gates.

In the bathhouse, concubines wallow in bronze tubs of petal-bestrewn water. Maidservants pour water over their mistresses from pretty cloisonné jugs. It cascades over dark raven's hair, shoulders and breasts. The elder concubines wag their tongues. The younger novices are silent out of respect. "Toilet!" I call before I bathe. A chamber pot appears. A maid offers, on a velvet pillow, a silken sheet manufactured by the Department of Toilet Paper. They shroud me with screens as I crouch over the pot. When I am finished, they whisk away my leavings for the eunuch scribe to record in the Ledger of Bowel Movements and Menstrual Cycles of the Concubines. I lower my chilled, goosepimpled skin into the water, slipping into the circling conversation. Steeping in our baths, we poach ourselves pink and talk of the famine that blights the empire.

"The gods disapprove of the Emperor Jiajing. They punish his subjects with poor harvests and starvation. Millions have died."

You, recent arrival from the famine-stricken world beyond the Forbidden City, pipe up excitedly. "I saw, I saw! The peasants stagger from countryside to town, begging for work. They sell their children for a bowl of rice. They clutter the roadside with their heaped corpses. Flies buzz around them."

"Who spoke? Apprentice concubines should not speak! Someone ought to spank the saucy bitch."

Daggers fly and silence you.

"The Department of Astrology has charted many ill omens. On the Terrace of Spirits they observed with astrological instruments a star crashing from the sky in portent of war, the merging of lakes on the moon in portent of floods."

"Japanese pirates attack the east coast of the Celestial Kingdom. The Mongol army loot and raid us from the north. The gods are angry indeed."

"The Stone Lions weep at the palace gates. Tears of stone drip from their manes. They weep over the ruination of the empire."

"The reign of Emperor Jiajing is inauspicious indeed."

"Indeed, indeed."

Twenty bronze tubs of concubines in ponderous silence. Forty knees above water. Forty submerged three-quarter-moon breasts.

"His Majesty has no interest in the affairs of his empire. He neglects his imperial duties. He is obsessed with his Daoist longevity ceremonies and immortality elixirs of arsenic and silver that turn his skin yellow, his breath like that of a corpse . . ."

"He dreams of eternal life. He disappears for days in dark temples of incense smoke and Daoist monks chanting immortality prayers . . ."

"I hear His Majesty has invited the hermit sage Filthy Zhang to his quarters," I say. "The pills of filth collected by Filthy Zhang as he rubs his finger on his skin are said to lengthen life. I believe Emperor Jiajing has imbibed a few of these."

Peals of laughter. The maids' smiles show teeth, which they hastily conceal. Drumbeat in Drum Tower signals Second Watch. Bathtime is over. Bodies rise from the water into kang-warmed towels. The older concubines, with our Leopard Room–scarred flesh, are grotesque to behold. Your virginal body is pure and pale as almond milk. You shudder at the sight of what awaits. A whisper: "They are building his tomb in the valley of Mount Tianshou."

"Then pray he outlives us. Pray he doesn't die. For we'll be immolated with him when he does. And should we accompany him to the afterlife, he will torment us there with knives."

IV

Alone in my chamber in the Palace of All Sunshine. A bedchamber not shared with others now that I am a concubine of first rank who has borne Emperor Jiajing three daughters. Princesses aged two, five and eleven, reared by nurses in the palace nursery. Princesses who cry and wriggle out of Mama's arms during my brief visits. Alone in my chamber, but for my dearest companions, opium and wine, I am thinking with regret of my daughters, Lily, Chrysanthemum and Azalea, when there is a knock at my door. Swaying and inebriated, I open the door to my eldest, Lily. O beloved Lily, come to Mama at last! Then I blink my wine-befuddled eyes, and I see it is not Lily, but you, Concubine Bamboo, a winter mink over your shoulders, shivering in the courtyard.

"Honourable Elder Sister Concubine Swallow. Forgive my grave insolence, but may I speak with you?"

Surly hostess swings wider the door. "Come in."

I go to the dresser, my back turned on you. I drag a gem-studded comb through my tangled mane.

"The Emperor has summoned me to his chambers tomorrow night. To the Leopard Room."

"Oh?"

You stammer on, "I hear he carved out Concubine Jasmine's bellybutton. Used the flesh for a soup for eternal life. The eunuch physicians attend to the . . . cavity he made."

You stammer on, "I hear the Jiajing Emperor favours you. Pardons you from the Leopard Room. I hear, Elder Sister Swallow, that you are his luncheon companion on the twelfth day of the first lunar month. Tomorrow. Honourable Elder Sister, would it be possible for you to ask him to spare me? Please? I am only fourteen. I am too young, not ready to suffer and die . . ."

I loosen my sash and shrug my shoulders so my robe slides to my feet. The stitches that crisscross my body are like puckered seams, holding together my patchwork of skin. "Do these scars count as evidence that His Majesty favours me?"

Mesmerized, not appalled by my scars, you murmur, "I hear Emperor Jiajing has allowed you special privileges for years."

"By speaking on your behalf, I may provoke his ire. Concubine Bamboo, what will you give me in return?"

As we both know, you have only one thing worth giving and, having researched my predilections, you give it. I fondle and taste every part of your lithe, paler-than-moonlight body. I bury my teeth in you without breaking the skin. You lick the cleft between my legs until I am sated and permit you to stop. It is daybreak by the time it is over. You peel apart from me, sticky with my fluids, my sweat. Can't look me in the eye.

"Why so humiliated? I am not a man. I did not pierce you or touch you there. I know the folly of depriving you of the trickle of blood that must stain his sheets. Why are you crying, Concubine Bamboo? You miss your mother? Forget her. She's to blame you are here in the first place."

Naked, you stare into emptiness, knees hugged to chest. I scrape my long and tapered fingernails across your scalp. Clutch a fistful of hair. I promise to speak to the Emperor for you; I promise to do my best.

V

The drum bangs to signal dawn. Lanterns are lit all across the Palace of Heavenly Purity and Emperor Jiajing rises. "Ten Thousand Blessings to His Majesty!" cry the eunuchs as they attend to his morning ablutions. They bathe him, comb and trim his beard and clean the wax from his ears. They dress him in a padded blue silk, fox-fur-trimmed robe, brocade leggings and sheepskin-lined boots (recorded by a eunuch scribe in the Ledger for the Department of Wardrobes). The winter day is cold. All across the Forbidden City eunuch servants swish brooms back and forth, sweeping clean the courtyards. The Go-Betweens of the Grand Secretaries present to the Emperor trays of scrolls, reporting of famines, droughts, peasant uprisings and warlord rebellions across the empire; trays of official decrees for His Majesty to approve and sign to quell these calamities. But Emperor Jiajing waves the triple-kowtowing Go-Betweens away. He has a meeting with a Daoist sage who has journeyed from Yunnan with the waters of a legendary stream, promised to add to a lifespan fifty years.

The Hall of Literary Brilliance. One hundred serving eunuchs march in holding silver platters aloft. They cry, "Transmitting the viands! Transmitting the viands!"

The eunuchs lower the one hundred silver platters on six round tables before His Majesty, then withdraw to the edges of the room. Heavy-lidded on his throne, Emperor Jiajing scarcely stirs as the serving eunuchs whirl around him, pouring his much-loved elk-horn and deer-penis brew into a porcelain cup. He scarcely acknowledges Concubine What's Her Name, mother of three of his daughters, genuflecting on her hands and knees, touching her forehead to the cold stone floor. The she-goat bleats, "Ten thousand blessings to Your Majesty! There is no greater honour than to be invited to dine with our Supreme Ruler today!"

Wretched Concubine What's Her Name, with her defective girl-bearing uterus. Her man-hating womb, castrating his foetal sons so only daughters are born. Arising from her knees, Concubine What's Her Name, head bowed with humility and deference, goes to stand at His Majesty's shoulder. His rage blows over. The Emperor is hungry; his stomach growls with impatience.

"Remove the covers!" commands the Chief Serving Eunuch.

One hundred serving eunuchs scurry from the peripheries of the Hall of Literary Brilliance, remove the silver-domed platter lids and carry them away. What a feast! The Emperor licks his lips and points at a dish of noodles. The Eunuch Food Taster cries, "Appraising the viands!" and pincers some dangling threads of noodles with his chopsticks. The Eunuch Food Taster nibbles, nods that the noodles are unpoisoned and the Emperor proceeds to eat. Concubine What's Her Name hovers out of eyeshot, at the shoulder of His Majesty's fox-fur-trimmed robes. Concubine

Meek and Timid. O how ashamed of her I am. But to behave in any other manner is to provoke his wrath. To dine with Emperor Jiajing is not to eat oneself but to stand beside him, encouraging him and praising him for every mouthful he masticates. A sip of elk-horn and deer-penis brewed tea necessitates a cry of, "O how this revives the blood, enhances potency, O Emperor of Ten Thousand Years!"

(The Hall of Literary Brilliance is a curious venue for luncheon, as the Jiajing Emperor does not possess a scholarly bent, never reads the accumulated works of Chinese civilization crowding the shelves . . .)

"Your Excellency, why not have some steamed one-hundred-year-old turtle in ginseng soup? Ginseng strengthens cardiac function, will keep your heart beating vigorous and strong!"

(. . . the five-thousand-volume encyclopaedia, the Tang Dynasty poetry and the scrolls of Song Dynasty paintings . . .)

"Your Majesty, may I be so bold as to suggest some wolfberries and snow peas to aid digestion? Though I must say, Your Majesty's selection thus far has been exemplary!"

(The Emperor does not care about ancestor worship, or the historical records of the empire. Emperor Jiajing's solipsism limits pursuit of knowledge to mortality cures . . .)

"I see now that His Majesty is sated. I must compliment His Majesty on the judicious array of delicacies of earth and sea selected for his luncheon today!"

(Selfish as a newborn, nothing that exists beyond His Majesty is worth a moment's thought.)

Emperor Jiajing toothpicks from his canines shreds of pork and flicks them aside. One of the serving eunuchs falls upon the sacred toothpicked debris, gathering them to stow in a locket around his neck, thus bringing this mere castrato closer to Heaven's Son. Emperor Jiajing speaks to me for the first time, his back to me as I stand behind his throne.

"Imperial Consort, you do not dine. You have my permission to do so now."

"Your Majesty, to dine is nigh impossible when you are near.

When you are near all corporeal need flees my body. All thoughts leave my head."

"As one expects. Women's brains are anatomically very tiny. I expect scant few thoughts rattle about the confines of your skull to begin with. Thoughts of dressmaking and other silly frivolities."

"Your Excellency is correct. I am dim-witted as a she-goat. 'Tis a pity, but there is nothing to be done."

"How are my daughters?"

"Your daughters fare well. Azalea has recently been weaned from the breast, Chrysanthemum had her feet bound last week and everyone is of the opinion that Lily's embroidery is the finest of all the princesses'!"

The Emperor yawns wide his rotting-molars-and-gum-pits-stinking breath.

"Imperial Consort, you bore me tremendously. Do you have anything of noteworthy interest to say to me at all?"

Armpits sweating, the seams of my sapphire silk gown straining. My breath resists my attempts to reduce its speed, to make breathing inconspicuous.

"Actually, Your Majesty, I do have one suggestion, if Your Majesty would do me the honour of lending his much revered ears. My lowly opinion concerns Imperial Consort Bamboo. I think she is unworthy of serving the Emperor. The low-breed slut ought to be demoted to a maidservant."

The Emperor lifts his porcelain cup and drains the last of his elk-horn and deer-penis beverage.

"Is that all?"

"That is all, Your Majesty."

Emperor Jiajing gestures that luncheon is over with a wave of the hand. He moves to the doorway where the sedan chair bearers await, without glancing backwards at Concubine What's Her Name, who is nervously wringing her hands. The servants part the curtains and the Emperor enters the silk-veiled carriage. He murmurs his destination, the Palace of Heavenly Purity, and the bearers lift the poles and carry him away through the courtyards of the Forbidden City.

*   *   *

Alone in my bedchamber, I seek solace in the opium pipe and wine and I strum upon my zither a melody called "The Calamitous Golden Eel." I doze and dream of you, my fingers fiddling under my skirts, masquerading as your tongue, and I wake to emptiness, aching temples and a dry mouth. Dusk has cloaked the Palace of All Sunshine. There is a knock at the door. Eunuch Li of the Bureau of Affairs of the Bedchamber has come.

"Concubine Swallow, the Emperor Jiajing requests your attendance tonight in the Leopard Room."

Heart stops, breath caught in throat. Nearly three years since I was last impaled on the imperial cock.

"Shall I go to the bathhouse and have the maidservants prepare me?"

"His Majesty has requested you as you are."

"Then the Emperor's wish shall be granted."

I strip out of my robe. Legs shaking so much I can barely stand, I rinse my stale mouth with water and splash my face. Naked but for slippered feet and a feather duvet worn as a cloak, I climb on Eunuch Li's back and we proceed thusly to the Leopard Room.

VI

In the vermilion-pillared Leopard Room magical cranes fly across the lapis lazuli ceiling panels. Blazing lanterns dangling silk tassels hang from hooks. On the four-poster bed is Concubine Bamboo, naked but for a jewelled tiara. Your eyes are vacant, your pale skin unsullied but for some slight discolourations where I feasted too keenly the night before. Eunuch Li takes my feathered duvet and backs out of the room. His conscience is besmirched by what occurs in the Leopard Room, the concubines he carries out to be stitched up afterwards, and the ones that pass away. But what is to be done? The Emperor's wishes must be granted, his every desire fulfilled.

Emperor Jiajing emerges from an annex with silk rope and I am palsied with terror. He orders me to stand against a vermilion pillar and binds my wrists around the pillar behind my back. I tremble, grovelling like a whipped dog. "O Your Excellency, I beg your forgiveness. I sincerely regret having spoken this afternoon. Please be compassionate to the mother of your three daughters . . ."

"Quiet."

His Majesty turns to you on the bed. The maidservants have bathed you, prepared your toilette for the Leopard Room. Perfume scents your pulse beats and your lips are red as rubies. Emperor Jiajing directs a question to the pale masque of your face. "Concubine Bamboo, your elder sister Concubine Swallow has been spitting vinegar. Do you know why?"

You shake your head with those ever-vacant eyes. The precious gems of your headpiece glitter with the changing angle of striking light. Emperor Jiajing laughs.

"Sweet Bamboo, how innocent you are! Let us take a look at your elder sister. Do you know she has given birth to three children? Do you know what childbearing does to a woman's body? The teats sag like cow udders, the stomach flops and folds over. As for her cunt, well . . ." His Majesty chuckles. ". . . if the barbarians invade Beijing, we have a vacant storehouse for the imperial jewels! I have not lusted for her for years, but the wretched hag still lusts for me. So much so she has tried to warn me away from you, my sweet Concubine Bamboo. We'll teach her a lesson, shall we?"

Barely perceptibly, you nod. To me, the Emperor hisses, "Now watch me split the bamboo."

His Majesty throws off his padded blue silk, fox-fur-trimmed robe, proceeds towards you. Emperor Jiajing is underweight, asthmatic, feeble and sickly weak, but after smearing his erection with verdigris and snake dung and snorting powdery aphrodisiacs up the nose, he is convinced of his invincibility. The only man in the Forbidden City with his genitalia intact, His Majesty is virility itself. You are quiet as he parts your legs and mounts you. Perfectly still, but wincing in virginal pain as yet another member of the imperial household makes use of your young body. Despite my fear of what post-coital punishment awaits, the sound of him sliding up and down inside you and your whimpers and moans arouse me, make me want you too. After the snake has spat he collapses on you, as though his heart has arrested and he has died a little death. Beneath him, you lie still. You roll your head to the side. Your eyes are still blank. Let this be it, I beg the Heavens above. Let my only punishment be to watch him writhe above another. Let his ego imagine my "jealousy" is torture enough.

Emperor Jiajing slowly revives on the bed, conceitedly muttering of his sexual prowess in your ear, prodding you there and dabbing his bloody fingerprints on your collar bone. He molests you in this way for a while, then calls to me from across the room.

"See? You don't compare to sweet young Bamboo. Confronted with your haggard body, my cock dies a whimpering death."

I hang my head as though tormented, and the Emperor quotes from *The Book of Odes*:

> Women with long tongues
> Are harbingers of evil.
> Disasters are not sent down from Heaven
> But originate in the female of the species.

"See how pale she is, my sweet Bamboo? The god-awful pallor of her lips and cheeks? I think we ought to rouge them for her, don't you?"

He whispers in your ear and you giggle impishly. The Emperor smacks your bare bottom as you slide from the silk sheets. You scamper over to me, touch your finger to the bleeding palette between your legs, then smear the blood on my lips and rub your finger in circular motions on my cheeks. I stare into your traitorous eyes. You are blank as ever, though you turn to the Emperor to giggle every so often. The Emperor stands, walks away from the bed.

"What do you think, Concubine Bamboo? Do you think her complexion has improved?"

You shake your head no. Emperor Jiajing walks to the dresser and opens a jewellery box of knives and other sharp instruments of torture. The Emperor removes a silver scalpel from the velvet-lined case. Acrid wine-tasting vomit spills down my chest. The

Emperor laments, "Oh dear, she is paler than ever now! What do you think, Concubine Bamboo?"

He hands you the silver scalpel. You turn to me and treacherously utter, "More rouge."

VII

Concubine Jasmine spoons herbal soup between my parted lips and I struggle to choke it down.

"One more spoonful, dear sister Concubine Swallow," she encourages, dabbing my chin with lace cloth. "You need nourishment to strengthen and heal."

Concubine Jasmine smooths the cotton bedsheet that covers my torso, bound tight by bandages. Her beauty and kindness contrast starkly with the portrait of the Emperor of Knives staring at me from the wall opposite the infirmary bed. Though I am no longer in the Leopard Room, my torture is ongoing, for every night the eunuchs unwind the gauze from my crudely stitched chest and douse my flayed skin with fiery medicinal concoctions. My teeth bite down on rags stuffed in my mouth and my hands claw the bedsheets, until a tide of darkness comes, sweeping the pallid, tittering eunuchs away.

Imperial Consort Jasmine, a high-ranking concubine like me, knows the monotony of the infirmary, has spent weeks convalescing there herself. So she smuggles in a Siamese kitten to amuse me by chasing balls of yarn, and some bamboo paper, ink brush and ink, so this recuperating concubine can churn out imitation Song Dynasty landscapes. Puffing on the opium pipe together, we transcend into a giggling realm of lightness and ease as Concubine Jasmine reads to me from illicit, bootlegged erotic novellas (swearing me to secrecy, for if the eunuchs knew she was literate, they'd gouge out her eyes). She reads the tale of a cuckolding wife who romps with a gang of servant boys behind her master's back, and she acts out each part with comic timing, changing her voice for each character, exaggerating carnal moans. Spellbound by her deft tongue moving behind her luscious lips and her eyes widening during climactic scenes, I reach and touch her lovely breasts. Concubine Jasmine ceases reading. She takes my hand in hers and kisses it tenderly.

"O dearest beloved sister Concubine Swallow. Believe me, I wish I could. But it is my misfortune that I am not that way inclined."

VIII

When I am pronounced well enough to return to the Palace of All Sunshine, Concubine Jasmine and I celebrate by wandering arm in arm about the Imperial Gardens. The spring thaw has begun. Many species of flowers are budding and numerous winged insects hover about the shrubs. Our little bound feet, three silk-cocooned inches peeping from under the hems of our robes, *tap tap tap* along the winding pebble-mosaic path as we admire the songbirds on the branches of the cypress, catalpa and scholar trees. Under my bandages, the stitched lesions protest movement with lacerating pain, but I hobble on. Concubine Jasmine has sought permission for us to enter the Emperor's Menagerie to see the tributes from the kings of other lands: the elephant from Laos, the African zebras and the strutting ostriches with feathery bums and uppity beaks thrust to the sky. We stroke the zebras' black-and-white-striped hides and laugh and clap our hands as the stable boy climbs astride the elephant and gets a backward hosing from the wrinkled grey trunk.

Back in the Imperial Gardens in the late afternoon we hear a tinkling of voices in the Pavilion of Melancholy Clouds.

"Ah, who might that be?" stage queries Jasmine.

On the circular stone bench within is a gathering of palace ladies, resplendent in shimmering robes, jewelled combs in their impeccably coiffed hair. They arise as we enter the pavilion. "Concubine Swallow!" they cry, and flock to me.

"O precious Concubine Swallow, we prayed to the Goddess of Mercy for your swift recovery. We requested permission to visit you, but the eunuchs wouldn't allow it."

They embrace me and caress my chilled early-spring cheeks. Fourteen of my harem sisters, each a faded beauty of more than thirty years with age-spun webs around her eyes. A stove blazes in the corner and on the table are porcelain teapots and cakes baked in the moulds of butterflies. The party is in my honour. They present me with gifts prepared during my convalescence: peony-stitched satin slippers, pouches embroidered with Buddhist emblems and a balm of crushed petals to perfume my wrists. Silly frivolities that show how limited in skill and artistic expression the harem women are, but I battle my inner contempt and express gratitude for the gifts. For years I have rejected my sisters, and superiority is a hard habit to break. We sit on the circular bench. Surreptitious breezes sneak through gaps in the wax-paper windows to stir the pavilion air. Concubine Jasmine begins, "We may speak without restraint, Concubine Swallow. Maidservants have been dispatched along the paths to look out for spies such as Hunchback Guo." She lays a hand on the carved gully where her bellybutton used to reside. The afternoon stroll has aggravated Concubine Jasmine's wound.

"We have news of a tragedy that occurred last week," continues Concubine Autumn Rains. "Imperial Consorts Tranquillity, Heavenly Orchid, Bamboo and Joyous Abundance were summoned by Emperor Jiajing to the Leopard Room. As the Emperor engaged in coitus with each in turn, he became convinced they were giggling at him. His Majesty confronted them with his paranoid imaginings, then handed them each a knife and ordered them to commit suicide. Tranquillity, Heavenly Orchid and Joyous Abundance successfully put themselves to death. But Concubine Bamboo survives in the infirmary."

Under my bandages, the lesions on my chest scream as the maggots of ire writhe. "Bamboo is not dead? She survives? Indeed, that is a tragedy! I must go at once and finish the job!"

Elegantly coiffed heads shake at me in dismay. Concubine Emerald reaches and squeezes my hand. "Forgive her, Concubine Swallow. Every one of us has incised the flesh of others. Who amongst us has been brave enough to refuse the torturer's blade? The tyrant must be obeyed under pain of death. You must forgive Concubine Bamboo."

"Forgive her, forgive her," the she-goats bleat. But I can't. Fury chokes the gullet at the mere thought of you.

"Concubine Bamboo was no unwilling torturer," I spit. "Her eyes lit up as she spilt my blood, and with every incision she grew ever more ambitious with the blade."

"She is a child of only fourteen years old."

I hiss, "A demonic child. A satanic nymph with a thirst for blood."

"At the Emperor's bidding she slashed her own throat," says Concubine Tender Willow. "How many cups of blood do you think poured down her gullet? Enough to quench her thirst for good, I should think."

"Concubine Swallow," Jasmine says sternly, "you must let the desire to take revenge on the child go. We have more urgent concerns. Do you know of the Daoist monk One Hundred Trees?"

"The hermit sage who lives in the enchanted forest on Mount Emei?"

"Yes. Him."

Melodious Songbird, Tender Willow and Emerald each speak in turn:

"One Hundred Trees has come to the Forbidden City to tell Emperor Jiajing of a new cure for mortality . . ."

"The hermit sage says it is the blood that thickens the uterus then seeps from our womanly orifice every moon cycle."

"One Hundred Trees told Emperor Jiajing that a cupful every day will prolong his life."

"Every day the harem keepers consult the Ledger of Menstrual Cycles of the Concubines. Those menstruating are ordered to a chamber by the Gate of Obedience. They are forced to lie on a wooden bed, their ankles hooked in stirrups that hang from the ceiling . . ."

"A long, hook-ended needle is the tool that is used. Sometimes the bleeding cannot be staunched afterwards, and some have bled to death."

"No one is safe. Not even the princesses."

My eldest, Lily, is eleven. Has the curse struck her down yet? I must protect her from this atrocity! Outraged, I spit, "We must end this barbarous practice! We must bribe the eunuchs to trick Emperor Jiajing with chicken's blood!"

"Bribery has been attempted. Concubine Splendid Jade is now subject to torture in the Palace of Punishments."

"But something must be done," I cry. "If Emperor Jiajing harms my daughters, I shall . . . I shall . . ."

"Murder him?" suggests Concubine Jasmine with a wry smile.

I look at the fifteen palace ladies on the circular bench, their hands clasped on laps. They look back at me, their eyes glittering and fierce. Together, we are the sixteen mothers of the twenty-six princesses. Now I see. Concubine Emerald continues, "We are plotting now, the ways and means. We each accept the sacrifice of our lives, for assassination of the Emperor won't come without this penalty."

My heart beats swiftly beneath my flayed and bandaged chest. For the eighteen years I have lived in the Inner Palace, I have shunned my harem sisters. High on my lofty perch of lonely self-regard, I dismissed them as empty-headed and vain. How wrong I was. My courageous sisters are far nobler than I.

"We invite you to join us, Concubine Swallow," says Concubine Jasmine. "Will you accept?"

Murdering Emperor Jiajing is a recurring fantasy of mine, but am I willing to die for it? I dwell for a moment upon my wretched and lonely existence. So what of death? I decide. Better to die nobly than to live on wretchedly, listlessly wandering about the Garden of Dispossessed Favourites, slowly wasting from the rot of old age. Better to die having saved my daughters and the entire Celestial Kingdom from the worst Emperor ever to reign.

"I will be honoured to," I tell them, tears glistening in my eyes.

On a circular stone bench in the Pavilion of Melancholy Clouds, we clasp our pale-as-ivory hands together in solidarity, our pact to kill the Emperor now commenced.

IX

Evening in the palace infirmary. Eunuch physicians unbind my tightly bandaged chest. I lie on the bed and the eunuchs dab at the bleeding and pus-weeping wounds with cotton gauze in tweezers, tutting at my slowness to heal. They unplug the stopper from a bottle of herbal potion, and I claw the sheets as my doused chest blazes like oil set alight.

I go back to the Palace of All Sunshine, aching for the opium pipe, and snow flutters unexpectedly out of the night sky. I gaze up at the spiralling snow, falling to sabotage the winged debut of creatures from cocoons and the burgeoning buds of spring. What does this portend? I wonder. The gods must be angry indeed, to gust the icy breath of disapproval upon the Imperial City after the coming of spring.

Mesmerized by the snow drifting out of the dark void of sky, I nearly don't see the girl kneeling in the courtyard of the Palace of All Sunshine. It is Lily, my eldest, and I hasten over, stricken by her bled-dry pallor and the bandages around her neck. But as I draw nearer, my maternal instinct turns to horror and abhorrence. The deceitful night has tricked me again, for it is not Lily, but you. Concubine Bamboo. You shiver in the cold, your shawl of winter mink a pelt of icy tufts. Repentant eyes look up and meet mine. It's the first time I have seen you since the Leopard Room, and my screams are gagged and bound in my throat. I clench my spitting muscles, gathering saliva. Spittle drips down your cheek, but you don't wipe it away.

"Elder Sister Concubine Swallow," you cry, "I can no longer live with my abominable sins against you. I beg you to forgive me after I am gone . . ."

Out of your shawl you withdraw a dagger. Both hands on the ivory handle, you point the blade at your heart and plunge it down. Shocked, I instinctively leap and catch your wrists before the blade penetrates your chest. I grapple the dagger out of your suicidal grip and cast it into the darkness on the other side of the courtyard. Whetstone-sharpened steel clatters unseen upon stone. The pale beauty of your face is seized by shock. You whisper, "Concubine Swallow . . . *Why?*"

"They'll punish me for your murder, you snivelling brat!" Then I knock your head sideways with a furious slap. "Now go! Get out of my sight!"

I go into my bedchamber and stumble to my dresser, knocking over the bottles of mandrake extract and honeysuckle balm for masking my decay as I grope for my vial of sleeping draught. Unplugging the stopper, I down three nights' worth in one long swallow. I put out the spluttering oil lamp and sink on my bed into a fathomless sleep.

Spring tide ebbs and the icicles of winter make one last stab. Night and day you kneel in the courtyard of the Palace of All Sunshine, head bowed as though in prayer. Eye to the peephole in my wax-paper window, I watch you risk pneumonia and death to kneel in the snow and prove your remorse, forsaking meals and sleep and clean bandages for the deep cut in your throat, to become a sculpture of ice. I watch you through the peephole and your pain and subjugation sate a dark species of desire within.

On the third night of your vigil you are swaying on your knees, as though struggling not to faint. She won't survive the night, I think, smiling thinly. Then I put out my oil lamp and go to bed, expecting to sink into a deep, contented slumber. But sleep does not come. Under my quilt my limbs twitch as though possessed by the demons of fidgetiness and, after an hour of restlessness, I get up and go to my dresser. I pull the stopper out of my sleeping draught, upend the bottle between my lips, but not one drop trickles out. I rummage about in my jewellery box, but the opium is gone too. Cursing, I prepare to go out and bribe one of the guardsmen to smuggle a bottle of wine out of the storehouse for me. I throw a fox-fur cape on over my nightgown and unlatch the door, much aggrieved at having to go out into the freezing night.

Out in the courtyard you are lying on the ground. *Don't go near her!* warns a vengeful voice in my head. *Death is what she deserves!* But my three-inch bound feet shuffle nearer and I crouch to peer at you. Your skin is pale as ice and your stillness that of a corpse. Are you sleeping or are you dead? Whereas my breath emerges in thick white puffs, yours isn't visible. You look so much like my eldest, Lily, I can't bear it. *Leave her!* warns the voice. *Remember how sadistically she carved up your breasts!* But I can't leave you. My bandaged wounds in agony, I heave you into my arms and carry you into my chamber. How can I let you die when you look so much like my own child?

I lay your frozen body on my bed and you revive in the warmth of the briquette stove. Your blood thaws and circulates again, flowing back to your cheeks. You wake, blinking with eyes that wonder, Where am I? then shine with gratitude as they meet mine. Knowing you have not had any water for three days, I pour a glass from my carafe. Now throw her out! I think as you sip feebly at the water. Bamboo is a frozen snake brought in from the cold. Now recovered, she will sink in her fangs! But you are so sickly I daren't send you back into the bitterly cold night. I cover you with my goose-feather quilt, cursing my sentimental heart.

I drowse until the hour before dawn, when you wake me by loosening my foot bindings to rub my humpbacked arches and toe claws. At the deft touch of your hands, that cruel mistress lust stirs within and I don't resist as your lips flutter like moth wings against my legs and thighs. You pilgrimage to my sacred place and worship there, the lapping waves of pleasure rising to a crescendo and my shuddering release.

The drum bangs to signal dawn. The sun rises over the Forbidden City and the fearful symmetry of courtyards and palaces within. Your weary head on the pillow, you murmur that you love me. That you loved me before we even met. Your eyelids droop shut and I stroke your raven's tresses back from your inauspicious widow's peak. I am tranquil as I watch you slumber. The fury I was certain would seethe unto the grave is gone.

How did my defences fall so swiftly? I wonder. You came for my forgiveness, and how willingly I gave it away.

X

In the Palace of Sleeping Cicada fifteen aspiring murderesses gather in a sewing circle, embroidering silken slippers for our broken, mutilated hooves. Steam rises from our cups of aromatic tea. Lotus blossoms and golden peonies bloom from our needles and thread. More sinister things bloom from our tongues and mouths. How will His Majesty die? By poison or the dagger? Or, if time kindly permits, by the Death by a Thousand Cuts?

Out in the Garden of Dispossessed Favourites bronze bells are tolling in the fitful breeze. There's a knock on the door of the Palace of Sleeping Cicada and our sixteenth sister, Concubine Jasmine, rushes in. Her eyes are shining bright and her tongue is taut as an archer's bow drawn to fire arrows of speech.

"My beloved sisters! Our time has come! Tonight we are summoned to the Leopard Room. Tonight the reign of the Emperor Jiajing will end!"

Fifteen wagging tongues are stilled. Fifteen needles freeze midstitch. Fifteen hearts leap up into throats. "*How?*" we gasp. Concubine Jasmine lowers herself onto the kang in a perfumed cloud of silk. Kingfisher feathers of silver filigree tremble in her hair.

"Today I had the honour of luncheon with His Majesty in the Belvedere of Ancient Catalpa."

Concubine Jasmine piously widens her eyes and reverentially bleats, "O Supreme Ruler! O Lord of Mankind and all under Heaven! There is no greater honour than to be invited to dine with His Majesty today! Well . . . as His Majesty feasted on a dish of stewed meat dumplings, I crawled under the table, lifted up the imperial robes and feasted on His Majesty's dumplings. At first he was outraged . . . not to mention flustered, in front of the one hundred serving eunuchs!"

Fifteen aspiring murderesses titter to imagine the horror of the pallorous castrati.

"But he soon surrendered with moans of pleasure and, by the time I had imbibed His Majesty's seed, his luncheon had cooled on his plate. Then, whilst he was in an agreeable mood, I suggested a rendezvous in the Leopard Room tonight. I begged permission to choose his bedmates, promising His Majesty seductresses versed in the erotic arts who will send him to Heaven on clouds of transcendent bliss. Emperor Jiajing consented and waved me away, and I rushed at once to the Bureau of the Affairs of the Bedchamber and named our sixteen names. Tonight we will each be summoned to the Leopard Room! Tonight the Jiajing reign will end!"

Our sewing circle of fifteen concubines is effusive in its praise.

"Oh how brave you are, Concubine Jasmine!"

"How audacious! How sly and cunning!"

"Our hearts are brimming with admiration—truly they are!"

"Beloved sisters," Concubine Jasmine says warmly, "it was our sisterhood that lent me the courage and the strength."

Then silence descends upon the Palace of Sleeping Cicada. Our regicidal fantasy is about to be fulfilled, but His Majesty's death is our death too, and fear and sorrow drum loudly in our chests. Concubine Emerald wrings her hands in her lap and whispers, "Beloved sisters, I must confess that I am afraid . . ."

"Afraid of what?"

I speak before I know I am speaking, with a scathing that can't be reined in: "Of death? Isn't life as a harem slave already a waking death? Punished for the sin of pulchritude, we are prisoners here in this gilded cage, subject to the tyrant's every sadistic whim! My sisters, we died long ago. Each of us died the moment we were borne by palanquin through the Forbidden City's western gates."

Concubine Jasmine reaches and clasps both of Concubine Emerald's hands in hers. "We will be duly rewarded in Heaven for protecting our daughters and taking revenge on him for our murdered ancestresses," she says. "The gods approve of our plot to end his tyrannical reign. The gods have revoked the Mandate of Heaven and tonight we act in their stead . . ."

A pause. A muffled cough from the periphery of the chamber. Embroidery hoops tumble from laps as concubines flutter up like birds startled by a gunpowder shot.

"Who? Where?"

"An intruder! A spy!"

"Under the lid of the tea chest!

Concubine Moonbeam bounds over to the teakwood chest and throws the dragon-engraved lid open on creaking hinges. A colourful tumult of finely woven robes are flung through the air as she rummages for the interloper, whom she hauls up by her braids.

"Concubine Bamboo!" the sewing circle hiss.

You wince in pain as Concubine Moonbeam drags you to the centre of the Palace of Sleeping Cicada by your plaits. Sixteen elder sisters gather around you, and you cower beneath sixteen pairs of glaring eyes.

"Who sent you?" Concubine Melodious Songbird demands.

"Why are you spying on us?"

Your innocent eyes brim with tears and you lisp childishly, "I was playing hide and seek with the other novice concubines and . . ."

Concubine Jasmine laughs incredulously, then slaps you hard across the cheek. "Your lies insult us. Speak the truth!"

Your cheek reddens with the mark of her hand. Recognizing that your elder sisters won't be duped, you start again.

"Honourable Elder Sisters, I beg you to forgive my trespassing. I suspected that Concubine Swallow was part of a secret plot and, fearing for her safety, I hid in the tea chest to learn what it was. Now that I know, I swear on my ancestors' graves to keep your secret." You narrow your eyes with enmity. "I hate the Emperor of Knives as much as you do and will rejoice with the rest of the Celestial Kingdom to see him dead."

The sisterhood of sixteen exchange wary looks over your fourteen-year-old head. Concubine Jasmine turns to me, the one who unwittingly led you to us. "Is the child to be trusted, Concubine Swallow?" she asks.

Before I can speak, Concubine Melodious Songbird cries, "The devious Bamboo is in league with the vile castrati! I have seen her in the Pavilion of Immortal Birds, conniving with Hunchback Guo. We must bind her with ropes and drown her in the well. Or she'll sabotage our plans!"

Concubine Autumn Rains nods in vehement agreement. "Concubine Bamboo will betray our plot to murder Emperor Jiajing for her own gain! We must hand her the silken cord and order her to hang herself!"

As more of our sisters vociferously demand that you choke down poison or slit your own wrists, you are strangely calm. You speak to Concubine Jasmine, tremorless and clear. "I am prepared to die by whichever method my elder sisters decide upon . . ." Your tormented eyes then seek out mine. ". . . for what do I have to live for after Concubine Swallow has been executed?"

Your willingness to die for the sake of our harem sisters' paranoid fears provokes my heart into furious dissent. Your murder is an injustice I won't allow.

"What proof is there that Concubine Bamboo is in league with the eunuchs?" I challenge. "Emperor Jiajing is the one who deserves to be murdered, not this child. Why don't we just gag her and bind her and lock her in the tea chest? That should be enough."

Outraged, my sisters turn on me. Spittle flits from their lips as they vilify and slander me.

"How cleverly the child has manipulated Concubine Swallow!"

"Everyone knows the way to Swallow's heart is through her voracious cunt. The sly little whore now has Swallow eating out of her palm . . ."

"Give them both the silken cord to hang from the rafters!"

Mercifully, wise and compassionate Concubine Jasmine has heard my appeal. She claps her hands, silencing our harem sisters' vicious attack. Commanding of stature, Concubine Jasmine asserts her leadership without raising her voice. "Enough. We won't have the murder of a child on our conscience. We will bind her up and lock her in the tea chest. By the time they find her, Emperor Jiajing will be dead, and nothing she can say will bring him back."

Twelve rolls of foot-binding cloth truss your ankles and wrists. Scarves of silk stuff your gagged mouth. Sixteen pale and baleful faces stare down at you, in the bottom of the teakwood box. I lean into the chest and whisper, "Farewell, Concubine Bamboo. May the rest of your days be peaceful after the tyrant's death. I wish you a long, prosperous life, and I pray that we will meet again in the afterlife."

A suffocating heap of silk robes is thrown upon the gagged, bound concubine. The dragon-engraved lid thuds down and you are entombed in dark.

XI

Shadow of dusk inches stealthily across the Forbidden City. A flock of black crows soars over the shadowed courts of the Great Within, cawing and thrashing their wings. The end of the Jiajing reign is nigh. The timbers and beams in the Palace of Heavenly Purity creak and sigh of it. The weeping willows by the outer walls whisper sibilantly of it, trailing their branches in the moat. The tormented spirits of those who died in the Leopard Room sing of it, breezing through the chambers, rejoicing at His Majesty's comeuppance.

Drumbeat in Drum Tower signals the beginning of First Watch. Harem keepers go through the courts to the Palace of Modest Ladies, over slabs of stone polished smooth by a hundred and twenty years of servants scurrying to and fro. Sixteen concubines, naked but for slippered feet and goose-feather quilts, clamber upon the backs of the eunuchs, who carry them to His Majesty's chambers.

Lanterns blaze in the Leopard Room. His Majesty reclines on the bed, under a canopy of cicada-wing gauze. The sixteenth palace lady is lowered before him, and the last of the eunuchs retreats with her goose-feather quilt. The nine-dragon bolt shudders across the Leopard Room door, locking us in. Sixteen concubines, naked but for our slippered feet, our lips red as rubies, our faces powdered white and our hair elaborately arranged with jewelled pins. Kneeling before His Majesty, we kowtow and touch our foreheads to the cold marble floor.

"Ten thousand blessings to Emperor Jiajing! Ten thousand blessings to Emperor Jiajing!" we chorus.

Emperor Jiajing beckons Tender Willow to join him on the bed.

We are mute witnesses as he fondles her breasts then removes a slipper and unwinds her foot-bindings, exposing her pig's-trotter foot. The Emperor's red-silk-dragon robe slides open. He squeezes Tender Willow's broken-arched foot so toes meet heel, and she stifles her screams as he penetrates the crevice with his engorged cock. A few bored thrusts and he withdraws his wilting erection and sprinkles it with aphrodisiac powders from a snuff box. He kicks Tender Willow, who is writhing in pain, from the bed, and she thuds onto the marble floor. Regicidal desire burns in every one of our hearts.

The Emperor of Knives casts his gaze over our bodies, stitched up by eunuchs after the massacres he perpetrated upon them. Years of incarceration and torture have eroded our beauty, and we have toiled over our toilette, smearing nightingale's excrement and other pigments of white on our scarred skin. But the Emperor is not fooled. He snorts in contempt at our cowering nakedness. Jade goblet of wine raised to his lips, he sips and sneers, "How the winds of time have torn the blossoms of youth from the ugly, crooked branches! Imperial Consort Jasmine, what is the meaning of this moth-eaten coven of hags? Where are the airy sylphs? The earthbound goddesses with sweet-as-morning's-dew cunts? These wrinkles and sagging teats are offensive to me."

The wine-fuddled Emperor's speech is slurred. Our exquisitely painted eyelids are lowered demurely throughout his insults, but Concubine Jasmine gazes level with His Majesty, her smile a tranquil crescent moon.

"Ten thousand blessings to Emperor Jiajing! I beseech our Supreme Ruler to look beyond our repugnance, for we are devoted to the fulfillment of His Majesty's every desire. To elevating our Lord of Ten Thousand Years to the heavens on clouds of erotic delight."

Emperor Jiajing narrows his eyes. "Look at these haggard bodies! These ogresses' countenances! Clouds of erotic delight indeed! What brazen lies you tell. I am dangerously close, Concubine Jasmine, to calling the Imperial Guards to escort you to the Palace of Punishments to be flayed for deception with horsehair whips!"

In the chill of the Leopard Room, the sweat of foreboding seeps upon my skin. But Concubine Jasmine is serene and unmenaced by his brutal threats. "O Lord of Ten Thousand Years, I beg on behalf of your most devoted concubines for a chance to worship you. Has Your Excellency ever had sixteen tongues lapping at him simultaneously? Would Your Majesty consent to try it? If our Supreme Ruler is dissatisfied, then I will willingly submit to being flogged by the Imperial Guards, for brutal torture would be nothing less than I deserve."

Emperor Jiajing sighs, grudgingly opens his robe and lies on his back, and the sixteen concubines crawl, meek and subservient, upon the Emperor's vast bed. We surround His Majesty, lowering our mouths to his emaciated, biliously yellow body. The Emperor is vile and bitter-tasting from the arsenic and mercury elixirs secreted through his pores, but our tongues lap passionately, pretending lusty eagerness.

"Close your eyes, Emperor Jiajing," Concubine Jasmine murmurs, hypnotically. "There's no need for Your Majesty to torment his sight with our odiousness."

The Son of Heaven lowers his eyelids, succumbing to the sensual pleasure. Tongues incessantly licking, we slide our slippers from our feet and work our foot-binding strips loose. His Majesty's serpent rears up and stares at us with his lone Cyclops eye but, fortunately, does not report its findings to his master. When Concubine Jasmine sees that every one of us has a length of foot-binding cloth in her hands, she ceases licking and raises a phoenix-embroidered pillow over Emperor Jiajing's head. "Now!" she cries, and smothers the Emperor with the satin pillow, suppressing his screams as three or four concubines restrain each limb and lash it, with foot-binding strips, to a bedpost. Jasmine lifts the pillow and I stuff his mouth with silk scarves and gag him with the sash of his dragon's robe.

Emperor Jiajing is apoplectic, his bulging eyes threatening to leap out of their sockets. His Majesty struggles against the restraints but, weakened by poisonous elixirs, he barely strains the knots.

Our sisterhood of sixteen leaps from the Emperor's bed and dances around the Leopard Room. As we dance, we parade around His Majesty's bed as though we are Heavenly enchantresses. As we dance, the spirits of our ancestresses descend into us, and our levity is as though we dance upon air. Amusingly, the Emperor's serpent rears up in defiance of his master's fury, staring with its Cyclops eye as though beguiled. As we dance, we serenade Emperor Jiajing with sacrilegious song. We sing the truth that sycophantic officials daren't speak:

"You are the worst Emperor the Ming Dynasty has known."

"The worst Emperor the Celestial Kingdom has ever known."

"The history books will condemn you, Emperor Jiajing."

"You are a tyrannical despot, atrocious and weak."

"Your subjects will not mourn you and your crippling taxes."

The truth is like bamboo splints in Emperor Jiajing's ears. His Majesty turns a livid shade of purple, and he thrashes against the foot-binding strips that fetter him to the bedposts, his groin bucking up and down and his shoulders nearly wrenching out of their sockets.

Concubine Jasmine cries, "Bid your kingdom farewell, Emperor Jiajing! The time has come to die!"

The sisterhood of sixteen leaps back on the vast bed, and our Son of Heaven goes limp. Now that His Majesty is staring death in the face, he's so petrified he can't move. Splendid Jade and Autumn Rains fasten the strangling cord around his neck, and tears of desperation leak from Emperor Jiajing's eyes. We tug on the ends of the foot-binding cloth with all our strength.

"Pull!" we cry. "*Pull . . . pull . . . pull!*"

The Emperor chokes and chokes. Enough time passes to kill a man, but still he won't lose consciousness. We are panicking and confused.

"The slipknot is wrong!" cries Concubine Melodious Songbird. "He is still able to breathe. We must tie it again. Quick!"

But it's too late. Heavy boots stampede across the Great Within, and the door of the Leopard Room bursts open. Troops of armoured Imperial Guards charge in with spears.

Pandemonium. Shrieking terror and wails of dismay. Some concubines scatter by the instinct of flight to the peripheries of the chamber. Others weep piteously in each other's arms. Enraged that the Emperor of Knives has escaped death, I pull a silver hairpin out of the hair spiralled up on my head and stab it in Emperor Jiajing's wildly staring left eye. Blood spurts out and I smile. The Imperial Guards then drag me from the bed and slash through the fetters that lash Emperor Jiajing to the bedposts. They remove the gag from his mouth, and the Son of Heaven, more mortal than divinity, lets out a howl of agony.

They destroy us as the God of Thunder smashes tofu. They blacken our eyes, shatter our ribs and stave our skulls against the vermilion pillars. They beat us nearly to death, then haul our limp, insensible bodies out of the Leopard Room. As they drag me through the courtyard of the Palace of Heavenly Purity, my haze of excruciating pain parts long enough for me to see the saboteurs of our murder plot watching by the marble wall. Hunchback Guo and his mistress in a shawl of winter mink. Imperial Consort Bamboo. Concubine, fifth rank.

XII

On the day of the executions the Forbidden City is lost in opaque fog as the spirits of our ancestresses weave around the sixteen concubines, gathered in the courtyard by the Meridian Gate. Our ancestresses caress us and stroke our hair, soothing in whispers, "You have honoured us. We are proud of you. You will be rewarded in Heaven."

A distinguished crowd attends the executions. Empresses and princes and princesses. Grand secretaries and high-ranking officials in resplendent padded silk robes. Emperor Jiajing, however, has not come. Humiliated by the empty socket of his eye, His Majesty has withdrawn into exile in the Inner Palaces. His Majesty's third wife, Empress Bamboo, attends in his stead. High upon your throne, with the symbols of double happiness emblazoning your robe. What lurks behind your impervious mask, unknown.

The executioner swings his axe, and I weep and shake as each of my sisters is put to death. But when it is my turn to kneel before the blood-sodden chopping block, I am calm. As the axe swoops down through my neck, I do not regret departing this life.

When we are dead and dismembered, the distinguished crowd goes back to their sedan chairs, keen to return to their stove-heated chambers, opium pipes and pots of aromatic teas. Emancipated from our remains, the sisterhood of sixteen rises up too. We soar over the Meridian Gate, where our heads are soon to be exhibited on spikes, and at the Gate of Heavenly Purity, we go our separate ways. My fifteen sisters soar onwards to the Otherworld, and I soar through the Forbidden City in pursuit of you: Empress Bamboo in her palanquin, borne upon the shoulders of gelded men. I pursue you to the Palace of Earthly Tranquillity, and linger in your chamber after your ladies-in-waiting have been dismissed.

You stand before the bronze mirror, admiring the sapphire crown in the dark tresses swept up from your widow's peak. I weave around you in your embroidered robes. I soar through you, again and again, determined to break through the vault of your heart.

"Concubine Bamboo. This is your elder sister, Swallow. Does your conscience pain you? Was it worth betraying us for the crown on your head?"

As you gaze in the mirror, you sense my presence. Your piercingly dark eyes light up as you smile: "It's Empress Bamboo now."

And I soar through you again and again, but your conscience remains as stone.

19

Retaliation

Wang walks through the night, breathing the exhaust fumes from the heavy trucks rumbling by, sending tremors through the asphalt under his feet. He walks by scaffolding and rubble and billboards of adverts promising sex appeal, glamour and success to those who can afford the latest skin-whitening cream or Nokia phone. He walks by mechanical diggers steering around a floodlit pit and men in hard hats crouched by a gas ring outside the workers' barracks, cooking rice. He walks by the neon of a Japanese restaurant, the gate of Tuan Jie Hu Park and a pedicab driver begging a policeman not to confiscate his unlicensed vehicle. Wang walks on, through concrete, traffic and dust. Though he had set out with a strong sense of purpose, by the time he reaches the turning to the Public Security Bureau, his will falters. Better he solve his problems on his own.

Wang follows the ring road south, all the way to the China Central TV Towers. He stops and stares at the broadcasting HQ of Party propaganda and the strange architectural design of the towers leaning into each other, as though half collapsed. The city has changed radically in the decade Wang has been driving a taxi, the monuments to capitalism soaring up. Wang's own growth, in contrast, has been stunted. China may be rising, but he is not.

Walking west to Tiananmen, he passes an entrance to the underground city, dug in the era of Chairman Mao and Soviet nuclear threat, tens of metres deep under his feet. When he was a child, his mother told him about the thousands of workers sent down with pickaxes and shovels to carve out a subterranean city under Beijing. The conscripted diggers were sworn to secrecy and how far the tunnels extend is not known (Shuxiang had said as far as the city of Tianjin). She told him she'd like to live down there one day.

"But won't it be dark?" he asked.

"The darkness down there is no worse than the darkness up here" was Shuxiang's reply.

Perhaps Shuxiang was right, Wang thinks. Perhaps the city above the ground is as dark as the one below. He remembers some of the stories he read that day in the *Beijing Evening News* left by a passenger in his cab. Twenty underage prostitutes arrested in a Shunyi karaoke bar. A cooking-oil-manufacturing company fined for selling "gutter oil" recycled from kitchen drains. A clinically depressed man leaps from the thirtieth floor of a tower block in Fengtai District. A jilted girl breaks into her ex-boyfriend's home, douses herself in gasoline and sets herself alight. There were photos of a mangled car wreck on page three, with a sheet-covered corpse on the tarmac and a crowd taking pictures with their phones.

East of Tiananmen Square, a gigantic digital clock counts down the days, hours and minutes to the Olympic Games. *Civilized Olympics. Harmonious Olympics. One World, One Dream.* The corporate-sponsor logos and slogans are everywhere. Over the past week a patrol of Olympic Security Volunteers has sprung up in Maizidian to monitor the community and report any suspicious activity to the Public Security Bureau. That morning, Wang had seen Granny Ping on a low stool by the bicycle shed, vigilantly watching the comings and goings of the housing compound, with a red *Olympic Security Volunteer* armband strapped over her sleeve. Wang had thought there was something defiant about her squatting posture and ageing body, her sagging breasts and her flaccid upper arms and varicose-veined legs, uncaringly exposed. The widow of a Ministry of Agriculture official, Granny Ping can afford tasteful clothes, but prefers to go to the supermarket in cheap polyester nighties, her perm straggly and uncombed.

"Tell me, Wang Jun," she had called out to him, "are any of Ma Yida's folk visiting from Anhui?"

Wang shook his head. "There's just the three of us, and Echo's two pet turtles."

Granny Ping frowned at him. "*What?*"

"The Olympic Security Volunteers came last Tuesday," Wang said, loud and slow. "They checked our hukou and looked around. There are *no illegals* in Apartment 404."

"There's no reason to take my questions personally," Granny Ping sniffed. "No one is above suspicion when our national security is at stake. Not even the Olympic Security Volunteers themselves."

Wang decided to humour her. "Have you found any threats to national security yet?" he asked.

Granny Ping hesitated, looking Wang up and down. "There are some Uighurs in Building 8 who work in Yabao Market," she said, hushed and low. "*Muslims.* They have residence cards, but they come and go at strange hours . . . And there are two laowai in Building 14 who have Tibetan prayer flags on their walls."

Wang laughed. "Since when were Tibetan prayer flags a crime?"

"Laowai worship the Dalai Lama!" Granny Ping cried. "Who knows what they are plotting? They'll wait until the Olympics to strike, though. They'll wait until the eyes of the world are on Beijing and then make a scene."

Wang thinks of Granny Ping's warning as he walks by Tiananmen Square, closed to the public at night and empty of the camera-clicking tourists following the tour guides with loudspeakers. Wang can't imagine the westerners who ride in his taxi risking arrest and deportation to stage a protest for the Dalai Lama. They are too lazy and content, stuffing themselves with hot pot on Gui Street and chasing Chinese girls in Sanlitun. Any dissent would come from petitioners from out of town, or Beijing residents like him. Ordinary citizens with grievances against the City Administration to vent.

When he reaches Qianmen, Wang has had enough of walking. He can't put off confronting Zeng Yan for any longer. He goes to the bus stand to catch a bus headed east.

Outside the Xinjiang restaurant strings of lights blink on and off above the men drinking, smoking and swearing at the folding tables. Smoke billows from the hole-in-the-wall grill. A cook shakes spices over skewers of lamb and a wok of oil over flames suffuses the air with grease. The cook is watching a portable TV, showing the new National Stadium from various angles. "The steel rods of the lattice are designed like a bird's nest . . ." the voice-over says. "Modern avant-garde architecture with Chinese characteristics . . ." An old man taps cigarette ash in the drain and scoffs, "About as much Chinese characteristics as a donkey turd." Behind the glass of the Heavenly Massage parlour, girls made alluring by the sheen of lipstick and glittering sequined tops drift to and fro in the shadows. No one notices Wang.

The spiralling pole of red, white and blue spins by the barber's door, open during the peak hours of night. Wang lights a Flying Horse cigarette tapped out of a carton left by a fare and stares into the low-rent shop. Zeng Yan, in a white vest and low-slung jeans, leans on the counter and talks with two men. The faded ink of his dragon tattoo bulges slightly on his arm and his hair is swept over one eye. Wu Fei stands over a man whose jaw is slathered with shaving foam and glides a cut-throat razor over his stubble with confident, steady-handed expertise. The customer is relaxed as the steel blade moves up his neck, though Wu Fei could kill him with a flick of his wrist. Zeng's crow's feet deepen as he laughs at one of his friends. Wang grinds his half-smoked cigarette out with his heel.

Though the night is chilly, Wang is perspiring. The canister of lighter fluid sloshes in his pocket and, out of nowhere, a proverb taught to him in elementary school comes back to him: "Control oneself in a moment of anger, avoid a thousand days of sorrow."

Wang pulls Zeng's letter out of his jacket and tosses the pages on the ground. He uncaps the lighter fluid and pours it out. Wang had read the tale of Emperor Jiajing and his concubines when he was a student, in an anthology of Ming Dynasty literature. He is convinced of it. The story had resonated so strongly in his memory. Zeng had stolen the plot and reproduced some of the passages word for word. A plagiarist, through and through.

Wang shakes out the last drops of lighter fluid, then drops the tin. Sniffing the fumes, the men drinking beer outside the Xinjiang restaurant look over at him. "What's he up to?" one of them asks. Wang scrolls through his phone, hits dial and watches as Zeng reaches into his jeans. The phone is brought to his ear.

"*Wei?*"

"I'm outside," Wang says, and hangs up.

Zeng squints at the window, but sees only the light and reflections in the glass. He strides to the door and looks out.

"Wang Jun? What are you doing here? Are you okay?"

Wang bends over, strikes a match and holds it to the flammable letter. The paper ignites and flames rush up. Zeng widens his eyes in the doorway.

"Wang? What are you doing?"

They both stare at the flames consuming the letter, the paper curling at the edges and disintegrating to ash. The canister then catches fire and Wang is forced to take a step back by the rising heat and noxious fumes. He coughs, his eyes reddening.

The fire, though small, has attracted the attention of the hustlers in the alley. Vendors of fake booze and pirated DVDs peer out from where they work. "Madman," mutters the cook at the Xinjiang grill. But the alley is not a place of order and propriety. No one shouts at Wang to stamp the fire out. No one has any of the community spirit or civic virtue the government posters encourage. Wang's fire is a distraction from the monotony of the night. They watch him cough the smoke out of his lungs. They watch to see what happens next.

The flames lower to glowing embers and ash. Zeng leaves the doorway and goes to him.

"Wang Jun," he says, "why don't you come inside? Come and drink a beer with me, and we can talk about what's wrong."

But Wang shakes his head. He kicks at the charred ashes. "I warned you not to send any more letters."

"I didn't," Zeng says.

"One more letter, Zeng," Wang warns, "and I will come back and burn down your shop. One more letter and I will burn down your *life*."

Then Wang steps back. The boy has barged out of the barber's and is waving the long cut-throat razor about. He pushes in front of Zeng, his neck tendons standing out as he slashes the blade. The weapon is no less threatening for the shaving foam stuck to it.

"Get out of here! Get out of here, psycho, and don't come back!"

"Wu Fei!" yells Zeng, grabbing the boy's shoulders. "Get back inside!"

Everyone in the alley is staring at Wang, and if he leaves now, it will look as though Wu Fei has scared him off. But the boy's fury is like the heat of a raging fire, forcing him to retreat. The boy wouldn't hesitate to stab him. He wouldn't hesitate to go to jail to "defend" Zeng Yan. So Wang backs off.

"Remember what I said," he says. Then turns and leaves.

20

Yida

Chauffeur's hat on head, white-gloved hands on the steering wheel, Driver Mao was proud to serve the Communist Party cadres. He was proud to lend a hand in the cadres' messy domestic affairs and drive their clinically depressed wives to the psychiatrist's, their homesick six-year-olds to boarding school and pregnant mistresses to the abortion clinic. One of these mistresses, escorted against her will, was Lin Hong. She had told her stepson about it, the summer they were friends. Lin Hong had wept and spat at Driver Mao, and told him his conscience had been eaten by wolves. And Driver Mao had wiped her saliva from his cheek with a white-gloved hand and calmly said, "I have orders to stay with you until the general anaesthetic. It's my duty." This is how Driver Mao serves the nation and protects the image of the Party. He had no moral calling higher than that.

On the day Wang left the hospital, the same Driver Mao was waiting outside. He drove him to the building in Maizidian where he had grown up and handed him a set of keys. "Do you need assistance with your luggage?" he asked. Wang, who had nothing but a rucksack, said he could manage.

* * *

Wang let himself in and saw that Apartment 404 was its same dark self: the furniture arranged as it was nearly a decade ago, the curtains drawn. He dropped his backpack with a thud, and breathed the stagnant air. He sensed the atmosphere shifting around him to accommodate his human form. Uninhabited for ten years, stillness had reigned over his childhood home.

The bedroom was not the same, though, for every trace of Li Shuxiang had been removed. The hangers in her wardrobe were empty and her hundreds of novels and books of poetry missing from the shelves. Wang's father must have arranged for a recycling collector to clear out her things. He would never dirty his own hands with the task.

In the kitchen, Wang held the tea kettle under the tap and the pipes shuddered as water came through. He put the kettle on the stove, next to the battered wok, and sparked the gas ring. Then he stared out of the window, watching the grannies and retired Ministry of Agriculture cadres in the yard as the water came to a boil. He recognized some faces from ten years ago, and the familiarity both comforted Wang and filled him with despair.

The tea kettle was whistling when the key clattered in the front door, the pressured shriek of steam, metal vibrations and rattling door coming together as one. The door slammed and a flamenco stamp of heels came across the cement floor. Lin Hong stood in the kitchen doorway, wearing large sunglasses and a cocktail dress like a throwback from her eighties hostessing days. Her perfume was so overpowering, Wang thought the only explanation for it was that it was sprayed on as a weapon, meant to asphyxiate him. She did not smile at her stepson, or remove her sunglasses. "You're back then," she said.

Lin Hong put a shopping bag on the table and pulled out a bottle of Great Wall red wine, paper cups and a Styrofoam box of noodles.

"Lunch," she said. "Your father cannot come to see you today. He has important meetings all day. He sends his regards."

Hungry, Wang sat at the table to eat, and Lin Hong removed

a corkscrew from her leather bag, uncorked the wine bottle and tipped some into a paper cup. Now that he was closer to her, Wang saw that Lin Hong had been meddling with her face, bleaching her skin and injecting collagen in her lips. She lifted her cup.

"To your freedom! *Ganbei!*"

Lin Hong knocked the wine back, then reached for the bottle and poured a refill. Sipping on her second cup, she watched from behind her sunglasses as her stepson opened the Styrofoam container and dug into the noodles stir-fried with green pepper and pork.

"Tell me about the lunatics," she said. "Do they bark like dogs? Do they think they are Mao Zedong?"

"No," said Wang.

Many are more sane than you, he thought. Lin Hong smiled, and asked more questions. What caused his breakdown? Academic pressures? Dumped by a lover? Or was it hereditary, from his crazy mother? Wang stuffed noodles into his mouth with his chopsticks and did not reply.

"We heard from Dr. Fu that you had a little friend in the hospital." Wang looked warily up. Behind her dark glasses, Lin Hong's eyes were glittering. "Now it all makes sense. You were so *strange* as a teenager," she laughed. "I knew something wasn't right."

"Dr. Fu doesn't know what he is talking about," Wang said.

Lin Hong smirked. "Frankly, I find it disgusting. Most normal people do."

Wang's cheeks burned. He pushed his noodles away and mentally willed her to go. Lin Hong reached into her leather bag and pulled out some forms, stapled at the corner. She tossed them over to him.

"Registration forms. Your father met with the head of your history department last week. They are going to let you repeat your final year. You can go and register in August."

"I don't want to repeat my final year," Wang said. "I'm not going back."

His stepmother laughed. "Not going back? What will you do instead? You can't stay here. Your father wants to give up the lease."

"I will find a job," Wang said.

Lin Hong shook her head, her sleek bob shimmering. "Your father will be furious. He wined and dined the head of the history department for you. Not to mention the other expenses the arrangement incurred."

"I don't care," Wang said. "Going back to university is not what I want."

Lin Hong shrugged again. Whether or not her stepson got a degree was of no concern to her. She gathered up her bag, and said she had an appointment. "Do you have any money?" she asked.

Wang looked away and said nothing. "Of course not," she smiled, and flung some 100-RMB notes on the table.

Not looking at the money but at his stepmother's dark glasses, Wang asked suddenly, "Why the sunglasses, Lin Hong?"

She removed them, exposing her swollen eyelids and the post-surgery stitches on her widened epicanthus folds. She fixed him with a defiant stare. "Why are you so determined to be a loser, Wang Jun? You could take advantage of being your father's son. You could be successful like him. But instead you prefer to do nothing and be nobody." She slid the sunglasses back over her eyes and walked out, her stilettos clattering like shots fired from a pellet gun.

After she'd gone Wang unlatched the windows and opened them wide on hinges creaking from lack of use. The stench of her perfume had overrun the apartment like a malodorous cat scratching the furniture and pissing everywhere. It bothered him that Lin Hong had a copy of the key. It bothered him that she could come back when she pleased.

Solitude. Long, hot showers. The spaciousness of the double bed. Wang did not take for granted the simple things denied to him in hospital. He chopped vegetables and listened to the local radio station, slow-cooking soups on the hob. He swept and mopped the dust of inhabitation from the floor. The apartment had remained undecorated since the block went up in the seventies, and the walls were drab and needed a coat of paint, so he bought tins of white and painted compulsively for nine hours straight. When he finished he stood back, woozy with fumes, his joints and muscles sore, and admired the whitewashed walls. Wang had the sense that his past was contained within those walls. That his former life with Shuxiang had been absorbed by the concrete and was interred there still, under the coats of white.

On the nights Wang couldn't sleep, he thought of Zeng and masturbated. When he came, his remorse was immediate and his longing to be normal again intense. But he was not normal. He couldn't stop fantasizing about living with Zeng and sharing a bed and the rituals of everyday life. During the day the idea of him and Zeng living together was absurd. But in the hours of darkness it seemed like a chance of happiness he was foolish not to pursue.

To end the sleepless nights Wang set his alarm for six every morning, and dragged himself up when it rang. Groggy, he spread a folding map of Beijing out on the table and circled his forefinger above the districts of the city. Then Wang would bring the finger down on a random place, and that would be his destination for the day. He washed, shaved and dressed and then set out, the map folded in the back pocket of his jeans.

Tens of kilometres per day. Hundreds of kilometres per week. As he roamed across the city thousands of sensory impressions passed through him: the din of traffic, the *put-put* of motorized rickshaws and strange-tasting chemicals in the air. Perceptions that entered his senses fleetingly resided in him, then vanished without a trace. At the end of each day he went home and showered, rinsing the sweat and grime away. He would cook and eat a simple meal, then tumble into bed and fall asleep without a single thought in his head.

It was on the walks across Beijing that he decided to become a taxi driver. To drive to every part of the city and meet people from every walk of life. Wang got a driver's licence and, with his father's string pulling, signed up with a taxi company (vowing he'd never again ask for his help). By the end of the summer he was co-renting a Xiali sedan with another driver and supporting himself with his earnings. The next phase of his life was underway.

*   *   *

The day he met her, the clouds had been congregating since dawn, oppressive and tenebrous and gathering negative charge. Though it was late September, Wang had the windows rolled down and was perspiring as he drove about the city, thirsting for a cold beer. When the city darkened as though in premature dusk, and lightning forked the sky, Wang was relieved. The tension in the atmosphere dissipated as the storm broke loose.

The girl stood near Dongzhimen Subway, conspicuously still as those around her ran for shelter as though bombs were falling out of the sky. The downpour had soaked her to the skin, but she didn't appear to care about catching a cold. Though she hadn't flagged him down, Wang swerved over to her, his windscreen wipers slashing full speed. She pulled the latch of the passenger door and climbed in the front seat, as though his taxi was exactly what she'd been waiting for. The girl was twentyish, the same age as Wang. Her T-shirt and skirt were wringing, but she was unapologetic as her damp shadow seeped across the upholstery. She moved her feet and her canvas shoes squelched.

"Where to?" he asked.

She looked at him dismissively and named a street in the south. Her voice was husky and low, her accent that of someone who'd grown up far from Beijing. Wang pulled away from the kerb.

The wind shook the trees on Dongzhimen Avenue, stripping the branches of leaves. Lightning splintered the sky and water crashed on the windscreen faster than the wipers could clear it away. Wang stole glances at the girl, illuminated by the halogen arcs of streetlights slanting into the car. She was wringing out her hair, both hands squeezing it into a rope that dripped onto her denim-skirted lap. Then she stared straight ahead, biting her lower lip, raindrops studding her nose, her eyelashes in wet spikes. Wang shifted awkwardly in the driver's seat. He had been a driver for three weeks and hoped the girl wouldn't notice his inexperience. He hoped he wouldn't lose his way and have to consult a map.

The girl shivered beside him. A sneeze threw her towards the dashboard, and Wang turned the heater on full. Nervous of her prettiness, he asked her where she was from.

"Anhui," she said. How long had she been in Beijing? "Two years."

"Why were you standing in the rain without an umbrella?" he asked.

"Just because."

Her reticence had nothing to do with shyness, and they lapsed into a silence during which Wang imagined tugging her clinging T-shirt over her head and stroking and fondling her damp breasts.

The rain came down harder. It crashed down on the windscreen as though they were passing under a waterfall. The wiper blades slashed uselessly. Visibility was down to a few metres and Wang could barely see the taillights of the car in front. He held the steering wheel steady and slowed his speed.

"*Fuck!*" cursed the girl. "Drive carefully. Don't crash the fucking car!"

"You can get out here if you want," Wang said.

They were driving through a desolate region of the city, a wasteland of construction sites with industrial cranes and crater lakes of rain and sand. The girl scowled and said nothing else.

Minutes later, Wang pulled up at the street of run-down buildings that was her destination. "Thirty kuai," he said, reading the meter. Then he waited for her to pay the fare and disappear back into the city of twelve million strangers. Good, he thought. He couldn't wait for her to go. Outside, the storm raged on, battering the streets. The girl stared into her lap.

"I don't have any money," she said eventually.

Wang turned to look at her. "Never mind," he said. "You can pay me another time."

His kindness was too much for her, and the girl shuddered with a deep sob. She pressed her hands to her mouth and shook. Wang watched her awkwardly.

"Something bad happen to you today?" he asked.

"They fired me from my job."

"Don't worry. You'll find another job. There are lots of jobs in Beijing."

"I hated it anyway. I worked in the toilets in Dongzhimen Subway Station. Worst job I've done in my life."

Wang laughed, and the girl looked at him properly for the first time.

"You're young to be a taxi driver," she sniffed, wiping her eyes.

Wang shook his head. "I'm old. I'm twenty-two. I have wrinkles around my eyes."

The girl squinted at his face. "So you do," she agreed. "I'll call you lao shifu then."

Then she smiled, but as though her heart was breaking, and Wang knew that she needed saving from more than the rain.

Her name was Ma Yida. "*Yida*," Wang whispered in his head, liking the sound of it. She slapped the table, leaning towards him in a conspiratorial manner.

"Let's get drunk," she suggested. "Let's get so drunk we pass out in the gutter."

The waitress, pen hovering over order pad, narrowed her eyes. Yida's smile was beatific and wide: "Bring us four bottles of Tsingtao!"

Other refugees crowded the restaurant, fleeing the storm to order pots of tea and watch the red lanterns swinging wildly from the awning in the wind. In the kitchen, visible through a hatch in the wall, the chef pulled noodles from strands of dough and dumplings steamed in baskets of woven bamboo. Yida's clothes were drenched. When Wang suggested she dry them, she shrugged. "They'll dry eventually." So Wang offered her his jacket and was relieved when she accepted, covering her see-through wet T-shirt clinging to her bra-cupped breasts. When the beer came, she poured it out carelessly, frothing the glasses up with spilling foam.

"*Ganbei!* To the Beijing Subway Authority!" she cried, holding up her glass.

She knocked it back, then poured another. She wrinkled her nose at Wang's offer of a cigarette, denouncing the brand as "filthy-tasting," then lit one, and over the course of the evening chain-smoked most of the pack. "I'm not hungry," she insisted as Wang ordered. "All I want is to drink enough to fall down drunk." But when the dishes arrived, Yida stuffed herself like a starving peasant. Wang ate a bowl of noodles then lit a cigarette, leaning back in his chair to watch her eating dumplings. The stark fluorescent lighting stripped away the shadowy mystery she'd had in his taxi, exposing the odd pimple, chapped, flaking lips and other imperfections that in no way diminished her looks. She had arresting eyes, mostly brown, but with splinters of jade glinting in her irises. Spirals of curls sprung up about her head as her hair became drier, and Wang wanted to reach out and touch them. When she went for napkins, heads turned in appreciation of her pretty face and bare legs in a short skirt. And though he'd known her for less than two hours, Wang felt a mixture of possessiveness and pride.

When the dishes were empty, Yida put a hand on her stomach and groaned, "I'm stuffed!" Then she lit a cigarette and began to talk. Wang liked the low, husky pitch of her voice. He liked her strong Anhui accent and flawed command of Mandarin. There was a hint of performance in her outpourings, the theatricality of a lonely girl keen to keep her audience captive, now that someone cared enough to listen.

"Girls don't matter as much as boys," she told him. "That's why my parents didn't care that I went so far away. They have my younger brother. Married couples in our village are allowed two if the firstborn is a girl."

She had failed the high school entrance exams—not that her parents could afford to send her anyway.

"They are saving all their money for *his* education," Yida said. "I bought a fake high school certificate once, but never used it. Who needs qualifications anyway? *Eating bitter*—that's the only qualification I need in life."

Ma Yida's first job was in a factory when she was fifteen, attaching plastic blond hair to pink dolls. She moved to Beijing at seventeen. "I sent money home for a year or two, and I used to call them too. But now my family and I are out of touch." She shrugged. "I'll go back there one day. Not now, though. Unfilial, aren't I?"

Yida had worked two years of jobs that native Beijingers don't want to do. She'd been lied to, tricked and exploited, cheated out of her wages and abused. She'd left her job as a lift attendant after spending a night trapped in a lift which had ground to a mechanical halt (the caretaker, to save on the night call-out fee, had waited until the morning to call a repairman). She'd left her job as a waitress when the boss groped her in the storeroom, amongst the rice sacks and aluminium drums of oil.

"I kicked him in the balls," Yida said, stabbing the air with her lit cigarette. "He never fucked with any waitresses ever again."

Wang nodded, not sure whether to believe her. Yida slept on a mattress in a room shared by six migrant workers, all of them from Anhui Province, all of them dirt poor. When it came to workers' rights, they had none at all.

Yida had been a toilet attendant in Dongzhimen Subway Station for six weeks. The toilets were on the underground platform, between the tracks and the trains rumbling north and south. Yida's supervisor was an overweight, overbearing man in his fifties. "All men are equal; everyone has to take a shit" was his motto. It was supposed to make them feel better about the job.

"He hated me on sight. Accused me of having a bad attitude. Tell me, Driver Wang, what kind of attitude would *you* have being around all that pissing and shitting, day in, day out? Every night I go home and stand under the shower for half an hour, but I can't rinse off the filth. That's why I was standing in the rain: to get clean."

Working in the subway, Yida got to know the beggars who worked the circular line tunnelling clockwise and anticlockwise beneath Beijing, shaking their money-collecting tins as they limped through the carriages, frightening commuters with their deformities.

"The cripples. The burnt ones. The blind ones. Some are so

disgusting they made me want to puke. But when you get to know them, they are just like us. Some are mean bastards, of course, but some I get on really well with. Some of them are really funny. You need a sense of humour when your legs are amputated and you are dragging yourself about by your hands."

Her supervisor had seen the beggars hanging about by the hand-washing sinks, chatting with Yida as she mopped the floor. "They smell bad," he told Yida. "They scare the commuters." He warned her that if he saw the beggars loitering by the toilets again, he'd fire her, and Yida hadn't had the heart to tell them to go away.

It was close to midnight when they left the restaurant, the waitresses stacking chairs and sweeping around them. The streets were still after the storm, with only the odd drip of rainwater falling from the branches of trees. They swayed with drunkenness, laughing and splashing each other in puddles. Then they got into Wang's taxi and drove to his apartment in Maizidian, where Yida finally removed her damp clothes and Wang got to run his fingers through her long and tangled curls. The next morning they drove to Yida's place for her things. It took her ten minutes to pack everything she owned into two woven-plastic bags and bring them down to his cab.

Back then, she was a miracle. She moved into his lonely bachelor apartment and her laughter chased out the bad memories and ghosts. She sang along to Faye Wong cassettes, smoked cigarettes and painted her toenails on the bed. She strolled out of the shower wearing nothing but glistening beads of water running down her skin, and it stopped his heart. Yida was not a housewife. She let the dishes pile up in the sink and burnt the pan when cooking rice, covering the stove top with starchy, boiled-over scum. But under her spell of chemicals and lust, Wang couldn't care less. Every night he held her lithe and slender body in his arms, and never once thought of Zeng Yan.

Yida turned her back on the migrant community she had lived amongst. She threw herself at Wang with every molecule of

her being. Wang was her salvation, though she pretended otherwise.

"When you get sick of me, just tell me to go away," she said
breezily. "I'll pack up my things and you'll never see me again. It
will be as if I never even existed. No hard feelings—I *swear*."

Wang didn't believe her for a second. Yida was fooling nobody.
Yida had come to stay.

The first time he took her to meet his father, he was surprised by
how intimidated Yida was by the foyer of his building, with its
doormen, faux-crystal chandeliers and marble floor. In the lift,
on the way up, she was quiet. The wind had blown her curls into
messiness on the walk there, and she frowned in the mirrored lift
walls, combing them through with her fingers.

"I wish I'd brought a hairbrush," she fretted.

"Don't worry," said Wang. "They're idiots. You'll see. Once we
get what we want out of him, we'll get out of here."

The maid answered the door, and they exchanged their shoes
for guest slippers and padded down the lushly carpeted hall.
Glamour photos of Lin Hong, taken at a professional portrait studio, decorated the walls. There was Lin Hong posing as a thirties
Shanghai movie star in a silk qipao. Lin Hong swinging a lasso
as a cowgirl in jeans and gingham blouse. Lin Hong as a high-
kicking showgirl, with feathers in her hair. Wang had to stifle
his laughter at this photographic vanity project, which seemed to
offer a glimpse into his stepmother's fantasy lives.

Bright lamps banished the wintry gloom from the dining room
as Wang's father and Lin Hong sat at the table, chopsticks dip-
ping Cantonese dim sum in saucers of sauce. They both looked up
when Wang and his new girlfriend entered the room.

"Driver Wang!" father greeted son. "Come in. Sit! Eat! Introduce us to your new friend."

Seats were taken, introductions were made. Wang Hu asked
Yida where she was from, then spoke nostalgically of trips to
Anhui, with a charm and eloquence he never used with his wife
or son. Lin Hong sipped tea and watched her husband flirting

with the girl. Lin Hong knew she was superior to the Anhui girl in many ways. The girl had bronze skin and wiry curly hair and was swamped in a baggy jumper borrowed from her stepson. In contrast, Lin Hong's skin was flawless with Estée Lauder foundation, her hair sleek and her elegant cashmere sweater dress clung in all the right places. But the girl was twenty, and Lin Hong was thirty-two. And even if she sat in the beautician's round the clock, Lin Hong would never be twenty again. She picked up a prawn dumpling with her chopsticks and put it on Yida's plate.

"Please eat!" she smiled. "We ordered these dumplings from the finest dim-sum restaurant in Beijing. Wang Jun could never afford to take you there on his taxi driver's salary. Eat as much of this as you can!"

Yida smiled uncertainly and thanked Lin Hong. Wang Hu bit into an egg-custard tart. The pastry flaked and custard oozed down his chin.

"How's the taxi driving going?" he asked his son.

"Fine," said Wang.

In reality, the twelve-hour days behind the wheel were stressful and exhausting, and the romanticism Wang had attached to the profession was fading fast. But he kept this from his father.

"How's the salary? Earning enough?"

"We get by."

"How much are you earning per month exactly? One thousand five hundred? Two thousand?"

"We get by."

"*We get by*," mimicked his father. "*We get by*. I would never have sent you to such an expensive boarding school if I'd known you were going to end up as an urban peasant and *get by*."

Wang shrugged. Love had inoculated him against his father's jibes. "Actually, we came to tell you some news," he said. His eyes met Yida's and a smile broke across her face. "Yida and I are getting married."

Wang Hu took the news in his stride. He bared his tobacco-stained teeth in a wide and magnanimous grin.

"Congratulations! You are a lucky man!" Then he smiled at Yida and joked, "Are you sure about marrying my son? Driving a taxi is hardly the Iron Rice Bowl, is it?"

Lin Hong's tight smile did nothing to conceal her dismay. What poor taste Wang Jun had. The Anhui girl was pretty, she had to concede, but that was all she had going for her. It wouldn't last. She could just tell.

"This calls for a toast!" she said. "Let's open a bottle of champagne!" She shouted some instructions to the maid, and Wang cleared his throat, dreading what he had to ask next.

"Ba . . . we need some help with Yida's hukou," he said. "Do you know some people who can help us?"

His father smiled and, to Wang's relief, assured them he would take care of it first thing Monday morning. The maid came in with a bottle of chilled, imported sparkling white wine and poured it into narrow, long-stemmed glasses. They raised their drinks.

"To your future happiness," said Wang Hu.

Lin Hong knocked back her glass. As soon as the alcohol was inside her, diffusing into her bloodstream, her mood lifted.

"Do you have a job?" she asked Yida, careful not to afford her the dignity of calling her by her name.

"I am looking for one," Yida said.

"Maybe they need cleaners or toilet attendants in this building. Shall I ask?"

"That's okay. I can look myself."

Yida met Lin Hong's eyes with a steady, level gaze. Wang Hu grinned and raised his glass again.

"To my beautiful new daughter-in-law. May she find employment soon!"

Lin Hong glared at her husband and his open show of lust. Noticing his stepmother's foul mood, Wang began to plan their exit. Now that his father had agreed to help with Yida's residence papers, there was no reason to stay.

"Why don't you look for a job in a karaoke parlour?" Lin Hong said to Yida. "The Lucky Eight Club or the Executive Club?"

Yida stared at her plate, her cheeks turning red, and Wang Hu chuckled. Both clubs were notorious for whisky-soused businessmen and prostitutes. He knew them well. Lin Hong's eyes gleamed. She reeled off the names of some more brothels, and Wang Jun looked at her sharply.

"That's enough, Lin Hong!" he said.

Lin Hong widened her eyes at him.

"Why are you so upset? If she doesn't have a high school diploma, then she can't be too fussy . . ."

Yida pushed her chair back and stood up.

"Wang Jun told me about your past," she said to Lin Hong, "and I'd rather be poor than spread my legs for officials the way you used to. Just because I didn't graduate from high school doesn't mean I have to become a whore!"

Then she turned and stormed out. Wang Hu laughed and clapped his hands.

"You've picked a fiery one!" he called after his son, now chasing after Yida. "Your marriage is going to be interesting, that's for sure!"

Lin Hong sat in her chair. Ten years ago she'd have chased after the girl. Ten years ago she'd have fought her and scratched out her eyes. But Lin Hong wasn't as tough as she used to be, and her loss of nerve dismayed her as much as her loss of youth. The front door slammed, and Lin Hong turned to her husband.

"You should have seen how pathetic you looked! A wrinkled old man like you, lusting after his son's girlfriend."

Before she could finish, Wang Hu leant across the table and slapped her. He slapped her with a look of boredom and irritation, as though swatting a fly, or a minor pest he wanted to silence. Then he stood up and turned away from his wife's tedious melodrama, the wounded look in her eyes, the hand clasped to her cheek. He walked out of the dining room, yawning as he headed to the bedroom to sleep off his lunch.

Out in the street, they were laughing so hard they couldn't stand. Wang had a painful stitch in his side, and Yida's eyes streamed with tears. "I think I just peed myself," she sobbed, making them laugh even harder. They started walking in the direction of Maizidian but didn't get far before recalling Lin Hong's shock and collapsing into laughter again.

"I warned you they were idiots, didn't I?" said Wang. He pulled her close, his laughter dying down as he cupped her cold face between his hands. "Let's get married tomorrow. I don't want to wait any longer. I want you to be my wife."

21

The Sixth Letter

Where were you when it happened, Driver Wang? I was in my room, feeding words into the whirring machine. My blood sang with the force of it, and equilibrium wavered in my inner ears. Thinking the disturbance was physiological, I spread my hands on the table and took a breath. Then I saw the water swaying in the glass on the window ledge and realized it was not coming from within. When everything became still again, I put on my coat and went out. I walked to a nearby electronics shop, where the sales assistants were crowded around a TV, watching the breaking news.

Though we now live in rational, scientific times, the earthquake has revived my old superstitious beliefs in the seismic condemnation of the gods. But who has invoked their wrath this time? The Great, Glorious and Correct Communist Party? Or the citizens of the People's Republic themselves? The darkness and corruption is everywhere, at every level of society. Greed is the beating heart of our people, and morality is overruled by the worship of money. Anyone can be bought and sold, Driver Wang. Even your own wife.

How well do you know her, Driver Wang? How well do you know the woman you sleep beside every night? What I am about to relate to you is no exaggeration of events. The findings of my investigation into who she really is, an exposé of her disturbed mind.

I requested her by number at the reception of the Dragonfly Massage. The receptionist informed me that she was with a customer. The session would be over in forty-five minutes. Would I mind waiting? Driver Wang, I did not mind.

Poverty. Ill health. Someone on society's lowest rung. I know what Yida saw through her judgemental eyes. She saw no reason to be polite as she led me down the hall. But, inside the private room, I withdrew the pile of banknotes from my pocket and put it on the massage table, and her opinion of me changed. Yida stared at the money. Sixty portraits of the late dictator Chairman Mao, each worth one hundred yuan. Her nose twitched at the scent of ink and the mechanical processing of ATMs. Her eyes were no longer so dismissive.

"Six thousand yuan," I said.

"What do you want?"

"For you to strip," I said. "I only want to look. Not to touch."

"I'm going to call my boss," Yida threatened.

We waited. She didn't call her boss. Yida is no stranger to propositions. Half of her income comes from arrangements such as these. She peeled her eyes from the six thousand yuan and narrowed them in scrutiny of me. I didn't have the appearance of someone with money to throw about.

"Who are you?" she asked.

"No one of any importance," I said. "Do you want the money or not?"

She stared at it. "You only want to look?" she asked.

I nodded. Her mind was whirring. Calculating risk.

"I want the money in advance."

Stud buttons popped open. White uniform dropped to the floor. She reached back and unclasped her bra. Her thumbs hooked the elastic of her knickers and slid them down her legs. Cuffing her ankles before she kicked them off.

"On the table," I said.

She obeyed. Bare buttocks on white sheets. Yida didn't round her shoulders and hug her knees to her chest as any modest woman would. She arched her back as though posing for a pornographic shoot. She parted her lips and slit her eyes like a cat basking in the sun. She opened her legs, exhibiting the hole into which you plunge at night, stabbing blindly, sinking your hopelessness and despair.

Turned on by her own exhibitionism, your wife's posing became more and more explicit. She crouched on her hands and knees so her breasts hung like udders. Then she crawled to me, licking her lips with her pink, obscene tongue. She performed in this way, writhing and exposing her private parts, for several minutes. I watched her degrading herself until I could stand no more.

"That's enough," I said. "Get dressed."

Cold water thrown on her arousal, Yida was disappointed. But she had earned six thousand kuai for less than ten minutes' work. She'd nothing to complain about. Your wife reached for her bra, and I turned from the pathetic sight of her pulling the straps over her arms and covering her breasts. Six thousand yuan poorer, I turned and left without a word. I had proven what I had set out to prove. That Yida is disloyal. That Yida will betray you for a few thousand yuan. That your marriage is a sham.

You long for transcendence, Driver Wang. You long to escape the meaninglessness of your life. But first you must break free of the human bondage holding you down. For as the findings of my investigation have shown, these bonds are worthless.

22

Sirens

The passengers are from Henan. A man and wife, and a baby wrapped in a shawl. Recent arrivals at Beijing Railway Station, smelling of long train journeys in cheap, hard seats, sour milk and baby vomit. The woman cradles the squalling baby as her husband anxiously watches the fare on the meter rise, and Wang knows that, limited by poverty, they usually avoid taxis and struggle onto crowded buses, rousing the antipathy of Beijingers as they block the aisle with heavy bags. The baby is sickly and grizzles all the way to their destination, a run-down block in the south, where the man counts out the fare in one-yuan notes and coins, warm and sticky from being squeezed in his fist. He looks so wretched and pained to part with the money that Wang hands it back, telling him to buy medicine for the baby instead. He accepts the husband and wife's thanks, then watches them struggle away with their bags, relieved their stifling human misery is out of his cab.

Urgent. Come home now. The message comes as he is driving away. Wang calls her in confusion. Listens as her phone rings and rings. Yida should be home. She has every other Monday off from Dragonfly Massage and spends the day lazing about, watching Korean soaps. Wang hangs up and steers his taxi in the direction of Maizidian, worrying that Echo has had an accident. He

236

wonders if Yida's parents are ill or dying in Anhui. Yida has been estranged from her parents for years, and Wang has never met his mother- or father-in-law, nor Echo her grandparents. What impact their death would have on his wife, Wang has no idea.

The TV flickers in the shadows of the living room. Coffee cups and bowls, peeled eggshells and the walnuts Yida feeds Echo to improve her grades (persuaded by the superstition that they nourish the brain, because they are the same wrinkled, hemispherical shape) clutter the table from that morning's breakfast. There's earthquake coverage on TV. A child's limp hand in the rubble of a collapsed building. People's Liberation Army rescue workers heaving at the concrete slab trapping the child to a soundtrack of pulse beats that reminds Wang of the clock ticking on a game show. Then an orchestral swell as the child is freed. Dusty and semi-conscious, his legs bloody and mangled, a stretcher bearing him away. The clip is a week old and Wang has seen it before. He wants to know what has become of the boy. Has he recovered? Can he use his legs? But the story ends here.

"Yida?" he calls.

Silence. He goes into the bedroom to look for her. Disorder is the natural state of the room, and a second or two passes before Wang sees the chaos is worse than usual. The mattress has been flipped up, the wardrobe doors are open and Wang's shirts dragged from the wire hangers like guilty suspects and dumped in a heap. The underwear drawer has been capsized, and Wang's boxers, machine-washed to a shade of grey, cast out. Even his trouser pockets have been turned inside out, receipts and coins scattered on the rug.

"Yida!" he shouts.

Wang goes back to the living room. The laptop is still there, and Yida's handbag and wallet are on the chair. Nothing seems to have been stolen. He calls her phone again. Listens to it ring and ring. Celebrities on TV are asking for donations for an earthquake relief fund. The men are grave as they request that viewers call the hotline. The female performers are quivering and emotional. A songstress wipes her tears with pink acrylic fingernails. Wang hangs up.

He is debating whether to call the police when the sirens start wailing outside. The sirens rend the skies with a loudness that can only signal disaster—a fire, or flood or air-raid attack. Wang rushes to the window. Then he remembers the national mourning for Sichuan, and the three-minute "silence" scheduled one week to the minute after the earthquake struck.

The television screen has gone black as sirens call the nation to a halt. Workers gather outside every office and factory, hospital and bank. Teachers and students gather in the grounds of every university and school. Out in the yard, the security guards and residents stand by the gate to the Maizidian community, heads bowed, the guards with caps in hand. Out in the streets the traffic has stopped and drivers are pushing down on their horns, producing a fog of noise, like lowing herds of mechanical cows. The sirens are inescapable, and Wang stands by the window as though paralysed by the waves of sound.

When the sirens cease, the blackness of the TV screen brightens to a live broadcast of crowds in Tiananmen Square. Thousands of citizens stand facing the portrait of Chairman Mao on the Gate of Heavenly Peace, shouting, "*Zhongguo Jiayou! Go, China! Brave and strong!*" Thousands of citizens, grim-faced with defiance and national pride, punch their clenched fists to the sky as they chant. Wang watches the crowds for a moment, then reaches for the remote and switches the TV off.

Click click. Click click. Wang's head turns at the sound of the stove—the rings sparking to ignite the hissing gas. He goes to the kitchen, where Yida stands by the cooker, lighting one of his cigarettes from the ring of flames.

"Yida! Why didn't you say you were here?"

Yida stares at him from beneath the wildness of her hair. She is bare-legged, in an old, holey T-shirt, and her eyes are swollen and red. She takes a drag on the cigarette and, out of practice, coughs on the smoke. Yida quit smoking years ago and has been nagging her twenty-a-day husband to do the same.

"I got your message," Wang says. "What's happened? Why is the bedroom turned over like that?"

"Who are you?"

Yida asks the question slowly, cigarette smoke casting a veil over her face, a penetrating look in her eyes. Wang is confused. Yida is not in the habit of asking strange philosophical questions. *Where are the keys? Have you charged the electricity card?* These are the questions Yida asks.

"What do you mean, who am I?" he asks.

Yida glares at her husband. She grabs her mobile phone from the counter and throws it at him, hard. Wang catches the phone, fumbling as it nearly slips through his fingers. On the screen is a digital photograph, the resolution low and grainy. Wang squints to make sense of the pixels and, when he does, his insides lurch as though in a suddenly braking car. The photo is of two men side by side on a narrow bed, smoking and gazing at the ceiling as they lie on their backs.

"Who sent this?" he croaks.

Yida exhales from her cigarette and watches Wang squirm through the haze.

"I don't know who sent it," she says. "There's one more."

Wang scrolls to the next message, sick with dread. This time they are sitting on the bed, with Zeng's head inclined towards him. Wang checks the inbox. No more photos. Yet. Not that it matters. Wang looks at Yida and knows the damage has been done. She stands behind her fortress of smoke as though composed, but he knows she is fighting back tears.

"Are you sleeping with that man?" she asks.

"No!"

"Who is he?"

"His name is Zeng Yan."

"Your friend from the hospital?"

"Yes. I ran into him in the street the other day. He said he worked in a salon nearby and offered me a free haircut. So I went with him and he cut my hair. I'd slept badly the night before and was nodding off in the chair. So Zeng Yan said I could take a nap in his back room before going back to my taxi—"

"You expect me to believe this pack of lies?" Yida interrupts. "Don't pretend you didn't know it was a place men go to have sex with other men! Not even you are that stupid, Wang!"

"Look," Wang says, "I was tired and not thinking straight. I trusted this guy; I thought he was my friend. I lay down for a nap and woke up ten minutes later to find him next to me on the bed. I pushed him away, and then I got out of there as fast as I could . . ."

Wang hears his desperate, wheedling tone and knows Yida is not convinced. Sure enough, her stare remains cynical and hard.

"You don't look in any hurry to get out of there in that photo," she says. "You look very comfortable to me."

"Oh, come on! I bumped into an old friend, and made a stupid mistake," Wang says. "The thought of being with a man makes me physically *sick*. Yida, you have to trust me on this . . ."

"Trust you?"

Yida stubs her cigarette out on the window ledge. In her agitation she has flicked ash everywhere, on her T-shirt, on her bare feet and the kitchen floor—an offence she would rebuke her husband for. Her eyes darken, and she nods at a cardboard box on the counter.

"I've been reading your letters."

Wang had been so distracted by Yida and the photos, he hadn't noticed the box. He'd hidden it in the suitcase on top of the wardrobe—the suitcase they never use, because they never go anywhere. He thought the letters would be safe there. He'd never expected that Yida would one day turn the bedroom over. Yida grabs some loose papers, her hands trembling as she reads aloud:

"'Yida is a woman who stirs up in men the animal instinct to fuck and procreate. Tempting men as spoiled fruit tempts flies. But sleeping with Yida must be a sad and lonely experience . . . The thought of you with your wife repulses me too.'"

She chokes back a sob in her throat.

"They are from Zeng . . ." Wang stutters, thinking how odd it is to hear the letter read out in Yida's voice. "I meant to tell you about them, but I didn't know how to explain. They are harmless, I think . . . just strange."

Tears slide down Yida's cheeks.

"You think you are so much cleverer than me, don't you, Wang Jun?" she says. "Because you went to university and I dropped out of school at fifteen. Because you are the son of an official, and I am the daughter of peasants from the countryside."

Wang shakes his head and mumbles weakly, "*No.*" But what she says is true.

"But I am not so stupid that I don't know you wrote these let-ters *yourself,*" Yida cries. "This is what you do at night, isn't it? When you stay up late and don't come to bed. You are writing these crazy stories on the computer . . . writing nasty things about your wife!"

She crumples the letter up and throws it at Wang. The balled-up paper bounces from his chest.

"Yida, I swear I never wrote those letters," Wang protests. "Zeng Yan wrote them . . ."

Yida rubs her eyes, and for a moment looks as young and vul-nerable as when he first met her during the storm, and it pierces Wang's heart. He wants to go to her and put his arms around her—something he once did without a second thought. But now he hesitates, as he would before scaling a hazardous barbed-wire fence. He steps towards her, and Yida steps back.

"*Don't!*" she warns. "Don't come near me! Why did you marry me if you think so little of me? What does that say about *you,* Wang Jun?"

Wang shakes his head. He starts to tell her, No, he does re-spect her. Then stops as Yida snatches the cardboard box from the counter and hugs it to her chest.

"I am throwing these away!" she says.

"You can't!" Wang says. "They aren't yours!"

Wang lunges for the box as Yida spins to the window and leans over the ledge, holding the letters out over the yard below.

"Don't!" he yells.

But she lets go, and Wang reaches the ledge in time to see the lid come off and the letters tumble out into the car park four floors below. He turns back to his wife and shouts, "What have you done?"

Yida stares at her outraged husband. She bites her lip, eyes wide with the fear that she has gone too far. Then she bursts into giggles.

"Quick! Run down and fetch your precious stories, Wang Jun!" she says. "Hurry! Before Granny Ping reads them! Before the wind blows them away!"

Wang turns to go down and do exactly as she suggests. But Yida calls after him, stopping him in his tracks.

"Lin Hong warned me about you! Before we got married she came to see me, and warned me that you liked men. I thought she was making trouble, and I didn't listen to her. But now I wish I had. I hate to think of all the men you've been with behind my back over the years . . ."

Wang strides over to her. "Well, don't you offer *special services* to your customers at the Heavenly Massage? Didn't Zeng Yan pay you six thousand yuan to strip for him the other day?"

Yida gasps. "Wang, have you lost your mind? I don't work at the Heavenly Massage. And I've never met Zeng Yan in my life. What are you talking about?"

"You know *exactly* what I am talking about."

Wang hadn't believed the letter at first. He had thought the "exposé" of Yida was an imaginary scenario straight out of Zeng's perverted mind. But Wang now looks at Yida, gaping at him, lost for words, and knows the letter was telling the truth. Yida had stripped for Zeng. Not for the money, but to make a fool of him. To prove he didn't own her.

"You've been screwing your customers for years! You think you can hide it from me, but I've always known what you've been up to!"

Blood rushes to Yida's head as she leans towards him. She stabs her finger at the door and shouts, "Get out of my home! Get out! You're fucking crazy!"

Wang sets her straight. "It's not your home. It's mine. I brought you here off the streets, remember?"

Sobbing, Yida shoves him with both hands, pushing him out of the kitchen. But Wang won't be thrown out of his own home. He grabs Yida's shoulders and shakes her hard, with more strength than he knew he had. As he shakes her and shakes her, a strange thing happens. He somehow detaches from his body and hovers above them, watching him shaking Yida until she stops screaming, until she stops fighting him off and goes limp and insensible as a rag doll. When he stops shaking her, after a minute or two, his wife is silent. She stares at Wang as though she had glimpsed something nightmarish in his eyes.

"Who are you?" Yida whispers.

Wang smells the cigarette smoke on her breath. Even through his rage, he can still see how beautiful his wife is, desirable to any man. He takes her head in his hands and kisses her hard on the mouth, feeling her teeth beneath her lips. He knows he is hurting her, that later he will regret being so aggressive. But he takes her slack wrist and pulls her out of the kitchen. He is sick and tired of the dishonesty in their marriage; the time has finally come to show Yida who he really is.

23

Ah Qin and the Sea
Qing Dynasty, 1836

I

Slumbering beast. Yellow slit of eye. Slobbering on the cobbles of Hog Lane, as though gnashed up in the jaws of the Sea Daemon and spewed out. Hairy-knuckled hand, sleep-scratching the crotch-rot between his legs. Yellow matted hair like trampled straw. He should have been set ablaze, he was so crawling with filth and disease.

It was the hour of the ram and Hog Lane was empty. No pole-carrying porters, tinkers, rat catchers or peep-show men. Only toothless Ah Ling under the bamboo awning of his junk shop, whose sly grin said, "Go on, boy, fleece the barbarian!" Jack's Ale Tavern was rowdy with the beast's shipmates, who'd swagger out later with bladders full of firewater, looking for a whorehouse or a brawl. But first, the drinking had to be done.

I was a young boy then, and scared out of my wits. I crept over to the slobbering beast and whispered in Ghost People tongue, "Mister? How do you do, old boy?" The beast slumbered on. His breath stank of firewater—alcohol and tobacco juice, with a dash of arsenic, and something viler, as though a rat from the ship's hold had crawled into his guts to die. My hand shook as I reached for the coin purse in the barbarian's pocket. Blood crashed in my ears, and I was so intent on my thieving I didn't see one of his shipmates staggering out of the tavern.

"*Oi!*"

He shackled my wrist with his hairy hand and hauled me up so I was staring right into his snarling face, breath of firewater stinging my eyes. Coins jingled out of the stolen purse onto the ground as he walloped my backside like he was beating dust out of a rug. *Whack! Whack! Whack!* More beasts spilled out of the tavern to cheer as I howled. Down the lane, Ah Ling sniggered on his stool.

"Mister! Let me go!" I begged in Ghost People tongue.

I wriggled and kicked out backwards like a donkey with its hind leg and struck something soft. The beast squeaked, let go of my wrist, and I ran off.

I ran up Hog Lane, past the dens of opium smoke and sinful deeds. I ran past the shophouses of Old China Street, and the factories of Thirteen Hong Lane, where flags of other lands fluttered from the flagstaffs. I ran past the warehouses of tea and silk, porcelain and furs, and past a foreign devil squinting through a monocle, inspecting a pocket watch on a chain. Some of the drunken beasts gave chase, but I outran them.

I was running down a narrow alley leading out of Fanqui Town when I looked back at the herd lumbering behind. The next thing I knew I'd barrelled straight into one of the sailors. He grabbed me and twisted my arms behind my back, as the rest of the beasts, furnace red and out of breath from the chase, caught up. The one I'd kicked between the legs came over. Out of his pocket he took a knife, and flicked out the blade.

"Mister!" I pleaded. "Old boy, please!"

I was done for. A Tanka boy losing his life for kicking a white man—that was fairness in the barbarian's eyes. He leant in close, grabbed a fistful of my hair and brought the blade to my neck. The other beasts crowded round, and their calm was more chilling than the cheers in Hog Lane. I thought of poor Ma Qin in her wash boat, about to lose her only son.

But fate wasn't to have it that way. Fate had you waving your walking cane in the air and shouting at them instead. The sailors looked over at you, limping up the alley. You were odd looking, even by barbarian standards, with your ship's prow of a nose and orange hair and freckles on pale skin. One of those gweilos who even on the hottest days wore a waistcoat over a stiff-collared shirt, long breeches and shiny leather shoes. You hobbled over to us, your cane tapping, lame foot dragging. The sailors, not having much respect for cripples, sneered.

A drunken sailor's a barrel of gunpowder that can explode at the slightest spark, and so you spoke to them carefully. The barbarian with the knife yelled and stabbed the blade at you, but you stood your ground. Though thin and weedy as he was barrel-chested and burly, you had the cleverer tongue. The beast soon flipped the blade away and backed off. One last kick to my backside and they staggered back to the ale taverns of Hog Lane. You watched them go, leaning on your cane and dabbing your brow with a handkerchief.

Though you'd saved my thieving neck, I turned to run as far from Fanqui Town as my legs would carry me, without a word of thanks.

"*Wait!*" Cantonese, with a strong barbarian accent. "Are you hurt?"

I stared at you. Who knew foreign devils could speak? Most sail all the way to the Celestial Kingdom without even knowing how to say hello.

"Stealing is wrong," you scolded. "You shouldn't steal."

Ah, a Jesus Preacher, I thought, edging away. But the sermon ended there. I wanted to run, but something in your green-coloured eyes held me in the alley. You stroked your beard and side-whiskers and looked at me.

"What's your name?"

"Ah Qin."

"I am Ah Tom," you said. Another dab of your brow with the linen in your pale, freckled hand. "You're a Tanka, aren't you? Want to make some honest money? Come with me."

II

"This is the British factory." You pointed your bamboo cane to the sagging flag on the flagpole. "That is the British flag."

Your cane tapping the wooden floor, you led me through the factory, down the hall to the rear. Through one doorway I saw a dining room with silver candlesticks on a long cloth-covered table, and a portrait of the She-Emperor of England on the wall. I saw the Chinese servants, polishing silver things that I knew were called "forks and spoons," though I didn't know which were which. The servants frowned at me, the Tanka boatboy in rags, tagging after Master Tom. They frowned as though they'd seen the glint of thievery in my eyes.

You led me to a chamber of leather-bound books and sat at the desk behind the abacus, ink pot and quills and stuffed the bowl of a long-stemmed pipe with tobacco. A servant boy poured us tea and, puffing on your pipe, you told me you were a bookkeeper for the British factory.

"I am a writer too," you said, "writing a book about the people of China."

In the leather chair by the desk, I was ready to bolt. I hadn't seen a Red-Haired Devil up close before, and I stared at the red bristling from your head and chin. Were those orange freckles a skin disease? Could I catch them? What a hiding Ma Qin would give me if I went back to the wash boat with orange freckles caught off a gweilo. You cleared your throat.

"I want to write about the Tanka," you said, "but, as foreigners aren't allowed in the floating city, I can't find out much. Can you tell me about your people, Ah Qin? What are your customs? How do you marry, for instance? How do you bury your dead?"

Back then, I was ten years old. What did I know about "customs"? What did I know about marrying, or burying the dead? But you dipped your quill in an ink pot and gazed at me, feather poised over the blank page. So I opened my ten-year-old mouth, and this is what came out.

"The Tanka come from the sea," I said. "We were fish people long ago and lived in the ocean. Then we learnt to breathe the air, and walk on legs, and came out of the sea to live on boats . . ."

You nodded and wrote this down.

"Some Tanka are born with fish scales," I went on. "When a Tanka baby is born more fish than Tanka, it is thrown into the Pearl River and swims away to live in the sea."

"*Born with fish scales . . .*" you murmured, your feather spilling ink on the page. "*Swims to live in the sea . . .*"

Where had I heard such strange things? Pa Qin had told me before he died, back when I was small and waddled about the boat with a wooden float strapped to my back. Whether Pa Qin's tales were true or not, I had no idea. But you asked more questions about the Tanka people, and for another hour or so I told you what I could remember of my father's tales. And you listened, and wrote everything down with a seriousness that made me feel very important in that leather chair.

"What about Mazu, Goddess of the Sea and rescuer of ships in distress?" you asked. "Does your boat have a shrine to Mazu? Do you burn joss sticks for her?"

"I know Mazu," I said. "She came to our boat when I was little. She came with her two guards, Ears that Hear the Wind and Eyes that See across the Waves. She came in the night and the ship was bright as day. Ma and Pa didn't wake up."

"Did the Sea Goddess speak to you?" you asked.

I nodded. "She said that one day I would go to sea. Then she went away."

This was no Pa Qin story, but the truth. Ever since I was little, Mazu has been coming to tell me I will go to sea. That the sea is my destiny. You wrote this down, but had no more questions about Mazu. Then the British factory clock chimed five times, and you asked, "Do you have any questions for me, Ah Qin?"

There were many things I wondered about the gweilo. Was it true that your land was ruled by a little girl called Victoria? Were you barbarians bunged up from all the roast beef you eat? Could you smell as well as a dog, with that large nose? But I came over very stump tongued and shy. On your desk was a photo frame. Silver ovals with black-and-white photographs of two foreign she-devils. Seeing what had caught my gaze you smiled. "My wife and daughter."

The she-devils looked like barbarian men in wigs and dresses, but you looked at them fondly. Then you smiled at me. "Ah Qin, can you come back tomorrow and tell me more tales? Hour of the monkey?"

You handed me some coins, and I nodded. Then I ran home from Fanqui Town, my head jangling with the strange happenings of the day.

III

Ma Qin was sitting in our sampan, tangled up in the briny, sea-weedy nets the fishermen brought her to fix. Her nimble fingers picked through the knotted string, fish-scaly and slimy from the day's catch, finding and mending holes. First and Second Daughters were hard at work too, scrubbing up to their elbows in the washtubs. Every morning the Qin family washerwomen rowed up and down the Pearl River, calling up to the crew of junks for clothing to be washed, and by afternoon the bamboo airing racks were spread with cotton for the sun and wind to dry. My ma and sisters hardly ever set foot on the shore. The wash boat was where they did their living, cooking meals on a stove at the back and sleeping under the rattan shelter at night. Ma Qin walked splay footed on land, she was so used to the wobbliness of the waves.

"Ma," I said, "I earned four coppers today."

She squinted up from her fishing nets. "Whose pocket did you pick?" she asked suspiciously.

"I didn't steal it." I scowled. "A Red-Haired Devil called Ah Tom gave it to me. He wanted to know about the Tanka. He says I can go back tomorrow. He'll pay me again."

The boat swayed as Ma threw down her nets and stood up. Tanka womenfolk aren't the bound-footed, painted dolls that Han women are. Tanka women are tough as men, with the strength to row far out to sea and steer a boat through stormy, choppy waters. Ma Qin was a handsome and sturdy woman with braids thick as rope. She was twenty-four, but her knuckles, knobby from the washtubs, looked more than a hundred years old.

"Give me those coins."

I handed them over, and watched miserably as she threw them overboard, so they splashed and sank to the muddy riverbed. The boat then lurched from side to side as Ma Qin threw me over her knee for a spanking. My sisters giggled in the suds.

"Idiot!" she panted. "The foreign devils are our enemies! Pa Qin would be alive today if it weren't for the gweilo and their foreign mud. Now, go over there and don't speak. Betray your family again, and you are off this boat."

She cuffed me one last time, then got back to repairing the fishing nets, muttering, "Aya! Why has Heaven cursed me with such a fool for a son? What did I do to offend thee, Lord Buddha? Barrenness is what I wish for in my next life. Barrenness and blessed childlessness . . ."

IV

I lived with Ma Qin and my sisters in a city of ten thousand boats, swaying at anchor, to and fro. A city that every sweep of tide, or gust of wind, jiggled about. A city so crowded, if you saw it from dry land you'd be tricked into thinking it a forest of rigging and masts.

Those who lived in the walled city of Canton looked down on us low-caste Tanka people, but there was nothing on land that we lacked for on the water. Hawkers of every kind rowed up and down the Pearl River, banging drums and gongs and trading their wares, bone setters and tooth pullers, cobblers and ironmongers, and sellers of pigs and geese. There were school boats and theatre boats, opium barges and floating whorehouses. Up and down the Pearl River they rowed.

The law forbade us Tankas from building a home on the land, but that was no hardship in my mind. Being stuck on the same plot of land day after day—now *that's* hardship. When we wanted a change of scenery we'd thrust a barge pole into the riverbed and glide our boat to somewhere new. We may have been dirt poor and infested with water lice, but any time we wanted we could weigh anchor and sail away.

V

Pa Qin had lived with us on the wash boat before he died. When I was a baby, he worked as a porter in Canton Harbour. Then he saved enough for a duck boat and a hundred ducks and became Duck-Breeder Qin. Every morning he rowed the ducks out to a mudflat island in the Pearl River Bay so they could waddle and peck at the grass. Then every evening he herded the ducks up again and rowed them back to the floating city. Duck-Breeder Qin spent several years in this way, in the restful, mindless company of quacking ducks, earning a living from selling the eggs. He was fond of the ducks, and liked to stroke their feathery down, but he wasn't too fond to wring their necks for the cooking pot when his children's bellies growled.

Then one day the ducks caught a bird sickness and started dying. Pa Qin spent the last of his savings on herbal medicine he forced down their beaks, but he couldn't stop the duck boat becoming a graveyard of corpses with webbed feet. Pa Qin had lost his living. Grieving over this, he went onto an opium barge to drown his sorrows with wine and ended up having his first ever puff on an opium hookah. And it was that first puff, that first clack of teeth on the ivory mouthpiece and burbling of opium smoke through water and into his lungs, that marked the death of my father and the birth of Three Pipes Qin.

I've never had any foreign mud before, so I don't know it first-hand. But once, when he'd had a few pipes, Pa Qin told me what it was like.

"She's like a lover," he murmured, "cradling you in her arms . . . Or a mother . . . protecting you in her womb . . ."

Well, if opium's a lover or a mother, she's the kind hell-bent on destroying you, on tricking you into thinking you've gone to heaven while your body withers away. The fate of most opium smokers is the fate of drowning, and Three Pipes Qin was no exception to this. Every puff of the opium pipe brought him closer to death. But still he wouldn't quit.

Three Pipes Qin made promises, of course, but couldn't bear the fever and chills for more than a day before scurrying back to the opium barges. He stole Ma Qin's earnings from washing and mending. He sold the few sticks of furniture we had on the wash boat, and our cooking pots and stove. Three Pipes Qin wasn't ever sorry, not even when Ma Qin wept and raged. Eventually, at her wits' end, Ma Qin went at him with a boat oar. She chased him off the boat and shouted that he was banned until he was sober. He staggered ashore that night and never returned.

The last time I saw Three Pipes Qin was on Noise of the Tide Street. Scrag and bone, he was shaking his begging bowl at the Manchu-queued commoners. I stooped my head, but he saw me and limped over, rattling his wooden bowl.

"Firstborn son," he said, "spare your old pa some change?"

I handed over what I had. Three Pipes Qin grinned at me and looked so much like a grinning skull I turned and fled.

"Tell your ma that I'm on the mend," he called after me, "and I'll be back on the wash boat soon."

Three Pipes Qin had no pride. He cared for nothing but opium. That night he'd go to one of the floating opium dens and exchange his beggings for the blackened, once-smoked scrapings from a rich man's pipe. Just enough to ease Three Pipes Qin's cravings and allow him a few winks of sleep.

Pa Qin hadn't been lying about coming back to Ma Qin's wash boat, though. The day after I saw him on Noise of the Tide Street, two servants from one of the opium barges brought him in a wheelbarrow to the Qin family boat. They'd dragged him out of the Pearl River after he'd fallen in. Ma Qin checked to make sure the drowned man was the father of her three children. Then she told the servants to take Three Pipes Qin away again.

"Do what you like with him," she said. "He's no husband of mine."

VI

Though Ma Qin had spanked me and warned me not to "betray our family," I still planned to go back to the British factory to see you the next day. You'd saved my throat from being slashed, and I didn't want to break my word. And anyway, how would Ma Qin find out? Like most Tanka washerwomen, she never left the Pearl River.

But returning to Fanqui Town wasn't to be my fate. That night as Ma Qin and my sisters were sleeping, the Goddess of the Sea came and the boat became bright as day. Behind Mazu stood her guards, Ears that Hear the Wind and Eyes that See across the Waves, protecting her from any threat.

"Ah Qin," Mazu said, "your fate is to be at sea, not on land. You will meet that gweilo Ah Tom again one day, but first you must go to sea. The sea, remember, is your destiny."

Then the goddess vanished and the wash boat was in darkness once more. I lay awake for a while, thinking on what the Sea Goddess had said, then drifted back to sleep. Early the next morning I was woken by the sun-and-wind-grizzled Fisherman Po, who'd come by our wash boat. He was in need of a fisherboy, and would Ma Qin offer up her young lad for the job?

So off I went in Fisherman Po's leaky, two-masted fishing boat, to plough the waters and harvest our crop of fish. Just as Mazu had said.

VII

For the next five years I worked as a fisherboy, sailing out to sea at daybreak and sailing back at sundown. Out on the waves, Fisherman Po handed down to me the wisdom of his thirty years of sea fishing. He taught me how to steer the boat on stormy waters, and where to cast the nets out and trawl for the finest catch. He taught me how to spot a pirate junk from far away, and how to pray to the Gods of Wind and Rain to ward off typhoons. I soon became a skilled seafarer, sculling and manning the boat, my sea legs used to the pitch and roll of the roughest waves.

I grew taller, stronger and broader, and had my head shaved and plaited in the Manchu style. I became fond of a cheeky dimpled Tanka girl called Ah Moun, who rowed a sampan up and down the river, selling baskets of fruit. She'd smile and toss me an orange or banana when she passed us by, or splash me with her oar, and when I asked her to marry me, she laughed and said, "About time, Ah Qin. I thought I'd be throwing oranges at you until we were old and grey." We soon had our own boat and within a year her belly swelled with our first child. We had enough money to live on from our fishing and fruit selling, and were happy. By then I was coming up to sixteen years old.

It was around then that war broke out over the foreign mud, and iron-clad British warships, propelled by cartwheels and steam, charged into the Pearl River Bay. Our Emperor's fleet of "avenging dragons" had colourful streamers flying from the masts, and noisy gongs and bells but, lacking proper guns, didn't stand a chance. The thundering of cannons shook the hills surrounding the Pearl River Bay as the British warships blew our Emperor's fleet to bits. Smoky blazes poured forth into the sullen darkness of night, and panicking survivors trod water and clung to the shattered fragments of their blown-up junks.

I prayed to Mazu to protect our men and wreck the British men-o'-war. But I didn't join the Anti-barbarian Army with their pitchforks, scythes and rusty farming tools—useless against the double-barrelled guns of the red-coated barbarians. Why should we low-caste Tankas fight to defend the land we're forbidden to live on? I was soon to be a father, and wasn't going to risk my life.

The cannons were booming when Ah Moun got the pains of labour. Ma Qin came to our boat to help with the delivery (snapping at Ah Moun to "stop your hollering. You aren't the first to push a baby Tanka out of your muckhole."). The labour was very short, and the baby slipped right out. I could tell by Ma Qin's eyes that it hadn't been born right. Ma Qin wasn't the sort to take fright easy, but she turned pale, covered her mouth and said, "Oh, you poor thing." My heart shrinking, I went round to look at my firstborn child, and what I saw sickened me. Our baby had the eyes of a fish, and its legs were welded together like a tail. Our baby son gasped but, like a fish out of water, could not breathe and died.

Ah Moun changed after that, and her dimples went away because she no longer smiled. One day I came home from fishing and she wasn't there. She didn't return to our boat the next night or the next, and I heard from my mother-in-law that she'd gone off to work in a laundry in Macao. Fisherman Po offered to sail us over to Macao so I could "knock some sense into her, and see she behaves like a proper wife." But it didn't seem right to sail to Macao to fetch her back. Ah Moun wasn't the only one who'd had a change of heart.

VIII

Not long after Ah Moun had left, Old Fisherman Po and I were casting our nets out at sea when the sky turned the colour of bruises and a squally wind whipped the waves up to an unruly height. Out of nowhere a pirate junk appeared, and a scrambling dragon of sea bandits came towards us with scurrying oars. As we struggled to sail our boat against the fierce wind and back to Canton, Fisherman Po shouted up to the Heavens, "How have we offended thee, Sea Goddess, for you to visit such calamity upon our boat?" Fishermen Po never failed to burn a joss stick or two at her shrine before setting sail each morning. Truly, it was a mystery.

A boat hook caught the side of us, and the bandits leapt aboard, weaselly eyed and waving cutlasses about. All we had was our basket of wriggling catch, and feeling wronged for having chased us across the waves for such little reward, the sea robbers set fire to our sails. If the bandits had left us then, Fisherman Po and I could have put out the blaze and rowed back to Canton. But they stayed aboard to beat me up. Fiery sails gusting in the wind, they kicked me to the bottom of the boat. Fearing that they'd beat me to death, Fisherman Po shouted, "Leave the boy! There ain't no fairness in six against one."

"Life ain't fair, old man," growled one of the sea robbers.

Then he jerked Fisherman Po's head back by his queue, opened his throat from ear to ear with his blade and shoved him overboard without even looking to see how he fell. Then the sea robber came for me, and I thought, Now I'm done for. I thought of Fishwife Po and Ma Qin. Who'd tell our womenfolk what had become of us?

But the sea robbers didn't kill me. They took me aboard the pirate junk instead.

IX

Sixty men lived aboard the *Scourge of the Celestial Seas*, Tankas who'd turned to banditry after their property had been shipwrecked, fugitive Hakkas who'd withdrawn into the world of pirates to flee punishment for crimes on land and captives from hijacked fishing boats, like me. Chief Yang was the head of the *Scourge*, and then there were the bandits, who drank grog and puffed on opium pipes, threw knives at squealing rats and bet on sparring quails they tormented in cages (so they charged at each other, beaks stabbing to the blood-spattered death when set free). The kidnapped fisherboys were deckhands or galley slaves, hoisting the sails, sculling and manning the fast boats and obeying the bandits' orders. The sea bandits were a barbarous lot and the *Scourge* was rowdy with thrashing fists and spillages of tooth and blood. At night I slept on deck, preferring the wind and rain to the violence of the quarters below. But there were nights I was ordered down to Captain Yang's cabin and had no choice but to go.

I crawled up to the deck after the first time, torn and bleeding inside and out. I leant over the deck rail and heaved my guts up, down the side of the *Scourge*. I wasn't Ah Qin anymore. I was a battered piece of meat, skewered by Yang and his gang. I leant over the railing and stared out at the dark waves roaring and crashing over the depths as the *Scourge* tilted this way and that, days from land. I cursed the Goddess of the Sea for luring me away from Canton to this leaky vessel of brutes.

"My destiny is to be at sea, is it, Mazu? To be prisoner on this ship of thugs? To be raped by Chief Yang and his gang?"

The sea was silent, and I cursed Mazu again. Then I stared out over the dark, tumbling waves, tormented by the urge to leap. Thoughts of Ma Qin and my sisters were the only things that kept me on board. It was my duty as firstborn son to get back to the wash boat, and there was no going back as a drowned man. So I curled up behind a coil of rope, and the waves lapped at the broadside, swaying the filthy cradle of the *Scourge* and sending me into a fitful sleep.

There's a saying about Tanka sea bandits: "A dragon on the water, a maggot on land." Well, Captain Yang was a maggot on the land *and* water. He even looked like a maggot, with his shrunken head and weak, receded chin.

Yang was the grandson of the legendary Cheng I, who had ruled the waves fifty years back with his Red Flag Fleet and amassed a vast fortune from the vessels that trespassed upon "his" waters. In the days of Cheng I, the Red Flag Fleet had over forty ships armed by cannons and guns, and a thousand-strong crew. Half a century later, all that was left of the "fleet" was one ill-rigged, three-masted leaky junk, and Captain Yang had no vast fortune, because he was too scared to chase the merchant clippers for the cargoes of opium and gunpowder casks. Far from conquering the waves, the good ship *Scourge* had conquered only a few defence-less fishing boats.

Chief Yang was nothing but a barnacle clinging to his grandfa-ther's reputation, but he swaggered about in his turban and robes like Emperor of the Sea.

"Come here, slave," he'd order. "On your knees. Open your mouth."

If you were the "slave" he was speaking to, you had better

obey him. You had better go down on your knees and open your maw—*or else*. If you were lucky, he'd just spit in you, and have you swallow the gob of nastiness down. If you were not so lucky, he and his men would have a pissing contest, shooting streams of yellow down your throat. The *Scourge* was a black-hearted ship, and evil the stuff of everyday. Upon sighting a kidnapped Hakka hanging from the mast one early dawn, a noose choking his neck, Turtle Li had smirked, "He'd had too much of a good thing." They'd raped him with a broom handle the night before.

And so a year of my life went by on the *Scourge of the Celestial Seas*. We captives weren't fed much, and I became thin as bones, the strength and bulk of my days of sailing with Fisherman Po wasting away. My teeth loosened and my eyesight dimmed, as though the wickedness I saw on the *Scourge* was slowly turning me blind. Night after night I slept up on the deck, where the sea tempted me with her dark, crashing waves.

"Come to me, Ah Qin," she murmured, slapping the side of the *Scourge*. "Come swim in my depths. All of your suffering will be over in a few watery breaths . . ."

I thought of Ma Qin and my sisters, and that life's a blessing you shouldn't throw away. But the lure of those roaring waves was harder and harder to resist. I prayed to Mazu for strength, but the Sea Goddess had deafened her ears. The Sea Goddess had turned her back on me. So I turned my back on her and became a godless man.

Toughen up or be gnashed up in the jaws of the Sea Daemon. That was my choice. So I hardened my heart into a callus. When other kidnapped fisherboys were beaten and abused, I stopped worrying for them, and thought, Better them than me. When hostages from hijacked fishing boats were brought aboard the *Scourge*, I stood in the crowd and heckled as Yang's men set on them like snarling dogs. I got into the habit of spitting on and slapping about boys younger and weaker than myself. The honest and decent Ah Qin, who'd sailed with Fisherman Po, would have been ashamed of my bullying streak. But that Ah Qin had died a long time ago, leaving only the nasty dregs of me behind. Soon my viciousness was earning approving nods from Captain Yang, and I knew that I'd soon be one of his gang.

But then something happened that proved fate had other things in mind. Something that made me wonder if Mazu hadn't been watching over the *Scourge* all along.

X

"Foreign devils!" Turtle Li hollered. "Foreign devils lost at sea!"

The sea was smooth under a windless sky, unmarred by a ripple or a wave. The clouds hung low, and the air was hazy with saltwater. The sea gypsies on deck rushed to look where Turtle Li was pointing his spyglass. A rowboat was drifting on the water, carrying two gweilo without oars or guns or any means of defence, both slumped as though sleeping. Seven years had gone by since you'd saved my throat from being slashed, but I recognized you at once. One of them's Ah Tom! I thought, Ah Tom of Fanqui Town! What other gweilo had such fiery hair? That large and crooked nose? You and the other barbarian were woken by the racket of the sea bandits, lowering the fast boat into the sea, and you sat up and watched as the scrambling dragon rowed towards you, unable to protect yourselves or row away.

Terror leapt about your face as you were forced at knifepoint aboard the *Scourge*. You had more wrinkles now, and more baldness than hair, but there was no denying you were Ah Tom of Fanqui Town. You were crutchless and limped supported by the other barbarian, who was staring in fright at the seething horde of sea bandits, grinning and making throat-cutting gestures with their cutlasses. Too exhausted to stand, both of you sank to your knees at the stern. What a pitiful sight you were. The sun had blistered your nose and your skin was raw and peeling. Your beard was straggly and your shirt stiffened with sea spray and sweat. The days out at sea had reduced you to a beggar in rags.

Chief Maggot, swaggering about in his turban and robe, ordered cups of water, stagnant and spawning mosquito eggs, to be brought to you from the rain barrels. You and the other barbarian fell on that water, spilling it down your chins as you drank it. Some of the jackals went over and turned out your pockets and pouches onto the deck. Ink quills, a pocket watch, letters bound in red ribbon, a leather Jesus book and barbarian coins. Chief Yang bit one of the coins between his teeth.

"That's a British devil coin!" one of the sea gypsies called.

A loud hissing like water thrown on hot coals went through the crowd. Even the lawless men of the *Scourge* hated the British devils. "Kill 'em! Kill 'em dead!" some of the rabble shouted, and under your sunburn you turned pale. My bowels loosened out of nervousness for you as you spoke: "Thank you for rescuing us, Captain."

Chief Yang nearly leapt out of his skin. "Did that foreign devil just speak?" Chief Maggot cried. He stabbed his finger at you. "Did you just speak?"

"I have lived here for eight years, Captain. I can speak your language."

"What about him? Can he speak too?" Captain Maggot asked, pointing at your friend.

You said that he could not, then went on desperately, "My name is Ah Tom, and my friend is Ah Jack. We are merchants. Three days ago we were rowing to shore from our merchant vessel when we got caught in the storm. We lost our oars in the sea and need help to get back to Wangpo. We will pay you, Captain. We will give you as much money as you want."

Captain Maggot slashed his hand to silence you, then he muttered to one of his jackals, who went down the trapdoor to the galley. As I crouched in the crowd, I wanted to catch your eye, to let you know you had an ally on the *Scourge*. But your gaze skimmed over me, unable to tell me apart from the rest of the nasty, foul-stinking horde. Ah Jack, a handsome man with dark curls, about a decade younger than you, was speaking to you under his breath. Though the sun had scalded you red, he was brown as an Indian.

The jackal came back up through the trapdoor and handed

Captain Maggot some papers. "Who can read?" Maggot yelled, and a galley slave came forwards and said he'd had lessons on a school boat. Captain Maggot handed him the papers, and the boy read them out:

Reward for the capture of barbarians: Those who seize a barbarian steam vessel shall be rewarded six thousand dollars . . . Those who seize an ordinary man-o'-war will receive one thousand dollars per mast . . . Those who seize alive a native-born Englishman shall be rewarded two hundred dollars . . . Those who bring us the cut-off head of an Englishman will receive one hundred dollars.

Under his turban, Chief Yang frowned. "Two hundred dollars?" he muttered. "What miserly bastards the Manchu government are! I ought to ransom them to the British devils."

But to ransom you to the British was to risk one of the She-Emperor's warships coming after the *Scourge*, and, lacking his grandfather's bravery or guns, Captain Maggot turned to his helmsman and asked him to steer towards Canton. You panicked at this. Prison, interrogation and torture. This was the fate of British devils in Canton.

"Captain, if you row us to Wangpo I promise you will be paid twice as much as they will pay you in Canton!" you begged on your knees. "Eight hundred dollars! One thousand dollars! Captain, name your amount, and you shall have it . . ."

Captain Maggot threw a punch at your head, knocking you sideways on the splintery deck. "I don't like speaking gweilos," he told us, shaking out his hand. "If he speaks again, put out his eyes."

XI

Quail cages were brought to the foredeck, the bamboo bars smeared with quail shit and bloody feathers. You and Ah Jack were forced into a cage each, and the doors were latched and knotted with twine. The cages weren't meant for men, and you both sat hunched, your heads crooked and your knees to chests. Captain Yang then went down to his opium-fogged cabin, revelling in the prestige of barbarian captives for the Red Flag Fleet.

As the *Scourge* sailed to Canton under the overcast sky, the sea gypsies crowded around the cages and pestered you. "Ah Tom, you ever done it with a Tanka girl before?" "Ah Tom, you ever been captured by bandits before?" "Ah Tom, you ever heard of the 'Red Flag Fleet'?" The Tankas who'd picked up broken English from labouring in the port of Canton called out, "One! Two! Three! How you do, old boy?" then fell about laughing. They didn't get bored of teasing you and, stuck in your cages, you and Ah Jack just had to put up with it.

Around the hour of the ram, some galley slaves came up with bowls of rice, which you ate with your fingers, spitting out the tooth-cracking stones. Then Pockmark Wan let you out of the cages to stretch your legs and empty your bladders, as Turtle Li aimed a rusty flintlock at your head. Dusk came and the muggy closeness of the day was gusted away by wind. Cramped in his quail cage, Ah Jack bowed his handsome head over his clasped hands and moved his lips in prayer. You did not pray with him, but gazed seaward and skyward at the coming rain.

The night was cold, moonless and dark. Squalls of chilly wind whipped around the deck, and the timbers and mast heads creaked and groaned. Rain pattered down, dimpling the waves, and drummed on the rattan mats thrown over the quail cages. The Gods of Wind and Rain were on our side that night, chasing most of the sea bandits down to the underbelly of the ship. Up on deck the men on watchman's duty shivered around the feeble light of a spluttering oil lamp, huddling under hemp sacks and necking grog vile as bilge water to keep warm. In the quail cages, you and Ah Jack hugged your knees, shivering in your cotton shirts. I watched the watchmen from behind a rain barrel, my teeth chattering in the drizzle. A lazy ship of fools was the *Scourge*, and it wasn't long before the opium-spiked grog knocked them out.

When the last of them, Stinky Fu, was snoring, I sneaked out from behind the barrel. The last waking soul on deck.

The oil lamp had gone out, and the waves lapped the broadside in pitch black. Like a scurrying rat, I went over the deck to your cage and the dark, hunched shape of you.

"Ah Tom," I whispered. "*Shuush*. Quiet. Don't speak."

You woke from your shallow sleep at once. Your eyes opened and your neck bones cricked as you turned to look through the bars of bamboo, crooked hump of nose and straggly beard standing out in the shadows.

"Ah Tom," I whispered, "it's me, Ah Qin. Do you remember me?"

Your night-blind gaze flailed through the dark at me. "Who?"

"Ah Qin. You saved me from the sailors who wanted to cut my throat. Remember?"

I could smell the days lost at sea on you. Barbarian sweat, wrung out of you by the sun and blown stale by the breeze.

"No," you said, "I don't . . ."

But I knew the thieving ten-year-old Ah Qin was somewhere in that head of yours. Your memory needed a prod—that was all.

"I went with you to the British factory," I said, "to your room with the books. I told you about the Tanka people, and Mazu the Sea Goddess . . ."

You stared at me, your eyes straining through the dark. Then remembering crept into your voice.

"I waited for you the next day," you said, "but you didn't come. You were younger then. A child. Now you are . . . *older* . . ."

Older. Uglier. Stinkier. Thin as bones. Not much better than Three Pipes Qin before he drowned. But I had no time to waste grieving for the Ah Qin I used to be.

"I wanted to go back to you," I said, "but Mazu came to say I had to go to sea. So I went to sea with Fisherman Po and was a fisherboy for six years. Then Captain Yang's gang came on our fishing boat, murdered Old Po and brought me aboard the *Scourge*. I'm not a sea robber, but a prisoner like you."

In his cage, Ah Jack whimpered like a dog having a bad dream.

"I'm sorry, Ah Qin," you said.

But not that sorry, I could tell. A Tanka ends up on the *Scourge*—well, that's a pity. British devils like you and Ah Jack end up here, it's a tragedy. But, to tell you the truth, I was sadder for you and Ah Jack too. It cracked the callus of my heart to see you cramped in that cage.

Stinky Fu cursed and coughed in his sleep, and the *Scourge* tilted, the timbers and mast creaking as the Sea Goddess breathed on the back of my neck.

"Listen, Ah Tom," I said. "Mazu put your rowboat in the path of the *Scourge* for a reason."

"And what is that, Ah Qin?"

"You saved my life once before. Now it's my turn to save yours. Mazu has fated it."

There was a long pause from you.

"And how will you do that, Ah Qin?"

"Mazu will tell me when the time comes."

Another pause.

"I see."

Though you hadn't much faith in me, knowing you had an ally on the *Scourge* must've put some ease into your mind, for you leant your head against the bamboo bars and dozed off. I stayed by your cage for a while, worrying over you as you slept, until the Sea Goddess blew on the back of my neck, telling me what to do next.

Down the trapdoor to the galley I went, into the dank, stinking pit of Yang's cabin. Treading carefully so as not to creak the wooden boards, I stepped over Yang and his gang, snoring on rattan mats, my heart going berserk with fear. But the ruffians sleep deepest in the hour before dawn, and they slumbered on as I stole what Mazu told me to and slipped out.

Back on the deck of the *Scourge* I hid what I'd stolen in my robes, and prayed to Mazu to be long gone from the junk before they knew what was missing.

XII

The sun was midway in the sky when you and Ah Jack were let out of the quail cages. The galley slaves brought you bowls of rice, and the sea ruffians crowded round to stare at the gweilos at feeding time. Captain Yang came up in his turban and robes, and spoke to Pockmark Wan. The plan was to row you and Ah Jack to Hermit Crab Cove, then walk you across the mudflats to the authorities in Canton. The patrol boats on the Pearl River were as bad as sea bandits, and would steal the British devils from the Red Flag Fleet and reap the reward for themselves. The four hundred dollars was Captain Maggot's alone.

They needed men to row the scrambling dragon to Hermit Crab Cove, and Pockmark Wan chose oarsmen, pointing at chests. *You. You. You.* I rushed to the fore and thrust my chest in the path of his grime-blackened forefinger. *You.* Though I was not one of the gang, I had been chosen. The Sea Goddess's intervention, no doubt.

When this was settled, Captain Maggot strutted up to you, puffing his chest out to make up for the fact he was several heads shorter, waving his dagger about. He rubbed the cotton of your shirt between his grubby fingers, as though to check that it was up to his high standards, then, gesturing with his dagger, said, "Take off your shirts!" You and Ah Jack looked at each other with panicking eyes. But Yang had a dagger, and not wanting to be stabbed, you unbuttoned your shirts and handed them over to the outstretched hands of his lackeys. Then you stood there, bare-chested before the leering crowd.

"Look how hairy these barbarians are!" Captain Yang smirked. "More like beasts than men!"

Ah Jack's chest was broad and muscular, with whorls of dark hair. You were narrower, pale and freckled, with an overhang of belly. Both of you had more meat on you than any of us Hakkas and Tankas, and you couldn't count your ribs like ours. "Cow's milk bulks them up," one of the sea ruffians noted.

Chief Yang gestured again with his dagger. Off with your belts. Off with your trousers. Off with your boots. He wanted them all. I lowered my head in shame as you unbuckled your belt and slid your trousers down your hairy legs. The sea bandits grinned at the sight of you stripped to your underwear.

"Hairy down to their toes!" they laughed. "Like beasts! Like beasts!"

The sun beat down on the *Scourge* and waves slapped on the broadside, tilting the deck. You stooped and lowered your head, but Ah Jack stood with his chin up, refusing to part with his dignity. Captain Yang grinned at this, then reached to stroke Ah Jack's brown curls. The lecherous look in Maggot's eyes made my guts writhe, for now there was no denying what he wanted. Ah Jack looked murderous, but looks can't defend a man the way weapons can, and there was nothing he could do as Yang stroked his neck.

"Down on your knees," Captain Yang said.

Ah Jack had no understanding of what was being said to him, but you did.

"How much money do you want, Captain?" you cried out desperately. "I swear we will give you any amount you want if you leave him be!"

Chief Yang didn't even look at you. One of Yang's men jerked your head back by your hair to shut you up.

"On your knees," Chief Yang repeated. "Down!"

Yang then slapped Ah Jack and stabbed his blade at the wooden boards. Ah Jack reeled from the slap but stayed on his feet. His stubbornness had the jackals baying for his blood.

"Knock him down! Knock him down! Teach him respect for the Red Flag Fleet!"

Yang's henchmen went over to make Ah Jack kneel. They went to grab him, but Ah Jack shouted and thrashed out his arms, fending them off. "*Don't!*" you shouted. But Ah Jack kept throwing punches at Yang's men, until Chief Maggot moved into the fray and Ah Jack's knuckles struck his jaw, sending him lurching back. It was the first time anyone on the *Scourge* had seen the head of the Red Flag Fleet assaulted, and the sea ruffians' jaws dropped. The deck tilted, as though the *Scourge* itself was reeling in shock, and Chief Maggot roared and stuck his dagger in Ah Jack's guts.

He withdrew the blade and at last Ah Jack obeyed the order to get down, thudding to his knees and slumping on the splintery deck. Your mouth went round, as though you were saying "Oh!" and you clutched your sides as though you had been knifed too. The blood of Ah Jack's wound puddled around him, and parts of him twitched and he blinked as though he had dust in his eyes. Stabbing Ah Jack had lessened Maggot's rage none whatsoever. He touched the swelling at his jaw and yelled, "Get this British devil, bleeding his stinking barbarian blood everywhere, off my ship!" He nodded to the oarsmen chosen to row to Hermit Crab Cove, and waved his bloodstained blade at the taffrail. "Throw him over! Drown him in the sea!"

There's no disobeying orders on the *Scourge*, so we all went over to Ah Jack. He's dying anyway, I told myself. At least drowning will end his agony. We each grabbed one of Ah Jack's limbs and, as we heaved him up, he screamed. Then Turtle Li shouted, "*Wait!* Don't throw him yet! The head of an Englishman is worth a hundred dollars!"

Chief Yang looked startled. He had forgotten about the reward for an Englishman's head. "Boy! Come here!" he said.

The "boy" Yang was beckoning to was me. His bloodshot eyes pierced into mine as he put the sweaty handle of the cutlass into my hand. "Take off his head first, before you throw him in."

I turned back to Ah Jack. The oarsmen had lowered him back on the deck, where he lay bleeding, for his heart had not yet stopped beating. Ah Jack looked up as I went over to him, heavy and slow, as though my conscience was dragging in my feet. Ah Jack saw the dagger in my hand and shook his head and mumbled, "*No no no.*" His eyes begged me for mercy as I knelt on the blood-soaked boards beside him. But there was no mercy on the *Scourge*. No mercy for him, and no mercy for those who don't obey orders.

"Sorry," I whispered in Ghost People tongue. "Sorry, Ah Jack."

Ah Jack moaned and beat his hand against my chest, and two

of the oarsmen came and held his wrists down against the deck. Ah Jack turned his head this way and that, with terror in his eyes. So I grabbed his dark curls to hold him steady, and brought the blade to his throat.

"No!" you shouted somewhere behind me. "*No!*"

But what choice did I have?

XIII

We rowed you away from the *Scourge of the Celestial Seas*, the flag of the Red Flag Fleet wilting from the mizzenmast. Oars splashed through the waves and seabirds swooped and soared in the clouded sky above, and we rowed as though the rhythm of our strokes, our heaving chests, had sent us into a trance. My arms were loose and shaking as I pulled the oars. Though I had rinsed my hands, they still looked drenched in Ah Jack's blood.

Now in the robes of a galley slave, you were nothing like the scholar I had met in Fanqui Town. Bound up with rope and dumped in the bottom of the boat, you glared above your gag, your eyes deranged. Ah Jack's head was in the burlap sack beside you, stained where the severed part had bled. The seawater that leaked into the boat, sloshing around our feet, had his blood in it too. Turtle Li sat on the bench above you, smoking his pipe, his flintlock aimed at your head. "Behave," he warned, "or your head's going in that bag with your friend's."

We rowed up the Pearl River Bay to Hermit Crab Cove, then pulled the boat through the shoals and up the shore. We hid the boat and untied your ropes, and lent you a broken, splintery oar for a staff. We of the *Scourge* were wobbly at first on dry land; we were so used to pitching our weight to counter the up and down of waves. Mud squelched and splattered our staggery legs as we trudged over the mudflats. The rickety shacks of fisherfolk and pagodas stood out on hilltops in the distance, and further inland the scenery changed to lush green paddy fields, watered by streams of the Pearl River and tended to by crouching farmers in rice-planting hats. "Hurry up, *cripple*," growled Turtle Li, the muzzle of his gun prodding your back as you limped. Stinky Fu and Ah Xi had our rice and water, and Ah Chen and Scabby Rui each had a flintlock to ward off other bandits. Turtle Li had ordered me to carry Ah Jack's head in the sack and, as we trudged on, the memory of those eyes of his, begging for his life, haunted my mind.

At dusk the sky began to spit down on our heads, and Turtle Li cursed and spat back at the sky. Though the plan had been to hike overnight, the outlaws of the Red Flag Fleet weren't the sort for a gruelling slog through the cold and rain, and we detoured to a rocky outcrop Turtle Li knew from his time as a land bandit, where there was a cave.

We built a fire in the cave, under a hole like a chimney, borrowing driftwood left by those who'd sheltered there before. Scabby Rui bound you up with ropes again and dumped you in the shadows at the back of the cave, with the creatures that scuttle and bite. Though the stench of rotting meat was coming from the burlap sack, Ah Jack's head was thrown back there too. "So Ah Tom won't be lonesome," grinned Turtle Li. Back in the shadows you glared above the gag, looking keen to rip out his throat.

Stinky Fu heated some rice over the fire and we dug in with grubby hands. When our supper was eaten, they passed round a flask of grog, grimacing as they swigged. The time had come for me to reveal what I'd stolen from Chief Maggot. So I brought the wooden box out of my robes and opened the lid. I spoke for the first time since the *Scourge*: "Look what I got."

Turtle Li's eyes went round, and he choked on his liquor. "How did you come by *that*?" he spluttered.

"I found it on the deck."

"You don't find foreign mud lying about," said Turtle Li. "You stole it."

"That's Chief Yang's," added Ah Chen. "He'll flay you alive."

I said nothing and shrank back, leaving the opium out for the taking. They were opium fiends, every last one, and the opium was here and Yang and his jackals were not. There's no harm in smoking a pinch, they all soon agreed. Turtle Li stabbed his stubby finger at my chest.

"Anyone gets done for this, it's you, Tanka boy. Got that?" Then he pounced on the opium and stuffed some in his pipe.

And so they smoked and spent an hour or so bragging about the merchant ships they'd sailed on, and the faraway lands they'd been to, and guffawing about the sinner's boils they'd caught off the whores they'd poked. Smoke fogged the cave as they puffed on pipe after pipe and I had to crawl to the opening to clear my head.

The opium stole away their brains, or what they had of them, right before my eyes. They smoked themselves into a stupor, then stared into the fire, hypnotized by the leap of flames. When they spoke, it was the same foolishness Three Pipes Qin used to come out with after a pipe or two:

"I remember this cave from before I was born," said Ah Xi. "This cave's where all humans come from before they are born . . ."

"When we're back on the *Scourge*, I'll challenge Chief Yang to a duel and win," boasted Turtle Li. "Then I'll be head of the Red Flag Fleet. 'Tis the prophecy of the seagull with the ruby eyes!"

What a relief it was when one by one they lay down their opium-muddled heads and slept. Turtle Li was the last to go.

"Anyone's getting done for this," he slurred as he stabbed his finger at me, "it's you, Tanka boy . . ."

Then he was out cold, gone from the here and now.

In the gloom at the back of the cave, your eyes blinked in the dark.

XIV

I watched them by the light of the dying fire. Though they were strewn lifeless as bodies from a shipwreck, I watched to make sure they were properly out. Then, shuddering at the risk I was taking, I tugged Turtle Li's dagger out of the scabbard on his belt. At the back of the cave, you were wriggling on your side. Nervous you would wake the bandits, I crawled over and hacked through your bindings with Turtle Li's cutlass, breathing deeply to steady my shaking hands. You ripped off your gag and gasped. Then you grabbed Ah Jack's head in the sack and hobbled over to the sleeping bandits. You reached for Ah Chen's flintlock and limped out of the cave.

Silently we hobbled through the mud up the Pearl River Bay. You were using the broken, splintery oar as a staff and had thrown the flintlock in with Ah Jack's head and slung the sack over your shoulder. Under the cloudy and drizzly night sky we went as fast as our legs could go, Tanka fisherboy and Red-Haired Devil, knowing the more distance between us and the cave of sea bandits the better.

Grieving over Ah Jack, you didn't say a word as I led the way over the mudflats to the other British devils in Wangpo. But fleeing from the *Scourge* had lifted my spirits, and my heart had quickened with the eagerness to go back to Ma Qin's wash boat and show them I was alive. First and Second Sisters would shed some tears to see me again, and Ma Qin would tell me off for getting captured by sea bandits. "How was I cursed with such a fool for a son!" she'd scold. "No more seafaring for you, Ah Qin!" Then I would work as a porter in Canton Harbour and forget the *Scourge* and lose my sea-ruffian ways. I'd do my duty as firstborn son and look after Ma Qin and my sisters, and never leave the Pearl River again. I'd had enough of the sea for this life, no matter what the Sea Goddess had foreseen.

We hiked through the mud of the Pearl River Bay until sunrise, when we stopped to catch our breath. We could see Wangpo in the distance and, though you were soon to be with your British-devil kin again, you looked miserably at the sun rising over the sea and shimmering on the waves. "Are you thirsty, Ah Tom?" I asked, wondering where we might find some drinking water. You did not respond but dropped the sack you'd been carrying on the muddy ground, reached in and pulled out the flintlock. Then you spun around, and pain cracked in my skull as you hit me with the butt. You cocked the gun and upped the barrel level with my chest.

"Get back," you hissed. Your eyes were possessed by fury, your finger on the trigger. Clutching my head, nearly blinded with pain, I stumbled back a step.

"What is it, Ah Tom?" I asked. "What have I done?"

You glared and nodded at Ah Jack's head in the burlap sack. "Jack was a good man. Now I have to tell his wife and children that he is dead. That his head was cut off on a pirate ship and his remains are in the South China Sea."

"Chief Yang ordered me to," I cried. "I didn't want to. I had no choice."

You shook your head in disgust, and I saw no trace of the kind and decent Ah Tom I'd met seven years ago in Fanqui Town. Not much difference between a civilized man and a savage. A few days at sea and a skirmish with bandits can turn the former into the latter. Even the likes of you.

"Get back," you sneered. "You Chinamen are all the same." Then you pulled the trigger of the gun.

24

Bruises

The rush-hour crowds disappear into the subway, the masses, shrieking into cell phones, treading on heels and fighting their way through the scrum. Stalled in traffic, Wang watches them, his head throbbing with the engine. There's no harmonious society, he thinks, only the chaos of people with crooked teeth and no manners, trampling on each other.

Deciding to call it a day, Wang turns off the for-hire sign and moves with the traffic down Workers Stadium Road. Near the exhaust-blackened iron and concrete of Long Rainbow Bridge, Wang hears screeching brakes, the crunch of metal and a woman's scream. One by one the cars ahead of him stagger to a halt, and the drivers slam out and hurry over to the intersection. Wang stays behind the wheel, not wanting to run and stare. But it isn't long before the strange anxiety of missing out has him abandoning his car like everybody else.

A crowd of fifty or so has gathered beside a 707 bus, people at the back standing on toes and straining for a better view. Wang can't see much, but a report of the accident makes its way through the crowd. The 707 knocked into a cyclist and sent him soaring through the air, to land metres away from the crumpled metal of his bike. The boy's head has cracked against the asphalt, and those who can see him are certain he is dead. Wang can't see the cyclist, only the driver of the now-empty 707, a fiftyish man with a deathly pale face, his thin wail of protest rising above the crowd. *He flew into me! He wasn't looking where he was going!* The driver pleads his innocence as though the bystanders are the jury at his trial, and he must prove he is not culpable there and then. But the jury are not convinced. "He was driving like a maniac," an old man near Wang remarks. "He should be locked up." Others grumble in agreement.

The epidemic of staring infects more people on their way home from work. Some turn their heads as they walk by, looking casually at the blood-splattered scene without breaking their stride. Others push to the front of the crowd, one man holding up his cell phone to photograph the dead cyclist and his mangled bike. "Seventy percent of people in China are immoral," Baldy Zhang had once joked to Wang. "The other thirty percent are screwed over. That's a fact from the National Bureau of Statistics." Watching the jostling crowd, Wang almost believes Baldy Zhang's statistics, and he goes back to his taxi, wondering if he is part of the seventy percent too.

When he's back behind the wheel, the driver of the BMW on his right slams on his horn without letting up. *Hooonnnnkk.* The honking gets on Wang's nerves, and he leans out of the passenger-side window and yells, "Hey! Cut that out!" The driver, a teenager in a baseball cap, glances at him, glances away. He blasts the horn again. *Hoooonnnnnkk.* Leaving the keys in the ignition, Wang gets out. The driver looks up nonchalantly at Wang's approach. His window is open and, through the heat and traffic fumes, Wang smells new leather upholstery and the perfume of the girl in the passenger seat, who is batting her mascara-clogged lashes at him. Wang sees the contempt in the BMW driver's eyes. That the scruffy, middle-aged taxi driver isn't worthy of his respect.

"What's your problem?" the teenager asks.

"You," says Wang. "Stop honking on your horn."

"Why?" the boy pretends confusion. "There's no law against it, is there? It's not illegal."

Wang points to the intersection. An ambulance has now pulled up, paramedics bringing out a stretcher as several policemen herd the crowd away.

"Someone has been knocked down and killed," Wang says. "Show some respect, will you?"

The boy shrugs, his conscience unmoved. The death of a man twenty metres down the road is of no consequence to him, beyond the inconvenience of a traffic jam.

"Too bad for him. He should've looked where he was going." Then, ignoring Wang and staring through the windscreen, he slams down on the horn again. *Hooonnnnkk.* The girlfriend swats his arm and giggles at him to stop. Wang is sick of these Little Emperors, with their bulging wallets and expensive cars Daddy bought them.

"You're a piece of shit," he says when the honking stops. "You know you're a shit, deep down. That's why you act the way you do."

The teenager laughs.

"You know nothing about me," he says, pressing a button so his window rolls up.

Wang stoops and stares through the rising barrier of glass. When the window is nearly sealed, he hears the teenager mutter, "*Loser.*" Blood rushes in Wang's ears, and he slams his fist into the tinted, shuddering glass. "*Oh my God!*" squeals the girl, jolting in her seat. The boy sparks the ignition and the BMW lurches forwards a metre or so. The roaring in Wang's head subsides and he stands there, his knuckles throbbing.

Workers Stadium Road is moving again, and the police are directing traffic around the cordoned-off area. The white van behind Wang's taxi is beeping and shouting at him to move, and Wang goes back to his car, confused by the driver's anger. He had confronted the teenager on behalf of everyone there. Why is the van driver acting like he's in the wrong?

Baldy Zhang hunches over noodles in broth with chopped-up sheep's intestines, feeding before the long and solitary night shift ahead. Beside the bowl of noodles are Baldy Zhang's garlic cloves and a half-smoked pack of Dongfanghong, the favourite brand of his hero, Mao Zedong ("I know millions died because of Mao and his policies. But he's still the greatest leader China's ever had!"). The night is sibilant with whirring insect wings. The bug zapper crackles, electrocuting those lured by its fluorescence to charred carcasses.

"Your mood's as foul as a woman with the curse," Baldy Zhang remarks through a mouthful of offal. "What's up?"

A Sichuan kitchen girl, hugely pregnant, waddles over with a plate of scallion pancakes. She dumps the plate in front of Wang then arches her lower back, pushing her bump out and sighing before waddling away. Baldy Zhang takes one of Wang's pancakes with his chopsticks. Tears into it with his teeth and chews.

"I need somewhere to stay," Wang says.

"Why's that?"

"Yida has kicked me out."

Baldy Zhang guffaws, spraying the table. "What've you done? You been screwing around?"

"No."

"She cheated on you?"

Has she? Wang is not sure. Baldy Zhang sighs and shakes his head.

"Here's my advice, Wang Jun. Knock her about, then shaft her till she's bleeding and senseless. She'll *respect* you for it. Society had it right back in the days of foot-binding and concubines. I don't know why they had to go changing the laws. Back then, women *behaved* . . ."

"You ever been married?" Wang asks.

"Never," Baldy Zhang says. "'Marriage is the grave of love,' as they say. Mind you, I've never been in love either. Women are more trouble than they're worth. A bachelor's life is the life for me . . ."

Baldy Zhang furrows his heavy ledge of brow and slaps at a mosquito biting his scalp. "Bastard," he spits at the smear of blood and dead insect in his palm. Wang nods politely, thinking "bachelor's life" captures none of the bleakness of Baldy Zhang's existence.

"Can I stay at your place for a night or two?" he asks.

"Well . . ." Baldy Zhang digs his little finger into his ear, wiggles it about. ". . . You can't stay for free. There's the cost of overheads . . . Electricity for the light and fan. Water for the shower. Gas for the stove. It adds up . . ." He pulls out the long fingernail and inspects the contents. "Twenty kuai per night sound reasonable to you? I'm giving you a discount, by the way, on account of the rough time your wife is giving you."

"That sounds very reasonable," says Wang, pulling two ten-RMB notes out of his wallet.

"There's three bottles of Red Star erguotou in the kitchen," says Baldy Zhang, pocketing the notes. "I'll know if one goes missing."

"I won't go near them," promises Wang.

Old men stroll about the Maizidian compound, vests rolled up over Buddha bellies they slap proudly in the summer heat. The security guard naps in his booth, his cap on the desk beside his drowsing head. Air-conditioning units weep down the side of Building 16, dripping on Wang's shoulder as he goes inside.

In the stairwell, Wang sees the stuffed rubbish bags dumped outside Apartment 404. He can imagine Yida storming about the bedroom, emptying drawers of socks and underwear into the black bin liners, breaking into a sweat in her determination to be rid of him. Wang can imagine her grim satisfaction as she knotted the bags and slung them out like trash.

Audience laughter roars behind the door. Yida wants him to stay out. She wants him to take the bags and slink away like a dog with its tail between its legs. Well, too bad. He wants to say goodbye to Echo. But, as he slides the key in the lock, Wang can't shake off the feeling he is trespassing.

"Yida," Wang says.

Though the windows are open and the blades of the fan spinning, the living room is muggy and hot. Yida hugs her knees, her heels on the seat, her legs bare in denim cutoffs. The TV screen illuminates her hostility as she stares at the variety-show host in his spangly suit.

"Yida?" Wang says again.

Her slender neck is vaulted by tendons under her chin. Her head is still, her eyes refusing to look at him. Wang is exasperated. But he aches with tenderness for her too. For that same stubborn, headstrong spirit he fell in love with.

Echo does not join her mother in the pretence that Wang isn't there. She bounds out of the bedroom in her school uniform and frayed Young Pioneers scarf.

"Ba, you're back!"

She smiles, pleased to see him, but the nervous twitch of her lip betrays her anxiety. They stand by the table, messy with Echo's comics and bubblegum wrappers, until Wang scrapes out a chair and they both sit. Wang sees Echo's bleeding hangnails, the shredded skin peeled back with her teeth, and winces.

"You must stop doing that," he says.

Echo curls her bloodied fingers into her palms and looks at her mother, her back turned against them. The fan breezes the curls back from Yida's temples as acrobats on trapezes perform for her on the TV stage. Echo looks back at her father, her young face wrought.

"Ba," she says, "are you going away?"

"I'm going to stay at Uncle Zhang's for a few days."

"When will you come back?"

"I don't know."

"Tomorrow?"

"Not tomorrow."

"Next week?"

"I don't know."

Yida points the remote at the TV, tapping the volume up. Echo tugs at the frayed end of her Young Pioneers scarf.

"When then?"

She bites her lower lip with her rabbit's teeth as she waits for his answer. Wang can't say when and is heartsick to be letting Echo down.

"Don't worry, Echo," he says. "I'll see you often. Every day if you like."

"But it won't be the same!"

"You'll get used to it."

"Why? Are you going to get divorced?"

Echo's chin wobbles and tears prick her eyes. Where Yida comes from, a divorced woman is a failed and dissolute woman, and Wang doesn't think she'll divorce him. But what happens instead of divorce, he has no idea. Wang shakes his head. He reaches for and squeezes Echo's small hand on the table, hoping to reassure her.

"Then why do you have to go?" Echo says.

"It's not my choice."

Yida abandons the pretence of watching TV. She spins round to confront her husband and daughter, gripping the back of her chair as she sets them straight.

"It's not my choice that he has to leave," she says, her eyes fierce. "Your father is not well. He's become abusive!"

"Ba," Echo says, "what's wrong? You're sick? Have you been to a doctor?"

Wang glares at his wife. "There's nothing wrong with me," he says. "Your mother is exaggerating."

Yida stands up in her denim cutoffs and yanks her vest up to show Echo the fading bruise on her flat stomach. "Look at this, Echo! Look what he did to me! Before you go begging your father to stay, you should know who he really is. It's not my fault that he can't stay here!"

Yida storms out of the room. The bedroom door slams and the TV bursts into a round of applause. The fan breezes at her empty chair. Echo looks at her father, her eyes tearful.

"It was an accident," Wang tells Echo. "I would never hurt her on purpose."

Wang remembers the day Yida threw his letters out of the kitchen window. They had fought, but Yida had done more damage to Wang than the other way round. Yida had slapped and scratched at him, clawing with her nails. Wang had wrestled her onto the bed to keep her under control. He may have been heavy-handed, but he has no memory of hitting her. They had struggled on the bed until Yida had gone limp beneath him, the fight draining out of her. Then Wang stroked his subdued wife. He kissed her full on the mouth then, aroused, unbuttoned her shirt. Yida hadn't resisted at all.

The spangly suited host banters into a microphone and the audience claps and laughs. Echo bites a hangnail, stripping the bleeding skin. Wang can't bear to see her so upset. He reaches over the table to comfort his daughter, squeezing her shoulder.

"I'm sorry," he tells her. "Things will get better soon. I promise."

Echo pushes her chair back, pulling away from him. "I have to go and do my homework," she mumbles, not looking at him. Then she goes to the bedroom, to her mother.

Wang stands up and notices the bare patch on the wall, where his and Yida's wedding photo had hung for the past nine years. He stares at the empty rectangle, paler than the rest of the smoke-yellowed paintwork. Then Wang reaches to turn off the TV. He can't stand walking out on them. He can't stand walking out on Yida, who, for all her wrongs, he still loves. But he can't think of what to do, other than collect the rubbish bags and leave.

25

Liars

The slammed door wakes him in the morning. "Off!" Baldy Zhang orders, kicking the mattress, as though Wang is a dog sneaked onto the furniture in his master's absence. "Off!" By the time Wang has washed and changed in the mildewed bathroom, Baldy Zhang is slumped in his place, in his vest and sagging underpants, swigging from a bottle of Tsingtao and waiting for his laptop to boot up. Every morning Wang walks out, swearing to find another place to live. But signing a lease would be to admit the separation is long term, and he can't do that, though he's still not ready to reconcile.

So every night he returns to Baldy Zhang's room and the mattress, where he drinks beer and clicks about on the virus-ridden laptop. Baldy Zhang has warned Wang not to clean the room or tidy up his stuff, so the most Wang has been able to do to make living there bearable is to scatter poison pellets for the cockroaches, who, instead of dying, swagger about as though drunk or stoned. Though Baldy Zhang's room is a mess, his porn collection is very organized, his downloads saved in desktop folders labelled "girl on girl," "gang bangs," "anal," "orgies" and "bondage and whips." Out of boredom, Wang has clicked through the files, but the mental images of Baldy Zhang jerking off usually has him shutting them again.

Late at night, he stares into the dark, kept awake by the foreboding that he will end up like Baldy Zhang one day. Most of the time Wang thinks the way Baldy Zhang lives his life is selfish and wrong. But he has darker moments. Moments when he thinks the co-renter of his taxi has merely hit upon the solution to the pain and irritation of other human beings.

The sky is lightening by the time he sleeps. He is woken not much later by Baldy Zhang barging in with his morning beers and territorial attitude, kicking the mattress with a shout—"Off!"— and beginning his day over again.

On his third night in Baldy Zhang's room his phone buzzes. Lin Hong is calling to tell him she wants to see him.

"I heard that your wife has thrown you out."

Wang hears the malice in his stepmother's voice. Echo must have told her.

"So?" he says. "It's not your concern."

"Echo is our concern," Lin Hong says. "Should you and your wife divorce we can make sure you get custody of her. We can hire a lawyer who can guarantee it."

Wang thinks resentfully of Yida. He thinks of how depressed he is to be spending another night on Baldy Zhang's mattress.

"Well? Are you coming or not?"

Wang hesitates, then tells her he will be there in thirty minutes.

Lin Hong is feeding his father when Wang arrives. Wang Hu is slumped in his wheelchair as she feeds him, in blue pyjamas with fluffy white clouds, his hair, no longer politburo black, neatly combed and parted to the side. An electric massage pad for boosting circulation and preventing bedsores is vibrating beneath his bottom and thighs. Seated on the sofa, Wang averts his gaze from his emasculated father being spoon-fed mashed-up vegetables and looks through the wall of glass at the dazzling lights in the east of the city. He shivers as the air conditioner blasts, the thermostat set to a meat-cabinet chill, as though his father would spoil and go rotten in the summer heat. He glances at Lin Hong in her short skirt and chiffon top and wonders at the lack of goosebumps on her slender legs. She sways her hips as she moves about his father's wheelchair, tossing her auburn-tinted hair.

Wang Hu's jaw muscles lack the strength to chew properly, and partially masticated green beans slide out of his mouth and onto the towelling bib tucked under his chin.

"Chew properly!" Lin Hong scolds. "Swallow! Don't drool!"

She scrapes the dribble and mashed-up green beans from his chin with the spoon and stuffs it back in his mouth. Wang's father shakes his head and pulls back with a moan of resistance.

"He's not hungry," Wang says. "You shouldn't force food down his throat if he's not hungry."

Lin Hong turns on Wang with a glare. She stabs the spoon at him, as though threatening to thrust it down his throat.

"Your father was on the toilet for forty minutes this morning. I had to give him a suppository. Unless you are willing to come and squeeze a suppository up your father's anus every time he's constipated, keep your opinions to yourself." Lin Hong turns back to her wheelchair-bound husband with the spoon of green mush. "Open!" she commands.

And as the electric massage pad vibrates and buzzes under his thighs, Wang Hu obediently opens wide.

After Wang's father is in bed, Lin Hong returns to the living room, her nose powdered and a fresh coat of lipstick on her collagen-plumped lips. "Whisky?" she asks, sashaying over to the drinks cabinet. Lin Hong holds heavy-bottomed tumblers under the ice machine and several cubes rattle out then fissure and crack as she pours the whisky in. She hands Wang his tumbler and flops onto an armchair opposite him, making a show of her exhaustion with a weary sigh. Wang swallows his drink gratefully, the flames of alcohol burning in his chest. Lin Hong's skirt rides up her thighs as she crosses her legs. She drinks half her whisky, then taps the glass with her wine-red talons.

"What do you want, Lin Hong?" Wang asks, wanting to get straight to the point.

Lin Hong looks at him gravely. "Your father's condition is worsening. The burden of caring for him is becoming too much for me."

"Hire a full-time nurse then," Wang suggests. Why Lin Hong took on full responsibility for caring for his father has always been a mystery to him.

"He needs more than a nurse," Lin Hong says. "I want to move him to a residential care home for elderly people with disabilities."

She hands Wang the glossy promotional brochure on the coffee table and, as he flips through, Lin Hong gives him the hard sell. Full-time doctors and nurses on site. State-of-the-art medical equipment. Physiotherapists and dieticians. Peaceful environment with carp ponds and landscaped gardens. Wang needs no selling on the idea. Having sat through half an hour of his father's evening routine, he doesn't doubt that Wang Hu will receive more respectful care in a home.

"Can't you see how exhausted I am?" Lin Hong says, pointing a manicured finger at her chest. "Day in, day out, I attend to *his* needs. I deserve a break. It's time for a change. When I heard that you and your wife had separated—"

"We haven't separated," Wang corrects. "It's only temporary, while we sort out our differences."

"When I heard that you had *separated*," Lin Hong repeats, "I was inspired to take a look at my own life. I am forty-two. That's not so old, is it? There is still time for me to *do* something with my life and *be* somebody. I have so much *potential* . . ."

Her self-help-manual-speak makes Wang wince. Though Lin Hong's eyes are earnest beneath her lash extensions, he doubts that his stepmother will ever do anything with her "potential." Despite the money and resources she has had at her disposal, Lin Hong has done nothing for the last twenty years but visit the beauty spa and watch Korean soaps. His stepmother's mean streak makes her seem interesting, but really she's vapid and dim.

Wang suspects she'll be lost without the routine of caring for and bullying her invalid husband.

"What will you do?" Wang asks.

Lin Hong tosses her auburn hair. "Oh, you know, something creative. Interior design, or fashion. I am a very artistic person—everyone compliments my great taste. I want to renovate and re-decorate this place too—knock down some walls and change the colour scheme. I want to convert the home gym into a bedroom for Echo, so she can come and live here after your divorce. Echo should have her own bedroom. It's wrong for her to share with her mother at her age."

Wang baulks at her plan for Echo to live with her. But Lin Hong doesn't notice.

"Echo and I will decorate the room together, then I will take her to Ikea to choose new furniture. It will be so much fun! You can move in here too, Wang Jun. Once your father has moved out to the private care home, there will be plenty of room for the three of us . . ."

Wang drains the last of his whisky for the courage he needs to step between Lin Hong and her delusions. "Yida will never agree to Echo living here," he says. "And as for me . . . well, I think my living here would be . . . impractical . . ."

Lin Hong sighs. "Yida won't have any say in the matter," she says. "I will hire the very best lawyers to handle the divorce pro-ceedings and guarantee you custody of Echo. And how can you say that living here will be impractical?" Lin Hong laughs and sweeps her hands at the high ceiling and vast floor space. "Look how spacious it is! And we have a maid to cook and clean and do the laundry. You and Echo will be very comfortable. Much more so than in that cramped hovel in Maizidian. *Ugh*—so filthy! Does that woman ever clean? I'll do a much better job of taking care of you and Echo than she ever did . . ."

Wang doesn't know what to say. He has a sudden resurgence of loyalty to Yida, who, for all her faults, at least hasn't parted company with reality.

"If Yida and I divorce, Yida can have custody of Echo," he says firmly. "She's a good mother and I won't take Echo away from her. And please understand, Lin Hong . . . we won't ever move in here. Echo won't want to leave Yida. And I'd rather live on my own . . ."

Lin Hong narrows her eyes at this, and Wang regrets not having another glass of whisky to fortify himself against what is to come.

"Every choice you have ever made, Wang Jun—dropping out of university, becoming a taxi driver, marrying that woman and now *this*—has been *wrong*," she says. She brings her whisky to her mouth and chokes it down. Wang knows he should stand up and leave now. But part of him wants to stay and see how low-down and dirty she will fight. "You are very selfish to deprive Echo of the opportunity to have her own bedroom with furniture from Ikea," she continues. "She would have so much fun staying here! You should stop being so selfish and let Echo decide for herself where she lives."

Wang smiles. "We'll let Echo decide then, shall we? You know, Lin Hong, Echo doesn't like coming here. I have to drag her here most times. You are very pushy and overbearing, Lin Hong. You are a very *hard* woman to be around . . ."

Lin Hong looks as though she's been slapped. Then she rears up, hissing like a cornered cat. "A hard woman, am I? Well, at least I don't have a mental illness. You are not fit to be a father, Wang Jun! You should be back in a psychiatric hospital. The police should lock you up with the other madmen they are rounding up before the Olympics. I ought to report you to the Public Security Bureau as a threat to national security!"

Wang laughs at this. He laughs at her viciousness. The bloodletting is cathartic, even though the blood spraying about is his own. "Listen to yourself, Lin Hong! You are poisonous! I wouldn't let Echo stay with you for even one night."

Lin Hong leans towards him. She spills whisky on her chiffon top as she shouts, "You are a *bad father*, Wang Jun! They should never have let you have a child! They should have sterilized you in the hospital! They should have locked you up like your mother! You are just as insane as she was!"

Wang straightens up, as though a low voltage has run up his spine to his skull.

"What do you mean, 'locked up like your mother'?"

Lin Hong smiles. She had not meant to say what she said. It had slipped out. Her stepson's expression is so gratifying, however, she is glad it did. "Your father put her in a hospital. The same one you were in."

"No," Wang says. "She died from pneumonia."

"She didn't die," Lin Hong corrects. "She recovered, and then she was moved to the mental hospital. She was there for a year or two, then she ran away."

Lin Hong's voice is no longer shrill. Back in control, she is smooth and dulcet as a late-night radio show host. Wang is faint. The room spins as though he has drunk a bottle of whisky, not a glass.

"She's still alive?"

"Dead," Lin Hong says. "A week after she ran away from the hospital, your father got a phone call from a town in Heilongjiang. The police had found her in the streets, frozen to death in the night. They cremated her and posted your father the death certificate."

Wang is short of breath. His chest has narrowed and he can't get air inside. "When was that?"

"1992."

"But he told me she died years before then, when I was twelve. I don't understand . . ."

Lin Hong sips her whisky, relishing his confusion and anguish, taking her time.

"Your father wanted to protect you," she says. "After you were sent to boarding school her madness got worse. She was like a wild animal. In the hospital she was howling and biting the other patients and doctors. She couldn't speak. She didn't know her own name. The doctors said that she would never recover. No child should ever have to see his mother in that condition."

"But he told me she was *dead*."

Lin Hong raises her eyebrows. "Why are you so upset? Your father said she was a bad, abusive mother and you were better off thinking she was dead. So what if she died later than you thought? She's dead now, isn't she? What difference does it make?"

"I want to see the death certificate," Wang says. "Bring it to me."

"Why?"

"Bring it to me!"

Lin Hong gets up and goes to the study. She returns and hands Wang a green booklet. Wang looks inside the government document, stamped with red stars and filled out in ballpoint pen by a small-town clerk. It's all there. His mother's name, age, weight, blood type. The cause of death is cited as hypothermia. Place of death, a town called Langxiang. Why Heilongjiang? he wonders. She had been a Sent-Down Youth in Heilongjiang in the 1960s and had hated it. Wang's eyes blur with tears at the thought of Shuxiang freezing to death in a small northern town. At the thought of himself at the age of twelve, under cold damp sheets in the boarding-school dormitory on the day his father told him she had died.

"Why are you crying?" Lin Hong asks. "Wasn't she a bad mother? Didn't she abuse you? Your father told me he once walked in on the two of you in bed together! For a mother to do that to her son is unforgivable . . ."

Wang puts the death certificate in his pocket and stands up. Tears are sliding down his cheeks. "You will never see Echo again," he tells Lin Hong. "You are dead to her now. You are dead to all of us."

He leaves the room before his stepmother can say another word.

He goes into the bedroom and flips on the light. Wang Hu is awake in his bed, pillows propping up his grey, wrinkled head, the duvet up to his chest. He looks nervously at his son. He has been listening.

"Why did you tell me she was dead?" Wang asks.

Wang Hu doesn't answer him but shrinks back against the pillows. But Wang is not fooled by the defenceless-old-man act. He knows what his father is really like.

"Why did you lie about her?" he shouts.

He reaches for a wooden dresser near the door and pushes it over so the drawers slide out and the large oval mirror shatters as it crashes to the floor. His father's eyes go wide with fright. He parts his dribbling lips and a low moan comes out. He tugs on the duvet with his semi-paralysed hand and pulls it over his head. Pathetic, Wang thinks. He has no pity for him. Reverse the effects of the stroke, restore his ability to walk and talk, and he'd be back to his bullying ways tomorrow. By rights, he should drag his father out of bed. He should drag him about and pull his shoulder out of joint, like his father did to him when he was twelve.

"*Get out!* Or I will call the *police*!" Lin Hong rushes past Wang to stand between him and the old man hiding under the bedcovers. She waves a cell phone at Wang. "I am dialling now! I will tell them you are having a psychotic episode and they will throw you back in the hospital!"

The dial pad beeps as she presses the keys. Wang shakes his head at his stepmother, and steps back. "You deserve each other," he says. "I couldn't wish any worse for you both than the lives you have now."

Then he turns and walks out of the apartment, slamming the door.

Out in the street, he is shaking. They are not humans but monsters hiding behind human masks. He won't speak to his father for as long as he lives. Or as long as his father lives. Whoever is first to die.

26

Train Station

Wang had showered, dragged a razor over his stubble and changed before meeting Echo, hoping to counter Yida's slander by looking the part of a respectable father. But he's not sure this has worked. Opposite him, Echo is paler than usual, with dark circles around eyes that don't seem to trust him. Since leaving her and Yida, he has not seen her as often as he said. Over the past fortnight he has seen her three times, and each time Echo has been more like a stranger to him. She hands the menu back, solemn in her T-shirt and dungarees.

"I'm not hungry."

"Are you sure?" Wang says. "You can order whatever you like . . ."

But she's not even tempted by fizzy drinks, so he orders for them both and then asks in an over-bright voice about school and her plans for the summer holidays. Echo scratches at a mosquito bite on her arm and gazes at the table of sunburnt American tourists and the laoban in polo shirts and suit trousers clinking glasses of baijiu to celebrate a business deal. When the dishes arrive, Echo nibbles at a lamb kebab while Wang eats from an earthenware pot of spicy chicken and potatoes. He swigs some beer from his glass and belches gently.

"How's your ma?" he asks.

Echo looks guiltily at the half-eaten kebab on her plate. She says in a small voice, "She says I'm not to talk to you about her."

"Really?" Echo reaches for a napkin and Wang frowns at her nails, bitten to the quick, the cuticles ragged and raw. "What's she been saying about me?" he asks. "Don't worry. You can tell me. She won't find out . . ."

Echo doesn't look up as she folds the napkin into origami.

"I can't say."

Wang smiles tightly. He should shut up. He shouldn't drag Echo into this. But when it comes to Yida, he has no restraint; he can't do what's right.

"Bad-mouthing me every chance she gets, eh?" Wang says. "Is she still saying that I am ill?" Echo puts her origami crane on the table, looking miserable. "Well, there's nothing wrong with me," Wang says. "Your mother is making it up. *You* don't think I am ill, do you?"

Echo looks up at her father. "No," she says quietly.

Wang is stung by her lack of conviction. "Listen, Echo, there are two sides to every story. There are lots of bad things I could tell you about your mother. But I won't, because I don't want to upset you." Wang drinks the last of his beer, choking back the urge to rant on. Then he pushes back his chair and leaves the table.

In the bathroom he splashes water on his face over the sink. He hasn't slept properly in days and is in a dark, irritable mood. How much had his mother suffered during the last two years of her life? Why was she homeless on the streets of a town in Heilongjiang? These questions go around his mind at night, sabotaging sleep. He wipes his face with a scratchy paper towel from the dispenser. After leaving his father's, he called Yida to warn her to keep Echo away from them, and explained why. Yida needed no persuading. That his father and Lin Hong were despicable was one thing on which they agreed.

When Wang returns to the table, Echo is looking through one of her own comics, illustrated in black and white.

"Can I see?" Wang asks.

Echo hands over the stapled sheets, and Wang flips through them. *The Watcher* is the title of the comic, and it is about a girl called Moonbird who is stalked by a dark shadow only she can see. The shadow, crosshatched in ink and swarming with strange, demoniac eyes, lurks in the corner of each panel, watching Moonbird in the classroom, on the way home from school and in her bedroom at night. No one—not her parents, teachers or classmates—sees the shadow except Moonbird, whose isolation worsens her fear. Eventually Moonbird confronts the shadow. "Who are you?" she asks. "What do you want?" The second-to-last panel shows Moonbird disappearing into the shadow. Whether the shadow is devouring her or she is entering of her own volition, Wang can't tell. The last panel shows Moonbird's mother and father calling for their missing child. *The End*. Wang hands the comic back, unsettled.

"What a sad story," he says. "You're only eight. Why don't you write a story with a happy ending?"

"It's just a story," Echo says.

She stuffs *The Watcher* back in her shoulder bag. Seeing he has hurt her, Wang says, "The illustrations are really good. I don't know where you get your artistic talent from. Not from me or your ma . . ." Echo shrugs and pushes her half-eaten kebab away. "Look, Echo . . . I know we are going through a rough time right now," Wang says, "but don't worry too much about it. Things will get better soon. Don't upset yourself."

Echo winces and puts her hand on her stomach. "My belly hurts," she tells her father. "Can we go?"

Not sure how to put things right, Wang calls the waitress for the bill.

Morning. Wang is woken by the slammed door and beer bottles clinking in a bag. "Off!" orders Baldy Zhang, kicking the mattress. Wang drags himself up and rummages through his bin liner of clothes for a crumpled shirt. He is so exhausted after his night of sleeplessness, that if he had a gun he'd put himself out of his misery. He's so exhausted, even Baldy Zhang notices.

"Sleepless night, eh, Wang Jun?" he says, grinning with sulphur-coloured teeth. "Still angsting about your wife and kid, eh? Forget 'em, I say. You're better off without them!"

Wang goes into the bathroom, throws water on his face and drags a toothbrush about in his mouth. He knows he should take the day off work but can't think of where to go. At least driving the taxi will be a distraction from his wretched state of mind.

"Don't crash the car today," Baldy Zhang calls from the mattress as Wang picks up his keys and walks out the door. "You're paying for the damage if you do!"

Behind the wheel, buzzing with nicotine and caffeinated energy drinks, Wang barely feels the steering wheel in his hands or the pedals under his feet. His driving is shaky at first, but autopilot soon takes over, controlling his steering and braking. Wang works on automaton too, picking up fares and driving them to their destinations, as though in a surreal dream of a working day.

By late afternoon, he can't remember one thing about the ten hours he has worked. He can't remember where in Beijing he has driven to, or any of the passengers he has had. So when he sees Zeng through the windscreen, in the crowds outside Beijing West Station, he thinks he must be hallucinating. He swerves over to the kerb anyway, and slams on the brakes, sending the man in the passenger seat lurching to the dashboard. Wang then snatches up the keys and bounds out the door. "Where are you going?" his passenger calls, aggrieved. Wang ignores him. He runs past construction workers digging up the roadside and fights his way through the station crowds, determined not to lose him. "Zeng Yan! Stop!"

Zeng Yan, backpack on his back, turns around, and Wang is shocked for a moment that he is not a trick of the light or the mind, but flesh and blood and real. He stares at Zeng and his stomach turns over with the sense that this is no coincidence. But how did Zeng know where he would be driving his taxi that day? How had Zeng timed his movements so he would be in Wang's line of sight at that moment in time? Who *is* Zeng exactly? Smoker's wrinkles deepen around Zeng's eyes, dazzled by the sun. Then he shades his shrinking pupils with his hand.

"Wang Jun? Is that you?" Zeng breaks into a wide smile. "I just got off the train from Guangzhou. Forty-eight hours in a hard seat. What are you doing here?"

Wang doesn't smile back. "I've been looking for you."

Travellers leaving Beijing West Station push past them, fatigued from long journeys on trains with strangers and now stumbling out on cramped legs into the traffic-honking chaos of Beijing. They have reached the point of exhaustion where other people are no longer people. They bump against Wang and Zeng. "Stop blocking the way," says an old man, hunched under heavy bags. Zeng looks strung out too, and gaunter than the last time Wang saw him. He nods, Wang's hostility chasing away his smile.

"Feifei said you were looking for me at the salon. I was back in my hometown for a few weeks. Wang Jun, my mother died. She had ovarian cancer . . ."

My mother has cancer . . . Zeng had used this story on the CEOs when he was a nightclub host, to con them out of money for "hospital fees." Wang doesn't waste time on his deceit.

"Why did you send the photos to my wife's phone?"

Zeng looks confused. "Huh?"

A man pushing a cart of wholesale clothes cuts between them. Zeng backs out of his way, only to be shunted by someone rushing for a train. He holds onto his backpack straps, swaying on his feet.

"The photos you took with the hidden camera in the back room. The photos you sent to her phone."

Zeng looks at him blankly. "What are you talking about? What photos?"

"You know what photos," Wang says. "The ones you sent to my wife's phone!"

Zeng stares at Wang as though he is speaking another language. He rakes a hand through his jagged hair. "I have no idea what you are talking about. I never sent any photos to your wife's phone. I don't know her phone number. I don't even know her *name*."

Horns beep and a pneumatic drill starts up in the road, shattering concrete. As Wang stares back at Zeng, he feels a pulsing in his temple and tension mounting behind the eyes. Somebody treads on his heel, and he glares over his shoulder. But the offender has merged back into the masses streaming around them, chattering, smoking cigarettes, squinting up at the train timetable or down at their phones. He turns back to Zeng.

"Because of your photos, my wife and I have separated. She threw me out."

Zeng frowns as though concerned. He reaches out the arm he scarred by punching out a window many years ago, to comfort Wang, his hand hovering near his shoulder.

"Do you need somewhere to stay?" he asks. "You can come and stay with me. You can stay as long as you like . . ."

Wang sees the longing in Zeng's eyes and his heart quickens in spite of himself. He resents Zeng then, for the complicated feelings he wrings out of him. The jackhammer continues to break up the road, and the tension behind Wang's eyes sharpens into pain. "Are you crazy?" he says. "Do you really think I want to stay with you at the barber's? After you broke up my marriage?"

Zeng shakes his head at this. He opens his mouth and hesitates for a second. Then he takes a breath and says, "Your marriage was broken long before your wife saw any photos. Your marriage was broken from day one. I see men like you all the time, Wang Jun. Men who are living a lie. Men who think they can get away with hiding who they are. But we are born this way, and to deny it is to betray yourself."

Though Wang can feel his own pounding heart and panting breath, there is something disembodying about his rage, knocking him out of himself. Though he can feel the thud of Zeng's flesh and bones beneath his knuckles, he hovers above them, watching one man striking another, throwing punch after punch, as his victim fends off his blows. When it is over, Wang stumbles back from Zeng dizzy and out of breath, shaking out his numb and tingling hand. Zeng is bending over with both hands on the bright mess of red streaming out of his nose, splashing down his chin and vest.

Though it had lasted only a few seconds, Wang's fit of rage had attracted a crowd like a magnet pulling iron filings. Those standing around them stare at Wang in shock and fear.

"Are you okay? Do you need to go to the hospital?" a boy in a KFC uniform asks Zeng.

Zeng shakes his head.

"Someone should call the police," says a girl with a fake Louis Vuitton bag over her arm, looking nervously at Wang.

"*No no no*," Zeng says. "Don't call the police. He's my friend. He didn't mean it."

Wang nearly laughs. "We're not friends. And here's some advice for chasing men in the future. Don't write them letters. Don't stalk them, and don't break up their marriages. It's the wrong way to go about things."

Zeng says nothing in his defence. Blood seeps through the fingers clamped to his nose, and there's hurt and confusion in his eyes.

"Now get out of my sight," Wang says.

But it's Wang who turns to walk away, pushing back through the crowds, bumping into a woman carrying a toddler in split pants and mumbling an apology. When he gets back to his taxi, the passenger-side door is wide open, and the passenger gone, leaving 20 RMB on the meter, unpaid. Wang gets back in the driver's seat and lights a cigarette with shaking hands, his knuckles grazed and smeared with his own blood and Zeng Yan's. He inhales long and deep, but the lungfuls of smoke don't calm him. The confrontation has changed nothing, of that he is sure. Nothing short of death or a jail sentence will keep Zeng away.

27

The Fire

Night. Out in the street, traffic murmurs. Halogen lamps glow through the curtains, and the bantering of drunks rises up from below. The July night is hot, and Wang can't sleep. He smokes a cigarette on the mattress and watches the spirals of smoke rising up, then diffusing to the corners of the room.

Knock. Knock. Knock . . . Someone has the wrong door, Wang thinks. No one ever visits Baldy Zhang. Wang ignores the knocking and wills the caller to go away. But the striking of the knuckles becomes louder, more demanding. *Knock. Knock. Knock . . . Knock. Knock. Knock . . .* Wang stubs out his cigarette and drags himself to the door.

"Who is it?" he calls, pulling down the latch.

The woman standing in the hall is in her forties, shabby as a poor migrant worker, with threads of grey in her hair, face as round and pale and impassive as the moon. Wang knows at once there's something not right about her. Though the night is sweltering, over thirty degrees, she wears a padded Mao jacket and looks cold to the touch. Her piercing eyes settle on Wang, waiting for him to recognize her. When recognition comes, Wang is light-headed, and he holds the doorframe to steady himself.

"Ma?" he says.

Shuxiang nods. Wang speechlessly pulls the door wider and she walks in. Under the 30-watt bulb she looks younger than Wang remembers, and he understands that while he has aged twenty years, Shuxiang has stayed the same. He is catching up to her. Wang drags a chair over for her. Though old and creaky, the chair makes no sound as Shuxiang lowers her substanceless body onto the seat.

"Can I have some water?" she asks. "I have walked very far today, and I am thirsty."

Wang's throat constricts at the sound of his deceased mother's voice, and his hands are shaking as he pours a cup of boiled water from the thermos by the mattress. He passes the cup to her, careful not to brush her hands, which look icy and repellent to the touch. He watches his mother take cautious sips, as though the water is not room temperature but scalding.

"Are you a ghost, Ma?" Wang asks.

Shuxiang pretends not to hear, and Wang remembers her habit of "not hearing" questions she didn't want to answer from his childhood. She gazes at the beer bottles, pellets of cockroach poison and the stuffed bin liners "packed" by Yida before her eyes come to rest on her son. Wang shifts awkwardly in his T-shirt and boxers.

"I don't live here. I am staying here for a week or two while I work out some problems with my wife . . ."

"I know."

How much does Shuxiang see of his life from beyond the grave? Wang wonders, with a creeping sense of shame. But Shuxiang knows the truth about what people are like. She has seen humans at their worst, and nothing much shocks her. Wang thinks of where they put her before she died.

"I'm sorry about what happened to you, Ma," he says. "Father lied to me. He told me you were dead. I only found out the truth last week . . ."

Wang thinks of Shuxiang, drugged and incarcerated in the hospital. He thinks of his twelve-year-old self, grieving on cold, damp dormitory sheets, and tears flow down his cheeks. Irritation stirs the blankness of Shuxiang's face. Even when Wang was a child, she had no patience with tears.

"Why get upset over that now?" Shuxiang says. "Even had you known the truth, what could you have done? You were twelve. That's in the past, anyway. That's not why I came to see you. I am here because of a danger in the present."

"Danger?"

Wang notices for the first time the strange humming in the air, as though the atmosphere is agitated by Shuxiang's presence, the molecules vibrating, tense and volatile.

"That man," Shuxiang says, "is worse than you thought."

"Who?" Wang asks. "Father?"

"Not him. Your friend. You must go and check on Yida and Echo. They are in trouble."

There's a sickening thud in Wang's chest. Zeng Yan. She must mean Zeng Yan.

"What do you mean?"

"Go to them," Shuxiang urges. "Before it's too late."

Wang curses, pulls his trousers from a bin liner, staggers into them and zips up the fly. He grabs his keys and wallet and runs out of the door.

"Hurry," Shuxiang calls after him as he runs on panicking legs down the hall. "Hurry, Xiao Jun . . ."

The phone is ringing, shrill and electrifying as it jolts him awake. Wang sits up in the dark. "Ma?" he says. The chair is empty, Shuxiang no longer there. Disappeared upon waking from the strange dream. Wang gropes for the ringing phone. It's Yida, and she is hysterical. Wang can't make sense of her breathless torrent of words. He hasn't heard her so distraught since that harrowing night nine years ago, when they woke to blood-soaked sheets and the miscarriage of their first child.

"Slow down, Yida. What did you say?"

She repeats herself. Wang can't believe what he is hearing. If he didn't know Yida better, he'd think it was a sick practical joke.

"I am coming now," he tells her. He hangs up and heads out into the night.

* * *

SUSAN BARKER

Echo is in a private room at the hospital, on a white-sheeted bed. A high-flow oxygen mask is strapped over her nose and mouth and connected to a ventilation machine by a long corrugated plastic tube. Wang touches his hand to her clammy forehead, and her eyelids, pale and faintly blue-veined, remain shut. Her hair is spread across the pillow, and the pallor of her face, partially obscured by the transparent muzzle of the oxygen mask, is as though her blood drained in fright and has yet to return. The odour of fire clings to her. Smoke and the chemical fumes of burnt plastics: toxic and harmful to the lungs of little girls.

The last time he'd seen Echo in the hospital was the day of her birth. Wang had watched the midwife pull her out and hold her up in her latex-gloved hands under the fluorescent strip light. Echo had wailed, and Wang had sympathized with her protest at being wrenched out of the womb. He understood the terror of her ears, hearing for the first time the stainless-steel clatter of the delivery room. He understood the terror of her lungs, breathing the chill, disinfectant-scented air. Echo had wailed and kicked her tiny feet and Wang had vowed then to protect his newborn daughter. A vow that, standing over Echo's hospital bed eight years later, he knows he has not honoured.

Dr. Shu waits quietly, allowing the father time with his child, before explaining, "The smoke inhalation is unlikely to cause any lasting damage. We will prescribe your daughter some anti-inflammatory drugs, and the irritation in her lungs and respiratory tract should be gone in a week or two. Echo is a very lucky girl. Her mother was very brave and quick-thinking to get her out of there as fast as she did."

Wang nods and, without pulling his gaze away from Echo's sleeping face, says, "The police suspect an electrical fault?"

"That's what I heard," the doctor says. "Your wife is talking to them now. She will have a clearer idea of what is going on . . ."

Wang can't hear the rest. Who once bragged in a letter about going to Apartment 404? Who was once convicted of arson for setting fire to a shed he thought his ex-lover was inside? Who is deranged enough to attempt to burn a woman and child to death

300

in their beds? When he sees Zeng, Wang doesn't know what he will do.

The door to the private room opens and Yida enters, her eyes dazed under the craziness of her hair. The smoke of the fire clings to her as it does to Echo, ashes smudging her cheeks. She wears the floral polyester nightdress Wang bought her for her birthday, and must have fled without shoes, as she has disposable hospital slippers on her feet. Yida stiffens when she sees Wang, who walks to her, reaching out his arms.

"Yida . . . what's wrong?"

She glares at him, her smoke-inflamed eyes shot through with red. "I don't want to speak to you."

"Yida? You don't blame me for the fire, do you? That makes no sense. I wasn't even at home!"

Dr. Shu clears his throat, excuses himself and slips out the door. Yida strides past her husband to Echo's bedside. Her chest heaving under her nightdress, she turns and points a shaking finger at him.

"I warned you the wiring in the bathroom was dangerous. I warned you we had to get it fixed. But you were too lazy. We accidently left the water heater on tonight, and look what happened!"

"So it's my fault then? That's what you're saying? If you were concerned about the wiring, Yida, why didn't you report it to the landlord yourself?"

Though Wang thinks he's made a valid point, Yida reacts as though he has said something offensive. She stabs a finger at the door. "Get out! Now! I can't stand the sight of you."

Wang takes a deep breath. He reminds himself of what Yida has been through. How she woke in the night to suffocating heat and smoke and had to escape with Echo onto the neighbour's balcony. Apartment 404 has been gutted by fire, and everything they own destroyed. She has nowhere to live, and her only child is in a hospital bed, hooked up to a machine. Yida is too shaken up to think straight, and Wang aches for his wife. She should be turning to him for support, not turning against him.

"I'm sorry that I wasn't there, Yida," he says. "I thank God that you and Echo got out of there safely. I owe you for rescuing Echo. You were very brave."

Wang's words, the tremor in his voice, break down her animosity. She lowers her shaking hand. "I thank God I woke up," she says. "It frightens me to think what would have happened if I hadn't woken . . ."

A sob catches in Yida's throat and she throws a hand over her mouth. Wang goes to her, and she doesn't resist as he takes her in his arms, embracing her for the first time in weeks. He strokes the back of his wife's messy head as she quietly weeps on his shoulder. The fire has destroyed everything they have, but at least it has brought them back together, Wang thinks, as a family once more.

"We shouldn't blame each other," he says soberly. "The fire had nothing to do with the wiring."

"What are you saying?" Yida pulls back to look at her husband at arm's length. There is a wary look in her bloodshot eyes. "That it was arson?"

Wang nods. "I know who did it."

Yida laughs, shoves his chest with both hands and steps backwards out of his arms. "Let me guess," she says. "Your friend? The man who wrote the letters?"

"The police couldn't do anything about him before," Wang says, "but now that he has harmed us they can arrest him."

Yida laughs again, harsh and cynical. She goes back to their daughter's bedside. Leaning over Echo, she strokes the hair at her temples, as though to close ranks against him.

"You think it's all in my head, don't you, Yida?" Wang says.

"Yes," Yida says. "The fire started in the bathroom. The firemen said it was the wiring. I can't take any more of your madness, Wang Jun. I'm sick to death of it. The police are waiting to speak to you in the hall. Go and tell them your arson theory! Go!"

Echo is waking. She coughs faintly into the breathing apparatus over her mouth, the sound muffled by the plastic. Her eyes flutter open up at her mother, standing over the bed, and she attempts to raise her head from the pillow. "*Ma?*" she croaks up at Yida. Wang's heart contracts and he wants to stay with his daughter, to reassure her that she is safe. But the last thing Echo needs right now is to see her parents fighting. So he leaves to speak to the police. Yida will come round.

The policeman is sleeping in the chair outside Echo's room, called off duty by his three-in-the-morning fatigue. Wang looks up and down the otherwise empty hallway. He hears the policeman's colleague in the examination room. "This one's a bullet wound. I was chasing a gangster," he boasts. The nurse giggles. "What bullet wound needs . . . ten stitches?" Wang stares at the policeman sleeping in the chair. What if he tells the police he suspects arson and they suspect him? What if they look up his records, see that he was once a psychiatric patient and arrest him? He has heard how the police solve their cases. They will take him to the station and throw him about an interrogation room until he confesses. The investigation will begin and end with him.

Wang walks back to reception, where a mother hugs her asthmatic, wheezing toddler and a drunk smiles, bleeding from a head wound but too numbed by baijiu to feel the pain. The sliding glass doors part for him as he leaves, and out in the hospital car park Wang starts to run, past the ambulances and parked cars. At the hospital gate, he looks back at the emergency-room entrance. No one is coming for him but, not wanting to take any chances, he keeps on running down the street.

Morning. The sky, cleared of pollution by pre-Olympic closures of coal-burning factories outside Beijing, is blue and streaked with cirrus clouds. The alley, however, is its same sordid self, smelling of beer, gutter urine and the sweet rot of cabbage in bins. The barber's is closed, the red, white and blue pole not spinning, the cord unplugged. Wang turns off the taxi engine and calls Zeng. The phone rings and rings. Wang is on the verge of hanging up when Zeng picks up.

"Wei?"

Zeng is sleepy, his tongue groggy on the bed of his mouth. Ten past seven and he probably hasn't been in bed for long.

"I need to speak to you," Wang says. "Come outside." He hangs up.

As he waits, Wang smokes a Red Pagoda Mountain, tugging nicotine and tar, the only stuff his body won't reject with nausea, deep into his lungs. He has smoked it down to the butt by the time Zeng appears. Yawning. Bare-chested in boxers. The bruises on his nose and cheeks darkened to purplish black, making him look like a featherweight boxer staggering out of the ring. Zeng walks to the taxi, the emerald scales of his dragon tattoo glinting in the sun. The waistband of his boxers hangs from his narrow hips, and his lean and sinewy body looks vulnerable and undefended.

Wang leans out of the driver's-side window. "Get in."

"What is it? Why have you come to see me?" Zeng asks. He touches his hand to the bruises that Wang beat into him the day before.

Wang chokes back his anger, struggling to bring his voice under control. His heart is beating hard and sweat dampening his brow. He looks straight ahead through the windscreen.

"You know why. Get in."

Zeng goes to the passenger-side door, unconcerned that he is barefoot and in his underwear. He slides into the passenger seat, slams the door and turns to Wang. "I don't understand you, Wang Jun," he says. "The way you . . . *attacked* me yesterday. I thought you never wanted to see me again . . ."

Wang shuts his eyes and grips the steering wheel with all his strength. He thinks of Echo in the hospital bed, wearing an oxygen mask so she can breathe. The nearness of Zeng in the taxi is unbearable. Wang can't release the steering wheel from his white-knuckle grip, out of fear of what his hands would otherwise do.

"Did you get another letter? Is this what this is about? I swear, it wasn't me . . ."

Wang opens his eyes. Zeng is stroking his scarred forearm as he looks at him, as though his fingers are unconsciously drawn to his past self-destruction and pain. Wang is sure Zeng knows why he has come for him. Where is his sense of self-preservation? His sense of threat?

"I worry about you, Wang Jun," Zeng says. "I know you are under a lot of stress. If you want to talk, I am here for you . . ."

Wu Fei comes flying out of the barber's. Barefoot. Naked from the waist up. His underdeveloped chest and pale adolescent nipples make him appear younger than Wang had first thought. Seventeen, or even sixteen.

"Yanyan! Stop!"

Wang hits central locking. The boy won't let Zeng go without a fight.

"Roll up your window," he tells Zeng.

Wu Fei dashes in front of the taxi, to the passenger side. He pulls uselessly on the door latch then thrusts his fingers through the narrow gap above Zeng's window, tugging on the glass.

"Don't go with him, Yanyan!" he yells at Zeng. "He's dangerous! He will beat you again. He only wants to hurt you."

"Feifei," Zeng says firmly, "we are just going for a drive. There's something Wang and I have to talk about."

Clinging with his fingers, the boy shouts into the gap above the window glass. "Please, Xiao Yan. Please get out of the taxi. Don't go with him. Get out of the taxi now!"

Zeng Yan sighs. "Feifei, go back to bed. I'll be back soon and we'll get breakfast together."

"No." Wu Fei shakes his head. "Let me come with you. I will sit in the back seat and be quiet. You won't know I'm there—I promise. I just want to make sure you are okay."

"Feifei, stop acting like a child!"

But he is a child—Wang sees that now. He is a boy in a dark adult world, and Zeng is his protector, the one person he has. Wu Fei clings to him with a child's fear of abandonment.

"Please, Yanyan, don't go! He's crazy and wants to hurt you! Why can't you see that?"

Zeng turns to Wang, embarrassed. "I'm sorry about this."

He turns back to Wu Fei, and Wang waits as they quarrel. The boy presses his forehead to the passenger-side window, desperately pleading with Zeng through the glass. Frustrated tears well in the boy's eyes and Wang feels sorry for him then. It must hurt to love someone so much. Wu Fei shouts over the passenger seat at Wang, "Let me in, or I'll send more photos to your wife! I'll send the worst ones I have!"

Wang turns the key in the ignition. At the sound of the engine starting up, the boy dashes to the front of the car and leans over the bonnet. For a moment Wang is afraid he will climb on the taxi and cling on to the windscreen. But Wu Fei stares him down instead. He spits on the windscreen, vicious and hard. Saliva slithers down the glass and Wang fights the urge to turn the windscreen wipers on.

"I know your taxi company!" the boy shouts. "I know your licence-plate number! If Zeng Yan doesn't come back soon, I'll call the police. I'll tell them you've kidnapped him, and they'll go after you!"

He thumps the bonnet, the vibrations passing through the chassis to the driver's seat. Wu Fei glowers at Wang. But he is conceding defeat. Backing off.

"If you hurt him, I will kill you," he shouts. "I'll kill you, Driver Wang!"

Wang doesn't doubt it. He lowers his foot to the accelerator and the car lurches forwards. The boy moves aside, and as they drive away Wang watches him recede out of sight in the rearview. Wu Fei stands in the alley, watching them, desolate and grief-stricken as Wang drives his lover to an unknown fate. You are still young, Wang thinks. You'll get over him.

"He has problems with his temper," Zeng says. "His father used to beat him a lot . . ."

Wang shakes his head and mutters, "I should've run him over for sending those photos to my wife."

28

The Anti-capitalist School for Revolutionary Girls
People's Republic of China, 1966

I

The peasant is old and shrunken, his clothes sewn out of Plentiful Harvest rice sacks. He hawks and spits on the classroom floor, and rows of fifteen-year-old girls in padded-cotton jackets and trousers wrinkle their noses at their desks. Most of my classmates are from good Beijing families, and some are daughters of the Communist elite. Their fathers use spittoons.

The peasant shuffles up onto the teaching platform, and Teacher Zhao introduces him as Comrade Po.

"Comrade Po is from a village outside Beijing," Teacher Zhao says, "and in today's lesson, 'Recalling with Bitterness the Exploitation of the Peasant Classes by Evil Landlords,' Comrade Po will tell us about his suffering during the Nationalist era."

Comrade Po grins with overcrowded, never-been-brushed-looking teeth, and starts lecturing us in his guttural, rural dialect. A quarter of an hour goes by before Teacher Zhao realizes we can't understand and translates:

"One year the sorghum harvest was so bad, Comrade Po couldn't pay the rent. He begged the landlord not to evict him, as he and his wife and children would freeze to death. The landlord told Comrade Po that he could stay if he gave him his eldest daughter. Well, what choice did Comrade Po have? To save his wife and eight other children, he gave his eldest daughter away. The landlord raped her, and Comrade Po's daughter was so ashamed she drank insecticide and died. She was eleven years old."

The tragedy of Comrade Po's life under the Nationalists reduces our class to tears. Red Star weeps onto her desk lid, and Soviet Chen shakes with her head in her hands. My eyes remain stubbornly dry, and I panic because I don't feel sorrow for Comrade Po as he stands on the teaching platform, wiggling a finger about in his nose. So I think of my father, sent to a labour camp in Qinghai because his department had to expel a quota of rightists in the latest anti-rightist campaign. Ma and I haven't had a letter from Father in over a year. Though we daren't say it, we fear he is dead. Tears drip onto my desk and I am relieved. Now in the eyes of others my conscience is politically correct.

A spinster devoted to Communism, Teacher Zhao is deeply moved by Comrade Po's tales. Behind the thick magnifying lenses of her glasses, her eyes well up.

"Comrades!" Teacher Zhao cries. "Let Comrade Po's tragic story remind us why we must be revolutionary and fight!"

Teacher Zhao punches her fist to the ceiling, a damp patch of revolutionary fervour in the armpit of her chalk-dusty Mao jacket, and our class applauds. Comrade Po grins and flicks his nose pickings, and above the blackboard, Chairman Mao watches approvingly from his gilded frame.

The winter sun is setting, the alley shadows lengthening into dusk. I walk briskly, my satchel bouncing at my side, my breath fogging in the freezing air. I am nearly home and out of the cold when a shout turns my head.

"Yi Moon! Stop!"

Red Star, Long March, Patriotic Hua and all their hangers-on stride down Vinegar Makers Alley towards me. Hair in braids. Padded-cotton jackets buttoned up. Trousers long and grey. They crowd around me, exhaling white clouds of contempt and backing me up against a wall.

"Why were you smirking during Comrade Po's story?" Long March asks. "You thought he was smelly and backward, didn't you? You thought his daughter's suicide was funny."

Though speaking back to Long March only makes matters worse, I say, "I wasn't smirking. Comrade Po's daughter's suicide was very sad. I was crying like the rest of the class."

"No, you weren't," Resist America says. "I saw you and you didn't shed a tear."

"I cried."

"How dare you accuse Resist America of being a liar!" Long March says, her eyes flashing in outrage. "Rightist bitch! Your father deserves to be worked to death in that labour camp!"

"*Everyone* saw you laughing at Comrade Po," says Red Star.

The others nod and chime in that they saw me laughing too, and I shrink back. There is not one girl not complicit in this group lie. A shy girl called Socialist Flower steps towards me with a glass bottle of red paint. Socialist Flower's shyness, and the fact that her father was once condemned as a rightist too, had led me to think she was a secret ally of mine. But I was mistaken. Socialist Flower's nose twitches as she holds the bottle, excited to be one of Long March's gang.

"Yi Moon is a capitalist parasite, sucking the blood of the masses!" Red Star says. "The time has come to cure her blood thirst once and for all!"

I look at the red liquid in Socialist Flower's glass bottle, sedimented at the bottom, clearer at the top. That's actual blood, I think, shocked. Resist America and Patriotic Hua grab my arms. "Please! No!" I cry. Socialist Flower giggles nervously as she moves the bottle to my lips.

"Drink, Rightist!" Long March commands. "Drink!"

I jerk my head back and clamp my lips.

"Throw it at her!" Resist America shouts.

There are gasps of horror and delight as Socialist Flower splashes blood over my mouth, down my chin and cotton jacket. The stench of blood fills my nose. Blood drips on the ground as I bend over and retch.

"Pour the blood over her, Socialist Flower!" Long March orders. "Over her head!"

Socialist Flower giggles as she lifts the bottle, still three quarters full. Resist America yanks my head back up by my hair, and I squeeze my eyes shut tight.

"Drink, Rightist!" she orders. "Open your mouth . . ."

Bells jangle and brakes screech, and I open my eyes instead.

"*Hey!*"

Your Flying Pigeon skids to a halt and the girls turn to look at you: Zhang Liya, leader of the Beijing No. 104 Middle School for Girls' detachment of the Communist Youth League. You straddle the saddle of your bike, hands squeezing the brakes. You arch your eyebrow at our scuffle. "Comrades," you say, "what are you up to with Yi Moon?"

Socialist Flower smiles uncertainly. She holds the bottle over my head, not sure what to do.

"We are disciplining Moon for laughing at Comrade Po during today's lesson in 'Recalling with Bitterness the Exploitation of the Peasant Classes by Evil Landlords,'" explains Long March. "Moon's laughter is evidence of her counter-revolutionary views."

"Moon's too timid to raise her hand, never mind laugh at a speaker in class," you say scornfully. "Leave her alone now. You've splashed blood on her already. You've gone far enough."

Frustration twists Long March's pretty face into ugliness. "But Liya," she says sharply, "Yi Moon is a class enemy and must be punished!"

"I said, 'Leave her alone,'" you repeat.

Silence. They let me go, and I wipe frantically at my mouth and chin. Long March fumes as though she wants to snatch the bottle from Socialist Flower and smash it over your head. But she doesn't dare protest. Your father is a high-ranking Party official, chauffeured to Zhongnanhai every morning in a black car that glides through the streets of Haidian. One word to your father and higher Communist powers would come down on Long March like a People's Liberation Army boot stamping on a cockroach. You command respect and obedience from every student in our school. But power hasn't corrupted you. Recognizing that Long March's pride has been wounded, you say in a conciliatory tone, "Go on ahead, Long March. Go and start the Youth League meeting without me. You can lead the meeting tonight."

Long March nods, placated to be put in charge. "Capitalist parasite," she hisses at me.

And our classmates walk away. They turn the corner of Vinegar Makers Alley, and we are alone. I stammer my thanks and you lean on the handlebars of your bike and regard me with your clear, strong gaze. Your short hair frames a striking face, with high cheekbones and eyes as determined as those of a heroine in a propaganda poster. Every year you are cast as the revolutionary lead in the school play, but this is as much down to your birthright as your good looks. Before he became a Party official, your father fought the Nationalists, then served as a commander in the Korean War (sacrificing his right eye during hand-to-hand combat with an American soldier in Pyongyang). Some people are born to stand out from the crowd and lead, I think, gazing at you in admiration. You gaze back as though thinking the opposite of me.

"Pig's blood," you say. "You better rinse your clothes in cold water when you get home."

Pig's blood. Nausea turns my stomach, and I wipe again at my blood-smeared mouth.

"Long March goes too far," you admit. "I'll speak to her. I'll ask her to stop these attacks."

"Why does she hate me so much?" I ask.

I expect you to say it's because Long March is a staunch Communist and vigilant with class enemies. But instead you say, "Long March is an unhappy person. People who are unhappy often hurt others."

I consider this, and then say dismally, "But I am unhappy. I don't go around bullying people."

"That's because you haven't had the chance."

Then you are gone. Pedalling up Vinegar Makers Alley to catch up with your friends, leaving me with the pale wisps of your strange remark lingering in the freezing air.

When I get home, I go straight to the communal standpipe in our courtyard and crouch by the spluttering tap to wash the blood from my hands and face. I strip off my jacket and throw it in the bucket underneath. Shivering in my vest, I plunge my hands in the near-frozen water to scrub out the blood before my mother catches me. But my timing is bad, and she emerges from our room with a bowl of carrots to be rinsed.

"Why are you washing your jacket, Moon?" she asks.

"I spilled red paint in art class," I say. "We were painting political slogans and I knocked the paint pot over."

The wrinkles deepen around my mother's concerned eyes. "Little Moon," she says, "tell me the truth. What happened? Are your classmates picking on you again?"

I stare into the bucket, watching the blood eddying in the water. My mother puts down the soil-muddy carrots, places her hand on my shoulder, and asks, "Do you love Chairman Mao with all your heart?"

I nod. Of course I do.

"Well, Moon, you must let your love of Chairman Mao shine out. When those girls recognize that love, shining for Chairman Mao in your heart, they will leave you alone."

I nod. "Okay, Ma."

My mother smiles a drained, tired smile. Since my father was sent to Qinghai, her belief in Chairman Mao and the Party has become very devout. It's not enough, she says, to be revolutionary merely in action. It's not enough to take up a spade and toil for sixteen hours a day when the Party conscripts you to dig a reservoir by the Ming Tombs. It's not enough to spend every waking hour chasing sparrows, rats, mosquitoes and flies when the Party tells us the Four Pests must be eradicated. It's not enough to melt our pots and pans in backyard furnaces when the Party tells us our national iron production must overtake the West's. To be revolutionary merely in action is not enough. If you don't love Chairman Mao in your heart of hearts, the Party will find out, like they found my father out. They will arrest you and send you away to Qinghai.

My mother squats down and gently nudges me from the bucket. "Let me wash that for you, Moonbeam," she says. "Go indoors and warm up by the stove."

My mother plunges her arthritic hands into the pig's-blood-tainted water and scrubs. Shivering, I stand up, and as I cross the courtyard to our room, I see Granny Xi glaring at me out of her window. After my father was convicted as a rightist, Granny Xi organized a petition, calling on the Residents' Committee to evict us. Though the petition was signed by the other families in the courtyard, we haven't yet been served an eviction notice. Offended that we are still here, our neighbours refuse to look at my mother and me. Granny Xi glares right at us, though. She makes her hatred of class enemies known.

The next morning I wake at six, wash and get dressed. Mother serves breakfast, then scolds my lack of appetite as I struggle to eat her rice porridge ("Think of all the starving children in America!"). At seven I say goodbye and leave. But instead of going to the Beijing No. 104 Middle School for Girls, I go to the local junk-yard and wait until my mother leaves for her cleaning job. Then I return to our room and daydream the rest of my day away.

I don't go to school for three days. I know that Teacher Zhao will send a letter to my mother, and I will be caught. But whatever punishment lies in wait is worth the respite from my classmates' hate.

There is a knocking on our door in the evening. Mother stiffens and lowers the woollen sock she is knitting, and we exchange nervous looks. Since father was sent to the labour camp, no one has come to visit us. A knocking in the night can only be bad news.

"Who is it?" my mother calls anxiously.

"Zhang Liya. I have come to speak to Yi Moon."

My mother leaps up and throws open the door, as though to keep you waiting for even a second would be a grave discourtesy.

"Zhang Liya!" she cries. "What an honour! Come in!"

My mother trips over her feet as she fetches you a chair, then apologizes profusely for the chair's wobbly legs. You sit down and Mother brings you a cup of tea, which you politely accept and sip beneath my mother's astonished gaze. Though I am embarrassed by my mother's bowing and scraping, I am just as stunned to see Zhang Liya, daughter of an eminent Communist official, in our dingy, cramped room of broken furniture and smoke-sooty walls. Sensing that you want to talk to me privately, my mother says brightly, "Excuse me, Zhang Liya, but I must go to the store to buy some eggs!" And before we can point out that the shops closed hours ago, she grabs her coat and dashes out into the freezing night.

You sit, hands in lap, in the wobbly legged chair. Your deep-set eyes drift over the used tea leaves Ma has spread out to dry on newspaper (to brew second or third pots), and our damp underwear pegged on a line above the coal-burning stove, which leaks headachy fumes. Your gaze comes to rest on me.

"Yi Moon, Teacher Zhao wants to know why you haven't been in school."

"Oh . . ." I say, flushing. "Stomach flu . . ." I am a clumsy liar, and I look down at my lap, flustered.

"I spoke to Long March," you say, brushing aside my lie, "and Long March has given me her word that she won't bully you anymore. I spoke to Teacher Zhao too, and she has promised that if you are back at your desk tomorrow, you won't be disciplined for missing school."

I stare at you, speechless. How did you convince Teacher Zhao to bend the rules for another pupil? How can a fifteen-year-old have such power and sway?

"You *must* go back to school, Yi Moon," you urge, "or you will make everything worse for yourself . . ."

What could be worse than school? I think. But I nod and say, "Thank you, Zhang Liya. I will be back in class tomorrow."

You nod back, satisfied. Then you stand and go to the door. Out in the courtyard, I watch you kick up the kickstand of your Flying Pigeon. Your eyes obscured in the darkness, I am suddenly emboldened enough to ask, "Zhang Liya, why are you being so kind to me?"

You look at me uncertainly. Then you wheel your bicycle out the gate, leaving my question unanswered in the night.

Back at school, everything is as you said. Teacher Zhao nods her salt-and-pepper head in approval when she sees me at my desk. Though I have no note from my mother, she doesn't ask about my absence. Long March and her gang don't ask either and go on braiding each other's hair and singing "The East Is Red" before the morning bell. The day goes on and no one shoots me any hateful looks. No one "accidentally" barges into me or trips me up. No one hisses "Stinking Rightist" in the hall. There's no opening of my desk lid to find a pot of glue poured over my books. It's as though there's an invisible circle around me that no one dares cross.

During the breaks from lessons, I roam the playground on my own then read in a corner of the library. Most girls would be miserable to be cast out by their classmates. Most girls would be forlorn. But after Long March and her gang's long campaign of hate, I am relieved.

On Sunday morning, I am studying a history book about the Communists' defeat of the Japanese devils in the War of Resistance against Japan, when there is a knock at the door. My mother puts down the handkerchief she is embroidering with "Long Live Chairman Mao" and goes to answer. I hear your strong, distinctive voice, but don't catch your words.

"Wait a moment!" my mother shrills in excitement. "I'll ask her!" She turns back into our dark hovel, skirt and apron flaring. "Zhang Liya wants to know if you'll go on a bike ride with her!"

"But I don't own a bike."

Bells are trilling outside. I put my homework aside and go to the door. In the courtyard you stand holding two shiny, brand-new Flying Pigeons by the handlebars. Your short hair is tucked behind your ears and you look military and tough in your father's hand-me-down People's Liberation Army jacket.

"Which bicycle do you want, Moon?" you ask. "The red one, or the blue?"

We cycle through Haidian, past Tsinghua University, to the ruins of the Old Summer Palace, torched by the British and French devils during the Qing Dynasty. We climb off our bikes and push them by the handlebars as we walk amongst the collapsed pillars and arches of the once-majestic palace, now desolate and overgrown with weeds. We trample through the withered grasses and you say sombrely, "These ruins symbolize how weak China was before Liberation. How fortunate we are that Chairman Mao taught our nation to stand up and be proud!"

I nod. I vehemently agree.

"Chairman Mao would never have let the foreign devils ransack our palaces! He would have sent out the People's Liberation Army, one million strong, to destroy them!"

You smile at this. The wind blows your short hair up from the roots, and your eyes shine with patriotic pride. "After high school I am going to join the army and fight to defend our motherland," you declare. "And when I can no longer fight, I will serve the people by becoming a Party official. I'm not going to university. I'd rather have adventures than learn from books."

Though I have no desire to be a soldier or politician, I envy your ambition. I envy your confidence that your ambitions will be fulfilled. "What about you, Yi Moon?" you ask. "What will you do after school?"

"The government will assign me a job," I say quietly. "I will most likely end up as a cleaner like my mother."

You frown at me, concerned. "Why are your ambitions so low?" you ask. "You are very clever. You could study at Tsinghua if you wanted. You could be more than a cleaner . . ."

I want to explain that I will never go to university because of my father. But I remember my mother's advice: *Before you so much as breathe, think about whether it could be misconstrued as a criticism about the Party.* "Misconstrued" because my mother and I have no criticisms. We support everything the Party does.

"Ordinary workers are important," I say. "They serve the people and the motherland too. I will be proud to be a cleaner, and will work my hardest at the job."

You nod, accepting that I will be content to mop floors for the rest of my life. And suddenly I am heavy of heart, for my future looks as bleak and hopeless as my life now.

At dusk we cycle to a noodle shop in Wet Nurse Alley, where the owner greets you like a visiting dignitary and immediately serves us two bowls of noodles with ground beef.

"This costs a week of my mother's wages," I gasp, reading the menu. "I can't afford this!"

"Don't worry," you say casually. "My father has an account here. He has accounts in most places in Haidian."

The delicious aroma of beef rises from the noodles. The last time I ate meat was during the Spring Festival, nearly a year ago, and I bury my head and chopsticks in the bowl, slurping up the noodles and broth. When the bowl is empty, I belch and wipe my mouth and am ashamed to see that you have been watching me. How greedy I must have looked. Your own noodles are untouched.

"We can't be friends at school, Moon," you say. "You understand why, don't you?"

I understand why. You are as red and glorious as our national flag, and I am as black as the grime under a convicted rightist's fingernails. Of course I understand why. But I still feel slapped.

"Then why be my friend at all, Liya?" I ask. "Why bother with a friendship that must be kept secret?"

You widen your eyes in surprise at my question. "How could I *not* want to be your friend, Moon?" you say. "When I am with you, I'm so at ease. It's as though I have known you all my life . . ."

Your praise makes me blush, and I forgive you at once. Your request is understandable, and it's selfish of me to take offence.

"I understand, Liya," I say. "It's important that you maintain your red status so you can one day fight for Chairman Mao and our motherland. I don't mind if we can't be friends at school. I am lucky to get to be your friend at all."

You smile at me, your deep-set eyes wells of gratitude. And I smile back, hoping that my understanding will last. Hoping resentment won't creep back in.

The next weekend, when your father is away on Party business in Beidaihe and your stepmother visiting relatives in Tianjin, you invite me to stay at your home. You live in a courtyard like me, but whereas six families are crowded into our ramshackle building, the Zhang family have the entire property to themselves. You show me around, and I sigh with envy. The furniture in every room is elegant and skilfully crafted, and as well as portraits of Chairman Mao, delicate bird and flower paintings by a famous Hangzhou artist decorate the walls. But what I envy most is the privacy. Never do you have to listen to your neighbours rowing, or making noisy love, weeping or sneezing, or beating their kids in the next room. You even have your own private bathroom, with a flushing toilet, hot and cold running water and a wooden bathtub—sparing you trips to the stinking public convenience and the lice-ridden communal bathhouse, crowded with other people's naked bodies.

"You bathe in your own home?" I ask.

"Every night," you say. "Let's have a bath now." And you turn on the hot tap and strip.

The water is cleaner and hotter than in the communal baths, and we steep at opposite ends of the wooden tub, speechless with pleasure. Submerged in water, I hug my knees to my chest, conscious of how skinny I am. The Three Years of Natural Disasters, and the food shortages that ensued, stunted my growth. The hundreds of meals I went without during those hardscrabble years have left me as underdeveloped as a child. One look at your healthy, womanly body, however, flushed a radiant pink, tells me you were never kept awake at night by a growling stomach. You smile at me through the rising steam, then surprise me by wistfully saying, "Moon, you have such lovely long hair. Can I wash it for you?"

I turn my back to you, slide up the tub and sit between your legs. You unbraid my hair and comb it out with your fingers. You lather up a bar of soap.

"Your hair is like silk . . ." you praise, fingers massaging my scalp. "So lustrous and soft."

"Why don't you grow your own hair?" I ask, thinking of your short bob, cut to the earlobes.

"No way," you laugh. "Long hair is bourgeois."

I hear the shudder in your voice, and I say, "Well, in that case, I ought to cut mine short like yours."

"Don't you dare!" you joke in a warning tone. "Don't touch a strand!"

I slide down the tub and slip underwater, swishing my hair about to rinse out the soap. How strange and contradictory you are, I think, to admire my hair and condemn it at the same time.

After a meal of pork dumplings, cooked for us by your servant, we go to spend the evening in your bedroom. The room has a bed, a desk and chair, a white bust of Chairman Mao and no character to speak of. Though you must sleep there every night, the room has a bare and utilitarian air, as though purged of your girlhood things to prepare for life in the Liberation Army barracks. I sit by the record player and flip through the collection of vinyl. "The East Is Red." "Ode to the Motherland." "The Night-Soil Collectors Are Coming Down the Mountain." Revolutionary anthems with rosy-cheeked workers holding their hoes and scythes aloft on the cardboard sleeves.

"You can listen to any record you like," you say.

"Um . . . that's okay."

Sensing my boredom with your record collection, you ask hesitantly, "Do you want to hear a different kind of music?"

I look up from "Raise the Red Flag for the Soldiers, Peasants and Workers." "All right."

You go to your bed and grope under your bedding for a screwdriver. You then use the screwdriver to pry up a loose floorboard and reach beneath to pull out a battered cardboard box.

"A servant was cleaning out a store cupboard a few years ago," you say, "and found some of my mother's things. My father said they were decadent trophies of the Nationalist era and threw them out. But I sneaked out in the night and got them out of the bin."

You tilt your chin and say defensively, "My mother died when I was six. This is all I have of her."

You pull the lid off the cardboard box and lift out a scarlet qipao, embroidered with golden flowers. I gasp and stroke the qipao, my fingers enjoying the sensation of pure silk.

"This was my mother's dress," you say. "Here is a photograph of her when she was twenty." You show me a black-and-white photo of a beautiful woman, posing with her hand under her chin. She has an enigmatic smile on her lips and a white gardenia in her hair.

"Your mother looks like a movie star," I sigh.

You modestly brush my compliment aside, though I can tell you are pleased. "Of course," you say sternly, "my mother would never doll herself up like a woman of loose morals if she was alive today. This photograph was taken in the Nationalist era, when women were exploited and oppressed by the shackles of beauty."

"Yes," I agree. "Thanks to Communism, women are now emancipated from the tyranny of lipstick and hair curlers." Though, gazing at your lovely mother, I can't help but think that lipstick and hair curlers weren't all bad.

There's one more object in the cardboard box: a record with not a worker, peasant or soldier on the sleeve but a glamorous woman with her hair in the stiff waves of a permanent and the same hand-under-chin pose as your mother.

"This is a love song from Hong Kong, where my mother grew up. She used to play it to me when I was little. I listen to it sometimes, when my father and stepmother aren't home . . ." Another hard and defensive stare. "It helps me remember her."

You lower the record onto the turntable and drop the needle in the groove. There is hissing and crackling, then a singer warbling in Cantonese to a big band. The melody is joyful, but with a hint of melancholy. You translate the lyrics for me.

"'I will make you mine . . . I will love you until the end of time . . .' The song is about a shop girl in love with the mail boy."

Though it's just a simple love ballad, it sends shivers down my spine and I realize it's been years since I heard a song without a militant marching-band beat, rallying the masses to fight for the Socialist motherland. It has been years since I heard a woman singing of love for a man who is not Chairman Mao.

I take a deep, steadying breath. This record is from Hong Kong, the prison island where the British devils have enslaved our Chinese brothers and sisters. A Marxist-Maoist analysis of this song would most certainly reveal its hidden anti-Communist agenda, that the song intends to lure us from the path of socialism by corrupting us with bourgeois longings for romantic love. Oblivious, you sway to the music, your eyes shut.

"Zhang Liya . . ." I say in a quiet but urgent tone, "maybe we shouldn't be listening to this anti-Communist Hong Kong music . . ."

You snap out of your trance and there's a warping sound as you stop the music, dragging the needle across the vinyl. You snatch the record from the turntable and shove it back into the sleeve. You seem shaken and upset.

"Thank you, Yi Moon," you say. "I will stop listening to this Hong Kong record. I will overcome my sentimental attachment to my mother's things. I will destroy these shameful, decadent possessions first thing tomorrow."

You put another record on the turntable, and the strident marching beat of "The Night-Soil Collectors Are Coming Down the Mountain" fills the room. You avoid my eyes, and I know that you won't destroy your mother's things tomorrow. You will continue to hide them under the floorboard and cherish them with all your heart.

* * *

Later, under thick bedcovers on your coal-heated bed you ask, "Do you miss your father?"

Our heads share a pillow, and your breath is warm and tickling on my cheek. At the mention of my father, my heart clenches with the fear he has died in the labour camp. But I don't speak this fear. I open my mouth and a well-rehearsed, politically correct answer comes out.

"He's no longer a father to me," I say. "Only when Class Enemy Yi Liang has been fully rehabilitated as a loyal citizen of the People's Republic of China will I accept him as a father again."

You are silent and doubtful in the darkness. Then you ask, "What was he like? Before he went away?"

When I was a child, my father read folktales to me. He gave me calligraphy lessons in the courtyard, writing on stone with a long brush dipped in a pail of water. He taught me to ride a bicycle, holding the saddle from behind ("Keep on pedalling, Little Moon! I'm here to catch you if you fall!"). He named me Little Moon because I was born with a "face as bright and round as the moon."

"He was a good father," I whisper. I squeeze my eyes shut, but tears squeak out. You hear my sniffles.

"Don't cry, Moon." You put your arms around me, holding me closer to the heat and pulse of your body. "Don't cry. Your father will be reformed and released soon."

You kiss my eyelids with light butterfly kisses that flutter down into the pit of my belly. It's so unexpected, I stop crying immediately. The last person who kissed me like this was my mother, and not since I was a little girl. You stop kissing me but don't move away. Your breath is humid on my face.

"What about your father?" I whisper. "What's he like?"

You laugh and say, "One-eyed Zhang gave me a good Communist upbringing. He was reading passages of *The Communist Manifesto* to me when I was still in the womb. When I was old enough to read, he made me memorize *People's Daily* editorials and recite them back to him. If I made too many mistakes, that one-eyed bastard would beat me." You laugh again. Bitter and without mirth.

"I should be grateful to Comrade Zhang, I suppose," you say. "Thanks to his strict ideological training, political speeches are effortless for me . . . My father wanted to call me Soviet Zhang"—you pause—"but my mother insisted on the name of Liya. She was much gentler than him. Not a day goes by when I don't miss her . . ."

You stroke my hair, your fingers tickling my scalp. It's past midnight, much later than I am used to. My eyelids are drooping, the tempo of my blood slowing down.

"You were looking at me in the bathtub," you say.

Your words shake me back to wakefulness.

"What?"

"My breasts," you say. "You were looking."

I laugh in surprise. "You were naked. How could I not look?"

I hear the muscles in your throat contract. "You can touch them if you like."

I laugh again, embarrassed, not sure whether you are joking. I don't move, so you grab my limp hand and place it on your pyjama top, over your left breast. I rest my hand there awkwardly for a moment, then I squeeze. "Much bigger than mine," I comment.

"You'll catch up, in a year or two," you say kindly.

I remove my hand, and it feels different somehow, as though the fullness of your breast has left an impression in my palm.

"Have you started yet?" you ask.

"Last year," I say, "but they aren't regular. Every three months or so."

"Mine came when I was twelve," you say. "I thought I was dying. I ran to the school nurse in tears, and she gave me some rags and explained what it was."

"I can't believe"—I nearly say, *your mother didn't tell you*, then I remember your mother is dead—"you didn't know." There's a tickling in my throat so I turn my head and lightly cough. Then I ask the question I wanted to ask when you put my hand on your breast: "Do you ever touch yourself?"

"Touch myself?"

"You don't ever touch yourself . . . ? Down there?"

"*No.*"

You sound appalled, and I regret mentioning it. But then you ask, "What's it like?"

I hesitate, then say, "It starts when I think of a man, like Teacher Wu, kissing me, and *down there* feels good. So I rub and rub and the feeling grows stronger, until this *spasm* comes . . . I sleep in the same bed as my mother, so I usually wait until she is snoring . . . Sometimes I stop halfway through, scared I have woken her . . ."

You don't say anything. What are you thinking? That I am a pervert? A sexual degenerate?

"I . . . I feel bad afterwards," I stammer. "So I will stop this bad habit. I will keep my thoughts Socialist and pure, and loyal to the motherland."

You remain silent and I start to panic. What was I thinking? You are Zhang Liya, leader of our school's detachment of the Communist Youth League. You will report me on Monday, and I will be ordered to write a confession of my bourgeois self-pleasuring and read it in assembly. Teacher Wu will be disgusted. I will be expelled and perhaps even sent to a prison for juvenile sex offenders. My mother will hang herself in shame.

"What do you rub?" you whisper. "What is this *spasm*?" You reach for my hand, resting on the pillow, and tug it down under the bedcovers. "Show me how."

At the Beijing No. 104 Middle School for Girls, you behave like a stranger to me. But though you shun me in the classrooms and halls, I know that I am your closest friend. Though you and Long March walk arm in arm in the yard, I know she is your rival and wants your position as leader of the Youth League. ("Long March would push me off a cliff if she had the chance.") Though you and Resist America share a bowl of noodles in the dining hall, you have never bathed with Resist America, or washed her hair with your stepmother's expensive shampoo. Though you and Patriotic Hua plan the agenda for Youth League meetings together, you have never shown Patriotic Hua the black-and-white photograph of your mother, or turned the white bust of Chairman Mao to the wall before dancing cheek to cheek with her to ballads from Hong Kong. Though you praise Soviet Chen's singing of the latest revolutionary opera, you have never hooked your leg over Soviet Chen's under the bedcovers and whispered, "We are like a pair of chopsticks. We belong together."

Though you ignore me, I know I am your most intimate friend. Though at school I am as ostracized as ever, the spring of 1966 is the happiest of my life.

We spend every Saturday night together until May, when I don't see you for three weekends in a row. There are rumours that the Party has handed down directives to the student leaders to be more revolutionary. There are rumours of a coming political storm. And I know these Party commands are keeping you away.

The first Saturday in June you knock for me, exhausted after a ten-hour Youth League meeting. The evening is hot, and we go to Ironmongers Lane and soak in a tub of tepid water. When I ask you about the rumours, you say, "There's going to be a reform of the education system. I am prohibited from saying any more than that. But don't worry, Moon. I will keep you safe."

After dinner, we lie on your bed and go to sleep. Hours later I am woken by the floorboards creaking as you pace up and down, lost in thought. The moon-cast shadows of the tree outside the window reach across your body, the branches stroking your breasts and hips and reaching as though to strangle your neck. I drift off again, and wake before daybreak to see you kneeling by the loose floorboard and staring at the black-and-white photo of your dead mother. Are you too excited to sleep? Or too scared?

I am scared. In every political campaign, it's the rightists who suffer most.

II

On Monday when I arrive at school the playground is crowded with girls gazing up at large sheets of paper dripping with black ink pasted to the gate and the school walls.

Long Live the Great Proletariat Cultural Revolution.
Time for a Revolution in Education.
The Rightist Intellectual Headteacher Yang Must No Longer Dominate Our School with Her Capitalist Agenda.

We stare at the posters, confused. Who vandalized the playground? Where are the teachers? Why hasn't the bell rung for lessons? Only the Youth League members look as though they know what is going on. You and Long March, Red Star and Patriotic Hua stand with authority, watching your classmates' reactions to the slogans in black ink.

"Why hasn't the bell rung?" someone asks.

"Lessons are cancelled," Long March says.

"But the high school entrance exams are next month," complains Ying Le, who wants to go to medical school and train to be a doctor. "How are we supposed to study for them?"

"The high school entrance exams have been abolished!" Long March snaps. "The education system is being reformed. The teachers have been teaching the revisionist anti-Party line for long enough!"

You stand on the stage in the auditorium in front of hundreds of girls. Your hair has been shorn like a boy's and you wear a PLA jacket over your uniform. You look very military and tough as you hold a loudspeaker to your mouth and say, "We have it on good authority that there are Ox Demons and Snake Ghosts on the faculty of our school."

There are outraged gasps. Fearful murmurs. Confusion. Ox Demons and Snake Ghosts are spirits from folktales and myths that assume human form and do mischief. Do you really believe that our teachers are evil spirits?

"Many of our teachers are counter-revolutionaries," you say, "pretending to support the Party while indoctrinating us with the anti-Party line. The education system must be reformed to weed these bad elements out. Until the Cultural Revolution Committee decides upon the next course of action, all teachers have been suspended."

The whispers of hundreds of girls sweep through the auditorium, as though your words are a strong breeze rustling the leaves of a tree. "The teachers are suspended?" "What about exams?" "What's the Cultural Revolution?"

"Class time will now be devoted to revolutionary activities," you say through the crackling loudspeaker. "Every student is to give her blood, sweat and tears to the Cultural Revolution!"

Long March strides towards you on the stage and you hand the loudspeaker over to her. "The black-category students, with rightist, landlord or capitalist blood lineage will not participate in the revolutionary activities!" she says. "The black-category students will be segregated to the back of every classroom. They will study the collected works of Mao Zedong. They will write self-criticisms and reform their thinking!"

Standing beside Long March, you nod as though in agreement. You nod as though our segregation is fair and right.

Our classroom becomes a Big-Character Poster production line. Black ink smudges the faces and hands of nearly every student as they use calligraphy brushes to make posters denouncing our former teachers. Red Star has been appointed a "Big-Character Poster Inspector" and Ying Le's poster does not meet her standards.

"'Teacher Zhao Must Evict Any Thoughts that Contradict the Party Line from Her Heart . . .'" Red Star reads scornfully. "What's this meant to be? A love poem?"

"But I can't think of any anti-Party crimes Teacher Zhao has committed," Ying Le says honestly. "She was a dedicated Communist."

"Stop thinking like an intellectual and think like a rebel," Red Star scolds. "Teacher Zhao deceived us into thinking she was a loyal Communist when really she was teaching us her revisionist curriculum!"

Ying Le bows her head. She wants to be a doctor, not a rebel. Red Star snatches the calligraphy brush from her and scrawls, "Teacher Zhao Must Be Torn Limb from Limb for Challenging the Doctrine of Chairman Mao!"

"There!" she says. "Political power grows out of the barrel of a gun, and you, *Dr. Ying*, better hurry up and learn which end goes bang. Or I'll put you at the back of class with those Stinking Rightists over there." Red Star looks over at the black-category students, and catches me looking up from my desk. "Who gave you permission to look at me?" she snaps. "Take your beady little capitalist eyes off me!"

I bury my head back in my exercise book.

Industriously Study Mao Zedong Thought, as Mao Zedong Thought Is the Sole Criterion of Truth.

Long March has ordered us to write this ten thousand times without mistakes, and I have just completed my hundredth line. If Mao Zedong Thought is the sole criterion of truth, I think, then what about the five thousand years of civilization before Chairman Mao? For five thousand years was everything *false*? Of course, I keep my doubts to myself.

"Women hold up half the sky. Women are as revolutionary as men. We of the Beijing No. 104 Middle School for Girls reject femininity. We will roll up our sleeves and spit and curse! We won't bathe or wash our clothes. Soap is bourgeois! The sweat of the masses is revolutionary! We will breed dirt under our fingernails and behind our ears! We will emancipate ourselves from the shackles of our sex!"

Waving scissors above her head, Little Miao lectures us from the teaching platform. Miao has no problem "rejecting femininity," as for years Miao has been as aggressive, foul-mouthed and unwashed as the roughest of boys. Shopkeepers call her "young man," and children in the street call her "Elder Brother." Proud to be a tomboy, Little Miao never corrects their mistake. And now, scissors in hand, she intends for the rest of us to "reject femininity" too.

The long-haired girls go to Little Miao and she turns them into short-haired girls, one by one, hacking with the scissors, steely eyed, as though hair itself is the enemy. The "revolutionary haircuts" are awful, but who dares complain? Little Miao holds up every severed pigtail and we cheer as though they are enemy scalps. When it is my turn, Little Miao is vicious with me.

"Times have changed, Daughter of a Rightist!" she shouts, cutting away. "From now on, haircuts must be short, practical and revolutionary!" When her scissors have done their worst, she shoves me off the teaching platform. "Not so pretty now, eh? Go weep some capitalist tears over your lovely bourgeois locks!" she calls after me.

But Little Miao is wrong. I couldn't care less about my hair. The only person who cares is you. As I go back to my desk, I catch you staring at my short and stubbly head with sad, sentimental eyes.

I want to laugh in your face. My hair is the least of my problems right now.

In July, Teacher Zhao shuffles back into class to go on trial for her counter-revolutionary crimes and we see she has lost weight and now has more salt than pepper in her hair. As Teacher Zhao stands before us in her thick spectacles and chalk-dusty Mao jacket, patched and patched again, I remember her passionate teachings about Communism and can't shake the conviction that Teacher Zhao is a loyal Maoist from my mind.

"Comrades!" Long March yells. "Teacher Zhao is a traitor to the People's Republic, and opposed to the correct policy of our Great Leader Chairman Mao! This meeting, on 16 July 1966, is to denounce Teacher Zhao and her anti-Party teachings. But before we start, let's give Teacher Zhao a chance to confess her crimes."

Confronted by the fury of her former students, Teacher Zhao is shaking. But she speaks with her chin up, righteous and strong. "Comrades," she begins, "I am the daughter of poor peasants. My family background is revolutionary. My father fought the Japanese devils in the Eighth Route Army. My brother fought the American running dogs in the Korean War. I live a humble spinster's life, devoted to the teaching and practice of Communism. I am not opposed to the Party, and I have never committed any crime. Therefore I have nothing to confess. *Long live Chairman Mao!*"

"Class Enemy Zhao!" Long March shouts. "You are in contempt of the People's Court! You must assume the correct attitude of repentance and confess!"

"Down with Teacher Zhao!" Red Star chants. "No leniency to those who won't confess!"

The rest of the class chants with Red Star, banging on desk lids and scaring Teacher Zhao out of her wits. When the chanting stops, Long March reads Teacher Zhao her crimes—the findings of the Cultural Revolution Committee's investigation into her teaching and conduct: "1. Teacher Zhao is a loyal running dog of the Nationalists. 2. Teacher Zhao is a Nationalist spy. 3. Teacher Zhao is part of the plot to overthrow the Communist Party by taking over the military."

Teacher Zhao stares at Long March, stunned. Long March then tells Teacher Zhao of the evidence we have. One day last October Teacher Zhao had chalked "Use Maoist Thought to Criticize *Maoist* Thought" on the blackboard instead of "Use Maoist Thought to Criticize *Bourgeois* Thought." Teacher Zhao had laughed and corrected her mistake. But it was too late. A slip of the chalk had shown us evidence of her secret anti-Party agenda.

"Well, Class Enemy Zhao?" Long March spits fiercely. "Did you or did you not write 'Use Maoist Thought to Criticize Maoist Thought' on the blackboard last October? Think carefully before you answer. There are twenty-eight witnesses here in this room who will testify that you did."

For the next three hours Teacher Zhao defends herself against the charges. Though she looks scared stiff when the class breaks into chanting "Down with Teacher Zhao!" she still won't confess. Eventually, Long March screams, "I am sick of this rightist whore!" and slaps Teacher Zhao so hard she knocks her glasses off and sends them shattering to the floor. The class descends into silence. For a student to hit a teacher is an unthinkable thing. But Teacher Zhao hangs her head and does not reprimand Long March.

"I am sick of Teacher Zhao's lies," Long March spits. "As the Great Helmsman said, 'To stain our hands with our enemies' blood is an honour!' Comrades! The Anti–Black Gang Capitalist rally has begun outside. Let's take her out!"

The Ox Freaks and Snake Monsters are paraded around the running track behind the school. Tall dunce hats are placed on their heads and placards hung around their necks: *Down with Head-teacher Yang! Down with Black Gangster Zhao!* The teachers are handed pots and pans, which they are forced to bang in percussion as they straggle around the field.

A third-year girl called Shaoli shrieks the headteacher's crimes through a loudspeaker: "Headteacher Yang Attempted to Overthrow the Communist Government and Take Over the Military! Headteacher Yang Attempted to Assassinate Chairman Mao!"

Headteacher Yang is stony-faced and unrepentant. Shaoli calls over Teacher Wu and tells him to slap the headteacher. When he refuses, a second-year girl beats him with a broom. They call over Teacher Zhao and, scared of being beaten too, she slaps Headteacher Yang to loud cheers. "*Harder! Harder!*" shout their former pupils. Shaoli orders Headteacher Yang and Teacher Zhao to knock heads, and they headbutt each other like rams. "*Harder!*" Shaoli shouts through the loudspeaker, like a ringmaster in a circus of humiliation and cruelty.

Keen to lead the Anti–Black Gang Capitalist rally, you take the loudspeaker from Shaoli, punch your fist in the air and shout, "The iron fist of the proletariat will crush the enemies of Chairman Mao! Heads will roll! Blood will flow! But we will never let go of Mao Zedong Thought! *Long Live the Great Proletarian Cultural Revolution!*"

And hundreds of girls punch their fists up to the sky and shout, "*Long Live the Great Proletarian Cultural Revolution!*"

You hurl your clenched fist up again: "*Long Live the Anti-capitalist School for Revolutionary Girls!*"

And I have no choice but to flail my fist to the heavens and shout with everyone else: "*Long Live the Anti-capitalist School for Revolutionary Girls!*"

* * *

331

That night I can't sleep. I close my eyes and see Teacher Wu bleeding from his head as the second-year girl beats him with a broom. I see Teacher Lin on her hands and knees, her tongue lapping at Resist America's boot leather. I see Teacher Zhao being slapped hard in the face by Long March, and her glasses shattering on the classroom floor.

I slip out of bed at daybreak and go to the Zhang residence in Ironmongers Lane. Though it's not yet six o'clock, you are up and seated on the bench in the yard. Comrade Zhang Liya, leader of the newly established Red Guard of the Anti-capitalist School for Revolutionary Girls, looking ready to fight the class enemies with your PLA uniform, red-star beret and militant gaze. Then you see me and break into a wide smile. We haven't spoken in weeks. Not since the Cultural Revolution began.

"Yi Moon," you smile. "How are you?"

I smile back thinly and say, "I am well, thank you. I have become very practised at writing Thought Reports and using the scalpel of Mao Zedong Thought to excise the malignant tumours of rightist thought from my mind. I can write Thought Reports in my sleep."

"Good," you say, ignoring my sarcasm. "Keep your political consciousness strong."

"How about you, Comrade Zhang?" I ask. "Is the revolution progressing as you hoped?"

"Progress has been satisfactory," you say, your eyes shining, "but there is more work to be done. For now we must spread the revolution beyond our schools, to the streets of Beijing. But we Red Guards will rise to the challenge. We Red Guards will fight to protect our Great Leader Chairman Mao from the capitalist roaders who attack him."

"I'd rather have adventures than learn from books," you told me in the ruins of the Old Summer Palace. Back then, your ambition had impressed me. Back then, I hadn't known "have adventures" meant persecuting and terrorizing innocent people.

"Liya . . ." I say, "do you really think that Teacher Zhao was spying for the Nationalists and plotting to overthrow the Communist Party?"

"The Cultural Revolution Committee of the Anti-capitalist School for Revolutionary Girls has these allegations under investigation," you respond.

"But what evidence is there?"

"The allegations are under investigation."

Frustrated by your stilted, official speech, I cry out, "Every time I close my eyes, I see Teacher Lin licking Resist America's boots, or Headteacher Yang being slapped in the face. Can't you see how awful it is? We have stopped being humans. We are worse than beasts!"

Under your red-star cap, your eyes are stern. "You sympathize with the rightists because your father is a rightist," you say. "Restore your red status, and you would throw yourself into the Cultural Revolution tomorrow."

"My father is not a rightist!" I correct. "My father's department had to expel a quota of rightists. That's why he was arrested and sent away. He did nothing wrong."

You shake your head, as though at my naivety, and say, "Do you really think they'd send your father to a labour camp if he hadn't committed a crime?"

A servant enters the courtyard with a teakwood tray of rice porridge, steamed buns and soy milk. The servant girl, who is our age, lowers the tray beside you on the bench then retreats, walking backwards like a eunuch before the Emperor. You don't thank her, or even nod to acknowledge her, your chin propped up high by your sense of entitlement. How can you pretend to be one of the masses? I think scornfully. How can you pretend to be one of the proletariat, when you live like *this*?

I turn to leave. I don't bother to say goodbye. "*Wait!*" you cry. You come after me, catching me by my shoulder at the gate. I turn around, expecting an apology for what you said about my father. Tenderness returns to your eyes as you stroke my head. "Sorry they cut your hair," you say. "You used to have such beautiful hair. But that bitch Miao *butchered* it."

Who gives a damn about my hair? I want to scream. I step back, disgusted, and your eyes turn sad.

"Yi Moon, I want you to know," you say, "I am protecting you and your mother. I am keeping you safe."

"My mother and I don't need you to protect us," I mutter as I turn and walk out the gate.

Your laughter pursues me down Ironmongers Lane: "If only you knew . . ."

The Smash the Four Olds movement begins, and the Red Guards take over the streets of Beijing, intent on destroying the Old Culture, Old Society, Old Education and Old Ways of Thinking. Red Guards stand at intersections, shouting the quotations of Chairman Mao through loudspeakers. Red Guards hijack buses and lecture the passengers about the Ox Freaks and Snake Monsters in their midst. Red Guards armed with knives chase after people in western clothes, slashing their American-style shirts and dresses to shreds.

Destroy the Capitalists Street. All Hail the Red Guards Lane. The East Is Red Boulevard. All over Beijing, street names are changed to revolutionary slogans. Shops selling paintings, ornaments and other "poisonous weeds of the capitalist classes" are smashed up and portraits of Chairman Mao displayed in the windows. Signs saying *Masses Beware! For Tens of Years This Shop Has Exploited the Sweat and Blood of the Workers!* appear over shop doorways. The Red Guards "liberate" the shop assistants from their managers, who are beaten to the floor. The Red Guards change the traffic-light system so revolutionary red means "go" and green means "stop." The Red Guards then persecute the victims of the resulting traffic accidents for "clinging to the Old Culture and Old Ways of Thinking."

Red Guards from Beijing University stand in our alley, halting passersby and ordering them to quote Chairman Mao. They stop my mother, who nervously stammers, "Serve the People!" (choosing the simplest quote, because those who misquote the Great Helmsman are beaten). The Red Guards stop Idiot Zhu from the junkyard, who, when asked for a quote, laughs and says, "Chairman Mao stinks of dog farts!" The students take off their leather belts and beat the giggling Idiot Zhu, yelling, "Enemy of Chairman Mao! You deserve to die!" They eventually drag Idiot Zhu off to jail, and we don't see or hear of him again.

The home raids begin. Teenage fists *bang bang bang* on our courtyard gate, and my mother and I rush panicking around our room, hiding bamboo mahjong tiles, father's calligraphy and anything that could be labelled "poisonous weeds." The Red Guards break the gate down and we are certain we are done for. But as we cower behind our locked door, we overhear them say, "What about the rightist Yi family?"

"Zhang Liya struck them off the list. Besides, the Yi family don't have a pot to piss in."

And the twenty or so Red Guards storm into Granny Xi's room instead.

Landscape paintings, Qing Dynasty vases, classic novels and land deeds to old properties in the city—the Red Guards drag a haul of riches out of Granny Xi's room. Though Granny Xi petitioned to have my mother and me evicted, I can't help but pity the old woman as she is dragged out and forced to kneel in the yard. Mother and I peek out the window as a pimply teenage boy slaps Granny Xi in the face with her Nationalist-era land deeds.

"You kept these land deeds hoping that the Nationalists would return, didn't you?" he accuses. "You are hoping the Nationalists will come back and restore your status as a landlord, aren't you?"

"No," says Granny Xi, "I hate the Nationalists. I just forgot to throw them away."

The Red Guard unbuckles his belt and tugs it out of the trouser loops. He lashes the strip of leather down on Granny Xi's back and my mother gasps, "She's *eighty-four*!"

They make a fire of Granny Xi's poisonous weeds and force her to kneel close to her burning furniture and books so that the smoke makes her cough and the heat blisters her skin. When the Red Guards leave, carting Granny Xi's valuables, or "Ill-Gotten

Gains of the Exploiting Classes," off in a wheelbarrow, we go outside to help Granny Xi to her feet. Though she has long detested us, Granny Xi does not resist as my mother and I bring her into our room. The old woman collapses on a chair, her cheeks smudged with smoke, and her white hair and eyebrows singed. Mother kneels by Granny Xi and squeezes her wrinkled hand.

"Do you love Chairman Mao with all your heart?" she asks gently. "If you let that love shine out of your heart, Red Guards will leave you alone."

And Granny Xi looks at my mother with such watery, defeated eyes I am nostalgic for the days they seethed at us with hate.

Every day the black-category students go to school. Every day we study Chairman Mao's *Little Red Book*, write our Thought Reports and clean the school building. I am put on toilet-cleaning duty. Though I scrub the toilet bowls with my toothbrush every day for weeks, the pubic hairs, bloody sanitary napkins and faecal smears never cease to make me gag. But I can't slack off, because Martial Spirit comes to inspect my work.

"Why the vinegar-drinking face, Stinking Rightist? Too bourgeois to clean toilets, are you?"

Comrade Martial Spirit, formerly my mousy, twitchy classmate Socialist Flower, has become a monster since her promotion to jailer-in-command of the Cattle Shed. As I crouch by the toilet with a toothbrush in my hand, Martial Spirit sneers, "Scrub harder, Rightist! Or I'll kick the capitalist airs and graces right out of you!"

My other duty is to feed the Black-Gang Capitalists, incarcerated in the Cattle Shed. The Cattle Shed is the former music room, and the Black-Gang Capitalists are our former teachers, now subject to interrogation for their crimes.

"Long Live Chairman Mao!" I yell, entering the Cattle Shed with a tray of rice bowls.

"Long Live Chairman Mao!" the teachers croak back, vocal cords ragged from screaming.

The Cattle Shed smells of unwashed bodies and fear-loosened

bladders and bowels. "Long Live the Red Terror!" has been finger-painted in blood on the wall, above the portrait of Chairman Mao. Weeks of intimidation have broken the teachers down. They cringe behind their desks with bruised eyes, obedient as whipped dogs. I serve the bowls of rice and their chopsticks tremble as they eat.

There are fewer Black-Gang Capitalists now than at the start of the Cultural Revolution. Headteacher Yang was the first to die. The Cattle Shed jailers accidentally kicked her to death during an interrogation, and were out of their minds with panic afterwards. But there were no repercussions, and the next time they murdered a teacher they knew they had nothing to fear. Some Black-Gang Capitalists commit suicide. I was the one who found Teacher Zhao's corpse in the toilets, swinging from the leaky water pipes. Her salt-and-pepper head was bent over the noose and her toes swayed over the damp cement floor. A suicide note was pinned to her chalk-dusty Mao jacket:

> I am an Enemy of the People.
> In order not to poison the masses, I will exterminate myself from society.
> Long Live the Great Proletarian Cultural Revolution!
> Long Live Chairman Mao!

I went to Headteacher Yang's former office, now the headquarters of the Cattle Shed jailers, to break the news. Comrade Martial Spirit reacted with dismay.

"Teacher Zhao is a traitor of the revolution," she spat. "Had I known she was going to commit suicide, I'd have strangled her first!"

Sometimes when I am cleaning the toilets, I remember the time we spent together and my chest becomes tight. I remember how your eyes shone in the darkness of your room and the spine-tingling caress of your words as you murmured, "If only I had been born a boy, Yi Moon. Then I could marry you one day." I remember the secret transactions our bodies made in your bed at night, and how your touch suffused every part of me with pleasure, unspoken of during the day. But now the Liya of that time no longer exists. Now you are a Red Guard, spreading terror throughout Beijing, and it's as though that time never was.

Since the suicide of Teacher Zhao, toilet-cleaning duty has become a break from the chaos of the Anti-capitalist School for Revolutionary Girls, for in spite of the brave new Socialist claims to not fear "Heaven or Hell, gods or ghosts," old superstitions die hard and girls stay away from the "haunted" toilet block in droves. I am not scared of Teacher Zhao's ghost though. Every time I scrub the stall where she dangled from the pipes, I speak to her.

"You were a good person, Teacher Zhao," I say. "You never committed any counter-revolutionary crimes. They were wrong to persecute you."

Silence.

"I don't blame you, Teacher Zhao," I say. "There's only so much suffering we can endure. I understand why you hanged yourself."

Silence.

"I envy you, Teacher Zhao. If I had the guts, I'd find a length of rope and betray the revolution too . . ."

The thought of "betraying the revolution" becomes more seductive by the day. I imagine affixing the rope to the pipes and kicking the upturned mop bucket out from under my feet. I imagine the noose squeezing my neck until the moment of release. It's only the thought of my mother that stops me, and I can't help but resent her for holding me back.

Autumn. The sky is bled dry of colour. Leaves wither and wilt from the branches of trees. They rustle under my shoes as I walk into the playground and see a new Big-Character Poster on the notice board:

Down with Zhang Liya! Daughter of a Loyal Running Dog of Liu Shaoqi!

Since the Cultural Revolution began there have been many sudden reversals in status. A people's hero one day can be persecuted as the people's enemy the next. But this is so unexpected I nearly fall down in shock.

Zhang Liya Must Be Brought to Justice for Her Anti-Party Crimes.

Down with Zhang Liya, Part of Liu Shaoqi's Plot to Assassinate Chairman Mao.

Girls crowd around the Big-Character Posters. There are some half-hearted murmurs—"How dare Zhang Liya betray us!" But most girls stare up at the posters in a subdued mood. After weeks of class struggle, revolutionary spirit is flagging.

The Red Guards are back. Long March, Patriotic Hua and Red Star—now known as Dare to Rebel, Red Soldier and Martial Warrior. The Red Guards have shaved their heads. Their khaki uniforms, unwashed or changed in weeks, are nearly black. Their eyes are hardened and they are more like veterans back from fighting a war than sixteen-year-old girls. Long March, or Comrade Dare to Rebel, has a loudspeaker in one hand and a *People's Daily* in the other, opened to an editorial about the latest Communist Party purge. She waves the newspaper about as she rants into the loudspeaker.

"Though her father has been expelled from the Party and is now in prison for anti-Party crimes, Zhang Liya remains free and hiding out in the bourgeois luxury of her home. Zhang Liya must be brought to justice. We must bring her into school for interrogation! *Down with Zhang Liya!*"

"*Down with Zhang Liya!*" Long March yells.

"*Down with Zhang Liya! Down with Zhang Liya!*" chant the schoolgirls in the playground—but obediently and bored.

The Red Guards, led by Comrade Dare to Rebel, turn and march out of the gate. Before I have the chance to think about what I am doing, I have caught up with Long March and tapped her on the shoulder. She wrinkles her nose at me, as though I am a cockroach or a rat.

"Comrade Dare to Rebel," I say, "I have been to the Zhang

family residence and have seen poisonous weeds of the Nationalist era hidden in Zhang Liya's bedroom."

I half expect to be cursed or slapped for daring to speak to her. But Long March frowns, thinking over what I said. "Then you must come with us, Comrade Yi Moon," she says urgently. "You must come with us and show us where the poisonous weeds are hidden. They will be used as evidence against Zhang Liya in her trial."

Pride swells in my chest. "Comrade Yi Moon," she called me. Not "Capitalist Roader" or "Daughter of a Rightist," but "Comrade Yi Moon."

I follow the Red Guards out of the playground, to Ironmongers Lane and your home.

The Red Guards' clenched fists *bang bang bang* on your front gate.

"Open up, you Sons of Bitches! Open up, you loyal running dogs of Liu Shaoqi!"

Your servant girl unlocks and opens the gate and cries, "*Long Live Chairman Mao! Long Live Chairman Mao!* Don't attack me! I am just a servant exploited by the bourgeois Zhang family!"

The Red Guards ignore the girl's whimpering and stampede to your room.

You are waiting in a chair by the window. Your striking face shows no sign of fear or intimidation as twenty Red Guards chanting "*Down with Zhang Liya!*" stomp their heavy boots into your room. You sit in your PLA uniform and regard the mob of Red Guards with the dignity and composure that made you the natural choice for their leader. You have been expecting them.

"Class Enemy Zhang!" Long March yells. "You must come with us for interrogation and trial. Do you know why?"

You nod. You look older. Like the other Red Guards, the weeks of destroying the Four Olds have aged you. "Yes, Comrade Dare to Rebel, I do."

Long March smirks. You have been her greatest rival for years, and your downfall is her triumphant rise. "Class Enemy Zhang

Liya. You and your father were loyal running dogs of Liu Shaoqi and part of his conspiracy plot to overthrow Chairman Mao. Your crimes will be punished severely!"

You nod once more. "I understand."

You don't deny the accusations. You know the futility of denial. Your restraint and strength of character are remarkable. But the Red Guards will break you. And if they can't break you with words, they will do it with knives.

"We have also been informed of your loyalty to the Nationalist Party," Long March says. She nods at me. "Comrade Yi Moon, can you show us the evidence?"

For the first time since the Red Guards stormed your room, you look surprised. You stare at me in shock. I stare back coldly. I stamp out my guilt by remembering the humiliating terms of our "friendship." How is this betrayal when there is no friendship to betray?

I go to your bed, reach for the screwdriver under the bedding and pry up the loose floorboard. I remove the cardboard box and turn your dead mother's possessions out onto the floor. Long March pounces on the black-and-white photograph. She holds it up to her eyes and laughs in your mother's lovely twenty-year-old face.

"Who is this syphilis-ridden whore? Why does Zhang Liya have a picture of an ugly Nationalist-era prostitute under her floor?"

Your eyes are blank as Long March rips the photograph up and scatters the torn pieces over your chair.

"Bring this loyal running dog of the Nationalists back to school!" she commands. "Bring the poisonous weeds too!"

The Red Guards lunge for you. They force you into aeroplane position, wrenching your arms back and shoving your head forwards, and march you out. Other Red Guards start ransacking your room. Patriotic Hua holds up your mother's scarlet-and-gold embroidered qipao. There is admiration in her eyes as she gazes at the shimmering silk. She strokes the fabric with her fingers, and the sensual pleasure of it softens her harsh face. Then she notices me watching her.

"Who gave you permission to look at me, Stinking Rightist?"

Patriotic Hua snaps. "Take your beady little capitalist eyes off me!"

Long March, who is staring at the glamorous singer on the Hong Kong record sleeve, glances at me and says casually, "So you think you are one of the Red Guards now, Yi Moon? Don't be so deluded. Go back to the black-category girls where you belong."

They lock you up in Headteacher Yang's former office. Red Guards go in and out, carrying water and food and the papers on which they have recorded your confession. Days and weeks go by, and I never once hear you scream or weep or beg. Your silence unnerves me more than the howls of the Cattle Shed. Your interrogator, Comrade Martial Spirit, prides herself on making class enemies scream. Screaming, she says, exorcizes the counter-revolutionary demons from the soul. Your silence will be seen as defiance. Your silence will provoke them to inflict even more pain.

Winter. The toilet block is unbearably cold and damp. I breathe out fog and shiver under the sinks, reading sheets of toilet paper. When the Red Guards came back to school, they ransacked the library, clearing the shelves of every book not authored by Chairman Mao. Most of the books were razed on a bonfire, but some were torn up for toilet paper, as "poisonous weeds" are fit only for "wiping our backsides." Though a sorry fate for literature, the sheets of toilet paper are my salvation during the bleak winter days, as I read *Journey to the West*, *Dream of the Red Chamber* and other banned volumes, escaping through the pages into illicit other worlds.

One day I am lost in *The Book of Odes* when footsteps approach the toilet block. Scared of being caught reading the Propaganda of the Capitalist Classes, I throw the toilet paper aside, grab a rag and pretend to be scrubbing the floor. Head down, on my knees, I scrub and wait for the unexpected visitor to go into a toilet stall. But the footsteps walk over to where I crouch instead. I look up.

"*Liya?*"

You stand in the pallid winter light coming through the window. Your eyes are blackened and swollen, the lids welded shut. There are bald patches on your head and cuts on your legs seeping blood and pus. Your mother's silk qipao hangs in shreds.

"Liya, *is that you*?"

You breathe in shallow exhalations. "Who else . . . would be wearing this dress?"

The high-ranking Party official's daughter is gone. They have persecuted the high status out of you. They have proved you are just like the rest of us, with hair that rips out and blood that leaves the body through wounds. I wince at the cuts on your legs. They need to be disinfected and stitched up at the hospital, or they won't heal. I take a deep, shaky breath.

"Liya," I say, "my mother has a bottle of iodine at home. I can run home and bring it for you . . ."

"Don't bring me iodine, Moon . . . Or I will report you for collaborating with a class enemy."

You smile bleakly. Are you joking? I can't tell from your empty gaze. They have persecuted the life out of your eyes.

"But your wounds are infected . . ."

You say nothing to this, seeming not to care about your limbs rotting away.

"How did you get out of Headteacher Yang's office?" I ask. "Have the Red Guards released you?"

You hold up your clenched fist. There's a toothbrush in its grip. "Reporting for duty, Comrade Yi," you say. "Long Live Chairman Mao!"

The sight of the toothbrush is so pitiful I start to cry. Is this what I hoped for when I led the Red Guards to the box hidden under your floorboard? For you to be beaten until your head swelled black and blue? For your hair to be dragged out at the roots, leaving your scalp bleeding and bare?

"I am sorry I betrayed you . . ." I whisper.

You stare back, unmoved. "My father was expelled from the Party and imprisoned for counter-revolutionary crimes," you state flatly. "They would have tortured me anyway."

Pipes leak and drip onto the cement floor. In the distance is the chanting of a denunciation rally. A teenage girl shrieks hysterically into a loudspeaker. The sound is exhausting to me.

"I don't blame you, Yi Moon . . ." you say. "I looked the other way when they persecuted you . . ."

"You stopped the Red Guards from raiding our home!"

"I could have done more, but I didn't want to risk my status . . . I was a bad friend . . . I deserve your hate."

I go and put my arms around you. "I've never hated you," I whisper.

I breathe in your rankness and the septic odour of your wounds. They have been starving you, and you are thin as a stalk of bamboo.

"Yi Moon . . ." your voice is a low mosquito hum in my ear ". . . I need your help . . ." You move out of my embrace. You press a hard, smooth metal object into my hand. I look down. A penknife. "I stole it when Martial Spirit wasn't looking," you say. "Don't worry. She won't miss it. She has plenty of knives."

My heart beats faster. I stare at the penknife and fear shunts my chest, knocking the air out of my lungs. I stare at you, bleeding, bruised and paler than the dead. But behind their swollen lids, your eyes are burning and intense. Brought back to life by your will to die.

"Why me?"

"My wrist is broken. A couple of my fingers are too. I don't have the strength . . ."

I turn the penknife over and click out the blade. Short, but brutal and sharp. I imagine it cutting your wrist. Slicing through skin, blood vessels and tendons. I shudder and retract it again.

"Liya," I say carefully, "the Cultural Revolution will be over in a few months, just like the anti-rightist campaign was. Your father will be released from prison and rehabilitated. Your wounds will heal. Life will get better."

"My father won't be released from prison," you say. "He died there yesterday."

"*Oh* . . ."

"I deserve to die, Yi Moon. I am a murderer. During the home raids I kicked people to death. I dragged a woman by a dog's leash around her neck until she was strangled dead. I gouged the eyes out of a dead man's head and crushed them in my bare hands."

What you say is sickening and can't be true. But I look into your eyes and know you are not lying. I say weakly, "All the Red Guards have blood on their hands . . ."

"Then we all deserve to die."

"I can't do it, Liya."

"You *can*." You go down on your knees on the damp cement. You hold out your thin, blue-veined wrists. You look up at me from this begging posture, your bruised eyes pleading with mine. "You *can* . . ."

You lift your wrists higher, baring them for the blade. Your arms are shaking from the exertion, and tears sting my eyes, because I know then that I will do it. I will do it out of mercy, because it is the most humane thing to do. I will do it out of love.

My breath shuddering, I reach for your left hand. I click out the blade and slash your inner wrist as hard as I can. You gasp, and your eyes go wide. I let your hand go, and we both stare as the thin line of red widens and drips, the cement darkening as your blood escapes. You breathe in sharp intakes of breath.

"The other one," you say. "Hurry."

You hold out the other wrist, and I reach for it and slash again. This time you don't gasp. This time you turn your head up, as though to God in Heaven, and yell, "Long Live Chairman Mao!"

You crawl to a metal bucket of stagnant water and plunge your wrists in. As you crouch there I want to rip my shirt up for tourniquets, to staunch death's flow. But I betrayed you once. I can't betray you again.

When you lose consciousness, you slump and the bucket capsizes, spilling a tide of red across the floor. I kneel over you and the mess of your wrists. You have stopped bleeding. Your heart has stopped beating.

"Sorry," I hear myself sob. "Sorry."

In the distance, a teenage girl shrieks through a loudspeaker and hundreds of schoolgirls chant. I touch my fingers to your bruised and battered face. *I deserve to die, Yi Moon. I am a murderer,* you said. Now I am a murderer too and cannot live with my conscience either.

The knife is within reaching distance. I grasp the handle before I lose my nerve, and turn the blade on my own wrists. Once. Twice. Shock numbs the pain. Struggling for breath, I lie down beside you and hold your hand. There's a roaring in my head. The roaring of our Great Helmsman, furious that I have betrayed him. The roaring of the masses, furious that I have taken my fate in my own hands. Then there is silence, darkness and reprieve.

29

Rebirth

Unfortunately, I did not die. I woke in a hospital bed, my head throbbing and my wrists aching beneath thick bandages. When she saw I was awake, the patient in the next bed yelled for the nurses, who rushed to my bedside and started chanting, "Down with Yi Moon! Down with Yi Moon!" Big-Character Posters condemning my suicide attempt covered the walls. I saw one that said, *The Masses Rejoice in the Death of the Counter-Revolutionary Zhang Liya.* And I was relieved that you were spared the persecution I was about to suffer.

I went back to school with my bandaged wrists and spent the first months of 1967 on the brink of another suicide attempt. Then the Red Guards of the Anti-capitalist School for Revolutionary Girls split up into rival factions—one headed by Comrade Dare to Rebel, the other by Comrade Martial Spirit—and, caught up in the civil war, they neglected the black-category students entirely. When I stopped going to school, none of the Red Guards bothered to come and get me. So every day I stayed at home with my mother and waited to see what the Party had in store for us next.

A year later I was sent to Repair the Earth in the countryside. My mother came to see me off at Beijing Railway Station. She gave me a box of rice and vegetables prepared for the long journey to Heilongjiang and wept as she hugged me goodbye.

"Be revolutionary!" she urged. "Love Chairman Mao and the Great, Glorious and Correct Communist Party with all your heart!"

By then I had lost my faith in Communism and willed the Great Helmsman dead, but I smiled and promised my mother I would. The train of Sent-Down Youth pulled away from the platform and the crowds of parents wailed to be losing their children to the Great Northern Waste. My waving mother receded into the distance and I started to cry. I had a premonition that I would never see her again.

The train journey was forty-seven hours long and every carriage was crowded with Sent-Down Youth, excited to be going "Up to the Mountains, Down to the Villages" to be educated by the peasants. They sang jubilant revolutionary songs all the way to Heilongjiang. The train moved us farther into exile, and the Beijing students chorused, "I'll Go Where Chairman Mao's Finger Points!" and "Long Live Our Sickles!" in joy.

I was one of twelve Sent-Down Youths sent to Three Ox Village, a few tumbledown shacks a six-hour hike from the town of Langxiang. During the day we laboured in the sorghum fields with the peasants, the wind and rain lashing away our youth. At night we slept in a barn so cold our tears of homesickness froze on our cheeks. The idealistic Beijing students organized political classes for the peasants of Three Ox Village and meetings for "Recalling with Bitterness the Exploitation of the Peasant Classes by the Evil Landlords of the Pre-liberation Era." Unfortunately, the illiterate villagers, far away from the sloganeering of the *People's Daily*, had not learnt the correct political script. The hardships they recalled—the deaths from starvation, the corrupt Party officials and crippling taxes—were from Mao Zedong's era. The Beijing students were shocked by the ignorance and backwardness of the villagers and the extent of political re-education they needed. But as the Educated Youth slowly came to understand the real reason they had been exiled in the Great Northern Waste—that the "rebellious youth" had served their political ends and Repairing the Earth was the Party's way of getting rid of us—the curriculum planned for Three Ox Village was abandoned. Consumed by hopelessness and loss of faith, the Sent-Down Youth went through a re-education of their own.

Year after year, I slaved in the fields, suffering chronic backache, stiff, inflamed joints and wind-chapped skin that cracked and bled. In the evenings I drank sorghum spirits to numb the ceaseless pain. One day in 1969 a letter came from my mother, informing me of my father's death in the Qinghai labour camp. Weeks later another letter came from Granny Xi, to tell me my mother had died. I requested permission to return to Beijing, but it was denied. Then the Sent-Down Youths started dying. One girl caught pneumonia, and by the time we had hiked to Langxiang and back to get her antibiotics, she had passed away. Another Sent-Down Youth died of rabies when bitten by a wild snarling dog. Another died of unknown causes in his sleep. The deaths were a warning to me that I had to get out of Three Ox Village and back to civilization. That if I continued stoically to "eat bitterness" and endure, I wouldn't last another year.

To leave Three Ox Village, I needed a local-government connection. Most of the local Party officials were no more than scruffy peasants themselves, but I remembered a regional Party secretary from Langxiang who had come to Three Ox Village to inspect the Sent-Down Youths when we first arrived. The official was bald and fat but well dressed and rumoured to own a car. I was twenty-three and had wasted six years of my life in Three Ox Village. I decided to go to him for help.

On my day off I got up before dawn, hiked three hours to the nearest road then hitchhiked to Langxiang. I went to the town hall and requested an appointment to meet with Party Secretary Lin. His secretary turned me away and, frustrated that I had spent over four hours travelling for nothing, I lost my temper with her, and Secretary Lin stepped out of his office to see what the commotion was. He knew at once what I had come for, and what I had to offer in exchange. The labouring and harsh weather hadn't quite robbed me of my looks, and I had bathed and washed my hair the night before to make myself presentable. He invited me into his office and locked the door. There was no discussion or negotiation of the terms—we just lay down on the floor behind his desk. Secretary Lin's round cheeks turned very red during the act, and as he climaxed he grunted like a hog. I remember he was very pleased by the blood, and that it was my first time.

I was Secretary Lin's mistress for a year before he got me the residence papers and job in Beijing, a year of his sweaty hands groping my breasts and cunt, a year of pretending not to care what the other Sent-Down Youth and villagers thought. The official eventually arranged for me to swap papers with a red-category girl my age, willing to sacrifice her life and status in Beijing to move to Langxiang to be with her repatriated fiancé. I was to take her name, Li Shuxiang, and she was to take mine, Yi Moon.

Secretary Lin nearly didn't let me go. He had fallen in love, and got it into his head to divorce his wife and marry me instead. To become Secretary Lin's second wife was the last thing I wanted, and I begged him to stay with his wife "for the sake of his family" until his sense of duty was restored. The official said I could come back to him if I was unhappy in Beijing. He said he would welcome me back to Langxiang with open arms. Lying through my teeth, I promised to return one day, and the lovesick man threw his head against my breasts and wept.

Seven years after leaving Beijing, I returned. Secretary Lin had found me a job as a tea lady in the Ministry of Agriculture, and I spent my days pushing a tea trolley about dreary government buildings and pouring hot water out of a thermos for the cadres. At night I slept in a workers' dormitory in Maizidian. I was only twenty-four, but an old woman inside. I had none of the spark and vivacity of other girls my age.

Your father was just a clerk back then, but ambitious and clever and certain to rise through the ranks. He was handsome and could have had any woman he wanted, so what did he see in me?

Your father saw subservience in the meek way I served him tea. He saw compliance in my diffident smile. I was the only tea lady who didn't flirt with the cadres, and this led to the expectation that I would be a loyal wife. He saw that I wouldn't be controlling or demanding and would stay out of his affairs. He saw that he wouldn't have to sacrifice his womanizing or late nights. And he was correct. I couldn't have cared less who he slept with or what time he came home. But I was not the sweet and deferential wife he expected.

Pregnancy. The birth of a son. When you were born, I was convinced there was something strange about you, that there was a cognizance in your eyes, as though you had been born with prior knowledge of the world beyond my womb. Yet, at the same time, you were defenceless and tiny. You couldn't stand up, or walk, or do anything for yourself. You were constantly crying for milk, or to be cradled in my arms, or for your vomit or shit to be wiped up. I was twenty-six. I went through the motions of being a mother but had no maternal instinct or feeling. Your needs were endless and I couldn't meet them. I was an inadequate mother. I saw this judgement of me in your eyes. Your father knew it too.

"Shuxiang, you are an unnatural woman!" he barked on the rare occasions he was home. "Pick the damned child up when he cries!"

Was it my lack of maternal instinct that led to the otherness I sensed about you? Or was it your otherness that corrupted my maternal instinct? I told myself the post-natal anxiety was because of my inexperience with babies and the more time I spent with you, the less strange you would seem. But, instead, time exaggerated my feelings of disquiet until they became an irrational fear that you weren't my own flesh and blood.

Once, I was breastfeeding you, and as you were suckling I had the uncanny sense that someone other than my four-month-old child was staring out at me from behind your gaze. I pulled you from my nipple, and milk and spittle dribbled from your mouth as I held you at arm's length. "Who are you?" I asked, my voice shaking, half expecting the imposter behind your eyes to speak. You spoke back in baby babble and I was as embarrassed as I was relieved. Four months earlier I had pushed you out of my own womb. I had seen the umbilical cord being cut with my own eyes. How could I suspect that you weren't my child?

The next time it happened you were six months old, and we were rolling a ball back and forth on the floor. You smiled and gurgled at the colourful ball, unaware of your mother's deathly boredom. "Back to Mama," I said, rolling the ball to you. But a change came over you and you suddenly lost interest in our game. You stared at me with the unmistakable gaze of someone from my past, and my panic was similar to the time I was an hour's hike from Three Ox Village and realized I was being stalked by a wild and rabid-eyed dog.

"Liya?" I whispered.

You stared back with cold, hostile, accusing eyes, still furious that I had betrayed you to the Red Guards, still furious I had taken your mother's possessions out of the secret hiding place. I couldn't stand it. I walked out of the living room. I put on my coat and left our apartment. I wandered the streets for hours, thinking, It can't be . . . It can't be . . . It can't be. Yet it was. How long had Liya been lurking inside you, biding her time? I shuddered to think.

The apartment was dark when I returned, and harrowing with a small child's crying. I went to the living room and turned on the light. You were a mess, crawling about in a puddle of urine, your cheeks and hands smeared with shit. When you saw me you threw back your head and bawled, your eyes accusing. But this time your accusation was that of an abandoned child. Liya had disappeared. Though I was wary of you still, I picked you up and washed you in a basin of lukewarm water. I towelled you dry and I fed you a bottle of formula milk. The whole time, I was nervous that Liya would reappear.

There were incidents like this throughout your babyhood, when I was overcome by the conviction that Liya, or some other im-poster, was stalking me through your eyes. I would walk away from you. I would shut myself in the bedroom or bathroom. When you scrabbled at the door and called, "Mama . . ." I covered my ears. Sometimes my panic was so overwhelming I would leave you splashing in the plastic tub, or in the kitchen with pans boiling on the stove, and flee the apartment and walk the streets until my heart stopped pounding and I was brave enough to go back. Fight or flight—that was my reflex when I was menaced by others in your gaze. And though walking out on you was irresponsible, not walking out on you would have been worse. I would have screamed and shaken you. I would have beaten you and staved in your baby-sized skull.

Fortunately, it didn't last. As you grew up into a chattering child, with a mind and character of your own, Liya and the others went away, and I soon forgot there was ever a time I suspected you weren't my son. My skills as a mother did not improve, though. I still forgot to cook dinner. I still forgot to tell you to go to bed. Your teachers wrote me notes, saying that your clothes needed washing, and your toes poked through the holes in your shoes. I never beat you or was intentionally cruel. But I didn't love you as a mother should love her son. And you, who loved me as a son should love his mother, could tell.

Life passed uneventfully, with my baijiu, cigarettes, novels (my love of "poisonous weeds" had stayed with me from reading the toilet paper during the Cultural Revolution) and young son. I had no ambitions. In the eighties, as televisions and fridge-freezers and other appliances appeared in the stores, I had no desire to consume. I had no interest in men or love affairs and would have been celibate but for your father, drunkenly mounting me once in a while.

"What other man would want you, Shuxiang?" he'd grunt. "Not even a dog would take a sniff at you. You should be grateful you are mine."

But your father was wrong. I wasn't his. His wife was Li Shuxiang, not me. Your father didn't know who I was. He didn't even know my real name.

*   *   *

I don't remember the breakdown. One day I was living with my son in Maizidian, and the next I was tranquillized and unable to go to the toilet without assistance. I don't remember much about the hospital either. I remember the odour of disinfectant on the wards. I remember a kindly nurse brushing my teeth and baring her own teeth to encourage me to do the same. I remember lying on my back with a wad of cotton between my teeth and paddles against my temples. I remember lightning striking. Once. Twice. Thrice. I remember your father coming to visit me. He sat over by the window, looking formidable in his work suit. Other patients from my ward stood drooling in the doorway, staring at him in fascination.

"Mister, haven't I seen you on TV?" one woman asked. "Aren't you the prime minister of Taiwan?"

Your father paid as much attention to them as to stray cats. He sat up straight in his chair, stiff-backed and tense with his loathing of me. "You deserve to rot in Hell for what you did to our son," he said.

When he said this, I had only a vague memory of having a son. How old was he? A baby? A walking and talking child? What did he look like? I certainly couldn't remember the thing I had done to him, for which I deserved to rot.

"You are dead to him now anyway," your father went on. "He thinks you are ashes in an urn." Then he stared out the window as though he couldn't stand the sight of me. He started smoking his way through another cigarette and muttering, "You are the sickest woman I know . . . You are rotting . . . You stink of death . . ." Then he looked right at me and sneered, "Hurry up and die, will you? We *can't wait.*"

By "we" I knew he meant himself and his teenaged mistress. Whether or not I lived or died was of interest to no one but them.

After your father had gone, I asked to borrow a mirror from a girl in my room. She opened her round powder compact and held it up, and I saw my reflection for the first time in over a year. I was not rotting, as your father had said, but I didn't recognize the woman staring back with vacant eyes. That wasn't me. Where had I gone? "Do I stink of death?" I asked the girl. She leant closer and sniffed me. "No, Shuxiang, you smell nice," she said. Then she patted the fluffy puff in her compact and tenderly powdered my nose.

That evening I didn't swallow my pills and, within hours, the medicated fog was clearing. I didn't swallow my pills the next day or the next, but was careful to keep up appearances as a dribbler who couldn't think for herself. After a week of no pills, I stole a wallet from one of the doctors' coats and hid it in my underwear. Two days later I was on a long-distance bus headed north to Heilongjiang.

Secretary Lin had retired now. Though eighteen years had passed, he recognized me straight away. He was speechless for a while, tears standing out in his eyes.

"Yi Moon, you came back," he whispered. "Finally, after all these years of waiting, you have come back to me."

He was older and fatter, and walked with difficulty due to complications from diabetes and gout. And I had aged too. I was no longer the young girl who had gone away to Beijing. I was over forty, and wrinkled with grey in my hair, and dazed-looking from all the electricity that had seared through my brain.

"I just got out of a mental hospital," I explained. "I look unwell."

And the sentimental man shook his head and smiled. "Yi Moon, you look exactly the same as the day we first met."

Secretary Lin rented a room for me on the outskirts of the town. Then, at my request, he bribed his friend at the local Public Security Bureau to contact your father with news of my passing and to forge a death certificate for Li Shuxiang, which I posted to Beijing. Your father accepted the lie. He didn't bother to make further enquiries, or send for the ashes. I had escaped his punishment and I was free.

I lived in Langxiang as I had lived in Beijing before my breakdown. Baijiu, cigarettes and novels. Solitude. But I was not free.

At night I dreamt of you. I dreamt of you at the age of two, crouching in split pants to peer at a dead spider in a drain. I dreamt of you aged four, standing on a stool and watching me stir a pot on the stove. I dreamt of you aged twelve, chewing on a pencil, doing your homework in your pyjamas. I had been an indifferent mother. But now, hundreds of kilometres north of Beijing, I woke from dreams of you, aching with loss. But what could I do? I had died in Langxiang, and couldn't come back from the dead. I had no choice but to stay beyond the grave, out of your life.

I had been in Langxiang for ten years when Secretary Lin was diagnosed with lung cancer. The doctors didn't even prescribe chemotherapy, the prognosis was so bad. In desperation, I went to a shaman I knew of near Three Ox Village, a toothless old man with skin loosened from the bones of his face, rumoured to be over two hundred years old. After selling me some herbs to "fight the demons" in my official's lungs, the shaman asked me if I knew I was a "reincarnate." Suspecting that he just wanted to sell me more medicine, I snapped, "I can't afford to buy more of your herbs." The shaman laughed, toothless and sly, and gave me a potion free of charge. "Drink it," he said, "and you will dream of your past lives." I put the bottle in my bag then rushed back to Langxiang and my dying official, who over the years I had come to care about a great deal.

I forgot about the two-hundred-year-old shaman and his herbal potion until after Secretary Lin's funeral. It was late at night, and I was drinking in my room when I ran out of spirits. Searching for more alcohol, I found the shaman's bottle in my bag, pulled out the stopper and drank it down, hoping it contained some intoxicating herbs that would knock me out, or at least numb my sadness. I passed out shortly afterwards and woke hours later from a dream so strange and disquieting that I had to turn on the light for reassurance that it wasn't real. I had dreamt I was being chased out of a hut by a fierce-eyed woman with a knife. I had run into a forest and hidden in the trees, my heart thudding with the conviction that the woman would find me and slit my throat. The dream was too powerful to not be of any significance. So, later that day, I found a notebook and wrote it down.

The next night, without imbibing any potions, I dreamt I was in a boat out at sea with a wrinkled old man, casting out fishing nets. This time, the dream was peaceful and serene, and I woke up with the taste of saltwater in my mouth and waves crashing in my blood. Though it was still dark, I went and sat at my desk and wrote what I remembered down in my notebook, and by the time I had finished the sun had risen in the sky.

For years my life was centred around the dreams and their documentation. I recorded obsessively, emptying pen after pen of ink, as though the past incarnations themselves were pushing my writing hand across the pages. Though the dreams were nothing more than random scenes that resisted order and interpretation, the need to record them was as consuming as hunger or thirst, a need that had to be sated in order for me to survive.

When I understood every dream was from one of four perspectives, I divided the dreams amongst four journals, each of which came to form a disjointed, non-chronological biography of one life. I dreamt haphazardly. Sometimes I dreamt of one incarnation for nights on end. Sometimes I dreamt of each incarnation in nightly succession. The dreams were exhilarating. The dreams were horrifying. The dreams were, without exception, more real to me than waking life.

Awareness that I was dreaming not only of my own past lives but those of the soul I lived in tandem with came slowly. The revelation that the recurring soul was yours, however, struck like lightning one day. The epiphany sent me out into the streets, where I walked for hours, mindless of where I was going, colliding with strangers in my shock. I thought about you as a baby. The strangeness I had sensed about you was not a young mother's paranoid imaginings. Those times I saw someone else lurking in the eyes of the four-month-old suckling at my breast, or the six-month-old playing on the floor, were not projections from my own mind.

Your other selves were surfacing from the depths, rising into the void of your unintelligent, not-yet-formed baby's mind. Your other selves were moving within the cavity of your skull and staring out through your eyes.

That day was a day of many regrets. Regret that I sent the death certificate to your father. Regret that I had stayed in Langxiang for fifteen years, thinking I could break with the past. That day I went to the bank and withdrew the last of Secretary Lin's money. Then I stood in a queue to buy a ticket from the train station booth. You have been dead for sixteen years, my conscience warned me. You can't go back . . . But what does my conscience know? I thought as I returned to my room to pack. What does my conscience know about the bond of souls entwined for over a thousand years?

As the train moved through the night to Beijing, I thought that suddenly to reappear in your life would be irresponsible. I had to enlighten you of your past lives first, as the shaman near Three Ox Village had enlightened me. But how? I had no herbal potions, for the shaman had years ago died, and the task seemed as impossible as moving a mountain one spadeful at a time. Yet it had to be done.

The day I returned to Beijing was the day I began the first letter to you. It was winter then, and now it is summer and this letter will be the last. Whether you are enlightened or not, the time has come to move into the here and now.

Once there was a time, when you were seven or eight, when you woke up crying in the night. "Ma . . ." you called through the dark. "Ma . . ." I got up and went over to your bed. "I had a dream you were dead," you whispered. "I was on my own . . ." I stroked your damp forehead and reassured you, "I am here, Xiao Jun. I am not dead, little one . . . I am here . . ." Then I tucked you back in and stood over you until you were sleeping once more.

I am here, Xiao Jun. Are you ready to see me again? Or am I too late?

30

The Wake

Lin Hong prowls amongst the guests, her loud and empty voice possessive of the attention in the room. She parades her new dress, the black ruche fabric sliding from her shoulders and clinging to her curves. "Fifty percent off in the sale," she boasts to those who compliment her, tossing her head and tinkling her chandelier earrings, as though showing off their deliberate bad taste.

News of the tragedy had spread about Maizidian. Though Wang hadn't been more than a nodding acquaintance to most, he'd been polite, unassuming and well liked, and many neighbours have come to pay their respects. Some taxi drivers who'd grumbled over noodles and beer with Wang, about traffic cops and extortionate fines, have come too. Baldy Zhang walks in and lets out a low whistle at the grandeur of the high ceiling and marble floors. ("Fuck me! Who knew that Wang's folks were so rich? What the fuck was he driving a taxi for?") The young girl from the convenience kiosk outside Building 12 comes and stands shyly at the door. "A pack of Red Pagoda Mountain, twice a week," she tells the other guests. "Mondays and Thursdays, usually. He always said thank you. Never forgot."

Wang Hu's former colleagues from the Ministry of Agriculture have come, ostensibly to offer condolences for the loss of his son, but mostly out of a morbid curiosity to see how the once larger-than-life Wang Hu, now semi-paralysed and wheelchair bound, is faring these days. Slumped in his chair, Wang Hu is miserable, doubly humiliated by the procession of witnesses to his debilitated state and the death of his son, unfilially passing away before him. The cadres slap him on the back, bantering and making witty jokes like back in the day, but Wang Hu, ashamed of his slurring, dribbling speech, doesn't join in. Though in their sixties, the cadres are strong and in robust health from golfing and extramarital affairs, and the stark contrast with his crippled impotence is more than he can bear. He's relieved when Lin Hong sashays over, hips swaying as though swinging a tail, and offers the cadres more drinks. "Tea? Beer? Anything you want . . ." The cadres' wives narrow their eyes at Lin Hong's convivial manner. Even to the most generous-minded of guests, the stepmother of the deceased looks in a celebratory mood.

A framed photograph of Wang, taken by Yida the year they were married, sits on an altar of burning candles and incense. The guests go to the altar and contemplate the handsome young man in the photograph—remembering him fondly, or not fondly, or not at all. Baldy Zhang chuckles at the photo and remarks, "When was that taken? Looks nothing like him! Where's the eye bags? Why so much hair?" There are no wailing mourners at the wake, or hired monks chanting verses of Buddhist scriptures, or burning of paper money for Wang's prosperity in the afterlife. The ashes were left at the crematorium. The guests murmur about the break with tradition, the subdued, modest affair. It's not as though Wang's family can't afford the expense.

Wang Hu and Lin Hong are nervous about the details of Wang's death coming to light. The police had estimated his taxi was speeding at 140 kilometres per hour when it crashed into the guard-rail of a vaulted flyover in the northeast of Beijing. The police had suspected more than reckless driving—that Wang had crashed intentionally. But the last thing Wang Hu wanted was the shame and embarrassment of a murderer and a suicide for a son.

"Perhaps," Lin Hong had suggested to the investigator, "the man in the passenger seat attacked my son-in-law, causing him to lose control of the wheel? Perhaps the man attempted to rob him, and that is why Wang accidently crashed the car?" Damage limitation. Both of them are used to limiting the damage Wang Jun has done to his father's reputation over the years. They've been cleaning up his messes all his life. Why should his death be any different? They were fortunate that the passenger, who'd catapulted through the windscreen and soared twenty metres above the ground before thudding to his death, was no one of any significance. A drifter and male prostitute from Guangzhou. The Zeng family had been difficult at first, pestering the Beijing police with questions about the car crash. Then Lin Hong had contacted them, and offered to cover the funeral expenses, and generously compensate them for their loss. The Zengs had accepted the offer and shut up.

Wang's taxi-driver friends are out of place at the wake, and hopeless at small talk. ("Fucked if I care," one mutters when Lin Hong asks if he is looking forward to the Olympics.) They retreat to the kitchen, where the caterers are preparing trays of snacks, and gather around a table with their cigarettes and smuggled bottles of baijiu. They talk fondly of Driver Wang, gallows humour soon kicking in.

"Crashed off a bridge! What an idiot!"

"Maybe he had an undiagnosed brain tumour. That would explain a lot . . ."

"Probably had a heart attack at the wheel. He was so out of shape . . ."

"His stepmother says his passenger robbed him at knifepoint. That's how he lost control of the taxi . . ."

Baldy Zhang pours Red Star baijiu into the other drivers' cups. They drink to the memory of Driver Wang.

"Seen his wife? She's a weeping mess."

"Not bad, though, as far as weeping messes go," Baldy Zhang says slyly. "Should the poor widow be in need of comfort, she can come and weep on old Uncle Zhang's shoulder . . ."

"Show some respect! At the dead man's wake!" Driver Liang laughs. He points to the kitchen ceiling. "Driver Wang is watching you now. He's grinding his teeth and getting ready to punch your lights out!"

Baldy Zhang calls up to the ceiling, "Now now, Driver Wang. You wouldn't want your wife to be lonely in her bed at night, would you? Old Uncle Zhang will keep her warm for you . . ."

Laughter, another splash of baijiu in the cups, and they change the subject.

The widow and child of the deceased are on a sofa and, as a dazed spectacle of grief, Yida does not disappoint. "Poor Ma Yida," the guests whisper. "First her home burnt down, and now she's widowed at thirty. It'll be impossible for her to find another husband now . . ."

Yida has been holding the same cup of tea on her lap for the past hour. Not sipped from once, the tea is stone cold. The wrinkled faces of elderly neighbours loom in and out of focus as they offer consoling words that Yida can't hear. Echo is troubled to see her mother unable to hold a gaze or finish a sentence. She looks sullenly at the middle-aged women who pat her on the head and say, "Oh, you poor child," and wills them to go away. They whisper to Lin Hong, "How your daughter-in-law is suffering. She looks like a ghost."

Lin Hong nods, her chandeliers tinkling. "Looks awful, doesn't she? Can't eat or sleep and is barely functioning. I had to get my doctor to prescribe her some tranquillizers, just so she can shut down for a few hours each night. Still, how frightful she looks!"

Yida's hair has not been washed in days, and her skin is blotchy and her eyes bloodshot from weeping. Lin Hong could advise Yida on how to reduce her eye swelling (with a few dabs of haemorrhoid cream), but she'll be damned if she'll pass on her beauty tips to the Anhui girl. Echo is the one Lin Hong is saving her advice for. She can't wait to straighten Echo's teeth and hair and give her lessons in how to use make-up to accentuate her eyes.

"We heard the mother and child's house burnt down. Where

are they living now?" a wife of one of Wang Hu's former colleagues asks.

"Why, here, of course!" Lin Hong says. "Where else would they go? They are *our* responsibility now. The mother has plans to take Echo back to Anhui, but that won't happen. Echo and I are very close and won't be parted. She is like a daughter to me. Maybe the mother will return to Anhui alone."

The cadre's wife looks at Yida and shivers. What will become of this poor widow, now that she has nothing left?

Yida rises from the sofa.

"Ma, where are you going?" asks Echo.

"Kitchen," says Yida, and stumbles away. Echo can tell by her mother's voice that she does not want her to follow.

Yida enters the kitchen. She walks up to the table of boozy taxi drivers, who look up at her in surprise.

"I need a cigarette," she announces. "And a glass of whatever you are drinking."

The six men leap to meet her need, nicotine-stained fingers fumbling for packs of cigarettes and lighters, proffering her the choice of three different brands. A glass is fetched and colourless grain alcohol poured in.

"Mind if I join you?" she asks.

They shake their heads and say they don't, so Yida sinks into an empty chair, inhaling the fog of smoke and the musky odour that reminds her of her late husband. The drivers continue chatting awkwardly, but Yida is so quiet, they forget her after a few minutes and resume their sweary, bawdy banter. Yida smokes cigarette after cigarette down to the butt and knocks back glasses of liquor. Some of the guests, when they hear of this, couldn't be more scandalized if the widow had squatted and peed on the kitchen floor. But Yida can't see their disapproving looks from the doorway. The alcohol is mixing with the tranquillizers she took that morning and her vision is blurring, the kitchen slanting at a tilt. She slurs to Baldy Zhang, "You were my husband's friend, weren't you?"

Baldy Zhang clears his throat and admits, "We weren't really friends. Your husband was a good man, but I don't make friends easy. I'm a mean bastard, truth be told."

A few knowing chuckles around the table. Yida is solemn as she waits for the laughter to die down. Then, her alcohol-limp tongue wrestling with words, struggling to shape them in her mouth, she says, "You are wrong . . . He was not a good man."

The drivers pause, then laugh uncertainly, spluttering smoke. A hysterical shrill to her voice, Yida continues, "He crashed that car on purpose to kill himself and the man in the passenger seat, who was his lover. He committed suicide, leaving his wife and child with not one fen to support themselves. So you are wrong, Baldy Zhang. My husband was not a good man."

Yida looks around the table at the stunned and speechless drivers then stands up to leave. But no sooner has she risen, she keels over as the blood drains from her head and her knees buckle. Driver Liang leaps up, frowning as he catches her by the shoulders and supports her. Yida slumps in his arms, rolls her head towards him and smiles—her first smile in days. Driver Liang is two decades older than her late husband, but something about his strong arms and concerned expression agitates the itch of lust in Yida. Take me to the spare bedroom, Driver Liang, Yida thinks, and she laughs at the lewdness of her thoughts. The taxi drivers watch her uncomfortably.

"*Oh my goodness!* Is everything all right?" Lin Hong rushes to drag Yida out of Driver Liang's arms, and attempts to stand her upright. "Accept my apologies. My daughter-in-law is not quite herself today. She needs to lie down. I hope she was not disturbing you."

The taxi drivers watch as Lin Hong steers Yida out of the kitchen. Out in the hall, Lin Hong throws open the door to the guest room and points at the single bed.

"Get in there and lie down," she snaps. "You are making a fool of yourself."

Yida sways in the doorway, woozy and unable to focus. Lin Hong pushes her inside and slams the door. Pathetic, she thinks. But at least the ignorant Anhui girl has the sense to do as she is told.

* * *

By four o'clock the incense has burnt to ashes and the candles melted to stumps. The guests start leaving their empty glasses on the sideboard or coffee table, saying their goodbyes and heading for the door. Lin Hong pursues them out to the hall, standing over them as they rummage through the shoe pile for the pair they came with, and making threats to invite them round again. Then she follows them to the lift, waving and calling, "Thank you for coming!" like a party hostess who doesn't want the party to end. As the elevator pings shut on another group of guests, a woman in her late fifties or early sixties shuffles out of the door leading from the stairwell, a shabby woman, whose padded Mao jacket and worn trousers remind Lin Hong of the days when everyone owned one set of hand-sewn clothes. Lin Hong looks at the woman's lined skin and thinning hair, brittle enough to break in the teeth of a comb. Who in their right mind would climb ten flights of stairs in the July heat? The woman, who is not breathless or perspiring from the climb, moves with a slightly arthritic gait towards the open door of Lin Hong's home.

"Excuse me. Who are you?" Lin Hong asks, her eyes polite but her mind wanting to shoo the woman back down the stairs.

The woman does not answer, but wanders into the apartment as though Lin Hong is someone of no importance at all. She must be one of Yida's relations from Anhui, Lin Hong thinks, wrinkling her nose as the woman traipses her mud-caked sandals down her hall. These peasants are so rude and uncivilized. Then the taxi drivers stumble out, headed to a local Sichuan restaurant for more booze and spicy food, and the unknown guest is forgotten as Lin Hong chases after them, calling her goodbyes and inviting them to come again.

On the sofa in her formal black dress, Echo watches the last of the guests gossiping and stuffing their mouths with the leftover snacks on the trays on the sideboard. She watches her grandfather squirming in his wheelchair as though his incontinence pad needs to be changed and she is wondering whether to raise the alarm when the downtrodden, grey-headed woman enters the room.

Echo lurches with recognition and fear. What is the Watcher doing here? At her father's wake? Echo hadn't thought the Watcher could exist so openly out of the shadows, or the shrubbery in the park, or the shopping crowds. But here she is now. In her grandfather's apartment, for everyone to see.

The Watcher gazes about the living room, but her eyes don't widen in envy and admiration like the other guests'. She heads directly to the altar, nodding curtly at Wang Hu as she passes his wheelchair. Wang Hu wheezes as though with the onset of an asthma attack then keels over, wracked by choking, hacking coughs. The guests rush over, crowding him. "Slap him on the back!" they cry. "Bring water!" "Loosen his tie!"

The drama of the choking man does not distract the Watcher as she stands at the shrine and, like the guests before her, contemplates the young man in the photograph. But, unlike the other guests, the Watcher starts to weep. From the sofa, Echo watches, realizing that the Watcher is only the second person she has seen crying for her father. The first was her mother, who, when the police informed her of the "bad news," crashed on the hospital floor and sobbed on her hands and knees like a wounded animal. The Watcher, however, is silent in her grief, tears streaming down her cheeks. She weeps for a few moments longer then reaches into her Mao jacket for a large manila envelope. The Watcher stands with the envelope in front of the altar, as though debating whether to leave it as an offering or not. She decides against it and turns away.

The Watcher stares at Echo with her piercing gaze, and Echo shrinks back. Caught up in the commotion of Wang Hu's seizure of hacking coughs ("Call an ambulance! Wang Hu is choking!"), none of the guests notice the strange latecomer approaching the daughter of the deceased, who is wide-eyed with fright. Echo has never seen the Watcher close up before. She can see the crow's feet wreathing her eyes and the tears glistening on her cheeks. She can see the large mending stitches on her jacket and her bedraggled trouser hems. The Watcher's accent, when she speaks, is not what Echo expected. Not that of an uneducated migrant from the countryside, but that of a well-educated person from Beijing.

"I knew your father," the Watcher says. "I knew him very well. Better than anyone."

Echo does not believe this. If this woman knew her father better than anyone, then why did she only ever watch him from afar? Why didn't she ever speak to him, or say hello? The Watcher is lying, but Echo holds her tongue.

"I know you too, Echo," the Watcher says. "I know you better than you know yourself. Recently, I have been dreaming of you."

Echo is silent. She dreams of the Watcher too. She dreams of the Watcher stalking her through the streets and lurking outside the door of 404. She dreams of the Watcher standing in the corner of her bedroom at night. And now the Watcher has stepped out of her dreams and into waking life, looming over Echo, smelling of old age and homelessness. Though her eyes are shrouded in wrinkles, they are sharp as knives, dissecting Echo with their gaze.

"The dreams show me who you were in the past," the Watcher says. "Once, you were a sorceress, and then a Mongol warrior with a battle-axe-scarred face. Once, you were Emperor and ruler of all under heaven, and then a Red Guard called Long March."

Echo shudders. The Watcher is mentally ill, she realizes. Though her eyes are shrewd and intelligent, her mind is deranged.

"And now in this life," the Watcher says, "you are my grandchild."

Though the madwoman is lying, Echo recoils at the thought of being her granddaughter.

"Here," the Watcher says, handing her two brown envelopes. "One letter I wrote to your father, before he died. The other I wrote for you. It's the story of your first incarnation. And there will be more, Echo . . . For it's my duty to enlighten you about your past."

Echo accepts the envelopes with both hands.

"Now you are only eight years old, and too young to understand my letters. But, one day, when you are older, you will read them, and you will know about the bond that has entwined us for over a thousand years. You are very clever, Echo. It won't be long."

The Watcher turns and leaves, and Granny Ping (her Olympic Security Volunteer armband strapped over her sleeve) looks up from Wang Hu's wheelchair and gasps, "Even the dead have come to pay their respects . . ." The Watcher walks out of the living room as Lin Hong walks back in. The women brush shoulders in the doorway.

"Lin Hong! Your husband won't stop coughing!" wails a guest. "What shall we do?"

Lin Hong ignores Wang Hu. She marches over to Echo. "Who was that woman? What did she give you? Let me see!"

Echo leaps up from the sofa, hugging the envelopes tightly to her chest. "No!" she shouts, with such force that Lin Hong steps back.

As Echo runs to the spare room, Lin Hong decides there are too many guests about to make a scene. She will discipline Echo later. The patriarchs of the Wang family are either crippled or dead, and she is in charge now. And as much as she adores Echo, it is important that she keep the child in line. No doubt Yida's breast milk poisoned Echo as a baby, contaminating her with her backward Anhui ways.

"*Lin Hong! Your husband!*"

Lin Hong smiles pleasantly and turns to the crowd panicking over the choking man. "Slap him on the back a few times. The harder the better. That will shut him up."

Echo goes into the guest room, where her mother is unconscious, sprawled with her face in the pillow under lank and unwashed curls. Yida's dress is hitched up over her buttocks and, though there's no one about to see, Echo tugs the dress down over her knickers. Seeing her mother like this, drunk and insensible, is worrying to her. How will she stand up to Lin Hong when she is so weak?

Echo kneels and reaches under the bed for a large metal security box. She turns the combination lock, clicks open the lid and deposits the brown envelopes inside with the others. Her mother gave her the letters. She said it was her inheritance from her father. "Your *only* inheritance," she had laughed. "Your father wrote them.

Once, when I was angry, I threw them out of the kitchen window. I thought they were lost, but a security guard saw me from below. He gathered them up and gave them back. Anyway . . . I thought maybe one day you will want to read them. You will want to know who your father was."

Echo crawls onto the bed next to her passed-out mother and wraps her arm around her. She touches her forehead to her mother's shoulder and is reassured by the life and blood she detects thrumming there. She lifts her mother's curls from her cheek, and leans in to kiss her. Her mother is different when she is sleeping. She is like a child.

Echo slides off the bed. She puts the security box in her backpack, zips it up and feeds her arms through the straps. Then, her heart racing, she waits with her ear against the guest-room door until there's no sound in the hall, and sneaks out. She slips on her flip-flops and runs out to the stairwell. As she flies down the ten flights of concrete steps, Echo thinks of the guests at the wake, feasting their mouths on the trays of snacks, and their eyes on her mother's burnt-out grief. She thinks of overbearing Lin Hong, with her over-plucked eyebrows and stretched-too-tight face. She hopes Yida will move them out of her grandfather's home soon. Otherwise, Echo will run away.

Echo runs through the marble-floored foyer, past the doormen and out of the revolving glass doors. Out in the street, her flip-flops slap the pavement as she runs, and her backpack thuds on her back. She can't believe that her father is not out there still, cursing the traffic and tapping cigarette ash out of the window. She can't shake the feeling that at any moment his taxi will pull up. That he will beep the horn and call, "Echo! Jump in! I'll drive you the rest of the way . . ."

At a bridge over Liangma River, Echo stops and leans over the railing, peering down at the shallow water below. She thinks of taking out the metal box and emptying the letters into the stagnant ditch, drowning the letters so the ink dissolves into illegibility. But she tightens the backpack straps and runs over the bridge instead.

Echo runs all the way to Xiu Xing's run-down apartment block and sinks down on a concrete step in the entryway, panting and sweating in the July heat. When she recovers her breath, she will knock on Xiu Xing's door and he will pause his video game and let her in. Xiu Xing will hide the letters for her in his bedroom, where Lin Hong won't be able to find them. He is her closest friend and can be trusted to keep her father's letters safe.

Echo unzips the backpack, takes out the metal box and puts it on her lap. As she turns the combination lock, set to the date of her father's birthday, she remembers how the Watcher had said, "Now you are only eight years old, and too young to understand . . ." Who says I am too young to understand? Echo thinks. And, burning with curiosity and defiance, she unfolds one of the Watcher's letters.

"'Sorceress Wu, Sui Dynasty, AD 606,'" Echo reads out loud. Straining her eyes through the shadows, she reads on.

Acknowledgments

Thank you to Jane Lawson for her support and encouragement over the years I was writing *The Incarnations*. Many thanks to Andrew Kidd and Marianne Velmans.

Thank you to Hubert Ho, Jennifer Yeo, Richard Dudas, Sal Attanasio, Liang Junhong, Julia Wang, Glen Brown, Emily Midorikawa and Zakia Uddin.

I am very grateful to the Royal Literary Fund for the fellowship that enabled me to keep writing this book, and to Tim Leadbeater and the wonderful staff at Leeds Trinity University. Thank you also to the Arts Council England and the Society of Authors for the grants I was awarded.

In 2010 I taught English as a volunteer to patients at the Beijing Chaoyang Mental Health Service Center and to civil servants at the Ministry of Health in Beijing. I would like to thank all those I taught, for their friendship and the insight I gained into China and their lives.

Many thanks to my fellow writers at the Beijing Writers' Group for reading the early chapters.

Thank you to the Corporation of Yaddo, the Red Gate Gallery in Beijing, the Hawthornden International Writers' Retreat and all the inspiring writers and artists I met on these residencies.

Thank you, as always, to my father, mother and sister.

Thank you most of all to Robert Powers, who supported me throughout the writing of this book, and to whom *The Incarnations* is dedicated.

The Incarnations

For Discussion

1. Consider Wang's relationship with Yida. How have social and cultural constraints affected their union? For example, early on we learn that Yida, like many Chinese parents, had wanted a boy but Wang "had shamed her into keeping the baby" (their daughter, Echo; page 13). Are there other examples of how social norms or constraints have affected their relationship dynamic?

2. The chapters telling the stories of Wang's past incarnations are written in the first person ("I") and the second person ("you"). How did this style affect your experience reading the story? Why do you think the author chose to frame these sections from this narrative perspective?

3. Wang initially views the histories as "folktales" (page 75). Do you think he eventually comes to believe that these stories are true representations of his past lives? Why or why not? Find moments in the text that support your answer.

4. Betrayal is a recurring theme throughout the novel. Is there any significance to who betrays whom as the two characters' lives proceed together over hundreds of years? Do you think that their actions in one life affect the next life? Or does each life stand apart? Refer to passages in the text to support your answers.

5. Consider the notion of madness in the novel. Which characters are seen as mad, and why? How does this classification affect those characters in Chinese society—both in the present and in the past?

6. In the fourth letter, the writer declares, "We must rebel against fate. . . . Fate must be outwitted. It must no longer stand in our way" (page 117). What role does fate play in the story? Do you think the characters succeed in rebelling against fate in the last incarnation? Why or why not?

7. In the fifth letter, the writer notes that this "third biography has been more punishing than the others" (page 179). And after reading it, Wang is convinced he read the story at some point in his schooling since "the story had resonated so strongly in his memory" (page 215). All of the histories are graphic and brutal stories; why do you think this one (Ming Dynasty, 1542) is the most difficult for the writer to relive? Which of the five histories do you see as the darkest or most agonizing?

8. Towards the end of the novel, we learn that Shuxiang is the letter writer. How does this change your understanding of Wang and Shuxiang's relationship as mother and son? Do you see her differently as a mother? Refer back to Wang's memories of his mother, and compare them to Shuxiang's own recollections.

9. In each of their incarnations, the two characters have complex and intense relationships with each other. After so much conflict and passion between them throughout the past thousand years, consider the significance of ending the novel with a mother and son relationship. Why do you think the author chose to end the novel on this note?

10. Consider Echo's role throughout the novel, and at the end; the author brings the novel full circle, placing Echo into the

same histories her father and grandmother lived. Despite her conviction that "the Watcher is mentally ill" (page 367), Echo begins to read the letters and stories of her past lives. As such a young child, how will Echo interpret these stories? Do you think Shuxiang was right to pass on her insight of previous incarnations to her granddaughter? Why or why not?

A Conversation
with Susan Barker

**How did you approach writing a novel that contains so many
other intricately weaved stories within itself?**

Compared to the writing of my previous novels, my approach
to writing *The Incarnations* was haphazard, disorganized and
lengthy. I moved to Beijing in the summer of 2007 in order to
research a new book. I wanted to write about modern China
and the impact of the rapid social and political change on ordinary Beijingers. I also wanted to interweave several historical
stories into the novel, as China's history is so fascinating and
rich with narrative possibility. I would like to say I approached
the research and writing of *The Incarnations* in an orderly
and systematic manner, but the truth is that I pretty much began researching all of the narratives at once, with only a hazy
idea of how they would be structured into a novel.

For years I kept many notebooks full of jottings I made
while walking round Beijing, or while reading about life during the Tang Dynasty, the Cultural Revolution and the other
eras in the novel. The contents of these notebooks slowly
evolved into Driver Wang's story and the five historical tales.
I wrote about five or six drafts of *The Incarnations* and the
process was disorderly—I returned to different sections at
random and in nonchronological order, figuring out how
they fit together along the way.

The stories from the incarnations throughout history are extremely vivid and distinct from one another. Did you find it difficult to switch from period to period? Did you change anything about your writing process to accommodate this narrative flow?

Once I had done the preliminary research it was fairly easy to switch between the historical eras—in fact it was quite invigorating and fun to be writing about seventh-century Tang Dynasty Chang'an one week, and then switch to the nineteenth century and the Opium War the next. Almost like time-traveling (albeit very slowly and limited by variables such as work ethic, imagination and typing speed).

Not only does the novel jump through history, it also moves backwards into Wang's life. Why did you decide to frame the story in this way?

We are the sum of our experiences; our present selves are shaped by the events that occurred in our past. I wanted to tell the story of Wang's childhood, his detainment in the mental institution and ill-fated relationship with Zeng Yan, in order to offer the reader more insight into Wang's behavior in the present day. Wang Jun is a very passive character, but this doesn't mean he is not multifaceted and complex. I wanted to show the reader the formative experiences that made Wang Jun who he is.

Describe your research methods for the novel. China has such a rich and long history from which to draw: how did you narrow down which time periods to include for the incarnations?

I researched the contemporary sections of the novel by exploring Beijing by bus, taxi and foot, and making notes about what I saw. I spent about five years living in China (on and off) between 2007 and 2014, and this observational method of research was ongoing throughout that time. I also read as many books on modern Chinese society, politics and culture as I could get my hands on.

Though I knew I wanted to weave historical stories into the novel, I initially wasn't sure which eras to write about, so I read books that gave an overview of the last two millennia of Chinese history from the Qin Dynasty to Chairman Mao. When I encountered a historical incident or figure that I found fascinating, for example Genghis Khan and the Mongol Invasions, or Emperor Jiajing of the Ming Dynasty, I would deepen my research into that individual or era. I found that as I read and made notes, ideas for plots and characters would emerge from my research. Sometimes straightaway, sometimes over several weeks or months.

Do you have a favorite of the incarnations? If so, which one and why?

My favorite incarnation is Concubine Swallow in the "Sixteen Concubines" story, which is based on an actual historical event. Emperor Jiajing was the eleventh emperor of the Ming dynasty and was alleged to have been a sexual sadist who tortured his concubines. One night in October 1542, sixteen of the concubines crept into his bedchamber in the Forbidden City and attempted to strangle him with a silken cord. However, the assassination plot was thwarted and the concubines were executed.

I wanted to fictionalize and write about this regicidal plot from the concubines' perspective because I admired how they fought back against the emperor, and were willing to sacrifice their lives to do so. I also enjoyed writing in the voice of Concubine Swallow—she is so scathing, darkly humorous and self-loathing.

The novel centers on the idea of reincarnation, but the characters do not directly grapple with whether or not they believe in it.

How did writing this novel affect your thoughts about reincarnation? Did you learn anything new about reincarnation from your research or through writing the novel?

At the risk of demystifying the novel, the use of reincarnation was initially a narrative device; a way of structuring and bringing together all of my separate research interests in China past and present. However over the years, as I wrote draft after draft of *The Incarnations*, the reincarnation aspect gained substance and became the essence of the book.

As well as structuring the novel, the idea of reincarnation and recurring souls also links to one of the themes of the book, which is the cyclical nature of history. The taxi driver Wang Jun keeps repeating the same destructive mistakes in each of his past lives, due to the innate flaws in his nature (wrath, self-interest, possessiveness, jealousy) that recur life after life. I also hoped to capture how the history of civilization is repetitive too, with the same vastly destructive power struggles playing out across the generations, arising from the same innate human flaws.

I am not sure whether or not I believe in reincarnation. Perhaps I do in my more irrational moments, but it's a vast leap of faith to believe you've had past lives. My sister once met a medium when we were teenagers, who said that she (my sister) and I have been linked together for several past lives, but obviously I am skeptical.

With so much history embedded in the story, readers cannot help but become intrigued by China's past. Were you aiming to incite readers' interest in Chinese history and culture? Is there anything in particular you hope for people to take away from reading this novel?

I wasn't aiming to incite readers' interest in China's past, but if *The Incarnations* encourages some readers to want to learn more about Chinese history, then that's fantastic. I hope that the historical sections of *The Incarnations* offer the reader a glimpse of each era (though my fiction often deviates from historical truth into more surreal and fantastical terrain). I mostly hope that readers are moved and engaged by *The Incarnations*, that the book entertains.

Are there any writers who stand out as influences for you?

When it comes to contemporary writers I really like Nicole Krauss, W. G. Sebald, Jonathan Lethem, Junot Díaz, Lydia Davis, Jenny Offill, David Mitchell, Peter Hessler, Sarah Hall, Zadie Smith. I can't say how much they influence me, but reading amazing fiction always inspires me to write.

The end of the novel brings Echo into the cycle of incarnations; have you thought about writing a sequel to *The Incarnations*?

I have no plans to write a sequel to *The Incarnations*, but I am half-tempted to write the Watcher's "Sorceress Wu" story (which is the title of the story in the letter Echo opens on the very last page of the novel). I really enjoyed writing the character of the Sorceress Wu (the mother in the *Night Coming* story)—she was just so vehemently evil! I'd like to tell the story of how the Sorceress Wu lost her husband to bandits and turned to witchcraft. She probably wasn't always evil. I imagine a series of tragic events made her that way.

What did you learn from writing this novel that may help you with future projects?

I spent six years writing *The Incarnations* and in the process of drafting and redrafting the book I probably learned myriad technical things about characterization, plotting and structuring multiple narratives and crafting prose. Other than aspects of craft, researching and writing *The Incarnations* was a lengthy and challenging undertaking (challenging for me at least) and completing one lengthy project always lends you courage to commence the next one—faith that, no matter how long it takes, it can be done.

Enhance Your Book Club

1. Research one of the time periods through which Wang lives and discuss how the stories fit into the historical context (Tang Dynasty—632 AD; Jin Dynasty—1213; Ming Dynasty—1542; Qing Dynasty—1836; or People's Republic of China—1966).

2. Wang dies before Shuxiang can reveal herself as the biographer of their past lives, and this is the only life in which the two do not witness one or the other's last moments alive. Write a short chapter or scene imagining a reunion between Wang and Shuxiang, or discuss why you think the author chose not to include their reunion in the novel.

Susan Barker grew up in East London. While writing *The Incarnations* she spent several years living in Beijing, researching ancient and modern China. She currently lives in London.

Follow her on Twitter @SusanKBarker.